Magnus McGrandle was born in 1975. He works as a television journalist and lives in London with his wife and two children. This is his first novel.

SHORT RIDE
ON A
FAST MACHINE

MAGNUS McGRANDLE

SANDSTONEPRESS
HIGHLAND | SCOTLAND

First published in Great Britain by
Sandstone Press Ltd
Dochcarty Road
Dingwall
Ross-shire
IV15 9UG
Scotland

www.sandstonepress.com

The publisher acknowledges subsidy from Creative Scotland
towards publication of this volume.

ISBN: 978-1-910985-68-7
ISBNe: 978-1-910985-69-4

Cover design by Mark Ecob
Typeset by Iolaire Typography Ltd, Newtonmore
Printed and bound by Totem, Poland

For my father, Leith

Contents

Part One

Sam Black   1

Part Two (the others)

Marta Olsen   135
Anna Vig   157
Jon Sorensen   179
Pushpendra Singh Poyntz   198
Mashtots Hambartzumian   207

Part Three

Sam Black   217

PART ONE

SAM BLACK

1

A CALLING CARD

To begin with I thought everything that happened was connected with my visit to Mr Bembo, the Oracle of Stepney Green, and that the whole business with Sorensen and the journey I made to Norway with my best friend Poyntz were just minor detours on the path towards truth, which the great soothsayer had set me upon. He was, on the face of it, a shaman of rare talent, and if a man's character is his fate then Mr Bembo had the measure of my character and the measure of my fate. Later, I wondered what had originally drawn me to his calling card, which was absurd and which dropped through my letterbox the day after Poyntz finally beat me at backgammon, breaking my winning streak. After all, this *God Gifted Spiritual Healer and Clairvoyant with Spiritual Power from his Ancestral Masters Spirit, 25 Years' Experience* boasted that:

> No matter how difficult your problems is Mr Bembo can solve it from one visit: for instance, love problem, business transaction, sexual problem, exams, and court cases. He can improve your life by making you confident, make your marriage life

better, give you good luck, and remove back magic.
He can eliminate bad habits and many more.

I was twenty-one years old and had no marriage, business, legal proceedings or examinations to speak of and regarding love, well, the episode with Kelly Zimmerman was in the past. I had known bad luck and sometimes lacked confidence but I required no back magic to be removed, or black magic for that matter. I had some bad habits but none which I particularly wanted to be rid of. And sexually I was fully functional, at least in the anatomical sense. I did, however, have a weakness for mumbo-jumbo and I'd been a little on the jittery side since Yelena Zykov had been run over by a truck a month or so previously. I felt a little vulnerable and was looking for clarity. I was also bored, waiting on a delivery that afternoon of a pair of new wheels for my bicycle, a Pinarello which was – sad to admit – the real love of my life.

So I called up Mr Bembo and made an appointment.

2

MR BEMBO, AT HOME

My consultation with the witch doctor would last precisely forty-two minutes and would cost me thirty-three pounds and nineteen pence, all the money I had in my pocket. Mr Bembo had asked for much more – one hundred and fifty – and in return he'd ensure that I'd never fall off my bike and if I did, no harm would come to me.

I can make this happen, he said. For just one hundred and fifty English pounds.

I put three tenners on the table plus the loose change. He counted the money and pronounced it a reasonable start and said that afterwards we would go to the cash machine around the corner and that there would be no funny business. He asked for my mobile phone as insurance against non-payment of dues. I insisted it be left on the table because I was expecting a call from Fat Barry.

Ok, he said, eyeing the phone. We have made a little deal. Now tell me about yourself.

So I told him. Not much. Just a little. A few important details. My name: Sam Black. My job: bicycle messenger. My bicycle: Pinarello Montello, 1989, Columbus SLX tubing, chrome forks, Campagnolo groupset, Alex soon-to-be Mavic wheels and multi-coloured paintwork in the *spumoni* style, *spumoni* being an Italian pudding of Neapolitan origin.

I didn't tell him everything about the bike. But I did tell him that a fellow courier of mine had been killed in an accident recently and that I was feeling spooked by the roads. I didn't say that the ghost of Yelena Zykov – aka the Black Goddess – was supposedly riding the streets of London. I didn't tell him this because I didn't like revealing my superstitions to anyone, not even a witch doctor.

I told him I was considering quitting my job as a courier for a more sedate existence (although riding bicycles was the only thing I knew) and I told him I'd just lost at backgammon for the first time in three months. He said, backgammon? What is this thing you call backgammon?

Backgammon, I said. It's a board game. A bit like chess.

Ah, he said. Chess. A game of pure luck.

After this he went into his kitchen and I went outside onto his balcony, eight floors up a block of flats that overlooked the Isle of Dogs. I smoked a cigarette and took in the view. It was a beautiful, still day, the first of September.

When I went back inside Mr Bembo was still in the kitchen and I could smell something burning, like incense, but a bitter, unusual smell. I picked up my phone from the table, put it back in my pocket and examined Mr Bembo's qualifications. They hung in gilt frames on his living room wall, degrees from the universities of Oxford, Yale, Paris-Sorbonne and Bulawayo. All his degrees were in Human Sciences.

When he returned he had changed into some robes and was carrying a tiny cloth bag. The consultation is over, he said. But for free, Samuel, I will tell you this:

beware of cars, and avoid riding your bicycle on the streets.

It was problematic advice for a courier. I asked him if there was anything else I should know and he said I was to avoid yellow cars in particular. He also said I would meet an old man who would determine my fortune, a man with money and large hands.

This man would turn out to be Sorensen.

Then Mr Bembo held up the cloth bag, which he called the gris-gris. For the extra money, he said, you can keep the gris-gris. It is a lucky bag. It is a talisman. It will save you from motor vehicles. It will make them slow down when they see you. It will make them stop when they are near you. It will protect your body from injury.

I asked him what was inside the gris-gris.

Herbs, he said, and other things. He told me to keep it on my person at all times or else it wouldn't work. Then he announced it was time to go to the cash machine. There is one in the convenience store next to the chicken shop, he said.

But in the pissy metal lift on our way down things fell apart. I told him my phone was staying in my pocket. He said I owed him three hundred. I told him he'd said one fifty. He said my situation was more serious than he'd thought. He added that I was in grave danger, especially from yellow cars.

I unlocked my Pinarello and wheeled her as I walked with Mr Bembo to the cash machine. I considered how much I really needed that gris-gris and concluded I needed it a lot. I didn't believe in everything Mr Bembo said but I was worried about believing in nothing. So I took one twenty out of the machine and gave it to him. You owe me three pounds and nineteen pence, I said. Now please can I have the voodoo bag?

But he insisted on three hundred. Three hundred, he said, and your problems will be solved. Then he started to play the game proper. He said he had seen my accident and that it was not pleasant to look at. He said he had seen me lying on the ground and that he had seen my bicycle in many parts. He said he had heard the sound of sirens and the sound of screaming too. None of it, he said, was nice.

I was worried my bank would get lockjaw but it was the first of the month: payday. I took a further one fifty from the cash machine, counted the notes, and handed them over. He took the gris-gris from a pocket inside his robes and passed it to me in exchange. I stuffed it into the bottom of my courier bag and asked him whether he did not want to double-check the money.

Of course! he said, friendly now. You are a good businessman like me.

So he started to count the whole lot, two hundred and seventy in tens, and as he counted aloud, I got onto my Pinarello and clipped in. One hundred and twenty, one hundred and thirty. I set my wheels in the direction of the main road. One hundred and sixty, one hundred and seventy. I rolled on the wheels, a perfect track stand. Two hundred and twenty, two hundred and thirty. I reversed maybe a quarter revolution. Two hundred and forty. Two hundred and fifty. Two hundred and sixty. Two hundred and —.

I didn't let him get right to the end. That would have been too risky. But I still managed to take the whole lot, swiped out of his hands and into mine in a moment of beautiful synchronicity: left arm swinging in to collect the cash, right arm on the handlebars directing the getaway and helping my legs with the pushing and the pulling. The crazy mountebank ran after me for as long as he could, puffing and yelling, shouting the words *big cunt,* and while I was looking back at him I almost collided with a yellow Honda Civic that was coming the other way. But it braked sharply and somehow I managed to swerve past it and I didn't stop until I got home, where my new wheels were waiting for me. The cash I put in a sock and half-hid. I made a promise to myself not to spend it. The voodoo bag smelt so bad I put it under the sink in an empty jam jar, lid on. And everything else was absolutely fine until the following morning when, riding into work past the junction where the second-hand Merc dealership comes eye-to-eye with the pink and black lap dancing club, I was hit by the Porsche Cayenne and flung high into the air.

3

BACKGAMMON

Did it all start then with Mr Bembo? Or was it the night before, in that sixth and final game at the Montmorency? I remember Poyntz hunched over the backgammon set, shoulders tense, elbows on table, hands clasped tight, fingers entwined and thumbs to lips as if in holy prayer. Nestled between his little fingers were the dice.

The sixth game had reached its climax after four turns of the doubling cube. In order to win the session, Poyntz required a double six or a double five on his final throw. All I needed was the minimum, a two and a one. But it was his turn to roll, not mine.

The Montmorency was a fringe operation which ran on a handful of regulars, which more-or-less included Poyntz and I. It was painted orange and had a door on the side that, in the old-fashioned way, sometimes opened when you knocked after closing time. That night the bar was bare, with only a few of the usual Hibernians there. I fetched the drinks while Poyntz rolled out the board, a square of worn black velvet with twelve triangles embroidered on each side. We found our corner and started a new session: six games. The first I won easily. I gammoned him on the second and third. Five up after three, I doubled on the fourth: he redoubled, I redoubled back, he resigned. The fifth game was trickier but I still took it by half a dozen pips.

A brief history of the Game that year: I was whipping his ass. Poyntz hadn't won a single session since June and he was down by at least three hundred quid. I was starting to think of new challenges, namely Salowitz, a wily Czech who rode for London Wheels and had a fierce reputation at the board. Twice in the past we'd played, twice he'd thrashed me. Both times I'd insisted no betting.

It was when he took on Salowitz in that game at the Crown that I first came across Poyntz. He was this tall, thin Indian guy with an earring and a crewcut who'd just that week started out at Rapid Couriers. He must have played backgammon before – he knew the rules – but he can't have played much and certainly never for money because he agreed to Salowitz's crazy stake: a pound-a-pip with doubles. It was a rudimentary hustle. I remember locking up my Pinarello and seeing the crowd inside, gathered round the game, doing the maths. The stake had been doubled and redoubled twice and Poyntz had two of his men out of play. If he'd been lucky he might have got Salowitz on the way back in but Salowitz bore off clean, winning the gammon by forty or so pips. With all the doubles it was a finger-singeing sum: nearly seven hundred quid. Poyntz asked to pay his debt in instalments but Salowitz refused. The following day Poyntz called his controller at Rapid and told him he'd smashed up his leg: *pothole, fractured tibia, eight to ten weeks.*

Getting knocked off is part of a courier's job, which gives us some leeway in faking injury. But earlier that year a couple of messengers had pulled a ruse and been discovered. Denied time off by their controller, they dreamt up a pair of two-week-long injuries and flew to Ibiza. When they returned to the office, tanned and skint, they were promptly given the boot. In the same vein Rapid's controller instantly demanded evidence of Poyntz's fractured tibia. When Poyntz stalled he was sacked.

Riders come and go and I assumed it was the same with Poyntz but two or three weeks later Joe Guzzman rolled up while I was waiting at some lights and asked if I remembered the dude fleeced by Salowitz.

I nodded my head. Guzz said he'd bumped into him a couple of nights back, riding up Liverpool Road, working. Nights were much more lucrative than days if you didn't mind stashing drugs down your pants and dealing with the dealers. The parties could be fun. But you couldn't ride round the clock so couriers who needed urgent cash often cooked up injuries to keep their contract, worked nights to make some quick money, then returned to days when they were done.

All that money he lost playing backgammon, I said.

Yep, Guzz replied. D'you know him?

No.

He was asking after you.

Me? I said. Are you sure?

Yep.

Do you know why? I asked.

Dunno. He just said he wanted to get in touch.

Same guy? I asked. Rides a Bianchi?

Same guy, he replied. Rides a Bianchi.

Sure enough the following day Poyntz walked into the offices of Zenith Couriers and asked my boss Fat Barry for a job. Fat Barry, rightly or wrongly, regarded Zenith's messengers as the crème de la crème of the

London courier scene. I don't take Rapid's cast-offs, he told Poyntz. Especially those with dodgy injuries.

But Poyntz had his answer in a large brown envelope which he passed to Fat Barry. Inside were a pair of pristine X-rays, feasibly dated, with the name PUSHPENDRA SINGH POYNTZ white-typed into the corners. Poyntz explained how he'd made a quick recovery. Fat Barry looked at the sheets and then back at Poyntz. This is definitely you? he asked.

Yeah, Poyntz replied. It's me.

You got a passport?

Poyntz laughed. I'm British, mate. Born and bred in Brum.

Don't *mate* me, said Fat Barry, who liked to call the shots. You'll have to prove this is you. I run a legit operation here, I can assure you.

I'm quick, said Poyntz.

Quick, repeated Fat Barry, shifting some bulk around his high-backed leather chair. Quick's good, he said, but you need to be above board as well. We run some very important clients here and I don't want my riders fucking me about.

Just look at the X-rays, said Poyntz.

Fat Barry held the sheets up to the light. They're kosher are they?

Totally.

And why didn't you show them to Rapid?

Poyntz shrugged. I wasn't given the chance, he said.

And now?

Poyntz shook his head. I'm not going back to that prick.

Fat Barry handed the prints back to Poyntz. Bike? he asked.

Bianchi.

Don't tell me, a fucking Pista?

Mega Pro.

What year?

2000.

Very nice, said Fat Barry, you're hired. Then he leant forward: listen, he said, I'm a generous soul who believes in second chances. More importantly Christmas is round the corner and I've got bottles of bubbly coming out of my arse. It's the usual rate – two fifty a drop – and you're on a month's probation. Don't push it or you'll never work again.

The bullshit story behind the X-rays? They were a favour from one of Poyntz's acquaintances, an acquaintance known only as the Armenian. The Armenian had contacts in radiology. But the bullshit story worked and the night-peddling paid off Salowitz's debt. Quick as promised, Poyntz became a fixture at Zenith and, knowing that I played backgammon, he plotted his revenge on Salowitz by pestering me for games. Over the board we quickly became friends.

4

THE BLACK GODDESS

Zenith Couriers was an independent, run on a shoestring from a double-roomed office two floors up in WC1 and Fat Barry was its thick-lensed, foul-mouthed boss and our controller. Under the wheels of a battered Coppi Campionissimo – a relic from his racing days – Fat Barry would sit at his desk, gubernatorial in style, and take calls from clients, murder his keyboard with a pair of chubby forefingers and dispatch his thirty or so trusty riders across the city. It was a haphazard operation founded in the early 1990s as *London's leading specialist cycle courier company*, its unofficial motto uttered periodically by its chief: *We keep well-lubricated the cogs of LAW, COMMERCE and the MEDIA ETC.* Despite clumsy self-presentation Zenith had just about survived the digital revolution. There was a flip side to technology's relentless advance, Fat Barry would explain to anyone bothered enough to listen: people wanted *secure handling* and in many cases *the personal touch*. Apparently clients found that legal documents and blueprints and commercially sensitive data was better delivered by hand than through the *information super fucking highway*, which was what Fat Barry called the internet.

Hard work and an unwillingness to employ any idiot-on-wheels had kept Fat Barry in touch with the competition. Dart and Gazelle were indie firms run on similar lines: all their riders were self-employed and paid per drop; insurance and benefits were non-existent. The only way to make decent cash as an independent courier was to be quick and take risks on the road. In that way some of the very best riders cleared three, even four hundred quid a week. Unlike the bigger corporates – Central, Rapid, Excelsior – the indies were strictly cycle-only and that brought kudos. Some messengers still went for the security of the big firms, a signed contract, some accident cover, decent radios, etc. A bunch of their riders were among the quickest: Spinks, Mitsu, Kowalski, John Heimerdinger, Byron – they always did well in alleycat races. But many were mountain bike monkeys with fluffy toys attached to their helmets.

Sometimes the big firms were tricky with alleycats. They didn't like their riders getting into trouble with the law. Megalomaniac controllers, like the one at Rapid who sacked Poyntz, would try to get rid of messengers they knew to be alleycatting. If you ever got done by the police in an alleycat – pretty rare but not unheard of – they always tried to get you to reveal your firm. So we all carried fake ID: I was Fabian Miller from Urban Couriers; Poyntz was an Alphabet rider called Grover Watrous.

Grover Watrous is not an Indian name, I told him.

Neither is Poyntz, he replied.

The indies were more relaxed about alleycats. Funnily enough, Fat Barry didn't have international offices or a board of directors to answer to when an employee got sandwiched trying to bisect a pair of HGVs on the way to a checkpoint. At your own risk, he told us. Being a former track racer he understood the buzz. His days of thunder weren't quite on the Lev Zykov scale although he'd harboured Olympic ambitions. Hanging on the wall next to the Coppi were a series of framed black-and-white snaps from earlier days: Fat Barry and the rest of his time-trial team, resplendent in vintage lycra; Fat Barry in profile, on his saddle and in full flow, greasing the velodrome; Fat Barry legs pumping, forearms bulging, quick and lean as a leopard. A broken collar bone, he claimed, prevented him from progressing to the GB squad for Seoul.

Lev Zykov, by the by, was Yelena Zykov's dad and Yelena Zykov was a legend in the messenger scene. She rode for Gazelle and was an alleycat champion. Lev had competed in the Individual Pursuit for the Russians at the Moscow Olympics and defected to the US in the mid-80s after some competition in Colorado. For a week and a thousand miles he cycled west ending up in San Francisco where he got a job as a mechanic and fell in love with an English girl, a hippy. The Anglo-Ukrainian Yelena was born some nine months later. The three of them busked the American Dream for a decade or so until Lev dropped dead from an infarction: who said cycling's good for the heart? Afterwards the English girl, no longer a hippy and no longer a girl, moved back to England with Yelena in tow.

So it went that one fine July morning, some time before my encounter with the Porsche Cayenne, Yelena was on her way to a pick-up somewhere south of the river when a dumper truck bumped her on Tower Bridge Road just where the train lines pass overhead and at thirty miles an hour her eighteen-year-old self was catapulted into a one hundred and fifty-year-old Victorian brick wall and that was that. The funeral was an anarchic affair, rammed as it was with messengers. The family had expected a small gathering but over two hundred riders turned up that day to say farewell. Farewell but not goodbye. Because after a period of sluggish deliveries – no courier could say they weren't a little bit spooked, least of all me – Yelena started springing up all over town.

The first sighting was on a street in Deptford. A rider called Antoine who'd once asked her out on a date said Yelena had cycled past him with a twinkle in her eye.

We all thought it was the grief talking.

But a couple of weeks later Early Man, who'd worked with Yelena at Gazelle, also claimed to have spotted her. Early was a gentle giant, nearly seven feet tall, with classic Neanderthal looks. At dusk, somewhere near Blackfriars, Yelena had overtaken him, eyes fixed on the road. The whole thing may have sounded too neat but Early was an honest soul and no casual liar. Still, few believed that the ghost of Yelena Zykov was really haunting the streets, least so when Fat Barry said he'd seen her too, in Camberwell Green of all places. This made everyone laugh but Fat Barry was adamant: Fuck you! he stormed. It was her! I saw her with my own eyes! The Black Goddess!

The Black Goddess. Fat Barry's secret moniker for Yelena stuck and with it her legend grew. Some, like me, thought Barry's conversion on the road to Tooting Bec might finally put an end to the nonsense but soon the Black Goddess was being spotted all over town: New Cross, Percy Circus, Chancery Lane, Swiss Cottage... And if the numerous sightings were genuine and not a giant conspiracy of fun from which I'd been excluded, then Yelena Zykov was, in death, much as she'd been in life: scuffed SIDIs, black shorts, black T-shirt, black Le Bourget stockings (woollens in winter,

16

fishnets in spring and late autumn). The problem for me was that the myth was difficult to cast aside when you took into account her legendary skills as a rider. The Black Goddess had made her own bikes at eight, run her dad's business at twelve, competed in alleycat races in California at thirteen and won outright our very own *Greenwich Mean Time* at sixteen. She could probably have followed Lev into some Olympic team or other but instead London was her track – she clocked up fifteen, twenty thousand miles a year and forged an unassailable reputation as one of the fastest messengers in town. The city she knew better than anyone and with all the backstreets attached. She understood its traffic flow, its lights, its crunch spaces. She knew the minds of the speed freaks and weekend geriatrics, the bus drivers, the minicabistas, the HGV kings and SUV queens and the jumped-up souped-up boyriders and scooterrorists. Her knowledge of drafting and aerodynamics, learnt at the velodrome in San Jose, drew her into the slipstreams of Omnidekkas and Kawasakis alike. Common to all of us she hitched lifts from buses and trucks but no one else took on the White Van Man with any seriousness or ever got close to the spoiler of a Lamborghini Diablo or, during a particular emergency, a fire engine which delivered her across town in record time. That was *the* classic provocation of a Section 26:

holding onto a vehicle in order to be towed

but she never had anyone to answer to because somehow – for such a prolific law-bender – the law never seemed to get to Yelena Zykov in the way that it got to other riders. Once she negotiated a whole bunch of alleycat riders out of a Section 31:

by claiming that a night-time alleycat from Alexandra to Crystal Palace was in fact a wake for a Spanish colleague who'd come off his bike in the Pyrenees and fallen down a ravine. Everyone arrived at the finish in quick succession to find a bunch of coppers, notebooks at the ready. Yelena let rip with Aristobulo's story, expounding on the arcane mourning rituals of our tribe. Bolo was indeed in the Pyrenees at the time, visiting relatives and preparing for an Iron Man. He'd met his end doing what he loved doing – so spun Yelena – and this was our collective tribute to him, a kind of funeral march carried out at speed. While the police chewed on this, a more important crime came screeching down their radios. They piled back into their van and sped off.

5

THE INCIDENT WITH THE PORSCHE CAYENNE

I had approached the crossroads that morning as I always did: two wheels on the ground and at speed, a fish eye focus on the world. From home I sprinted to the turn, determined to cast Yelena and Mr Bembo from my mind, and then accelerated past the cop shop, the graveyard, the bus depot and council buildings, up past the dank trendy Irish boozers, the ocakbasi holes and strip-lit Viet supermarkets, the horse-gutter-on-legs and the churches of the Seventh-day Adventists or Latter-day Saints or Brazilian Pentecostalists or whatever and then over the canal with its broken-bottle walls tagged by Nooz and Ja Rat and past all the Fried Chickens (Mississippi, Tennessee, Carolina) until I had moved from fifteen to twenty-two, to twenty-four, to twenty-six, to twenty-eight, to twenty-nine, to thirty, to thirty-one. And at thirty-two miles an hour – where the trains grind and squeal and where the spoiler and side skirt merchant Rude Mercs ogles London's Number One American-Style Gentlemen's Entertainment Club, Megalopolis – I was hit by a two-ton block of yellow metal, namely the Porsche Cayenne, and my body was sent soaring.

At the time, Megalopolis's very own Laetitia was lying provocatively in a sequinned bra-and-thong combo across forty-odd square feet of advertising space, blond and seeking attention. It was possible that whoever was behind the wheel of the yellow Cayenne had felt a surge of testosterone and hit the gas, jumped the lights and inadvertently catapulted me off my Pinarello. He was – in the split second I caught of him, through a gap in the Cayenne's windows – a typical Megalopolista, ecstatic in his leather and walnut-fasciaed world: heavy silver watch hanging loose at the wrist, bejewelled hand-like-a-ham knuckling the gearstick, skin the colour of a month in Dubai. A fat fucker he was but all muscle and sinew and with a murderous physiognomy: head shaven to bald, ears melded to skull, crushed nose, two rows of gritting spitting over-polished teeth and eyes like a Dobermann. What he appeared to be communicating: *I fucking hate cyclists.*

But I heard no words just the squeal of the Cayenne as it turned the corner and the whoosh as it missed my leg by inches: thank God, I thought, I am safe. Then as the car straightened up, its back swung round and it bit me scorpion-like, slamming my rear wheel into the frame and my front into the curb. I flipped unclipped out of my saddle and floated. I heard a gasp from the pavement and the Cayenne roar into the distance. As I hung in the air I waited for my entire life to play itself out in front of me, frame-by-frame, just like it does in the movies.

But this did not happen.

For instance, I did not see myself crowned with blood at the end of a stop-start labour which had started with my mother doubled-up in pain and my father in the pub and which had ended with him doubled-up himself, doubled-up with fear and alcohol and my mother walking home from hospital, me happily swaddled in her dark arms, an only child-to-be.

Neither did I see myself crawl into their bed and, in between their silent hulks, find space for sleep or play. How perfect they seemed as they struggled to find space enough for their own love and so quickly settled upon me instead. When I was old enough to realise this I battled to keep me for myself but I did not see the disappointment on their faces when I would not do as they wished. I didn't take to going to church or playing the violin and I had no interest in sitting by riverbanks, my mother being a battler of religion and Kreutzer and my father being a catcher of carp. Instead I fought kids at school with my bare fists and broke records with a football of black and white hexagons but I did not see the punch I landed on the boy as we fought under the oak tree or the goal I scored running up on the right, cutting through and lacing into the far corner.

If only it was all so glorious but neither did I see the two deaths I had witnessed up to that point: the overcoat who jumped in front of the goods train when I was ten and the priest whose haemorrhage in a cathedral nave was witnessed by God and a group of tittering teenagers of which I was one. Nor did I see the carving knife thrown at me by the rotisserie chef in the kitchens of the oil giant HQ where I learnt how to speed-peel carrots and stuff bread up my nose to combat onion tears: the knife clattered into a walk-in fridge next to me and spun on the floor, its tip pointing back at the maniac. A month later he was killed – knifed no less – in a brawl on the south coast.

I did not see myself kicking drainpipes in anger or

shitting in a taxi delirious after eating bad fish in Turkey or getting fleeced by a peep show merchant (the other peepsters were a tourist and an Arab but I was the only one who paid triple for my ignorance, triple for a minute watching a girl writhe on a turning dais). I did not see her face or the face of the only girl I have loved, Kelly Zimmerman. I did not see Kelly Zimmerman in the bathroom. I did not see her on the hill. I did not see her at the wheels of her Fiat Panda or smiling on Two Tree Island or looking up at the sky, predicting rain. I did not see the back of Kelly Zimmerman's neck or her dimples or her freckles and I did not see the indent on her pillow when she went for a piss first thing in the morning. I did not see her making cigarettes or tea or yellow rice and I did not see her heavily Kohled eyes run dirty tears when she threw me on the scrapheap and told me I was useless. But no hard feelings Kelly.

I did not see myself dressed up as an alligator, riding my bike weaving through traffic on the way to her party, the party where we kissed; I struggled to read the road through papiermâché. Or sweating in bed, on acid for the first and only time, my grandfather emerging out of the wafer-patterned ceiling. I did not see the dust on the springs of my bed or the grey-green carpet never replaced or the decrepit kitchen chairs or that vase or the paving slabs outside and I did not see the soft pack of Lucky Strike or the matches I used to light my first cigarette. I did not see bonfires at night or hear the call of the wood pigeon as I woke in a friend's house and I did not see the man who, seven years ago, asked me what I wanted to say. Neither did I see the woman on the bus all tits and tats two weeks ago, delivering me her own worldview in between swigs of Bacardi Breezer: I've been good in my life, she said, fuck 'em all. If she didn't want to back-adjust her life, then why the hell should I want to back-adjust mine, but all the same I did not see the look on my father's face when he left the house for the last time and the tears in my mother's eyes. And I did not see my own tears when they told me the news of my mother or the tears when I read to her at her bedside during the Greek Period of my life or indeed the tears afterwards that fell from my face when I was just seventeen years and one month old, when they told me she had died.

No: instead I saw Poyntz, fucking Poyntz, throwing dice in the sixth and final game of that backgammon session at the Montmorency. Yes, my big moment halfway between the curb and the Megalopolis's citrus trees and all I saw was Poyntz throwing fucking dice at the Montmorency. When he threw, the Montmorency froze. The stranger at the bar finishing his stout turned into a waxwork. The greasy speakers were cut, conversation fell silent. Phyllis the landlady stopped pulling pints, wiping the bar, loading the steam machine, drying glasses, going for a smoke round the back. She was perfectly still. The bar's colours dimmed to nothing and all I saw were the dice as they hit the board, jumped and settled.

When they settled so did I, on a citrus tree adorning the entrance to the lap dancing club. It wasn't that big a tree, four foot perhaps, and it didn't do much to break my fall but I held it all the same, kissed it and embraced it, and its thorns ended up multitudinously in my flesh: three in the arms, one in the neck, four in the face. Not that that was the worst of it: on the way down, the citrus and I hit a balustrade of grey marble. My brain could have split or quit or I could have had one of those deranging scars running crown to brow. But instead my helmet took all the pain for me, which was money well spent.

In the ambulance I regained consciousness and according to the doctors the first words I uttered were *double six* which of course meant the end of my winning streak and, depending on which way you look at it, the beginning of everything else that happened.

6

SORENSEN

It was a Monday, my first day back after the crash
and Sorensen was my fourth docket: the Hotel Priam
in Bayswater. All morning I had ridden slow, wary of
everything, stopping at every light. Yelena Zykov was
back riding around in my head and in the yellow Porsche
Cayenne I now had confirmation of Mr Bembo's psychic
powers. I had retrieved the gris-gris from under the sink
and stuffed it inside my seatpost.

My face was a fuck-up but the rest of my body was
more-or-less okay: collar bone good; scaphoids good;
ribs, knees, wrists: all good. My right-side elbow and
shoulder were bandaged-up with road rash and my
thigh too. It throbbed a little. My chin and cheekbone
were starting to heal but they were bloody to look at
and I had a little running of vital fluid in the left eye, like
a boxer the morning after. The doctor said this would
clear up in a few weeks. The thorns had been removed
from bicep, neck and face and placed in a kidney bowl
one-by-one, tiny razory fuckers that left apple-pip scabs
in their place. I'd had a CAT scan because I'd hit my
head but the picture was all hunky-dory. The doc told
me to come back if I got any dizziness or blackness or

lightness or sickness or loss of vision or anything in the head department that was giving me hassle. How long, I asked, before I can give myself the all-clear? The brain's a pretty complex organ, he replied. Sometimes you get a delayed reaction.

I didn't much like the sound of that. The idea of a reaction that I couldn't control filled me with anxiety and brought out my superstitious side.

It's not easy being a cyclist if you have a superstitious side. Sometimes I'd go out and tell myself that unless I touched a number 38 on the back brake light, left-hand side (and it had to be a Routemaster) I'd cop it later in the day. Other times I'd have to overtake every other rider on the road, even if it took me away from a job, or steer clear of roads and addresses featuring the letter Z, like Curzon Street or Maze Hill or Zenobia Mansions. Once I ended up riding the Westway at night while testing some cabbie's dumb theory that London has more left turns than right at a ratio of 4 to 3. I'd started at Old Street and headed west and by the time I got to Lisson Grove I'd counted forty lefts and fifty-five rights, which was the wrong way round so I carried on to Western Avenue to further test the theory, dick that I was. At Western Avenue my head told me Hanger Lane and after Hanger Lane it told me Target Roundabout and after Target Roundabout it was the dry ski slope at Hillingdon where my mother once dislocated a thumb and after that it was the M40 and when I got to the M40 it was dark and I was no longer in London so I turned around and headed back. By then I'd stopped counting because my maths is weak and because I eventually realised that logic dictates that every left is a right and every right is a left. When I got to the Westway it was all lit up so I went up onto the flyover with all London around me and I wondered what had made me carry on riding if it wasn't the left and right question, which it wasn't. The answer: superstition had glued me to my saddle. I can't even remember what the consequences of getting off would have been: no doubt they were apocalyptically bad. The consequences of cycling on the Westway was a ticket from the police, which felt like a let-off.

Don't get me wrong, it wasn't like this every day. Most days were normal. But some days the dickish impulse was too strong to resist. That Monday I'd felt the dickish impulse but repelled it, encouraged by the fact that my Pinarello had emerged from the crash remarkably unscathed: her frame was true, her wheels true, her headset was just a little wonky, her brakes were in need of only minor re-adjustment, and her *spumoni* paintwork was intact. I got on the saddle and headed into town. But straightaway I felt like I was pedalling squares and when I locked up outside the Priam I was happy to be off the roads. I announced myself to the hotel's receptionist, a Polish guy with what looked like cheese on his upper lip.

Delivery for Zenith Couriers, I said.

Zenit Courier?

Yup. Zenith Couriers.

The guy looked at me. What happened to your face? he asked. Accident?

Yes, I said, accident.

On your bike?

Yes.

It look real bad man.

Thanks, it's nothing.

Room 45, he said, pointing to the elevator.

The Priam's white stucco was grand but inside it was all fake mahogany and stained carpets. I'd done countless hotel pick-ups and drops but they tended to be bigger outfits than this and you rarely went beyond reception. I took the lift and wondered whether this might be a top five job. My top five jobs were as follows:

1. Whole pig, frozen, thawed en route.
2. Bricks. Heavy, a dozen of them. But a £50 tip.
3. Urine samples, one batch. Hospital to lab.
4. Salamanders, three, in takeaway boxes, pet shop to client.
5. Dildos, boutique, set of six, sex shop to client.

Also: false teeth, fancy dress, narcotics, bibles, ice, birthday cake, toupees, passports, wedding rings, car keys, fertiliser, fishing rods, chicken feed...

But most of the time it was just envelopes.

Room 45 was at the end of the corridor, the last room in the hotel. I knocked and a voice told me to come in. An American voice, elderly.

It was a small room, bathroom to the right, desk with a TV on top, windows curtained twice and looking out to nowhere, double bed round the corner. What hit me was the smell of the place, alcohol fumes and cigarettes, no air at all, and then its darkness: the only light was a chink where the curtains didn't meet and a tiny bedside lamp.

In the bed lay Sorensen, sitting upright, propped up by pillows, reading a book on taxidermy. Next to him on the bed a cigarette smoked itself out in an ashtray.

Half his body was covered by bedclothes but you could tell he was a giant, an enormous man, six foot ten or something crazy. He had a thin pocky face, long nose and great ears. I figured he was in his early seventies by the wrinkles and the veins and by the pure whiteness of his hair which was thin and ran neat, left to right, across his forehead. He wore a white vest of the kind old men wear but it was pristine, like he'd put it on new that morning, and in the wardrobe I saw hanging two dark suits and two crisp white shirts. Underneath them stood a pair of cowboy boots with patterned stitching.

Up against the desk leant a walking stick. Its handle was the head of an eagle. On the desk was the man's passport, another eagle confirming him to be a citizen of the United States of America. Poking out of the top of the passport was a boarding pass and next to the passport was a wallet of crimson crocodile skin. Next to the wallet sunglasses, next to the sunglasses paracetamol, next to the paracetamol bourbon and next to the bourbon a tower of duty free cigarettes.

These were the atmospherics.

As for him, he continued to read quite deliberately, aware of my presence but not looking up, and as he read I noticed the size of his hands, the huge digits wrapped around the tiny book he was reading. They were either stranglers' hands or they were more benign: a double bass player's, a chief woodsman, some kind of heavy lifter. I said hello twice and the second time he looked up. Do you like reading? he asked, after a moment's silence, and then afterwards: are you room service?

What the fuck. Did I like reading? Did I look like room service?

No, I replied. I am not room service.

Oh sorry, he said. I thought you were room service. Do they have room service here?

I don't know. Do I look like room service?

Not particularly. But this is a strange place. Not really what I was hoping for.

I'm sorry.

Don't be sorry. I asked for somewhere central and this

is where I ended up. I've stayed in worse but only in the third world. Who are you if you're not room service?

I'm from the courier company.

The courier company?

The courier company. Zenith Couriers. Do you have something for me?

Did I order a courier?

I don't know. Did you? Maybe I've got the wrong room.

He looked at me as if to consider whether I had indeed got the wrong room. Then he found a bookmark for his book and told me to hang on. Stay, he said. I may well need a courier. Take a seat. That's kind, I replied. But I have another job to get to.

Another job? he said. Can you be late?

It doesn't really work like that.

Oh, he said, how does it work?

Well I pick up stuff and take it to wherever it needs to go. And it needs to be there on time. Do you have something for me?

You pick things up?

Yes.

And deliver them?

Yes, I said. Do you have something for me?

I might well do.

You might?

Yes, I might do, the man said.

And when are you going to decide?

Do you smoke? he asked. Have a cigarette. My name is Jon Sorensen.

I'm Sam, I said, declining. It's a bit early thanks.

It's never too early, he replied. He reached for a half-finished pack on the bed and threw it at me. Good catch, he said. They're Danish. Would you pass me my stick?

I passed him his stick and with it he manoeuvred himself out of bed at the far side and limped the three metres to the bathroom. Sorry, he said, locking the bathroom door, I've got to take a leak.

Brilliant. I had myself a cripple in jockeys. This was not part of the contract. I checked my phone and thought about making a run for it. It was fourteen minutes past eleven. My next job was back in town at half past. It was possible but unlikely. I texted Poyntz: *Got myself a madman* and Poyntz texted back: *A good one or a bad one?*

I replied: *A crazy in white jockeys* and then the crazy in white jockeys returned from the bathroom, ablutions complete, joggers donned, a key in his right hand. It was seventeen minutes past eleven. If he cut to the chase I might still make it. What do you think of the cigarette? he asked.

Seriously, I told him, I've got to go.

Pass me one please, he replied, taking a shirt from the wardrobe and putting it on.

I handed him the pack and he moved over to the window, drew the curtains, opened a pane and lit up, dressing at the same time. They are made in Søborg, he said. Or at least they were. Søborg is an unremarkable place. I went there once many years ago, with a girlfriend of mine called Anna Vig. We drove the long way down, along the coast, through Gothenburg and beyond. Søborg is not far from Copenhagen. You will know Copenhagen. My aunt was ill. Dying too young. It was very awkward. The house was tiny, full of cheap things, china dogs, that kind of rubbish. We stayed too long. Every time we tried to say goodbye the poor woman would find some excuse to make us stay longer. Another cup of chocolate. More *wienerbrød*. We were too polite. There were endless photograph albums. Trips to

31

the beaches in this, that year. Do you know the beaches of Denmark?

No.

They are nice to visit if you are passing. But if you are passing, avoid Søborg. Of course my aunt went a bit crazy when we finally left. Weeping as we stood at the door. The fear of dying alone. What became of Anna I don't know. I remember us getting back to Copenhagen very hungry and having an argument because we didn't have enough money for a proper meal. Do you earn good money in your job?

No, I said. The money's shit.

What's the price of shit?

Two fifty a drop. I'm losing money as I speak.

Per week?

As I speak.

I heard you. I'm not deaf. How much do you earn per week?

Four hundred if I'm very lucky. Why?

He laughed. I am making conversation, he said.

I don't have time for conversation. I'm about to miss my next job.

I'll make your time worthwhile, he said.

How? I asked.

I'll pay you.

For my time?

Of course.

How much?

That depends.

Depends on what?

Depends on how long it takes.

How long what takes?

How long it takes to do the job.

Well tell me what the job is.

What do you want to know?

I want to know what I'm taking. The book?

No, no. Not the book.

The alcohol?

No. The liquor's mine.

Money?

No.

Drugs?

He laughed. Do I look like a junk merchant to you?

You thought I was room service.

Well that was a mistake.

So what is it then?

He paused. Here, he said, and he threw me the key.

It was three inches long, old, slightly warped, rusting, with white paint on its tip and the number seven inscribed into the bottom of the handle. What's it for? I asked.

What do you think?

I've no idea.

It's for opening a door.

Very funny. You want this delivered?

Not exactly.

You don't want this delivered?

No.

Fine, I said. You want me to go somewhere and pick something up. What will you pay me?

Whatever it takes.

I've already lost a day's work.

So how much do you want?

A day's work.

How much is that?

One hundred.

Ok, he said, pass me my wallet.

This was funny. I passed him his wallet and from it

he pulled out two crisp fifty pound notes – those lovely oversized red ones – and handed them over.

I might need one fifty, I said.

Really? One fifty?

One fifty all up. This being a freelance job.

Ok, he said. Then he gave me another fifty. But you'll probably need more, he added.

More? I said.

Yes. You'll need more.

Fine, I replied and I told him to hold on. I texted Fat Barry:

> Back too soon. I can't ride. Have finished job in
> W2. Please reassign W1. Sorry. Will call later

and straightaway my radio crackled. I turned it off. Then my phone went too. I silenced it.

Listen, I said, before I take any more of your money, do me a favour and tell me what you want me to do.

Okay, he replied. That's the key to my house in Norway. I want you to go there and pick something up.

Norway?

Yes. Norway.

You want me to go to Norway?

Yes. Norway.

The country of Norway?

Yes, the country of Norway.

And what do you want me to pick up? I asked.

An owl, he said.

An owl?

Yes, just an owl.

What do you mean an owl? I asked.

He looked indignant. What do you think I mean by an owl? An owl. An *owl*.

A real owl?

Yep. A real owl.

A real, live owl?

No, he said, the owl's dead.

Dead?

He's stuffed, he replied. I need him for a competition. But I can't get him myself.

This was straight in at number one. This beat the frozen pig, hands down. It was fucking brilliant, perfect, a major piece of work. A stuffed owl. In a foreign country. For a bunch of top denomination notes and the chance to escape the city.

Why can't you go there yourself? I asked.

It's complicated, he said.

Go on, I replied, I've got some time now.

Then take a seat, he said, and I took one. He carried on standing by the window, looking out.

What's your name again? he asked.

Sam, I said.

Sam what?

Sam Black.

Yesterday Sam, he said, I suffered a stroke. Yesterday, on the flight over from New York. Not a big one, just a little flicker. But the doctors say I can't travel for at least a week. They say I need to take things easy.

What doctors?

The doctors at the airport. They told me no air travel and no cigarettes.

You're smoking.

Sure. They can't stop me from smoking. But they can stop me from getting on a plane.

What happened? I asked. You look okay to me.

I'm fine. Totally fine. My vision just went a bit blurry. I don't know what it was. Maybe the Valium. I'd woken up and we were just about to land when boom my arm went numb and everything was fuzzy. Didn't last long. By the time the plane was on the runway and we'd taxied in I was already feeling better. But they'd noticed me looking shaky so they took me off to hospital in an ambulance and they did some tests. A mini-stroke is what they called it. Not a big one, just a little flicker. Fine, I told them, I want to go now. They said I could go but that I needed to rest, take it easy.

So you came here?

I'm already thinking of moving.

Then what's the problem? I asked. Stay in a hotel for a week, relax, then get on a plane.

I can't go in a week, he said. I'll run out of time.

Run out of time for what? I asked.

For the competition, he replied.

What's the competition?

The World Taxidermy Championships. They're taking place in a fortnight, in Springfield.

You're making this up, I said.

I wish I was, he replied. Category seven, non-game birds. First place ribbon in a subcategory means you go forward for Best in World. *Bubo scandiacus*. Mr Tecolote's one of the finest specimens of snowy owl —.

Mr what?

Mr Tecolote. You speak Spanish?

No.

Tecolote means owl in Spanish.

Great.

He's a male snowy and pretty much as pure white as they get. Hardly a speck of black on him at all.

And when's this competition?

Weekend after next.

Where did you say it was?

Springfield.

Where's that?

Illinois.

Sounds like you've got plenty of time. You wait a week, take a flight next Monday or Tuesday, pick up the owl, then fly back to the States.

No, he said. It's too tight. I need to go from London to Bergen, then back again, then to New York, then to Springfield. I need to be there on the Friday to register.

Bergen?

That's the closest airport.

And how far is it from there?

I'll give you some directions in a moment.

Actually d'you know what? I said. Forget it. I'm not sure this is one for me. I don't really do international dockets.

Oh, he said. That's a shame. You look like you could do with the money.

How much money? I asked.

Well. Let's say you leave tomorrow and it takes you a couple of days. Do you drive?

Yes, I lied.

You'll need to drive. You'll need money for the flights, something for the car hire and petrol, a bit of spending money, somewhere to stay. Plus whatever you'd be earning in your normal job.

One fifty a day, I lied.

Okay, so three hundred for the job and maybe three hundred for expenses, that's six hundred plus a bit extra when you bring back Mr Tecolote in a nice condition. Do you think you can do that?

I thought for a moment. What I thought was that if I cycled and saved on expenses and brought along Poyntz for the ride, I would definitely need more money.

I have some problems at work, I explained. I won't be able to go for a couple of days and then I can't just disappear. If I get caught bunking off or doing jobs on the side, I'll get the sack. You'll need to pay me a risk premium.

A risk premium? he said.

Yeah. I'm risking my job. So you need to pay me enough money to make that risk worth it.

How much is enough?

Pay me five days' work and the same in expenses.

He turned from the window and looked at me. You're asking me to pay you fifteen hundred pounds? he said.

Yes, I replied.

I'll pay you half now and half when you return the bird.

Seven fifty now, seven fifty later?

Yes, he said.

And the extra?

That will be discretionary. I'll need the bird by Friday.

I can't leave till Thursday, I lied, thinking about cycling.

Monday then.

What time? I asked.

Midday, he said.

Fine, I replied. And the house?

What about it?

Where is it?

A couple of hundred kilometres from Bergen. It's a mountain hut, near a lake. Very beautiful. I bought it years ago but then I had to move abroad. So I didn't go there much.

And the owl? I asked.

You can't miss him, he said. He's up on the wall, next to the northern hawk, Mr Scritch. There are three of them. A tawny, Mr Ker. A northern hawk, that's Scritch and then on the far side Mr Tecolote. Yellow eyes, black beak, perfect white plumage.

And what do I do?

What do you mean what do you do?

What do I do when I get there?

Let yourself in with the key, unscrew him off the wall, pack him up nice and careful with some bubble wrap and newspaper, lock up, and bring the owl to me. Simple.

Why don't you just get him shipped?

Shipped? Are you crazy? The bird is too important to be shipped. I had a bad experience with a moose's head, a few years back.

Problems with the law? I asked.

He looked sharply at me then relaxed. No no, he replied, problems with a broken antler.

7

ON THE PLANE TO NORWAY

It was the following day and we were on a plane, Poyntz and I, somewhere over the North Sea. Poyntz was in the window seat, I was in the aisle seat. Once more we were playing backgammon. I was losing. We'd played two games already and I'd been whopped both times. We were halfway through the third and I had two of my pieces stranded on the bar.

What d'you reckon? Poyntz was looking at one of the air hostesses. Every time she walked past he followed her with his eyes.

I shook my head. She was okay but no knockout.

Come on, Poyntz said.

Not my type, I replied.

He rolled sixty-four and moved. Maybe she has a bit too much make-up, he said. But she has amazing hips.

The flight was fine but there'd been trouble with our bikes at the airport. The Pinarello was in a United States Postal Service bag I'd borrowed from Early Man. It was the biggest bag in the airport, the people-smuggler's bag of choice. The guy at the desk had ordered me to detach the pedals and I'd argued with him for as long as I could but he just pointed to the queue behind us. I took the pedals off with a wrench.

(We'd brought few clothes, many tools.)

When the guy saw Poyntz's bike he let out a sort of death-sigh and told him he couldn't let it on board.

Oh, Poyntz said, genuinely surprised. What's the problem?

It is not appropriately contained, the man said. Our regulations clearly state that any bicycles taken on board must be fully enclosed within a bag or otherwise secured so no part, such as handlebars or pedals, is protruding.

Well I think I've done an okay job.

No, Sir.

It's fine, argued Poyntz.

No, Sir.

The handlebars may be a little conspicuous, Poyntz said, but I was in a major hurry. I didn't know I was flying till yesterday. I think it's good to go.

I'm afraid not Sir, said the man. Unless the bicycle is adequately packaged I cannot let it through.

Poyntz's Bianchi lay on the floor like a sick patient. It was in a brown cardboard bike box, patched up with gaffer tape. He'd left the wheels on and hadn't even bothered to lower the seat. Reluctantly he started to dismantle it. Pedals, wheels, post. The headset he twisted round. The wheels he carried.

When the man finally printed off Poyntz's boarding pass, he asked him whether he'd deflated his tyres.

No, replied Poyntz, I haven't.

Please do so, he said. The change in atmospheric pressure can cause the inner tubes to expand and burst.

8

Fish

An air hostess, not the one Poyntz liked, came around with tea. Poyntz had blitzed early in the third game and had started bearing off. I now had no less than three men stuck on the bar.

You're screwed, Poyntz said.

It was an understatement. Even if I hit his blots as he bore off I wouldn't roll enough big numbers to catch him. It was going to be the mother of all backgammons. But breakfast was arriving and the air hostess was telling us to put the game away.

What do you want to do? I asked Poyntz.

We'll eat later.

I'm hungry.

You just don't want to lose.

Maybe I can save the game.

Don't be dumb. Concede the backgammon.

No.

Concede the gammon at least.

No.

Well what d'you want to do then dipshit?

Let's just stick it under the seat and carry on after breakfast.

The board will get messed up.

Not if you're careful.

We won't be.

Jesus Christ, I said. Memorise positions then. Black's three on the bar, five on thirteen, three on eight, five on six.

Hold on, Poyntz said. White's more complicated. Two men off, two on one and five, three on two, three on three, three on —.

But before he'd finished the air hostess had carefully picked up the board and replaced it with a tin foil tray. I'll put it at the bottom of the trolley, she said. Come and pick it up when you've finished eating.

After finishing eating we finished the game, I lost, and then Poyntz took out his phrasebook. I want you to test me, he said. I've learnt Norwegian.

What? I said. The whole language?

Not quite. But I know the fish section off by heart.

That's useful.

Go on. Test me. It's all in my head.

Okay, I said. Give me the book.

The book covered Danish, Finnish, Icelandic, Norwegian and Swedish, in that order. They all looked the same. It called itself a language survival kit, as if the future of all Scandinavian dialects depended on it. *The traveller who speaks a few words in the local languages will be received with great enthusiasm and appreciation.* I found the fish section and went down the list.

Tuna?

Tunfisk.

Mackerel?

Makrell.

No shit. Cod?
Torsk.
Halibut?
Hellefisk or *kviete.*
Salmon?
Laks.
Jesus, I said. You really have learnt them. Anchovy?
Ansjos.
Lobster?
Hummer.
How about eel?
Eel is ål.
I checked his pronunciation. Annoyingly it was correct. How about cabbage? I asked. Vegetables were on the opposite page.
I only do fish, said Poyntz.
But it sounds just like eel. Have a guess.
Poyntz paused. Cabbol?
Kabul?
Cabbol.
Cabal?
Very funny. Fish is my subject not veg. What is it?
Kål. That's k, a with a circle on top, and l. You were close.
Kål. We'll order that when we get there. Eel and cabbage: ål and *kål.*
With soused herring.
Kryddersild.
I smiled and gave him back the book. So you've learnt some Norwegian, I said.
Go on, he said. Test me some more.
Later, I replied. I'm tired of Norwegian.
I closed my eyes and tried to sleep but I couldn't so I looked through my lashes at the man to my right. He

44

had a white ponytail and a T-shirt with a joke on it. I tried to make out the joke but the creases were in the way. Eventually he shifted and I got it. It said:

TEENAGERS!
Tired of being harassed by your stupid parents?
ACT NOW!
Move out, get a job and start paying your own bills
while you still know everything!

The guy was reading some kind of thriller: on the front cover a wolf with red eyes was sitting on its hind legs, howling its arse off, blood trickling from its fangs. Behind the wolf there was a full moon and a wood and above them, written in embossed gold, was the book's title and its author: *Skjebne* by Kjell Lid.

Skjebne. I turned to Poyntz. What does *skjebne* mean?
Skjebne? he repeated.
Yes, I said. *Skjebne*.
He paused. Is it some kind of flatfish?
I closed my eyes properly and considered the Game.

9

THE GAME

The Game had begun as a little exercise to bring Poyntz up to a standard where he could reasonably take on Salowitz and win back the cash he'd lost in that kamikaze match at the Crown. But it morphed into addiction. We played backgammon in most spare moments and spare nights, sometimes at my place, sometimes at Poyntz's, sometimes at the Montmorency, usually elsewhere. We'd meet up at lunch, laying out the board on pavements or tables or the footsteps of churches. Four sessions a week – twenty-four games – was our bread and butter although often we played more. Single games were worth a point, gammons two, backgammons three. Scores were multiplied up to a maximum of sixty-four by the doubling cube. The tally we kept in a little black book we called Heidi. Thirty thousand feet up, Heidi looked like this:

| Poyntz | 110 Netherlands Antilles guilders |
| Sam | 1003 Netherlands Antilles guilders |

The stake had moved around a little. We'd started with sterling but the maximum margin of victory at a pound a point we calculated to be two and a half grand, way beyond a courier's earning power. For a while we toyed with quarter and half stakes – twenty-five, fifty pence – but it was too complicated. Then Poyntz suggested international currencies so we opted for the dollar but when it rose against the pound the margins became unsustainable. We rejected the euro, the Brazilian real and the yen before eventually settling on the Liechtenstein franc, a currency of esoteric glamour that was pegged to the Swiss franc and thus largely immune to turmoil in the foreign exchange markets. The first series concluded in this way:

Poyntz	1320 Liechtenstein francs
Sam	1082 Liechtenstein francs

The sum of two hundred and thirty-eight Liechtenstein francs I handed over to Poyntz in a plain brown envelope. It hurt, being beaten by a rookie. My intention had been to pay up in the indigenous currency so Poyntz could go spend it in Vaduz. But conversion was costly so I bunged him a hundred quid and although he quibbled, once he saw the actual notes he shut up.

I suggested we lower the basic stake in Series Two. The Netherlands Antilles guilder had similar properties to the Liechtenstein franc but a slightly shorter rate of return on sterling. My argument was that the original payment had been high relative to the narrow margin of victory: a bigger win could have seen one of us – I didn't say *me* – seriously out of pocket. Poyntz accused me of running scared.

I've got nothing against the guilder, he explained, but if we play as we did last year, the stake will hardly be worth it. Last time it was close and I won a hundred quid. Perfect. If we'd bet guilders, I'd have only won fifty, sixty. After four, five hundred games, that's nothing. You're just worried I'll take you by a lot more: eight, nine hundred points. But if you want to be a pussy then fine. We'll change the stake to guilders.

We changed the stake to guilders but soon I was regretting it. One week in, my winning streak began, and it ran and ran. On the last day of August, the evening of the game at the Montmorency, I had won thirty-six consecutive sessions. I was three hundred quid to the good, in the currency of Curaçao. In Vaduz I would have been up four hundred, but it seemed that my luck was turning.

10

Luxury items

After we landed we buried our bags somewhere outside the airport then cycled north-west, knowing only
that north and west was roughly where we needed to
head. We had a compass which Poyntz had brought
and the Sorensen Directions and a map of the entire
country of Norway which I had printed off the internet.
But we had flown into Oslo, not Bergen as instructed:
my error.

I'd asked a man standing under a bus shelter for the
road to the Hardangerfjord. The Hardangerfjord was at
the top of the Sorensen Directions. The man was small
and white-haired with a wizened face. He wore a black
leather jacket and round wiry glasses. He was like Andy
Warhol.

When he heard my question he burst out laughing.
Very fun! he said. Hardangerfjord!

Yes, I replied. The Hardangerfjord. I was tired from
burying the bags and wanted to get riding.

Fun! the guy kept laughing. Very fun! Very fun!

I concluded that he was simple or that he was laughing at the scars on my face.

What's the deal? I asked. How many fingers? I held up four.

Four, he replied and stopped laughing. I am not an idiot, he said.

What's so funny then?

Nothing, he replied. But why do you fly into Oslo? Why do you not fly into Bergen? Or Haugesund? You fly into Oslo?

Yes.

From where?

London.

Why?

I shrugged my shoulders. He was rubbing it in. I didn't know exactly why we'd flown into Oslo. Oslo was the capital city wasn't it? Capital city of Norway = Oslo. I'd just looked at the flights and assumed that's where we needed to go. It was an automatic starting point. Plus, the tickets to Oslo were cheap. Plus, I hadn't consulted the map I'd printed off and I'd forgotten to write the word *Bergen* at the top of the Sorensen Directions.

Hardangerfjord is a long distance, Warhol said. Several hundred kilometres. It is best to leave your bicycle and take a bus. There is a good bus service here.

We're cyclists, I said.

You are madmans! Warhol replied. Then he wished us good luck and put his hands in his pockets.

I consulted Poyntz.

Why don't we ditch riding for today and go into Oslo and find a party? he suggested.

No. The man said it's hundreds of miles. We've got to be back in London in under a week.

A week's a long time.

You think so?

No. But we'll cycle fast and we can get lifts and stuff.

That's cheating.

I don't mind cheating.

We don't even have a decent map.

This map of Norway is a start.

You know the way to the Hardangerfjord do you?

I reckon so.

Of course you do.

I reckon I do, said Poyntz. This compass is epic. Much more useful than it looks.

The bags we'd buried round the corner using Poyntz's shit shovel – a military-issue portable spade which was one of many items he'd brought that were surplus to requirement. We chose a crooked tree to mark the spot, hoping it would still be crooked when we returned and in the big hole we interned the United States Postal Service bag and inside it:

- 1 poncho
- 1 rucksack
- 2 spare spanners, 15 mm and 10/8 mm respectively
- 1 spare chain extractor
- 1 cable cutter
- 1 chain checker
- 2 spare tyres, 700x23 cm, spare tubes
- 1 spare crank wrench
- 1 kettle
- 1 copy, paperback, *The Sorrows of Young Werther*
- 2 snakeskin neckties (spares)
- Nineteen pounds, seventy-five pence in sterling
- Tarpaulin, in case of rain

Kept aside for the journey, weight to be distributed equally between riders, were the following:

- 2 hammocks plus rope, carabinas, bungee cord
- 2 sleeping bags
- Lights
- Cycling caps, helmets
- Clothing, including bib shorts, base layers, leggings, gloves
- Woollen hats, balaclavas
- Crank wrench, spoke wrench, tubes, levers, pump, links, multi-tool
- 8, 9, 10, 15 mm spanners
- Matches, lighters, penknife
- Sunglasses
- 2 snakeskin neckties
- Backgammon plus Heidi
- Tin opener, cutlery, mugs, plates
- Shoes for socialising and dancing
- Tobacco etc.
- Painkillers, glucose tablets, chewing gum
- Locks (1 Kryptonite, 1 Abus) plus cables
- Stove, Butane, saucepan, stuff for coffee
- Walkman and iPod, headphones, headphone splitter
- The Sorensen Money and the Sorensen Directions

My luxury items, three permitted, were a big bottle of cognac, a small tub of anti-chafing cream and a notebook and pencil.

Poyntz's luxury items were his turban, a bottle of hot sauce, a pack of firelighters and a shit shovel. I told him he couldn't take the shit shovel.

Why not? he said.

It weighs a fucking kilo. It will slow you down big time.

I'll be quicker going down the hills.

Trust me. It's not worth it. You can bury shit with your hands.

That's not hygienic.

Jesus Christ. Since when have you been an ambassador for hygiene?

Listen I can take what I fucking want to take. That's the definition of a luxury item.

But you already have three, I said.

You've got four as well.

No I don't.

Cognac, crack cream, notebook, pencil? That's four in my book.

The notebook and pencil are part of the same package, I said.

So are the hot sauce and the shit shovel, he replied.

11

BALWANT SINGH

On the first night we found an empty boat shed on the banks of a massive lake. We'd ridden sixty miles and played one session of backgammon, which I'd lost. The sky was purple. We drank cognac and ate ravioli cold out of the tin.

The boat shed was empty of boats but there were oars that lay perpendicular on the rafters and there was fishing stuff scattered around – buoys and nets – in which Poyntz took a passing interest. Animal pelts hung from the walls. We hung our hammocks from the beams. The ropes we strung too long and the hammocks swung too much and were a little high and difficult to get into. We didn't change clothes, just added: we didn't know how cold it would get or how well our sleeping bags would fare, it being September. Swinging to pass the cognac, smoking in our bags, we played another session of backgammon on a board laid out on a wooden drum that stood between us. Once again I lost. Then Poyntz said he was going to clean his teeth and after that he was going to tell me about his trip to India to visit his disgraced grandfather Balwant Singh, the lingerie entrepreneur, and that if I fell asleep so be it but if I listened, so much the better.

Poyntz had been to see him the previous year, in spite of his parents. Balwant Singh was the lingerie entrepreneur on his father's side, not the one on his mother's side who was deemed to be respectable. Balwant Singh was a disgrace in the family but no one knew why because no one ever talked about it. The only things Poyntz knew about him was that he probably lived in Nagpur, that he was a former state squash champion and that he was totally fucking loaded.

Poyntz told his family he was flying to Mumbai and taking the first train to Rajasthan where he'd go to the usual places before flying south to Goa. That sounds acceptable, his father had said. He was told to send his mother a postcard from every city he went to and to avoid Nagpur, which was a dangerous place full of criminals.

Poyntz flew to Mumbai and took the first train to Nagpur. He turned up unannounced at a sports club in an upmarket neighbourhood where he was informed by an impeccably dressed receptionist that Balwant Singh was not about. But a message could be left. A message was then passed back to Poyntz's hotel, next to the train station, that he should attend an address, a villa in the suburb of Byramji, at noon the following day.

Certainly it had occurred to Poyntz that tracking down his grandfather in a country of over a billion people, with only three facts to go on, would be a difficult task. But Poyntz went to the place where rich people in Nagpur played sport and hit the jackpot straight away.

The journey to Nagpur had been uneventful until Poyntz was abruptly woken at six in the morning by a man entering his cabin. The cabin was meant to be private but this was India and there wasn't much Poyntz could do. The man had a certain authority. He'd removed

Poyntz's bag from the lower bunk, replaced it with his own case, aluminium and very large, took from the case a pack of mango-flavoured beedi and lying down on the bunk with his head on the pillow and his feet on the case, lit the flavoured cigarette, inhaled, and sighed. Poyntz decided to cut his losses and within half an hour the sun was up and he and his new acquaintance, who introduced himself as Mr Agarwal, were drinking chai and making their way through the flavours – strawberry, chocolate, cherry, clove, etc. The usual formalities were exchanged: Poyntz explained he was off to visit a long-lost relative in Nagpur and had slept most of the journey since Mumbai. Mr Agarwal explained he was getting off at Gondia, the end of the line, where before visiting his family whom he'd not seen for two weeks he was to report to his manager on the progress of his business trip. The trip had been a qualified success. Engaged on behalf of the Big Beedi Company – listed as suppliers of tobacco products such as cigarettes, cigars, raw tobacco, hand rolled beedi, gutkha and pan parag – he'd secured a larger-than-expected number of deals along the line. Deals are all okay apart from one, he said, slapping his hand down on his aluminium case. Poyntz asked what was in it. All my deals, Mr Agarwal replied, except one. The missing deal was with a local bigwig in Bhusarwal who worked for the Maharashtra State Electricity Board. The meeting had been arranged at a power plant along the banks of the Tapti, a longish tuk-tuk ride from the station. It wasn't the biggest deal on Mr Agarwal's list but Bhusawal was a market that had been specifically targeted by the Big Beedi Company. Mr Agarwal waited in the reception area an hour, then two hours, but the man did not come. The desk wallah made one call only, telling Mr Agarwal that the man had been alerted to his presence and would be down as soon as he was ready. The sun rose in the sky, gently baking Mr Agarwal. The reception area was not air-conditioned. There was a single, small, non-directional, non-oscillating fan pointing straight at the desk wallah but Mr Agarwal felt it would be rude to ask him to share the air. He likewise felt uneasy about going outside, where it would be cooler in the shade, in case the man came down to find nothing but an empty chair. For the same reason he didn't dare visit the bathroom. Neither did he risk reading the paper he'd bought in case the man came down to find him reading the paper; and he didn't dare close his eyes for fear of falling into slumber. His shirt was drenched, his Western suit unable to hide the sweat patches growing from his armpits like tumours. He imagined himself stripping off naked and diving into the broad, cool waters of the Tapti. It didn't matter that a thermal plant providing one-sixth of Maharashtra's electricity adjoined the river. He wouldn't have cared if the entire effluence of the state was piped into his swimming lane. I have made a series of major errors and this deal will not go through, thought Mr Agarwal. But after exactly three hours and thirty-three minutes, the man came down, apologised for his lateness, and took Mr Agarwal up to his office. The man's office was plush and severely air-conditioned. The contrast in temperature did something very strange to Mr Agarwal's body. As he was handing over his business card, in anticipation of the big pitch, he noticed his hand shaking violently, like it had been overtaken by a palsy. We are a blue-chip operation, said Mr Agarwal, and the shaking started in his legs. Our beedis are second-to-none, he continued, and his shoulders twitched uncontrollably. We distribute throughout the state, customers value our brand name as a mark of quality, he insisted, and his head jerked violently. What is the matter? said the client. Is the room at fault? I can turn the air down or open up the window? Do you like the view of the river? It is very peaceful: it makes up for all the heavy machinery. But are you epileptic? Should I call someone? A glass of water? Something to eat? Parkinson's? Leprosy? Or are you simply a little nervous? No no, replied Mr Agarwal, collecting himself. I am quite all right, Sir. Let me show you the product. But instead of opening up the case, which was crammed full of tobacco, he picked up his personal holdall, unzipped it, and began quite unconsciously to lay out its contents onto the man's imitation mahogany desk: wallet, underpants, a well-thumbed copy of *Devdas*, toothbrush, toothpaste, three shirts, ironed, one pair of cotton trousers, unironed, one half-empty bottle of aftershave, two condoms, pendants for his daughters, a bag of travel sweets, socks, a pencil sharpener, spare sandals, assorted ties, a foldaway umbrella, a penknife, mobile phone, toothpicks, one pair of sunglasses, two lemons, two handkerchiefs, V-neck jumpers (one brown, one grey), a plastic business card holder, a notebook, pencils tied together with string, six boxes of matches (one Triple Luck, three Triveni, two Fire Box), deodorant, two kurta pyjama (one for sleep, one for social), newspaper, fountain pen, writing paper, medicine (type unknown) and a single unopened packet of the Big Beedi Company's premium brand of cigarette: Happiness. In Mr Agarwal's fantasies thereafter the man picked open the packet of Happiness, savoured the smell of the leaves, tapped the filter on his desk, suavely lit the smoke with his on-desk marble lighter, inhaled – and then promptly ordered one lakh rupee's worth. But in reality he looked at his desk and sardonically enquired of Mr Agarwal which particular item he was looking to sell, the pencil sharpener? Or the condoms? Mr Agarwal passed out and when he came to, he was back in the reception and the desk wallah was explaining to him that the softener he'd set aside for the deal, as was custom, could be used to pay for the client's discretion. That the proposal came from the desk wallah suggested two things to Mr Agarwal: one, that the client was not discreet; and two, that the desk wallah had a more important role in the administration of the client's business than might normally be expected from a desk wallah. Either way, Mr Agarwal had to pay the softener or risk his entire career. From a hidden pocket in his aluminium suitcase he took four thousand rupees – in hindsight well over the odds – and handed them over. Then, as if in penance, he walked all the way back to the station, took the next train north and four days, eighteen hours and twenty-two minutes later – his graft money exhausted, *Devdas* once again read from cover to cover, his pack of toothpicks thirteen lighter and his plastic business card holder twenty-five heavier – Mr Agarwal walked into Poyntz's cabin and quickly decided that this was his final opportunity to recoup the money lost so shamefully to the man. He explained to Poyntz the elaborate practices and procedures of the accounts department of the Big Beedi Company; how the highest possible level of scrutiny was applied to the administration, in sales transactions, of the float; how the amount of money set aside for softening deals was carefully calculated according to factors such as the estimated liquidity of competing companies during the period in question, the malleability of target clients and the seniority of individual salesmen and their abilities at the big pitch; how the company's chief auditing officer had personally told him, Mr Agarwal, that every deal he made in which money had been used to ease negotiations could be discreetly checked with the client in question and that any surplus money should be handed back as soon as he returned to company headquarters and that any money unaccounted for would be thoroughly probed; how the previous year one of the company's star salesmen had gone missing during a trip to Madyha Pradesh with sixty thousand rupees' worth of facilitation money stitched into the lining of his suitcase; how when the salesman failed to return on time a private investigator was dispatched to trace him and the deals he had made, eventually tracking him down to a hotel on the outskirts of Indore; how the private investigator slipped into the salesman's room and carefully unstitched his case while the salesman was relaxing in the bar downstairs with a prostitute; how the private investigator found only a handful of minor notes and no evidence of deals having been made; how the private investigator then hid under the room's second bed with the aim of receiving intelligence as to the whereabouts of the missing money and how, two hours later, the salesman returned to the room with the prostitute and the two of them had sexual intercourse for twenty-five minutes – on the second bed – after which the prostitute left the room; how the private investigator waited until he was certain the salesman had fallen asleep before climbing out from under the second bed, locking the door, removing from his jacket a six-inch bladed kirpan, placing it in the right-hand back pocket of his blue jeans and flicking the light switch; how the salesman awoke abruptly with the private investigator standing over him, repeating the same question, namely what had he done with the sixty thousand; how the salesman, once he had put on his trousers, fixed his belt, smoothed his hair, taken a sip of mineral water and generally collected himself, told the private investigator that the money was untouched in his suitcase and there to be checked; how the private investigator said he'd checked the case already and the money wasn't there to which the salesman asked which pocket he'd checked, suggesting there was more than one; how the salesman then carefully unpicked a second hidden pocket and produced the sixty thousand; how he unpicked a third containing a further eighty thousand – emoluments from deals, he explained with a certain irony, which would be returned to the company in full – before unpicking a fourth and final pocket, hidden in the base of the case, in which he said was another bundle of cash which the salesman suggested might ease the private investigator's conscience but which instead contained a .22 revolver manufactured in West Bengal by Indian Ordnance Factories; how the salesman cocked the revolver, pointed it at the private investigator and told him to return to his superiors and tell them that the money was safe, that all was well with the deals and that he, the salesman, would be back in the office within the week; and how the private investigator responded by bowing deeply, emitting a short prayer to the Wondrous Master, and immediately leaving for Gondia, where he was never seen or heard of again. This, Mr Agarwal explained to Poyntz amid the giant cumulonimbus of beedi smoke that was now Poyntz's cabin, is a cautionary tale if ever there was one. Such is the way of the Big Beedi Company, employing spies to hide under your bed while you go about your private business. This, Mr Agarwal said, is why my aluminium suitcase has four hidden areas, the largest being in the base. But however cleverly constructed my suitcase is, it still lacks the four thousand I forfeited in shame and there is no way I can recoup that figure without a little charity from yourself. Only then can I return to the Big Beedi Company without fear of loss to myself and my family. Only then can my story be complete.

It is a preposterous story, interrupted Poyntz's grandfather, Balwant Singh, when Poyntz related it to him in the comfort of the luxury villa in Byramji.

Maybe, said Poyntz.

Maybe? You mean you believe that bullshit about the palpitations in the power plant? The knife-wielding private investigator? The swim in the foul fucking Tapti? The man was a confidence trickster. A thief. A vagabond. A fantasist. There are millions of them in this country. Don't tell me you gave him the money?

I did.

You did? You gave him four thousand rupees?

Yes, grandfather.

Then you are more stupid than I originally thought.

But you don't realise, grandfather.

Realise what?

He had a gun hidden at the bottom of his aluminium suitcase.

Nonsense dear boy: that was a ruse. He was as likely to have had a gun as he was to have been a tobacco salesman. Did you actually look inside the case?

It was full of cigarettes.

A suitable prop for a man addicted to smoking and thievery then. Now remind me, Poyntz's grandfather asked, taking a sip of whisky and selecting a cigar from his humidor, what exactly are you doing here in Nagpur?

12

TYRIFJORDEN

When I woke it was early and there was dew on my sleeping bag and a cigarette burn on my hammock. I looked over to Poyntz and he was sleeping like a baby, although he was wearing a balaclava. The animal pelts spooked me in the morning light. I imagined their skinner arriving back from a dawn hunting trip, weapons in one hand, dead animals in the other. I jumped out of the hammock, unzipped my sleeping bag, wrapped it around me to stay warm, checked the bicycles hadn't been stolen, lit a cigarette, and went to look at the lake.

It must have been half six or something. The water was vast and still and covered in a thin layer of mist. I couldn't make out the banks on the other side. I wanted to wash my face in the water but I was paranoid about my scabs coming off. The fat slug on the left by my chin was beginning to curl up around the corners; this was where I had hit the ground. The one on the other side ran cheekbone to jaw, disintegrating in stages, a red archipelago of scars; this was where I had hit the citrus. I didn't need to be clean for anyone and I was reconciled to a certain ugliness but still I wanted that water on my face. The bandages had been off two days now.

I felt bored waiting for Poyntz to wake up and a little lonely too so I picked up my Pinarello and carried her over to my side. Sometimes I felt she was my companion for life, the Pinarello. Previously when I'd had the Dawes and when the Dawes got totally piranha-ed – every single part nicked save the frame – I felt such deep pain I had trouble eating and I had recurring dreams of her complete. Then the week after I finished re-building her, imbecile that I was, I left her outside a shop as I went to buy a box of matches and when I came back out she was gone. That's the Super Galaxy for you: always in demand.

The Pinarello was in a different league though. Lots had happened since the Dawes got stolen. First her replacement, the Raleigh Professional. Then the business with my mother, which greatly amplified my previously narrow understanding of grief. The Pinarello came after all of this and was a kind of vessel for all my sadness and my love and my aspirations. She was like the perfect girlfriend I didn't have: love at first sight when unwrapped, a few heady months getting to know each other, then happy co-existence with the occasional hiccup (I had to overhaul her Campagnolo groupset for instance). Someone caught me talking to her once, not pillow talk, just something soft, about what I can't remember, maybe the replacement of a brake pad, and it came over all wrong, a little lustful, perverted even. After that I tried to tone things down, at least in public, but I really did love my Pinarello.

As soon as Poyntz had woken, we packed up and left. I took a quick look at the map. The plan was to head for a place called Kongsberg on the quickest route possible and from there make for the mountains and Sorensen's hut. But Poyntz wanted to go round the water riding east and south out of the peninsula instead of north and west. So all morning we hugged the lake, taking in the shimmering water, removing layers as the sun rose in the sky. Halfway round, through a gap in the pines, we found sand and swam.

Poyntz went in first: big strides bollock-naked, an actor's dive, then front crawl, head-down, breaths every four strokes like he was racing to the other side of the lake. After fifty metres he stopped, caught some air, treaded some water and shouted fucking pussy at me. I was on the shore, thinking about my face.

What the fuck are you doing? he shouted. Come on! It's amazing!

I told him I was worried about my scabs.

Forget about your scabs! he said. Come in!

I walked in slowly, the cold way, and breaststroked out to him. He was right. It was amazing. Everything was blue and the sun warmed my skin and made me forget the ice of the water.

This was a good decision, said Poyntz, when I caught up.

To swim?

To swim. To come here.

You could be riding in the pouring rain, Fat Barry calling your radio.

I could be managing a lingerie factory in Nagpur.

What?

Managing a lingerie factory in Nagpur.

I don't get it.

Were you listening to me last night?

I must have fallen asleep. Is this about your grandfather?

Of course.

He offered you a job in India?

Being in charge of one of his factories. In Nagpur.

Clearly you're very well qualified to do that.

I went to a top university.

You got chucked out.

He doesn't know that.

So what's the deal?

Jesus didn't I tell you all this?

No, I fell asleep. Tell me now.

It's too late. Besides, we're swimming.

Give me the short version.

What's there to say? My grandfather was a disgrace to the family because he couldn't keep his cock in his pants. His first wife left him three weeks after their wedding. His second tried to kill him, shot him in the left buttock: he showed me the scar to prove it. His third was clever when they came to divorce and that's how he ended up in the lingerie business, making a mint so he could pay her off, which he did. His fourth was one of his models and after that I lost count.

How many wives has he had?

I don't know but he says he's celibate now. He's in his eighties. But I don't believe him.

How long did you stay?

A month. His house is fucking massive.

And he offered you a job at the end of it?

Halfway through. He said he couldn't understand why I wanted to be a bicycle-wallah – his words – when I could be running one of his factories and driving a Mercedes-Benz.

It's a fair point.

I don't know. I like what I do. It's freedom. It's being able to do what you want to do, go where you want to go. That's why I'm here, having a fucking adventure. Sure I'm curious about Sorensen and what he wants with his dumb owl. Plus, I could do with a bit of extra money. Mostly though, I just like the fact that you've been asked to do this stupid random job and I like the fact that you've asked me to do it too. And I like the fact that to do it, I've only had to tell one lie, one lie only.

After this Poyntz swam off towards an island and I swam back to shore because I was getting cold.

13

KONGSBERG

When we got to Kongsberg it was mid-afternoon and too late to hit the mountains so we looked for somewhere to hang our hammocks. We ended up in a forest a couple of miles outside of town and locked our bikes to a fat branch ten feet up. Then we lay in our hammocks and counted our cash.

The Sorensen Money had consisted of seven fifty in sterling, four hundred of which had gone towards the flights. The rest, converted at the airport, came to three thousand five hundred kroner. But Norway was expensive. Already we'd eaten twelve hundred kroner's worth of food: lunch the day before when Poyntz had wiped out five hundred in the supermarket before realising he'd miscalculated the exchange rate by a factor of ten (we feasted on smoked salmon, cod cakes and Coca-Cola). The ravioli alone was ninety. Then there was breakfast, and we'd spent three hundred at lunchtime on meatballs.

You said the trip would be self-financing, said Poyntz.

As for Kongsberg, it was unpromising. We found a bar trying to be a pub and took a table in the corner. We drank beer at fifty kroner each, figuring there'd be nothing to drink in the hills, and played backgammon quickly and with maximum concentration.

Have you noticed something? said Poyntz, after about an hour.

That I'm losing again? I was.

No, he said. More interesting than that. Look around: this place is rammed with metal-heads.

Back turned, I'd been considering how best to play a roll of double three against Poyntz's back game. He had four men behind my blockade which was five deep but I was probably going to be exposed sooner rather than later. I had a man on fifteen which I could move to six then hit his blot on one, but that left me vulnerable. I could move 8/5 (2) or 7/4 (2) or I could move 7/1 (2) which is what I ended up playing. Then I looked round.

He wasn't wrong. They'd descended in a swarm of black and ranged from low-grade dabblers and wannabes to groups of hardcore Lucifers. There was flesh and tats and piercings galore plus chains, bum-length hair, coats to boots and tons of demonic make-up: black, black on black, black on white, blood on black, blood on white. They wore T-shirts emblazoned with the names of otherworldly bands: Gorgoroth, Dark Throne, Obtained Enslavement, Keep of Kalessin, Thou Shalt Suffer, Trollfest, Grimfist, Necrophagia, Mayhem. The women were kind of hot, kind of ugly, purple and white hair, morbid lips and colourings, lots of fishnets, studs and velvet. Some were prim and Victorian, some Jezebel-like, others tiptoed along the BDSM spectrum: there was a couple attached to each other by a chain and I couldn't tell who was meant to be dominant and who submissive but they both looked pissed off with each other. Most of the women were more goth than metal and most of the men were more metal than goth and as far as the Satanists were concerned they pretty much appeared to be all male, although it's never that straightforward with Satanists.

We need a gigantic slice of this, said Poyntz. Whatever's going on.

Go and find out, I told him.

I packed up the half-finished game of backgammon thinking I was more likely to lose than win and I waited. He came back ten minutes later with more beer and a grin on his face.

I've got some, he said.

Got what?

Got some fucking tickets.

What tickets?

Tickets to the gig all these freaks are going to.

What's the gig?

Check it out. He showed me the ticket. *Carpathian Forest. Support act: Nebular Mystik.*

Never heard of them, I said.

Me neither.

How much?

Poyntz leaned across the table and whispered: Nada.

Oh, I said. You nicked them.

He shrugged.

Poyntz. You shouldn't do that. Go and give them back.

No wait, he said, learning forward again. I nicked them from a Nazi.

You what?

I nicked them from a Nazi. They were poking out of his trench coat. There's no place for Nazis in society. Never has been.

How d'you know he was a Nazi?

He had the fucking giveaway letters SS on his collar.

Poyntz, most people here are in fucking fancy dress.

Just because they've got blood painted on their faces, it doesn't make them real life vampires. Just because he likes Nazi shit it doesn't mean he's a real life Nazi.

No no. This guy was definitely a Nazi. I know one when I see one. It's totally cool. He only would have spread bad karma. Now everyone can go to the gig and relax without the skinheads.

Everyone apart from the guy you stole the tickets off.

And his mate. Another Nazi. There were two of them. I asked them for a light.

Oh. So you befriended them and then you nicked their tickets.

Jesus Christ. Do I need to explain everything? I've just got you tickets to a fucking amazing black metal gig and you're still complaining. If you don't want to come, I'll go on my own.

No, I said. I'll come. Of course I want to come. I just wish you hadn't stolen the tickets. Why didn't you just go to the box office?

Sam, said Poyntz, this gig is the hottest ticket in town. It's sold out multiple times. It's not every day that a band like Carpathian Forest comes to a little town like this.

Like you really know.

I can tell. Look at their following. These aren't local fanatics. They've come from afar. Some of them are probably from Denmark.

Yeah, I nodded. Or Sweden or Finland or somewhere.

Shut up.

We're going to stand out big time, you especially.

It doesn't matter.

It might to the Nazis who are looking for their tickets.

They won't suspect a thing. I showed cunning. Anyway, the tickets aren't numbered.

They wouldn't need to be. Look at us. Two plimsoll-wearers, one ginger, one Asian, at a death metal gig. We don't have a single item of leather between us.

What about the ties?

They're snakeskin.

We've got bib shorts.

That's lycra and classified as sportswear.

Maybe they could be re-classified as bondage gear.

Maybe you could be re-classified as a dick.

Hey, said Poyntz, what about if we got our D-locks and hung them round our necks or something? Borrowed some make-up, drew massive sprockets on our face? We could pretend we were like at the vanguard of some black metal freako radical cyclist collective. You could wear an inner tube like a bandanna and I could pump it up to 120 PSI! I could wear a chain like a knuckleduster and hang a crank tool from my belt! They'd be so fucking scared of us! We'd probably get back stage passes as a result!

I'd laugh if I didn't think you were semi-serious, I said.

And he replied: You are so fucking boring at times.

14

Black Metal

(part one)

He may have been right: the first thing I did on entering the club was check the emergency exits (I concluded the place was a monumental fire hazard) and the first thing Poyntz did was go and get himself some face paint.

He came back re-classified as a dick. His face was white-washed and his eye sockets black and bruised and he wore blood dripping from his lips.

This time I laughed. He looked properly funny.

Shut up, he said. You shouldn't laugh at a member of a minority group.

Who the hell did it for you?

Some guy.

Some guy?

Some guy called Oddmund. He was in the loo with his mates.

And?

They were in front of the mirror like a bunch of girls, applying finishing touches to their zombie faces. Listen, I'm the only non-Caucasian here. I needed to blend in a little.

He didn't really blend in but it didn't matter. By the time Nebular Mystik took to the stage the place was heaving, three or four hundred punters strong and everyone too stoked to care about strangers in their midst. I lost Poyntz after the second or third song, when we forged to the mosh at the front and made signs of the horn with the rest of the maniacs. We became the crowd: sweat-drenched, covered in lager, hypnotised by extreme sound, moving as one.

If Nebular Mystik were one thing, Carpathian Forest were another. No offence but they were twice the band: the bassist carried seventeen stone of throbbing flesh and wore shorts; the drummer was possessed by demons; the rhythm guitarists – the standard-bearers of noise – patrolled stage left and right like a pair of Satanic bodyguards while the lead singer bedecked in leather and studs bossed the centre, upturned crucifix in one hand, mike in the other, and abused his faithful followers in Norwegian and poor English: *We are here to make fuck you! To make sex with you! We are here to drink your bloods and bring your worlds into total darkness!*

I wondered what these men were really like. They probably had mothers and fathers who were slightly disappointed in them and didn't get the whole black metal schtick. They probably had brothers and sisters who worked as lawyers and accountants. Maybe they too led middle-class lives, were polite in conversation, owned cars that were regularly taxed, had side interests in botany, ate cereal and toast in the morning. I wondered whether Sorensen ate cereal and toast in the morning. It was easy to assume you knew the characteristics of a black metallist: vampiric tendencies, devil worship, tinnitus, but in reality these people probably led normal lives. I wondered what Sorensen, with an apparently normal life, was actually like in reality.

15

LEIBNIZ

What's his story? Poyntz had asked. It was the evening of the Monday I met Sorensen and I was trying to persuade Poyntz to come to Norway. We were in his flat in Oast Court in Limehouse.

I don't really know, I replied. I guess he's like a regular owl-lover.

Oh, one of those.

Yeah. He's kind of old and interested in owls. Maybe a bit creepy.

You'd have to be, said Poyntz.

Poyntz was eating spaghetti hoops on toast. I'd given him the cigarette carton which Sorensen had put the money in and which was secured by a thick rubber band. I told him to take a look. Just tell me, he said. No, I said. Take a look.

He laughed. Seven hundred and fifty quid! Don't tell me you won this at backgammon because that would be too funny.

I told him everything and at the end I said he should come with me.

Is this because I can drive a car and you can't? he said.

It's true Poyntz had passed his test and I hadn't. I'd

never even bothered to learn. I'd never sat in the driver's seat and I didn't know which pedal was which. One day I'd get round to it but not while I was still riding the Pinarello.

Poyntz knew how to drive a car. He didn't own a car but he had keys to a Vauxhall Nova that one of his cousins owned and which he drove at breakneck speed. We went to Brighton in it once, to a house party where we took mushrooms. I got locked in a bathroom. It was awful. We spent the next morning being sick amongst the pebbles, trying to concentrate on the horizon. When exhaustion finally set in Poyntz annoyingly found a wrap of speed in his pocket and promptly took it. I got back into the Nova, which had a fully retractable passenger seat. It was immensely comfortable. I curled up, closed my eyes and tried to block out the music and forget about the fear. When I woke it was cold in the car and I was somewhere in Limehouse. It was nine in the evening and everything was bathed in streetlamp orange. The doors of the Nova were locked and Poyntz was nowhere to be seen.

Sure Poyntz could have driven us around Norway but I had bad visions of him on those narrow mountain roads. He drove too enthusiastically for narrow mountain roads. When he drove he thought he was a cyclist and when he rode he thought he was a motorist. He also had nine points on his licence.

I didn't discount it completely though. Riding would take the whole week; if we drove we could do everything in a couple of days. We'd save money not hiring a car but we wouldn't be away from work for so long. It would be easier to swing with Fat Barry.

I put the proposal to him – cycling not driving – and he laughed a lot and then suddenly took it very seriously.

But I have some questions, he said, so please can I meet him, this Sorensen guy?

No, I replied.

Why not?

You come over all bad.

Just let me meet him, said Poyntz. I'll be on my best behaviour.

No way.

Why not? he said. What difference does it make if two of us go instead of one? As long as he gets his owl he doesn't care does he? I need to meet the madman. What if you have an accident, how am I going to find him?

I'm not going to have an accident, I said, thinking about Mr Bembo. I'm not due another for a long time.

You know it doesn't work like that, he said.

(Once Solomon Weisendanger had three accidents in four days. The first was a simple case of dooring which left him with bruised ribs. The second was a pothole which he would have noticed had he not been looking at a girl walking on the opposite pavement. When he regained consciousness he carried on looking for her, chump that he was, but she'd gone. The third he skipped the lights at Bank and got hit by a bus. He was off work for six months with a fractured pelvis and his beloved 1971 Holdsworth was a write-off.)

I told Poyntz I'd tell him where Sorensen was staying once we were on the road.

You don't trust me then? he asked.

It's not that, I said. You just might get curious. I know what you're like.

He's paying well above the odds for a courier job.

I know.

Don't you think that's a bit weird?

Maybe. Perhaps he doesn't know the market. Besides,

he's wealthy. He just wants what he wants and he's decided that this is how he's going to get it.

When would we go?

Tomorrow.

Tomorrow?

Tomorrow. Tuesday.

And when are we back?

Sunday. We need to give him the owl the following Monday.

So we've got less than a week.

Yes.

And you've looked at the map?

Kind of.

And what's it saying?

If we cycle, we'll need to hit it.

How hard?

Sixty, seventy miles a day.

That sounds okay.

Exactly. But there'll be hills.

Hills?

Well, mountains.

Mountains are okay. What about flights?

We need to book them. Probably now. But there are flights to Oslo every day.

From where?

Stansted. Heathrow. Wherever. I don't know.

And what about Fat Barry?

Look at my face. I'll be okay. But you'll need to come up with something.

I'm out of bullshit excuses with Barry.

Can you take leave?

Taken it.

Injury?

Done it.

Bereavement?

Done it.

Jesus. Who died?

Loads of people have died. My uncle. My grandmother. My great aunt. I told him the Sikh religion requires me to attend a lot of funerals. Which is kind of true.

So some of these people have actually died?

No. Well yes. My grandmother is dead but she died before I was born. My great auntie Pooja is alive and so is my uncle Brian. In fact, everyone's alive apart from my grandmother. Maybe I'll go for a wedding. One of my nieces. I'll tell Fat Barry my niece Amandeep is finally getting married. In Scotland.

Great, I said. I'll book the flights.

Hold on, said Poyntz.

What?

I don't get time to think this through?

No.

None at all?

Not really.

Are you gonna book the flights now?

Yeah.

What airline?

I don't know. Scandy Air.

And our bikes?

We'll need a few things.

Weather?

What about it?

What's it going to be like?

I don't know. I'm not a meteorologist.

But it's going to be cold isn't it?

Maybe. I don't know.

You mean it's going to be freezing.

No. It's like the end of summer.

Oh. And when do I get my money?

At the same time I get mine.

You're not going to double-cross me?

For fuck's sake Poyntz. Your move.

He rolled sixty-five and moved off the bar to his nineteen-point and then moved 19/14 to hit the only man I hadn't got safely into my home board. (The chances of this roll are exactly one-in-eighteen. I know this because we'd both been learning maths in an attempt to outwit each other. It started when I caught Poyntz with *An Introduction to Probability* in his courier bag. Imagine this: you're after a blot your opponent has left exposed. It's ten pips away. Your chances of hitting it are slim. You can roll a double five or a sixty-four but that's it. Three rolls in thirty-six equates to an 8 per cent chance of hitting it. But if the blot's just six pips away, it's much easier. You can reach it on a double two or double three or a forty-two or a fifty-one or any combination of sixes:

twenty-two
thirty-three
forty-two
fifty-one
sixty-one
sixty-two
sixty-three
sixty-four
sixty-five
sixty-six

Yeah? This gives you seventeen combinations out of a possible thirty-six – that's just under a 50 per cent chance of hitting the blot. If the blot is seven pips away there are only six ways for it to be hit and if the blot's very close, say just one point away, there are only eleven possible combinations – five ones and another number, five other numbers and a one plus the double one – so around a 30 per cent chance. Boring, hey? No, because what this teaches you is to leave blots as far away from your opponent as possible and if you absolutely have to leave them near, then leave them very near and not four, five, six points away where the probability of being hit is much greater. Which is exactly what I had done. My blot was eleven pips from his man on the bar. He needed a sixty-five. Two rolls in thirty-six, a one-in-eighteen chance of hitting me. On the basis of these calculations I had redoubled the cube to four in my previous move. But he rolled his sixty-five, sent me back to the board, redoubled and bore off quickly, taking eight Dutch Antilles guilders in the process.)

Do you know this? said Poyntz, handing me a record after the game. Most of the money he'd made from his book-stealing business – which had got him kicked out of uni – he'd ploughed into a gigantic vinyl collection. Unfortunately, nearly all of it was jazz.

You know I hate jazz, I said.

I found it last week, said Poyntz. I've been looking for it for ages. I'll put something else on. That's wasted on you. Do you want spaghetti rings? What drugs are we going to take?

I looked at the record, some guy playing the double bass, and picked absently at my road rash. It was worst on my face but bad on my thigh and bad on my elbow. I'd taken the bandages off that morning and the scabs were starting to harden. I half-pulled down the leg of my jeans to inspect the damage and thought of the Cayenne and Laetitia's legs and I imagined her riding the Pinarello in her bunny tail or whatever, chasing after the Cayenne and swearing at the driver in Moldovan or Russian or Cockney or Scouse. High heels and cleats and gusset greasing an ergonomic saddle. Cocaine the stimulant of choice.

What were we going to take? The drugs the professionals took: in the early days mostly speed. Fausto took amphetamine mixed with Coca-Cola and caffeine: la bomba. He was one of the trailblazers. Tommy Simpson followed and it did for him, two tubes up his shirt as he lay dead on Mont Ventoux. Poyntz's hero Djamolidine Abdoujaparov tested positive for Clenbuterol which opens up your bronchioles during lung-busting sprint finishes. Some couriers took bronchodilators, mainly to show off, but mostly it was just alcohol, caffeine, maybe a spot of weed, bog-standard analgesics, growth promoters, glucose solutions and only now and then a little speed.

(Big Nuts was a messenger who took a bunch of steroids to help him win an alleycat with hills. His real name was Barnes and he was a meaty fuck, stupid as anything, with a big square ugly face and a northern lisp. He drank a lot of those putrid milkshakes and no one liked him very much. He won a few small races and his balls grew smaller and smaller because of the steroids. If you win races, girls like you – however dumb and ugly you are – and those who saw his balls spread the word. They were tiny: he became Tiny Nuts. When he got wind of his nickname he went back to his steroid dealer, a guy called Maguire, who prescribed him HCG but way too much. So his balls atrophied, went the other way: Big Nuts.)

I took a plate of spaghetti rings and below the words weed and coffee wrote a list of other things we needed and then I went out onto Poyntz's little balcony and smoked a cigarette and imagined having a support team like they have on the Tour. Team Sorensen. Fat Barry as Team Manager and driver of the lead car, a Merc estate with a lot of branding. Some unfriendly, taciturn French mechanics in the back. Dozens of kick-ass bikes on the roof. *Soigneurs* in the second car and the third full of supplies: la bomba in the glove compartment, an ice-making machine and a dozen boxes of Monster Munch.

Poyntz was talking to his budgerigar, Leibniz. Shall I go or shall I stay? he asked, addressing him in his cage.

Poyntz had developed an annoying habit of consulting his budgie on matters of importance. He'd even asked him about backgammon moves. He said Leibniz was a great sage. He claimed to have taught him how to speak but I'd heard only chirruping, never words. He claimed to receive signs from the bird but the only thing I ever saw the bird do was hop from one side of its cage to the other, eat seeds, and shit.

What's it telling you? I asked.

He's saying I should do it for the brotherhood of birds.

Excellent. I didn't know budgies and owls were so close.

They're both birds. They're part of the same bird family.

An owl would eat a budgie without blinking.

Not Leibniz. He's a fighter as well as a thinker.

Of course. But he says yes?

He says yes.

Which means you're saying yes.

Yes.

Great, I said. I'm going to go home and book the flights.

Wait, said Poyntz, and he went back up to the cage

and pretended to communicate once more with the bird.

    Leibniz says I need to look after the cash.

    Yeah right, I said. You'll get your cash later.

    Promise? he said.

    Of course, I replied.

16

BLACK METAL

(PART TWO)

Poyntz and I found each other around about the same time Carpathian Forest's go-go dancers came on stage. There were two of them, blubber-bellies who wore only knickers, bras and albino wigs and who danced completely out of time with the band: they moved dreamy and slow while the band headbanged and thrashed.

They were old, in their forties or something and ugly, and I was deeply impressed that this band of Satan-loving death-heads had recruited from their own type. It would have been too simple to have the usual kind of go-go girl up there. This was another way of saying shut the fuck up. It added comedy to the menace and I needed a bit of comedy because although swept up in a sea of mentalists and for the most part having a good time I was unnerved by the flame work that accompanied every new riff and was convinced that a nightclub inferno was just around the corner.

Poyntz had other things on his mind. The skinheads, he shouted, they're after me.

What skinheads? I shouted back.

There were a bunch of them at the bar.

And what did they want?

I don't know. They just looked at me.

How many of them?

Five or six. Enough for a proper beating.

Let's go, I said.

No no, Poyntz replied. It's fine. I can handle it.

I went to the bar to take a look and get away from the pyrotechnics but there were no skinheads just metalheads. I ordered two more beers, drank one, watched the band from afar, looked out for the skinheads, looked out for Poyntz, ordered two vodkas, thought about money, regretted ordering the vodkas, drank one of the vodkas, thought fuck it and ordered another, picked at my scabs, looked out for the skinheads, looked out for Poyntz, decided to go and find him, drank the second vodka, poured Poyntz's into his beer, regretted doing that, went for a pee in the rancid toilets then got back to the mosh.

It was thicker now, more difficult to penetrate. There was no sense in taking Poyntz's drink in so I necked it and straight away was less worried about fire and revenge beatings, feeling a little impervious, closer to the danger, more alive. The mosh was getting good. The placid go-go dancers had gone. Carpathian Forest's Satanist-in-chief was inciting bloodlust and perversion and devil worship and shouting the numbers as they went and the crowd were lapping it all up: 'Start Up The Incinerator...' 'Shut Up, There Is No Excuse To Live...' 'Doomed To Walk The Earth As Slaves Of The Living Dead...' 'Wings Over The Mountains Of Sighisoara...' 'Warlord of Misanthropy...' 'Pierced Genitalia...'.

The moshers were making sport with some low-intensity violence: shoving, stamping, hair-pulling, punching, elbows-to-the-ribs. The stage divers too seemed to want to inflict as much damage as possible and launched into the crowd with great zeal. Sometimes they got lucky and a face got in the way of their boot and fist. The fat ones crashed to the ground and took their support with them. Everyone swayed and toppled for a moment then got themselves upright and started to pogo again. It wasn't the best style of dancing for plimsolls with the floor properly glassed up. There was blood on the ground and there was blood in the air, or lager or sweat or water. The showers came every minute or so, from behind towards the stage or from the stage itself: Carpathian's singer had stubbed three cigarettes out on his arm and doused each wound with beer before chucking the rest of the can into the masses.

Amongst the masses I looked for Poyntz. I wanted to be with him at the end, take in the finale together. The band geared up towards the climax. The sound got immense then ear-splitting and then suddenly it died. They didn't relent to the baying crowd with their double horn signs to take to the stage once more: they quietly put their guitars back on their stands and walked offstage. The baying continued for five minutes but a gig eventually realises when a gig is over and people started wandering out. Amid the miasma of alcohol fumes and body odour I looked once more for Poyntz. When I couldn't find him I went outside to smoke a cigarette and looked for him there.

There had been no nightclub conflagration and all menace from the punters was imagined. The dial was back at zero. These were normal people dressed as freaks doing normal things. They said excuse me when you were in their way and sorry when they mistakenly bumped into you. The violence of the mosh pit was characteristic of the mosh pit not the moshers. I felt a bruise-in-waiting on my ribs and my right foot's big toe had been stamped upon. I wondered whether it would be difficult to put on my SIDIs in the morning. I picked at my scabs and made myself another cigarette, out of boredom, waiting for Poyntz. I called his mobile but there was no answer.

When I went back inside the roadies were clearing cables and the barman was restocking the bar and the cleaners were sweeping the floors and I looked in the loos which were empty and in the ladies too – I don't know why I looked in the ladies – and I shouted Poyntz's name and someone was in the ladies but it wasn't Poyntz. I thought if something really bad had happened I would probably know by now and I looked outside again and there were still plenty of people milling about but there was no sign of anything really bad having happened although neither was there any sign of Poyntz.

I thought about the gris-gris. Was I still protected when my Pinarello was up a tree a mile and a half away? How far away did the voodoo bag need to be before it lost its special powers? Certainly the distance between my flat and the lap dancing club: about a mile and a half. What had Mr Bembo actually said? He'd said the gris-gris would protect my body from injury and save me from cars, mostly yellow ones. It wasn't exactly a catch-all. He didn't mention friends disappearing at black metal gigs. He didn't mention trips to a foreign land or anything about owls. But he'd said the gris-gris was a talisman and I wondered if I returned to the woods, retrieved my bicycle, and cycled around, looking for Poyntz with the voodoo bag under my bum, I'd be miraculously directed to him. Then I thought if I returned to the woods I'd prob-ably just get into my hammock and fall asleep because I was tired and bored of worrying about Poyntz and so

I walked away from the gig and over the river with the idea of doing exactly that and halfway across the bridge Poyntz ran past me, in the opposite direction, sprinting in the way that he does: long strides, outstretched palms.

One thing to say about Poyntz: the boy can run. At the beginning of alleycats he's always up there at the front. He's got sharp elbows too. But seeing him run in normal shoes as opposed to cycling shoes was a minor revelation. He didn't even see me as he shot past, but I saw him. His T-shirt was torn and he had real blood on his made-up face and he was being pursued by four angry skinheads.

The problem with the skinheads was that they weren't particularly well dressed for pursuit: long coats, heavy boots. They were also pretty unfit. But I guessed they knew the territory better than Poyntz and if they cornered him, they'd certainly give him a proper beating. I figured out they'd figured out that it was Poyntz who'd nicked their tickets. I don't know how they'd figured this out but his chat when confronted must have sucked. Why else was he running like fuck?

Without my bicycle I felt vulnerable, not being able to escape quickly, and I was unkeen on intervention. I could have joined Poyntz in flight and we could have fled, together. Or I could have stopped him and squared up and the two of us could have tried it on with the four of them and got our heads smashed in, together. Or maybe I could have tried to reason with them, explain that Poyntz was a fuckwit, apologise, bung them some of the Sorensen Money, tell them the gig was crap, and call it quits. But everything happened so quickly and all these options felt just a little beyond my capabilities, being drunk, so in the end I just rolled another cigarette and walked back in the direction that I'd come, watching the action from afar, feeling all the time that everything was going to work out just fine.

It's a miracle that it did because at one stage – about halfway through my cigarette – they were bearing down on him and I was starting to think I might actually have to get involved. I really hate fighting plus I was naturally very worried about my scabs. But I didn't want Poyntz to get his head kicked in, even if he deserved it.

It was Carpathian Forest who saved the day. They walked up through the precinct where Poyntz and the four punks were playing cat and mouse. They carried holdalls which I guessed were full of crucifixes, anti-missionaries spreading the word of Satan. Except they were looking for a pizza restaurant. As soon as the punks saw the band they instantly dropped Poyntz. A greater prize was suddenly among them. Poyntz, seeing his moment, disappeared into the shadows. I wandered up, a casual observer, and watched the punks try to make conversation with the band.

The band weren't that interested. They wanted to eat pizza. The two albino dancers did most of the talking, all of it Norwegian talking. The punks were wide-eyed, meeting their heroes. But I felt sorry for them because their heroes were underwhelming, as heroes often are. Also, Poyntz had nicked their tickets and they weren't Nazis or neo-Nazis or any brand of fascist, they were just kids having a night out.

They wanted to get me, Poyntz said later, as we walked back to the forest.

I would have wanted to get you too, I replied. You stole their tickets.

They were Nazis.

They were not.

They could have killed me.

90

Fuck off. They were all front.

National Front.

They weren't fucking Nazis Poyntz! Those things on their shoulders were plain old epaulettes.

Nazi epaulettes.

Whatever.

They called me a Paki.

Really?

I think so.

Either they did or they didn't.

Well they were shouting in Norwegian most of time. What's Norwegian for Paki?

Hold on let me just get my dictionary. I don't fucking know. It's probably the same isn't it?

There you go. They called me a Paki.

How did they know you nicked their tickets?

They were all marked with cock drawings. They came up to me and said weren't you the guy who asked us for a light and I was like yeah and they said let's have a look at your ticket and I knew they weren't numbered so I handed it over like a dick and on the back there was this fucking drawing of a cock and it turns out they'd all been drawing cocks on the backs of their tickets and to prove it two of them got their tickets out and showed me.

I looked at my own ticket. It had a drawing of a cock on the back.

That's pretty damning evidence, I said.

Yep, said Poyntz. Still, I told them I'd found the ticket on the ground.

And of course they believed you.

They kept on asking what happened to the other ticket and of course I said I didn't know. I told them I'd only found one. Then they started shouting at me saying where is the other ticket where is the other ticket, like they really needed closure for fuck's sake. Then they started spitting at me and getting really close like they were about to hit me, so I ran.

What happened to your mouth? Poyntz's lip was bloody.

Oh my mouth, he said. I bit my lip.

You didn't get punched?

No no. I bit my lip in the mosh pit.

Right.

Yeah. So I ran up to the pedestrian area and they started chasing me but they were pretty slow so I thought if I made it over the river I could probably get out of sight and make it back to the wood. But I got to the other side of the bridge and lost my bearings big time and had to hide in an alley. It was like street combat without the guns.

Poyntz, I said, only you could end up in an imaginary firefight with a bunch of benevolent punks.

Sam. They were evil. Seriously evil.

And then what happened?

One of them saw me so I legged it back over the river.

Yeah that's when I saw you.

You saw me?

Yeah. I was on the bridge, walking back to the wood.

I ran past you?

Yeah.

And you didn't do anything?

I was monitoring the situation.

Monitoring the situation?

Yeah.

You didn't try to stop those motherfuckers from beating me up?

No.

Why the fuck not?

Well everything happened pretty quickly, I said. By the time I realised you were in grave danger you were no longer in grave danger.

You really wouldn't piss on me if I was on fire would you? asked Poyntz.

That would depend on whether I needed to go for a piss or not, I said.

Of course, said Poyntz, of course.

17

HAMMOCKS

Later we lay in our hammocks and listened to the buzz of
black metal in our ears and the wind rustle the branches
in the tall trees above us. Poyntz asked whether there
were bears in Norway.

Don't be a jerk, I said. Of course there are.

So what's your strategy? he said.

I don't know, I said, what's yours?

Well I have a knife. I would have to go for the eyes
first. If I could get to the eyes. Maybe the nose would be
easier. Smell, then sight.

But he'll come up and grab you from underneath.

So I'll get the knife and stab him in the belly.

That knife won't go deep enough.

What about rope?

What about rope?

While he's grabbing you from underneath I'll rope his
neck and garrotte him.

He's like ten foot tall.

I'll jump from the tree.

He's half a ton.

We're fucked.

Yep.

What do they sound like?

Dunno. They roar I guess. If we hear them roar, I said, climb a tree.

And bears don't climb trees?

They might not see us if we're up a tree.

And hyenas?

What about them?

Are there hyenas in Norway?

I guess so.

I hate hyenas, said Poyntz. I am actually more scared of hyenas than I am of bears. Hyenas are the most sociopathic animals in the world. They're fucking ugly, they make dumb noises, they're totally selfish and they're no good to anyone.

What about wolves? I said.

Wolves are okay. They keep themselves to themselves.

So how would you deal with a pack of wolves?

I wouldn't have to. As I said, they keep themselves to themselves.

Ok what if they're out tonight marauding and they're mad for a slice of inner tube?

I would reason with them. Explain we have a long journey ahead of us and that we need those tubes in case we get punctures.

And if they tell you to fuck off?

Fire. It's the only way.

It would take a while to get a fire going.

Light a cigarette then. Wolves are part of the anti-smoking lobby.

Of course, I said and lit a cigarette.

Where are we going tomorrow? Poyntz asked. I'm tired.

I got the map and put a torch to it. 37, I said.

37?

37. That's the road up north through the mountains to Sorensen's hut.

One road?

Not quite. But 37 is the one to hit. From Kongsberg we take it all the way till we hit 7 I think. After 7 we take another road and then we're there.

5?

Not 5. Another road. It's not marked on the map.

Do you think we'll make it tomorrow?

Maybe, I said. I think it's quite a long way.

Like how long?

Like over a hundred miles.

That's nothing.

That depends on the mountains.

True. I reckon we'll be okay though, said Poyntz.

Yeah, I said. I reckon we'll be just fine.

18

THE SORENSEN
DIRECTIONS

Write these words down in this order, Sorensen had
said. He had spelt them out slowly, letter by letter, and
I had copied them down.

Hardangerfjord.

Kvanndal.

Hagafoss.

Holsfjorden.

Hovsfjorden.

Strandavatnet.

From Bergen, he'd said, head east, towards the tip of
the Hardangerfjord. You will need to cross the fjord by
ferry, from Kvanndal. Once you are on the south side,
keep heading east until you reach Hagafoss. At the
church, take the road to the north. You will pass the two
fjords and then you will reach Strandavatnet. When you
get to the water you will see a little hut on the left and that
is where the houses begin. Keep going until you come to
a little white postbox with a number seven on it. You will
find it at the foot of a track, on the right-hand side of the

road. Follow the track to the top and you will find the hut. The windows are painted black and there is grass growing on the roof.

These were the Sorensen Directions.

19

SADDAM HUSSEIN

Of course the only problem with the Sorensen Directions was that we'd started from Oslo, not Bergen.

Oslo, in fact, could have been okay if we hadn't got blitzed in Kongsberg, lost the compass somewhere in the woods and taken the wrong turn the following morning. By the time we'd realised our mistake it was too late to turn back: we were already deep into a gigantic mountain plateau called the Hardangervidda. We thought the Hardangerfjord probably wasn't too far from the Hardangervidda, so we just carried on cycling. That night we hung our hammocks in the garden of a man called Piet and then rose early the following morning so we could make it to the hut by sundown. But we got stuck in an asphyxiating mountain tunnel – the Haukelitunnelen in fact – and ended by being rescued by a trucker with a clean white beard and strong arms. He was taking an industrial generator to Bergen, as it happened. Tunnels are dangerous, he said. We shared his cab with an Alsatian whom we were ordered not to touch. Then he dropped us in a place called Kinsarvik and pointed us towards Kvandall.

I am fed up with cycling, said Poyntz. When we get there, I am going to have a wank.

(Fat Barry once told me the story of a friend of his who'd fought in Iraq. The guy was a sergeant major in a platoon that liberated one of Saddam's palaces. They went through it room by room, knuckleheads demanding the spoils of war. But the place had already been stripped of its Babylonian treasures and trinketry and all that remained were portraits of the great Nebuchadnezzar himself. In the master bedroom with its balconies and views of the Tigris was a hidden prize: a bed big enough to sleep half the platoon or a middling al-Tikriti plus his harem. Its pristine silk sheets had been protected from mortar by plastic tarpaulin. Above, the ceiling sported a huge mosaic of Saddam: not in a homburg firing a rifle or in his customary khakis and beret but looking like the family man, open-necked and smiling. The sergeant major told his men to scram, kicked off his boots, unpeeled the dust sheet and settled down for a well-deserved nap. But he couldn't sleep with Saddam looking over him and so he decided to have a wank. Finding that equally difficult, he took masturbation to the enemy. Jumping on the bed, eyeballing the great leader, penis in one hand, semi-automatic in the other, he romped to the finishing line. His men, hearing shouting, raced up the marble staircase and burst in at the moment he crossed it. There was a primordial scream and gunfire. Tiles fell from the leader's face: an eye here, a bit of moustache there. The sergeant major dropped to the bed too, sated. His men made a tactical withdrawal.)

You cannot have a wank in Sorensen's house, I told Poyntz. It's not ethical.

20

THE HUT

I repeated this warning when we arrived at the little white postbox with the number seven on it. But Poyntz said he was not responsible to Sorensen.

And the money you'll end up getting? I asked.

It's money you're getting that you're giving to me. But I'm not here for the money, he said. I'm here for the thrill. I'm piggybacking your rollercoaster ride and if we crash you'll be the first to hit the ground.

So you're happy to take the spoils but none of the risk?

I'm here, aren't I? I'm not complaining. It's just that all the Sorensen stuff is your business. You wouldn't let me in on him so I'm bound to be a little sceptical. If you trust him and I trust you then that's enough for me. But you've got to ask the question: what he's doing paying you a grand and a half to pick up a dead owl from a hut in the middle of nowhere? Ok, he's old; old people are strange. And he's Norwegian, they're strange too. But he's not dumb is he? He's not some kind of fuckwit? He's not throwing money at you because he likes the look of your legs? At best he's misunderstood your job description, taken pity on your poverty, decided to redistribute some of his wealth and in the process is getting his owl back so he can take it to an animal stuffing competition.

And at worst?

I don't know. I guess that's what we're about to find out. I mean, isn't that the point? I'm not here to do an old man a favour. I'm here to find out why an old man wants a favour done. I want to know what's so important about that owl and why he wants it now. I want to know what else is in that house. I want to know who Sorensen is and who he isn't. I want to know why he chose Zenith Couriers to do his dirty work. I mean, come on. Zenith Couriers! Could there be a more inappropriate firm of messengers? Sam, you're one of the good ones! What if he'd copped Kowalski? Kowalski would have taken the money and run. Most messengers would have done the same, myself included. Free money and a fucking madcap scheme? But he lucky-dipped you. Ok, the money looked good and you wanted to get out of London for a bit. But you didn't have to go to Norway.

That's true. But now we're here don't fuck up. Please.

Jesus Christ. I won't. Just let me come with you when we get back.

No, I said.

Why not?

Because he'll suspect something.

What?

It will look odd.

So what?

I want the extra money he's going to give us.

The Bonus ?

Yep. I don't want him to get spooked.

Just say I'm your friend. I happened to be passing.

That already sounds like a lie.

Not a whopper though. We can fine-tune it.

He won't like it. He won't want anyone else there.

Exactly. Now ask yourself why he doesn't want anyone else knowing what you're doing.

I don't fucking know why. If I knew that we wouldn't be having this dumb conversation. Can we just do it?

Ok, he said, I'm ready. And as he threw his cigarette onto the road, a car – the first we'd seen in ages – approached from the right at speed and drove over the butt. We watched its lights until they disappeared around the side of the lake and then we turned round, picked our bikes off the ground, and walked up the track.

It was coming up to half past eight and the sun was thinking about setting. The house was no more than a hundred metres off the main road, at the end of the track as promised. There was woodland to the sides and back, sloping upwards, and at the front there was a small, overgrown garden, bordered by pines. The trees sloped downhill so the road couldn't be seen, only the lake and the mountains behind it. The only houses you could see were on the other side of the lake, little dots of light.

As for Sorensen's house it was not much different to the thousands we had passed over the past few days, but it seemed smaller. It took less than a minute to walk round. We tried to peer through the windows but they were shuttered-up.

It's cold, said Poyntz. You got the key?

I scurried about in my bag. The key was somewhere amongst the tools. When I stood up Poyntz was looking at something above the front door. Check it out, he said, here's your man. I walked over. He was shining his bike light onto one of the eaves. There was Sorensen's name carved into the wood.

JON SORENSEN 22 MARS 1980

I guess this must be the right place, I said. I put the key in the door and turned it. The door opened.

21

AQUAVIT

All I wanted was my vision of a perfect Scandinavian
interior to be realised: wood, lots of it; a rocking chair
opposite an open fire; an uncomfortable sofa; a large
kitchen table; shelves full of crockery and dried goods;
skis, poles and boots, lined neatly against a wall; fishing
rods and nets; pictures from the North Cape nailed into
the walls; maps and books on natural history; warm
jackets hanging from pegs; hats, snowshoes, fur-lined
gators; a stuffed owl on the wall...

What we got was the Gothic vision. A single light-
bulb hanging from the centre beam and a room that
looked like it had been ransacked. The rocking chair
was upturned; the uncomfortable sofa on its side; the
kitchen table pushed against the sink; skis, poles and
boots scattered on the floor; pictures awry and books
off their shelves; jackets and hats turned inside out.
Every single cupboard in the kitchen was open, their
contents displayed, tins of food and cleaning equipment and bottles of spirits and ashtrays and glasses and
kitchenware and crockery. The doors to an old oven and
a wood-burning stove were open too. In the bedrooms,
one big, one small, the beds had been stripped, both

mattresses lifted and dropped. The dusty wardrobe in the main bedroom had been shifted and its doors were ajar. Inside, a bunch of old shirts hung. One had fallen to the ground. The rugs in each room had been lifted and dropped and in the bathroom the medicine cupboard, full of pills, was open. The bath panel had been removed and a floorboard underneath had been jemmied and prised open. The only things that didn't look like they'd been touched were the animals, of which there were many, mounted on the walls: three reindeer heads, two elk heads, the head of a moose, the head of a wolf, a lynx, several foxes, half a dozen birds. Then separately, on a different wall, an owl, small and brown, another owl, big and brown and a third owl, big and white.

I went back outside to lock the bikes to a telegraph pole and when I returned Poyntz had found a pair of paraffin lamps and lit them. He was sitting at the kitchen table with a bottle of aquavit.

Make yourself at home, I said.

Someone had to. Here. Have a glass of potato juice.

I took it and sat down. Who the fuck has done this? I asked.

How the fuck would I know? Someone's come here looking for something and they've either found it or they haven't. No use worrying about it. Relax.

The place is a mess.

We'll tidy it up, light the fire, make it cosy. I could get used to it here, said Poyntz, lighting a cigarette. I could definitely stop for a couple of days. Fuck the owl, whichever one it is.

It's the white one.

Okay. Great. It's there. Nothing to worry about. Can we go fishing? It's been a while since I caught an ørret.

What?

Ørret. Trout.

Shut up. You've never caught a fish in your life.

What makes you so sure?

You grew up in Birmingham.

And? We've got the Grand Union.

It's full of shopping trolleys.

I bet there are some big ones in there. Anyway. What d'you think?

No.

Come on. It will be wicked. We could take a boat out. Borrow some of these garms. Catch some big game. There must be guns here somewhere.

What are you going to shoot?

Dunno. Some moose. Yaks. Maybe some bear. It's wild. They hunt ptarmigan here. I could bag us a couple for supper tomorrow.

You don't even know what they look like.

They're white and fluffy. Cute. Difficult to shoot.

So I hear.

Seriously.

No.

Why not?

Our flight's on Sunday.

We can put it back.

No we can't.

How much were they?

Two hundred quid each.

We can't swap them?

They're non-transferable.

And if we buy some more?

That's crazy.

Sorensen is giving us seven fifty, right?

Right.

So we'd still draw a profit?

Poyntz, we have to catch that flight. He wants the owl on Monday.

He told you that?

Yes.

How firm a yes? Firm or soft?

Poyntz, we need to be back Monday.

What time?

Noon on Monday.

So we could fly Monday morning?

No.

Why not?

Because our flights are on Sunday. And besides, you have to work Monday.

I'll call Fat Barry.

From Norway?

He won't notice.

Of course he'll notice. He'll say where the fuck ARE you anyway? And you'll forget and say, er, Norway.

Poyntz poured more aquavit. *Skål*, he said, lifting his glass.

Skål, I replied, lifting mine and thinking that was the end of it. But Poyntz persisted.

What about if we dick around here tomorrow and get a bus back in the evening?

You mean the bus that goes direct to Oslo and stops every fifteen minutes by the front door?

Come on, there must be buses going east.

When did you last see one?

We could hitch. We've done it before.

That guy saved us from death in a tunnel.

Nah. We were pretty close to the end of it. We'll find another tunnel to hitch another lift.

Listen, I said. We're not even meant to be here. We're

meant to be letting ourselves in, picking up the owl and letting ourselves out.

Relax, said Poyntz, assembling tins. We need to eat.

We'd not eaten properly all day. But I didn't want to get involved. The state of the hut was making me nervous. So I tidied up, putting shit back where I thought it ought to be and when I finished tidying up I went to look for the Northern Lights.

By the way, I said, on my way out.

What?

If you'd died in that tunnel...

Yeah?

Who's your next-of-kin?

My what?

Your nominated next-of-kin?

Oh, replied Poyntz, it's the Armenian.

Then he turned his back and carried on cooking and I went outside and looked for the Lights, realised we were too far south, smoked a cigarette and considered how I would have contacted the Armenian whom I knew nothing about, only that he lived near Poyntz, that he'd supplied him with the dodgy X-rays and that he'd done time for beating someone up (a miscarriage of justice, Poyntz claimed).

He's like Winston Wolf, Poyntz said later. He solves problems. He can do anything, fix whatever, sort shit, make stuff happen, find things, find people. He's like one of those wilderness tracker guys except he works the city not the bush. The perfect person to have as your next-of-kin, to spread news of your demise, to those who need to know.

You twat, I'd told him. He's a fucking goon.

Maybe, said Poyntz. But he's a nice goon. He's one of the good ones.

22

KELLY ZIMMERMAN

Kelly Zimmerman was still *my* nominated next-of-kin, an administrative error I had not got round to rectifying.

Fat Barry said girlfriends couldn't be your next-of-kin but Kelly wasn't my girlfriend then, she was my ex-girlfriend. Still I told him Kelly was my mum and that she'd divorced my dad and reverted to her maiden name. I don't believe you, Fat Barry said, although I have long suspected you were a yid. It's true, I lied.

Kelly Zimmerman loved me and then she hated me. To Kelly I was a god until she flicked a switch in that crazy brain of hers and I became a retard, a no-hoper. I was drawn to Kelly Zimmerman like a sailor to a mermaid but when the fin-haired pretty boy appeared on the horizon, Kelly Zimmerman flipped her scaly tail and cast me into the wine-dark sea.

Mr and Mrs Zimmerman were intellectuals. Every year they went to Germany to watch operas by Richard Wagner. Kelly, an only child, was given the run of the house. As soon as the call came through from Bayreuth, Kelly sent the word out. The best thing about the Zimmermans was that they weren't just intellectuals, they were *liberal* intellectuals which meant that Kelly's parties were always amazing. Her folks turned the blind eye as long as whatever went on didn't result in them being pulled from the final scene of *Tannhäuser*. So Kelly Zimmerman, privileged as she was, became highly privileged. High privilege is a good starting point for a house party.

I didn't know Kelly at all and I'm not sure how I ended up at her party although I remember biking there with Guzzman, who had just become a courier. We were quite drunk, both of us wearing papiermâché alligator heads because it was a fancy dress party (Kelly loved fancy dress) and because Guzzman had a pair of these heads kicking about in his flat. I remember walking in with him like we were guests of honour and I know Guzzman knew someone who was buddies with one of Kelly's friends but that was as far as it went. But if you are wearing a papiermâché alligator head I reckon you can get into most parties.

It was one of those relatively well-advanced house parties where all manner of strangeness and naughtiness was happening in most places but the best shit was happening on the stairs. The stairs are a house party's arteries. Make an initial survey of the scene, mix yourself a substandard cocktail in the kitchen (no ice but outside people are climbing trees), make your way through the crowd to the top of the house but not too quick: take it slowly, watch the traffic come and go.

Guzzman and I found a spot on the landing and talked shop in our alligator heads for as long as it took to realise that you can't smoke in an alligator head however hard you try. After that we retired our fancy dress and talked some more. Three times Kelly passed me and I looked at her not knowing who she was and she looked at me not knowing who I was and every time she passed she said hi and every time I said hi back and by the fourth time even I, an imbecile at reading signs, thought that possibly, just maybe...

In hindsight I was being dumber than normal because when Kelly Zimmerman wanted something well she got it and she wasn't very subtle about it. She was like the spoilt kid in the sweet shop who screamed her head off until she got the gobstopper. I never really figured out why she fixed her sights on me because all I was doing was chatting to Guzz. It wasn't like I'd spent all evening whispering poetry in her ear.

The following morning as we lay in Mr and Mrs Zimmerman's frankly massive bed I leafed through one of Mrs Zimmerman's books about art and asked Kelly what she'd been on, since everyone seemed to have been on something. Nothing, she replied. I was drunk but I had my wits about me, *of course*.

Of course. It was classic Kelly: adroit, self-assured. It's not like she had an answer to everything but she had an answer to most things and certainly an opinion on everything. That was the way she controlled things, through her views. That night, for whatever reason, she took the view that I was okay. And she held the same view for whatever it was, a year or something, until she decided, quite quixotically in my opinion, that this view was no longer sustainable – that *I* was no longer sustainable – and then she dumped me.

Poyntz said it was clearly a good thing that Kelly Zimmerman had dumped me because she sounded like a right bitch.

But I cried (there were tears on my pillow) because if the truth be told there was no one quite like Kelly Zimmerman. At least there was no one quite like her until Bella Meikels turned up (although Bella Meikels wasn't really like her at all).

After getting dumped I went cold turkey and didn't see her for months except inside my head when in the beginning I saw her all of the time and then, after a while, I saw her some of the time and then finally – it took ages – she more or less disappeared.

When I eventually saw her for real it was at another party and sure enough she was arm-in-arm with the fin-haired pretty boy and it was like *I've moved on Sam have you?* That was one big punch in the ribs. Later that evening I learnt she'd walked into some job where they were paying her four, five times what I'd just started earning as a courier, and that was another hit. That Kelly Zimmerman was still my nominated next-of-kin, that I'd even nominated her although we'd split up six months before: these facts created pain in my ribcage.

A few months into our relationship we drove up to Yorkshire in her Fiat Panda, metallic blue it was and old. I don't know why we went to Yorkshire. Neither of us had ever been to Yorkshire before. I guess it just sounded nice. We asked some people and found a waterfall. It was October, too cold for swimming. But the sun shone hard so we stripped off. I got naked: there was no one about. Kelly went down to her bra and knickers, to get some sun on her skin. We stood there at the top, near the ledge. It was about twenty feet, the drop.

Let's do it, I said. No fucking way, said Kelly. Don't be a queen, I said. Don't be an idiot, she said. Okay, I said, just hold my hand. Okay, she said and she smiled and she took my hand and held it for a moment and I squeezed it and she squeezed back and then quickly I grabbed her and jumped over the edge.

It was a long way to fall. The mind takes its time with new things. I remember colours: the green and red and ochre of the leaves; the greys of bark and mudstone; the pale blue of the sky and rushing white of the falls; the whiteness of Kelly's skin and the azures that she wore; and the dark-ale brown of the water, darker as we got deeper. At the deepest point, at the moment where the going down made way for the coming back up, our bodies lost contact and we were suddenly on our own and everything was black, pitch black and deathly silent too. No brushing of water against water, water against stone; no high-pitch screaming and crash-splashing of daredevil jumpers; no mute bubbling as they descend, ever slower, into the depths of the pool. Just silence and darkness.

It could have been a moment of panic, that fear of never returning to the surface, to light. A dumb-ass watery grave somewhere near Hebden Bridge. A lovers' leap, a suicide pact, a double death by misadventure. Of course when you have not slammed the river bed or gashed your leg or head or back or bum or half an arm on a murderous rock you know that you are going to be okay. When the only resistance you encounter is water itself, you know that you are going to break the surface again, complete. But still, for a split-second, you are unsure. Only when your body starts its inevitable ascent to the surface are you sure.

But I didn't want to return to the surface. I felt too happy, too ecstatic in that moment of uncertainty. I wanted everything to be suspended. If it meant death, then so be it. At least I was quitting in a good place. I'd reached the zenith. In the darkness and the cold, I felt warm and crystal clear: I realised I was in love and it felt too pure, too precious to let it slip from my grasp.

All the longing of the past was channelled into a single moment: my heart pumped double, my arms flailed, my mind raced and my dick pointed resolutely towards

Kelly. As for the future, I gave it no thought at all until it brought me, in a matter of seconds, to the surface of the water. My bubble burst and a thousand others beside me. There was Kelly Zimmerman, treading water, looking daggers.

You bastard, she gasped. I will always fucking hate you for that.

As we drove back home, I told her that I loved her and she told me that she loved me back but it felt different, the way she said it. Had she been a cyclist, which of course she was not, with me riding in her slipstream, I would have recognised this difference in cadence. Instead, I just assumed my *souplesse* was hers too; that her love was perfectly timed to mine.

But I didn't know anything about love. I'd have gone into the desert for her, eaten locusts and wild honey, just to keep things as they were. But that's not how it works. I ignored the pain that Kelly put in my ribs that day, thinking love would conquer all. I ignored it pretty much up until the moment she dumped me.

There is a triangle that links the Zimmerman's house, the pub we used to drink in and where I got dumped, and a tree on the Heath where we'd lie on summer nights and get high and watch the skies and fumble around. This triangle, almost an isosceles, I still carry somewhere in my soul.

The tree I remember being Kelly's favourite and I have always liked people who are categorical about seemingly unimportant things. I didn't really care for that tree *per se* but I liked what it stood for and the fact that the tree was liked by Kelly.

I did wonder, afterwards, if she'd had sex with other people under that tree. But so what if she had? It was Kelly's tree, not mine.

Anyway, the tree was like a leafy bower of old, private and secluded. It was ancient with a massive green canopy for shade on hot days and when the wind blew every single one of its leaves blew too and all the high wavering grasses around us. We lay together and smoked and kissed and then kissed and smoked a bit more and my heart was a Portuguese man-of-war. The tree was on high ground and had views of the city which made you feel super-connected and super-apart at the same time. At night when the street lights flickered and twinkled along with the stars, it felt like they were doing it for us. I know that's fucking corny because they weren't but it felt like they were and that's what counts.

The Zimmerman's house was full of art and had a grand piano that I wished I could play. Everything was in the best possible taste. Kelly's room had an en suite bathroom with antique taps. She would stand in front of the mirror and apply in tiny dabs the Italian or Japanese perfume she wore, I never remember which it was. I loved the smell it gave her neck, her clothes, her pillow.

The pub was down the road, a hard old boozer turned soft. For a year on and off we drank there, sometimes alone, sometimes with her friends. Kelly called the shots and killed me with her dimples. Then, slowly, we started seeing each other less and less – she made some magnificent, history-making excuses – but even when I felt it was coming it still surprised me, chump that I was, sitting in that pub. She insisted there was no one else but I knew otherwise. I had this terrific urge to pour my drink right over her head – that's how the movies would have done it. But I didn't have the balls or I was too paralysed by sadness. I'm glad I didn't in the end.

After the pub we returned to the Heath, to a bench not far from the tree. It was February or March, grey and cold. She strung out the drama for a while and then said goodbye and walked home, leaving me on my own. London looked at me unforgivingly. It was a miserable summer that year, every corner bringing up Kelly in happy times. I dulled the pain by cycling more and more, quicker and quicker, thinking that the quicker I passed the memory spots, the greater the chance I wouldn't notice them. I rode as hard as I could for six months, exorcising all the shit that was swilling around in my head, and at the end of the summer I became a courier.

23

KIRSBERRY

The meal that Poyntz prepared murdered any scruples I had. Together we ate monstrously and with little sense of consequence or taste: three rounds of sardines with dried biscuits; whole jars of pickled cucumbers and herring; bowls of vermicelli with ketchup; tinned mackerel and dried cheese; another bottle of aquavit, a bottle of something called Lakka and a bottle of something else called Kirsberry; cold rice pudding and tinned raspberries; black coffee and slabs of chocolate. More aquavit. All the food was beyond its sell-by date, in some cases by years. Afterwards Poyntz said we should go for a swim.

What about backgammon? I said. I didn't think much of swimming and thought we would sink after a big meal.

What about a swim then backgammon? Poyntz replied.

What about backgammon then a swim? I said, thinking he'd forget about the swim once the game got going. But neither of us were much able to play and after losing two in a row I suggested we pack it in. He suggested we head for the lake. It was a quarter to one in the morning. We could take the boat out, he said.

What boat?

There's one by the water. Opposite the track.

You saw one?

Of course I saw one. You think I'm lying?

What kind of boat?

A Sunseeker.

Shut up. What kind of boat?

A rowing boat.

With oars?

I guess so. We can have a look.

Okay, I said, reluctantly.

We grabbed a couple of heavy jackets off the pegs and found boots that fitted and a pair of fleecy headbands. Poyntz wanted to take the fishing rods but I told him he'd catch more fish at dawn.

The clouds had dispersed and the moon was out. We ran down the track to the road and over to a little stony beach where a boat was upturned and half-tied to a stake. We found the oars. Poyntz got in first, I pushed and jumped. Ten minutes later we were in the middle of the lake. We put the oars back in the boat and drifted.

The lake was calm, the boat still. There was some water in the bottom but there'd been a lot of splashing when we launched. It drifted very slowly. I lay down, my head on the prow. Poyntz did the same the other end. We lit cigarettes and passed the bottle of Kirsberry and looked for shooting stars.

After a while Poyntz said, If I fell in and this heavy jacket dragged me down would you jump in and save me?

Probably not, I replied. It's just the kind of romantic death you'd like.

I'd prefer to die in a fire, doing something heroic. Saving Leibniz for instance.

I think this place is okay, I said. It's quiet. You can see the mountains. If the jacket's heavy enough, you'll rest at the bottom and get eaten by the fishes before you get to them tomorrow.

Don't worry. I'll get to them tomorrow. You know, if we both went and stayed down no one would ever know. Imagine that. My family, your family, all our friends.

Poyntz stopped. I'm sorry, he said.

Don't worry, I replied. It's cool.

He paused, then continued. It's just that one day, he said, we're cycling around London amongst millions and next day we've disappeared off the face of the earth. No one knows we're here. It would take them ages to figure it out. Missing persons. Police. Passport control. Then a fucking mad trail around Norway which goes cold somewhere around the place that truck driver with the Alsatian dropped us off. And that's if they cared. Would they fucking care? Would they fuck. We're of no importance Sam. We could disappear and remain an eternal mystery. Think of all the theories. They'd say you knocked me off because you were jealous of my track standing abilities.

Nice, I said, but unlikely.

I can track stand and smoke at the same time. You can't.

I can track stand and eat a bowl of chop suey at the same time.

Okay. I can track stand, smoke, eat a bowl of chop suey, row a boat and conduct an orchestra just using my nose – all at the same time.

It's certainly big enough, your nose, I said.

That's my dad's fault, said Poyntz.

So your parents wouldn't care if you went missing?

Oh *they'd* care. I'm not saying my family wouldn't care. I'm saying the authorities wouldn't care. My family would go crazy. Or at least my mum would. My dad would say oh he'll turn up sooner or later but my mum would go properly mental. She'd send my cousins to scour the country for me. She'd make them learn Norwegian. They'd turn up here in a hired car with frogmen outfits in the boot. What about you? What about your dad?

Are you joking? I laughed. My dad wouldn't hear a thing. He's a fucking air traffic controller. In Aberdeen. He wears headphones twenty-four seven. Even if he heard, he wouldn't care that much. He'd do the bare minimum. Call up the embassy maybe. Nothing more.

When did you last speak to him?

A few months ago. We speak a couple of times a year. It's always me who calls.

And?

We more or less have the same conversation every time. I tell him where I'm living, what I'm doing. He says that sounds good, that he's proud of me. Then I ask him about his girlfriend. Sometimes it's the same one as before, sometimes it's a new one. Sometimes it's someone he's met at work, sometimes it's someone he's met in the pub. Sometimes it's someone who works in the Spar. Sometimes it's Laura. Sometimes it's Lorna.

Do you ever go up there?

Once, when I was sixteen. My mum said don't go but I wanted to. We argued about it for days until I just went. It was fucking awful. I hadn't seen him since I was a boy. He took me to his local and we sat there all afternoon drinking seventy shilling or bob or whatever it's called. Then we went out to a Chinese restaurant and met up with the woman he was seeing at the time.

I can't remember her name but she was big and brassy and dressed up. She wore leather: leather skirt, leather jacket, big hoop earrings, lots of make-up, heels. After the meal they half-tried to persuade me to go out with them – they were off to some club – but all I wanted to do was go back to London. They didn't want me to come anyway. I went back to his place and packed my bag and fell asleep on the sofa. When I woke up it was still early and he still hadn't come back. So I left a note on the kitchen table and let myself out.

And that was the last time you saw him?

Well not quite. I thought he must have gone back to her place but when I was walking to the station I saw him on the other side of the road, on his way home, staggering like a bastard. He was the most pissed I've ever seen anyone. His trousers were ripped and his face had dried blood on it and he was zigzagging across the pavement, stopping every thirty seconds to catch his breath so he could swear. He looked about ninety.

And what did you do?

I wasn't sure what to do. I wanted to help him but I also wanted to get the fuck away from him. I figured if I got him home and cleaned him up he'd make me stay. He'd want to try and undo the damage and I couldn't face that. I told myself he wouldn't want me to see him in this condition. So I watched him go and walked on. That was the last time.

There was a pause then Poyntz said, My family will look after you.

I laughed and said thanks.

No seriously, he said. My family are good like that. They know you as well. Once they know you, they like you.

(I'd gone to visit Poyntz's family earlier in the year.

He'd taken his earring off beforehand and I was under strict instructions not to let slip the fact that he worked as a courier. I told him he couldn't live a lie forever. He said he needed to live the lie a little bit longer. The official story was that Poyntz had left university with a first-class law degree and was spending a year as a postgrad before joining a firm of hotshot solicitors. Of course the real story was that Poyntz had been suspended from university in his final year after being caught stealing books. He stole them to order for fellow students. His downfall had been a book called *History of the Hohenstaufen*, a request from a PhD student. It was an unusual one for Poyntz since most of his orders were contemporary titles from specialist shops: design, art history, medicine, science – these were his bread and butter. The Hohenstaufen book was out of print so either an antiquarian or a library job. Poyntz told the dude to get the book out on loan but other people were always trying to read it and the medievalist wanted it for himself and offered good money. So he ordered the book but it was in six fucking volumes and in klepto terms quite a challenge. Poyntz thought he could snaffle all six in one go but the CCTV got him and he was hauled before the university authorities. They suspended him and gave him the option of returning the following year to sit his exams, knowing that he wouldn't. He didn't. He spent the rest of his student loans, ran out of money and got a job riding for Rapid. I found it pretty difficult to believe that Poyntz's family didn't suspect something but his parents seemed happy in the knowledge that he was succeeding and didn't ask so many questions. His little sister though was twelve years old, smart and about to get wise to the lie. This was a major problem for Poyntz. He thought he might have another six months' grace before he was forced to buy her silence. In exchange, he suspected she'd make him promise to sit his exams plus the rest of it. But he'd have to find the money first.)

How much cash did you make from the book racket? I asked him. I was staring at the stars and thinking about my own future.

It was a business, not a racket, said Poyntz.

How much?

Loads. In a good week I'd clear two, three hundred pounds. But then I'd stop for a while until I needed the money again or needed some new records. I worked in cycles. Took orders, delivered, then laid low. For special jobs I'd make exceptions.

Special jobs?

Girls mostly. They were always hard to turn down. Also, difficult jobs: the biggest, most expensive books. Books that weren't on the shelf. Books you'd need to order. Challenging books.

You ordered books then stole them?

Yeah.

How?

It's easy. You phone up and give an assumed name. I used a bunch of different names.

Grover Watrous?

Don't be dumb. Not with a fucking bookseller. That's like saying my name's David Copperfield. My name's Oliver fucking Twist. You give an innocuous name: Steven Hunt. They say it will be three days, Mr Hunt. You call in four and say sorry you don't need it any more or you've found a second-hand copy or whatever. Okay, they say, no problem. Next day you go in and it's on the shelf.

And then?

And then what?

What happens then?

Well you take the book don't you? You make sure it isn't alarm tagged – most of them aren't and if it's tagged you remove it. Then you stick it in your bag or under your arm or under a pile of books you've already brought in and out you walk.

And if the books are big?

They'd cost more. I'd add a big books surcharge. Anything with a spine longer than ten inches I'd slap an extra tenner on. That covered *Gray's Anatomy* and *Consumer Behaviour* and the *Big Book of Breasts* which always shifted and *Intermediate Macroeconomics* and *Frigates of the Napoleonic Wars* and—.

He stopped speaking and there was silence just the lapping of water and the still night air and an absence of shooting stars until very quietly, very slowly, Poyntz said: by the way I think we're sinking.

Indeed we were sinking and we knew it because when we both sat up our legs plunged into a foot and a half of icy lake and while the top of the boat was still above the waterline, the water in the boat was just below the seats. I started singing WHAT THE FUCK WHAT THE FUCK WHAT THE FUCK very loudly and very quickly while Poyntz shouted slowly and with false calm I AM NOT FUCKING PANICKING WHERE ARE THE FLARES WHERE ARE THE FUCKING BOAT FLARES and in the commotion we almost upturned. We cupped water and started bailing out but the more we bailed the more the boat rocked and the more the boat rocked the more the water flooded the boat. In one moment we lost an oar. (This was Poyntz's fault. He thought they were getting in the way of bailing so he picked them up and threw them to the back of the boat but he threw them in the lake instead. We got one back but not the other.) In another moment Poyntz lost Sergio Bianchi, his favourite cap, which was being used for bailing and which was involuntarily thrown in the water as well. I'VE FUCKING LOST SERGIO BIANCHI! I'VE LOST HIM! LOST HIM FOR GOOD! he shouted. FOR FUCK'S SAKE SAM! HE'S GONE FOR EVER! IN THE MIDDLE OF A LAKE! IN FUCKING NORWAY! THIS IS A FUCKING DISASTER! A CATASTROPHE! I told him to shut the fuck up and carry on bailing. Eventually we realised that if we stopped shouting and arguing about where the hole in the boat was – because clearly there was nothing we could do about it – and just sat at the ends of the boat and bailed out methodically, each to his left-hand side, then the volume of water exiting the boat might start to exceed the volume of water entering it. It did, and a little calm descended. But once the levels were back to a manageable depth and the immediate risk of sinking appeared to have passed, we noticed we had drifted a good distance from wherever we thought we'd been. And we didn't even know where that was.

One oar is fine, said Poyntz. We just need to hit the shore. You row twice on one side. Then you swap and row twice on the other side. Or one of us can sit at the back of the boat and use their hand as a rudder and keep their eye out for Sergio Bianchi.

That is a dumb idea, I said, using my hand as a rudder. I am fucking soaking wet. I haven't a clue how big this lake is and neither have you. We can hit the shore and walk round and the walk might take us all night. We'll certainly get hypothermia. Or we can try and work out where the hut is and row in that direction.

Ok, said Poyntz. I'm in your hands. But the boat has a hole in it.

No shit Poyntz! One of us bails, the other rows.

Fine. I'll row. You bail.

No, I said. I'll row. You bail.

So I rowed Amerindian style, at the bow of the boat, away from the mountains. When Poyntz stood up and shouted at the very top of his voice COME BACK TO ME SERGIO COME BACK, a light on the shore went on and I headed straight for that light. Behind me Poyntz bailed and didn't once ask to swap. In twenty minutes I had steered us onto shore, close to the light but not too close, and just a quarter of a mile from where we'd set off.

We dumped the boat and walked up, then changed and had cigarettes and schnapps to warm us up but really I cared for nothing more than bed. I took a pair of thick socks from a chest of drawers in the main bedroom and two shirts from the wardrobe, wrapped myself up in my hammock, and got into bed. As I hit the pillow I could hear Poyntz ranting in the kitchen. What the fuck are we doing here? he was asking. It's all your fucking fault, he said. Fucking cunt.

I thought he was talking to me. But in fact he was talking to the owl. He was talking to the owl, jabbing his finger at the owl. The owl, I thought, the owl. Sorensen's prize owl! But then I fell asleep.

24

THE OWL

Poyntz didn't go fishing in the morning. He got up as dawn broke, took the rods down to the shore, vomited, then returned to the hut and went back to bed.

When I woke a few hours later he was sprawled next to me, puke on his T-shirt.

I started to tidy up. My head was pounding. I worked at quarter speed. The whole thing took almost three hours. The place was a mess. It was full of rubbish and ashtrays and empty bottles. All of the liquor had been drunk. There were damp clothes everywhere. The kitchen was horrendous. There was puke on the sofa.

I moved all our crap outside and checked the bicycles were okay. I looked out towards the lake and tried to figure out where we might have got to the night before, but the lake simply shimmered at me with reproach.

I worked away under the watchful eye of the owls. Poyntz slept. I got everything ready to go, then kicked him awake.

Come on, I said, we're off.

Poyntz groaned.

Come on fuckface. It's almost tomorrow. We've got a flight to catch.

I can't move.

You have to.

Where are we?

In the hut.

What hut?

We need to move.

Didn't we almost drown last night? I feel awful.

You and me too. Everything's ready.

Ready for what?

Ready for us to go.

I don't think I can.

You have to.

I need water.

I'll get you some.

I need food.

It's all packed away. We'll get breakfast on the road.

No. I need an egg. At least six or seven eggs.

Come on. I need your help getting the owl down.

What owl?

That got him up, straight up. The owl! he shouted, then burst out laughing, evidently still drunk. We forgot about the fucking owl! Where is it?

It's stuck to the wall with all the others, I replied.

I felt nervous about the owl. I had left dealing with it to the last minute, probably on purpose. We could have arrived, taken it and left. Instead we dicked around, stayed the night, got drunk, went out in a boat, capsized.

We got the fishing rods and poked the thing a little. It was high up, perched on a stick and the stick was attached to a kind of platform thing which was attached to the wall. We had three options: to wrench its claws off the stick, to take the stick, or to take the platform.

I don't want the stick, said Poyntz. I just want the bird. What did Sorensen say?

He didn't say anything, I replied.

It's definitely not that one? Poyntz prodded the small brown owl.

No, it's definitely not that one.

Or that one? He prodded the big brown owl.

No, I said. It's the white one.

What if we take all three, just in case? You can take the white one. I'll take the two brownies. Then if we get there and it turns out to be the wrong one we can go, aha, but look what else is in my bag!

No listen, I said. It's the snowy owl. I promise.

Okay, Poyntz said, then let's get the table and take this motherfucker home.

So we got on the table, lifted it against the owl wall, and jumped up. Then we stepped back. It's not nice to be so close, said Poyntz. This one's the fucking worst, the tiny one.

It's a tawny owl, I said.

How do you know?

Sorensen told me. He said the small brown one was a tawny owl called Mr Ker.

They've got names?

Yeah. The titchy one is Mr Ker. This one's Mr Scritch, he's something called a northern hawk. And this one's Mr Tecolote, the snowy owl. That's our one.

It's fucked up. They're like his buddies. Except they're buddies he stuffs and nails to the wall. What's our one called again?

Mr Tecolote.

Tecolote?

Tecolote.

What the fuck does Tecolote mean?

It means owl in Spanish. *Mr Owl.*

How do we know he's a he? He could be a she. He

could be a girl owl. *She* could be a girl owl. *Mrs* Tecolote.
Do owls have vaginas?

Fucking hell Poyntz. I don't know. Why can't we just
get him and go?

And what's this one called? He flicked the tawny.

That's Mr Ker. Be careful.

Mr Ker. Hello Mr Ker you ugly cunt.

Then he started talking very loudly to the northern
hawk. Hello? he said, knocking on the bird's head. Anyone at home? Fancy a trip to London? Yes? Bad luck.
It's not you we're after, it's him. Sorry. Been here long?
Yeah? Anything good happening? No? Oh dear. Now
listen, we're taking your friend away. I know you're not
happy. Neither would I be. Nothing but a boring little
tawny to talk to. Well, hard luck. That's the way it is...

I let him carry on and started trying to take the snowy
off the wall. His claws were glued to the stick and the
stick was nailed to the platform. If I could take the nails
out I could probably keep him perched on his stick
which seemed the naturalistic approach but I needed
the right tool, a hammer or some pliers. I jumped off
the table and went outside to the bikes but none of the
bike tools would do. So I looked under the sink and in
places where you might keep tools while Poyntz carried
on abusing the northern hawk. There was nothing in
the kitchen and nothing in the living room and nothing in the bedroom. As I sat on the loo in the bathroom
wondering if my head would ever recover and wanting
simply to be back home in my bed, dreaming Dionysian
dreams, I saw in the cupboard in the corner, underneath
the boiler, a massive wooden box, the kind of box you
might keep tools in. When I looked in this box I found
all manner of gear needed, evidently, for the stuffing of
animals. There were knives and saws and scalpels and

wires and skinners and buckets and glues and gloves and brushes and combs and foams and pins and threads and nails and bands and cards and chemicals and staple guns and cotton wool and a whole load of other things besides. Next to a packet of cornmeal I found a claw hammer, the perfect instrument for removing nails from a stick to which a stuffed bird is attached.

But when I walked out of the bathroom Poyntz was standing by the front door with the owl already underneath his arm. Underneath the owl was the stick and underneath the stick was the platform and in the space on the wall where the owl had been there was a massive hole.

Come on, he said wearily, let's go back to London. Our job of work is done.

PART TWO
(THE OTHERS)

MARTA OLSEN

ANNA VIG

JON SORENSEN

PUSHPENDRA SINGH POYNTZ

MASHTOTS HAMBARTZUMIAN

Marta Olsen

Stien. You're snoring. Softly, with your head against the window. I don't like it. We'll be landing soon, in London, and I wanted to tell you about Magnussen first. I wanted to tell you about Magnussen before we got to London.

How did it all start? It started with the call. The call about the hut. First thing in the morning. But I was distracted. I hardly listened to it. The inspector's name was Blom. From Northern District headquarters, in Drammen. It sounded like provincial business. I don't deal with provincial business Stien, and neither do you.

Look at the big picture, the deputy director always says, and when he says it he turns around in his big swivel chair and points to the whole of Oslo, because from his office on the top floor there is a view of everything: you can see Lillestrøm in one direction and Sandvika in the other and then if you look south you can see all the way down to the outer fjord. For a moment, he says, imagine this city is your case. Hidden somewhere is the clue you are looking for. Unless you can see the big picture you will never find the clue.

Last year was bad for us. The worst. First there was the NOKAS robbery. One dead officer and fifty-seven and a half million kroner in used cash, stolen. Then the Munchmuseet. We were all focused on the NOKAS case – every single police officer in Norway seemed to be working on the NOKAS case – and then they stole those bloody pictures and everyone went crazy about Edvard Munch, the bastard. NOKAS was a big deal but the way those Munch thefts hit the headlines around the world, it was on a different scale. They walked in, took one of the Screams and then took one of the Madonnas, just because they could. Everyone looked stupid: the museum, the police, the whole of bloody Norway. The deputy director says the public needs those pictures back. We all need those pictures back, Mr Deputy·Director. But like the fifty-seven and a half million, they're probably gone forever. I'd be surprised if there's a single krone that hasn't been washed by now. Tenerife, Riga, Algiers...

Why are you asleep Stien? I need to tell you about Magnussen.

Anyway, God knows why it was me who got the call. There are procedures for reporting up to us. We're Økokrim, and as I said, we don't deal with provincial business. But I just kept the phone to my ear and when the officer at the other end stopped talking I took his details and told him someone would get back. When Magnussen turned up, late as usual, I gave the number to him. It is probably nothing, I said, just let me know, okay?

Okay, said Magnussen, in that sing-song way of his.

Why did I leave it with Magnussen? I left it with Magnussen because it did not seem an important matter and because Magnussen is not a good officer. He is lazy and he is getting fat. He is not curious. He lacks basic intelligence-gathering skills. He sits at his desk all day dreaming of a transfer to tactical operations. When I ask him to make enquiries about this or that, he comes back with phantom leads. Even the basic stuff he seems unable to do. The other day I asked him to run a simple check on an offshore account and when I passed by, later on, he was stuffing an egg sandwich into his mouth and he hadn't done a thing. Oh, he said, I'm waiting for a call from the Cayman Islands. Who's calling you? I asked. The regulator, he said.

The regulator! As if the regulator ever provides anything good!

Sometime late afternoon, Magnussen returned. He said the call from Drammen was linked to a live case. What live case? I asked. But Magnussen being Magnussen went into the same story I had avoided listening to earlier, about a telephone call from a man complaining his boat had gone missing and another complaint from a woman about some disturbance at a neighbour's house. A local officer had driven over and made some enquiries. The boat was found, the house was fine, shutters open, locks intact. But when the officer returned to Drammen to write up his report, he ran a check on the property. That's when we were alerted. It's a hut on the border of Buskerud and Sogn og Fjordane, Magnussen said. Strandavatnet, I said, the lake? And Magnussen looked at me all surprised and said, Yes Superintendent, Strandavatnet, the lake. How did you know?

Well, Stien, this was how I knew.

Back in April, I'd received a call from a source of mine, an art dealer called Holm. I'd come across Holm a few years ago when he helped me identify some pictures we'd confiscated in some warehouse raid. After the Munch thefts I'd left him a message. I told him to call if he heard any noises. Silence for eight months and then in April, he got in touch.

We met for coffee near the central station. We found a quiet little corner and then he started talking.

He told me how a man, an old man, had walked into his place the previous day, claiming to have a picture by Munch. The man didn't have it with him but he said the picture was genuine and that it had been given to him by a friend. Holm was immediately suspicious. He tried to press him for more details but the man wouldn't answer questions. Holm told him that unless he was able to see the picture, there was nothing he could do. So they arranged a meeting for the following Monday, for the man to bring the picture in. The dealer took the man's name and number. His name was Jon Sorensen and he was staying at the Bristol Hotel.

Jon Sorensen. A very ordinary name. I asked Holm if he knew anything more about the picture. No, said Holm, the man wouldn't reveal a thing. Anything to suggest it was recently acquired? Holm said the man didn't seem to know much. And how common was it for someone to walk in, claiming to have a Munch? Well, said Holm, Munch did a lot of stuff but it's all pretty well accounted for. What was the man like, I asked, what was his appearance? Tall and old, said Holm, smartly dressed, big hands, a little nervous. And you think he'll come on Monday? I asked. Could he be a crank, a fantasist? It's possible, Holm said. Could he be playing some kind of trick? What kind of trick? Holm asked. Could he be leading you to something, showing you his hand? I don't know, Holm replied. But it's all pretty unusual.

I told Holm to keep it to himself and promised to make some enquiries. I said I'd speak to him on the Monday, before his meeting. After that I headed back into the office.

It's delicate, Stien. The Munch thefts are your

investigation, not ours. I could have passed the information to you guys or I could have made some discreet enquiries of my own, firmed it up a bit, and then contacted Kripos. It was nothing more than a line of enquiry and of course it might have led to nothing. It might have been simply an old man selling a picture. But it might have been a signal, it might have been a tip-off, it might have led to something else which led to something else. As the deputy director says, the public needs those pictures back. He wasn't going to complain if we were the ones who provided the intelligence. So I called up the hotel and straightaway they confirmed there was a Jon Sorensen staying there.

The Bristol is around the corner. I tidied up some papers. It was late, nearly eleven o'clock. At the least, I could have a drink. I walked out, down Rozencrantz and onto Kristian IV. The lobby was empty. I asked to speak to the manager but the manager had gone home. I asked to speak to the night manager. I explained who I was, showed him my badge. We went into his office. He played difficult. He told me he needed to speak to his boss. I told him he didn't. Eventually he was persuaded and he told me what I wanted: room number, arrival and departure dates, hire car information, this kind of thing. Then, as I was leaving, he pointed to someone sitting by the bar, across the lobby. I'm pretty sure that's him, he said.

The man was on his own, hiding in a big chair, drinking whisky, reading the newspaper. I walked up to the bar and ordered a glass of white wine. It had been a while since I'd done this kind of thing. I was a little nervous to be honest. There was no one else about apart from the barman.

I walked over and asked if I could join him. He looked

up, surprised, and said yes. He put his newspaper down. In my head I trawled back for an old cover story, one I might have used when I worked at Kripos, undercover with Lønn. Stien, do people ever talk about Lønn? Poor man, he died two years ago. Drowned, while fishing in the Gudbrandsdalslågen. The river was swollen after rains.

Anyway, I was Pia Haugen and I was in Oslo to attend meetings. I worked as a sales representative for a shipping company based in Bergen. I had a husband – Lars Haugen, an accountant – and two children, Nils, nine and Thea, seven. Every summer we'd go to Denmark for a month. My mother's name was Christine. My father's name was Jens. My maiden name was Knudsen. They lived in Lillehammer, where I grew up. They owned a dog, a little lundehund, but the dog had not been well for a long time.

Stien, I got him talking. He said his name was Jon Sorensen and his cover story was more interesting than mine. He'd flown over the previous day from London and the day before that from New York. He had an apartment there and one in Mexico City and a little farm – the word he used was *finca* – in one of the Mexican states. But he was Norwegian, grew up in Stavanger. He worked there for Phillips, the oil company, and moved to the States to join their headquarters. He told me he barely knew a single person in Norway now, that he felt like a stranger. This was his first time back in five years, he said.

He owned a place in Buskerud, a little hut he used for holidays. He said he was going up there to prepare it for sale. I asked him how long he'd had the place. He said twenty-five years, that he'd bought it when he was working on the Ekofisk platform. He'd do two weeks on, four weeks off. He'd bought a big house in Stavanger but he wanted somewhere away from the city, somewhere close enough to drive but far enough not to get bothered. So he got himself a little hut in Buskerud, in the Hallingskarvet, by a lake called Strandavatnet. Do I know this part? he asked. No, I told him. Which parts do you know? he asked.

Well Stien, Pia knows many parts: around Bergen, of course, the Hardangerfjord, the Sognefjord, up the west coast. And the area around Lillehammer, she knows that area very well. Walking in the Omrtjernkampen and Rondane to the north. Summers on the Mjosa, winters in Espedalen.

Espedalen, he said. That is a name I have not heard for many many years.

Then he talked about Mexico and about Mexico City and about how he spent summer in the United States and winter on his farm in Oaxaca where he watched birds and collected butterflies and had a girlfriend.

Are you not a little old for girlfriends? I asked, teasing him.

We ordered two more drinks and he told me he was seventy-five years old and that his Mexican girlfriend was thirty-nine and that her name was Maria-Paz and that she owned a restaurant somewhere on the Pacific Coast. Then he started to talk about the different kinds of bird that live in the forests of the sierra including rare jays and hummingbirds and I started to consider the likelihood that this man could in any way be connected to the theft at the Munchmuseet. Why would he be sitting here in an upmarket hotel in Oslo, having flown in from London and New York? Why would he be talking to a stranger about his life in such an open, unguarded way? Why was he so different from the usual kind of lowlife we are used to dealing with?

Sometimes the clue is hidden right before your eyes, so close you cannot see it. Of course he could have been acting, acting like me. He might have been another decoy, sent to Holm to distract. He might be taking the first steps towards blowing the whistle, laying the ground for greater clues. Or he might have been innocent of everything. Soon, I thought, I would lose patience with all the pretty talk of birds. Soon I would need to go home, and I would need to go home with something more than this. But for the time being I sat back and listened.

He talked about New York, about the colours in autumn and about the time a few years ago when he lost himself in Manhattan although New York, he said, is not complicated. He'd asked for directions to wherever he was meant to be going, a museum, but every time the directions went out of his head. He walked and walked, getting more and more lost until he stopped to catch his breath, outside a barber's shop, and collapsed. An ambulance came very quickly and he was taken to the nearest hospital. He'd suffered a minor stroke. Well, he said, I was seventy years old then. He was meant to be flying to Mexico City the following day but the doctors told him not to fly. The doctors told him he needed to rest and he needed to stop smoking. He told the doctors he was seventy years old and this was the first time he'd ever been in hospital. And that was the only time I've ever been in hospital, he said, looking at me.

Then he talked about Mexico again, how if he'd suffered that stroke in Mexico City he'd have never made it to the hospital. He talked about places in Mexico City where he could have been, listing their names, their names in Spanish, places where they'd have robbed him and left him or robbed him then called the ambulance, places where the ambulance would have taken three quarters of an hour and left him in a hospital where you'd have to buy your own medical equipment.

But you must like it enough to live there, I said, ordering two last drinks, thinking I was about to leave with nothing. He replied that he used to like Mexico City because it was after all an amazing city, like New York, one of the great cities of the world. But these cities, for a man of his age – he was seventy-five now, he told me again – these cities can become a burden. Which is why, he said, he bought the place in Oaxaca. To live there, to die there.

Which is why you're selling your hut in the Hallingskarvet, I asked, trying to bring him back to the present. He said he'd decided to sell it when he bought the farm but that it had taken him years to get round to doing it. The apartment in Mexico City he used only to hop between his place in New York and the farm. He said Mexico City was too much for him these days.

And what is it like, I said, this place of yours in the Hallingskarvet? He described a very ordinary mountain hut, comfortable, good for walking, good for skiing, good for fishing, good for hunting, good for wildlife, set away from the road but not far from the shore of the lake, once much-loved, now much-neglected. I have not been there for a long time, he said. How long? I asked. A long time, he replied. So I said with only a little calculation how it must be sad to be selling a part of his past, a part of his history. But he looked at me very sharply as if I had said something quite unusual, quite different. I told him I had meant the hut, I said it must be sad for him to be letting the hut go, to be selling the hut. But he put down his drink and the atmosphere changed very suddenly and the way he looked at me suggested I had asked a very different question entirely. And the way I responded – by insisting I was talking about the hut – suggested I knew there was something else my question could have been referring to. Yes, he replied, life can be very sad. As I looked down at the table, cursing myself, he was already standing and had gathered up his copy of *Afterposten.*

After we said goodbye, I walked back to the office and ran a check on properties around Strandavatnet. You know how long these things take. Eventually I found a JON ARNE SORENSEN listed as the owner of a property on the east side of the lake. I ran the name through the national criminal database but nothing came up. He was on the registry as having been born in January 1930 in Stavanger. I called Holm then put the phone down before it started ringing. It was too late to call. But afterwards, I tried again. Holm sounded a bit drunk. The old man's certainly got something, I said, you've no sense of what it is? None at all, said Holm, definitely drunk. I asked him why an old man could be connected to something like the Munchmuseet theft? Holm laughed. You're the cop! he said. When you're a cop everyone's a suspect, aren't they?

Then Holm asked me if I knew of a case Klaus Clausen had been investigating a couple of years back. My heart sank because Klaus Clausen was famous for investigating lost causes. Did you ever come across him, Stien? A strange man. Holm started to tell me all about the case: how municipal authorities had been clearing out the flat of an old woman who'd died in some high rise in Tveita. Her name was Katharine Vig. Amongst the rubbish was a suitcase containing a painting by Ludvig Karsten. The work changed hands a couple of times before ending up in the flea market off Frogner Park and being bought by someone who knew his work and had paid five hundred for it and then got worried that it was stolen and called the police. It got passed to us and Clausen picked it up because he dealt with art crime. The picture by Karsten ended up back at the Petersen Museum. It had been part of his collection and had been registered missing in the 1970s. The woman who found it got some money and everyone was happy, except Klaus Clausen. He'd discovered that Katharine Vig had had a younger sister called Anna who'd worked for Petersen in the early 1950s. She'd been one of his assistants and helped catalogue his collection. Hakon Petersen was a well-known collector, very wealthy, influential, and working with him would have been a big deal. Clausen had looked through the Petersen archives and discovered that when his collection was donated to the public – in 1971, a few years before his death – a number of other pictures alongside the Karsten were also registered as missing. Most, like Karsten, were middling Norwegian artists but one was by Munch. Katharine Vig's flat had long been emptied but Klausen re-interviewed the house clearance people and market men. Nothing came of it. Clausen had discovered that Anna Vig had emigrated to the States after the war but that no one fitting her profile could be traced. When Clausen retired, the case was dropped.

I didn't give a shit about Klaus Clausen or his little case. He never solved anything important. That's why they put him in charge of art crime. What's your point? I asked Holm. Why are you telling me all this? I said. My point, he replied, is that if the picture's anything, it's more likely to be something on this scale, rather than anything stolen from the Munchmuseet. But what if he's laying a clue, I asked, telling us where to look? Or what if they've sent him as a decoy? Trying to make a distraction? These guys are bloody clever. Do you think he could be an insider, I asked, sending us a message? Or maybe he's been frozen out, he wants to pass on information?

Anything's possible, Holm replied. As I said, you're the cop not me.

I got back onto the national database and placed a marker on the old man and his property. All I said was that he was of operational interest to Økokrim and I left our numbers. Then I arranged for the car to be tracked through the hire company. My instinct told me that if he had anything it would be at the hut. He wouldn't keep it in the hotel. The car was due to be returned on the Sunday. I messaged Haugeland and Sundby and told them there was a job the following morning and they needed to be ready at seven.

What I told them in the morning was that it was a tip-off, not part of the main investigation, but that it had come through Økokrim and that we were to pursue the lead and pass on any intelligence that was gathered. I told them they needed to follow the vehicle once it had left the Bristol Hotel and report back all its movements. I told them they were authorised to make a single random interception of the vehicle, the timing of which I would decide. I told them the interception of the vehicle should be conducted as if it were a routine security matter and that they should show their national police identification rather than their Økokrim badges if asked. I told them that the vehicle must be thoroughly searched before the suspect was allowed to continue. Finally I told them what they were meant to be looking for.

But Stien, all day they were parked, the two of them, outside the Bristol, waiting for the car to emerge. Every time they checked with the hire company they were told the vehicle was still in the hotel's underground car park.

It wasn't until the afternoon when Haugeland went into the hotel that we discovered that the old man had switched firms and had already driven up to the hut in a different vehicle. And while I kicked myself for being fooled in such an obvious way, secretly I was pleased because I knew then that we were on to something, that we were on to something big. So I sent Huageland and Sundby straight up to Buskerud and I went back to the hotel myself. But when I swept his room there was nothing, just a suit hanging in the wardrobe and some empty cigarette cartons.

They stopped him on the road out of Hol the following morning. He didn't seem that surprised. They told him he was driving badly, which he probably was. I told them they should take at least twenty minutes searching the vehicle, but they let him go after ten. There was nothing in the car. Nothing at all? I asked. Well, said Haugeland, there was a book. A book? I said. A book on Munch, said Haugeland, written in German.

I took the details then sent them up to the hut. I told them to leave it as they found it. Three hours minimum, I said. But after two hours they said they'd done everything they could, carpets, floorboards, etc. and there was nothing there either.

The book told me we were on to something but it wasn't what we were looking for.

The next day I got a call from someone at the airport, informing me that he was checked-in to an early flight to London. They were asking if there was any reason why he couldn't proceed. I ordered them to search his luggage and explain that it was a routine security check. They called back an hour later and again there was nothing. Nothing at all. And so he disappeared off the radar. For five months.

147

I tried my best to forget about it all. I wasn't proud. Sundby would smile at me in the lift. Haugeland wanted to tease me. Don't tell me, he'd say, the old man that stole The Scream! In the evening I'd go home and pour myself a glass of wine and watch bad television and curse Holm who called me afterwards and said casually oh by the way that man never turned up. I know, I said to Holm, he left the country the day before you were meant to meet. And what did you find out? asked Holm. Not much, I replied.

In truth I'd found out nothing. So, to begin with, I did a good job of getting on with other things. God, it was no different to lots of other dead-end leads. But when the Munch case continued unsolved, with nothing from Kripos to suggest they were getting anywhere, I started to ask myself questions again. Where could he have gone after leaving the hotel? Where might he have stopped between Oslo and the hut? Or if he travelled to the hut to pick up the picture, did he leave it somewhere between the hut and the point where Haugesund and Sundby picked him up? How thoroughly did they search his car? How thoroughly did they search the hut? If I drove up now, what would I find? How easy would it have been to conceal? Could it have been in his hotel room as I went through it, drawer by drawer? And what was the story behind the book?

I considered again his character. How much of his conversation had been a game, how much genuine? If he'd nothing to hide then why had he left so abruptly, and changed his car hire company the following morning? Why was he unsurprised when stopped on the road out of Hol? Why had he left Norway all those years ago? What was the Mexican connection? How had he come to settle in New York? Did they have anything on file over there? What was his record at Phillips Petroleum? Had he really lived in Stavanger, worked the Ekofisk field?

I made some light enquiries. The best cover stories are sometimes the most truthful. He'd grown up an only child in Stavanger, studied at the cathedral school, then geology in Trondheim, joined the air force, quit after a decade, got a job at Phillips Petroleum, left Norway in the 1970s, returned a few years later, then left again in 1980. This was the year he bought the hut. Immigration records showed he returned very rarely, a few weeks here and there, often years apart. He had no federal record in the United States and the Mexican authorities had never even heard of him. Reason prevailed and I let it go.

Then about a month ago, Stien, you called. Here goes, I thought: Kripos. An investigator on the Munch case. Let's go and have a coffee, you said. We need to talk.

I wasn't worried. I knew it would only be a matter of time before someone from Kripos found out that I'd been sniffing around their case. I'd told Haugeland and Sundby to keep it quiet but I'd never expected it to remain that way. I'd not done much wrong. The lead came to nothing. No use passing on nothing.

When I saw you, Stien, I realised you were one of those classic Kripos guys. I mean you're all the same: bodybuilders, fascinated by firearms! It makes me laugh, these cops who want to play guns all the time. Don't you know which country you live in? We don't carry guns here, in case you haven't noticed. They're all under lock and key.

I didn't like you much at first. You started boasting about some big name crook you'd brought down recently. I told you I'd never heard of him. You looked at me as if to say, well you wouldn't if you work at Økokrim, that's white collar crime, isn't it? *White collar crime.* Then you went on about your last murder case. Some guy, you said, found garrotted on a fishing trawler not far from here. You must have read about the case, you said. We were sitting outside at one of those bars on Lille Stranden, overlooking the pretty boats. No, I said, I hadn't. And you shook your head and drew smoke from your cigarette and I thought fishing trawler not cruise liner, garrotted not thrown overboard. There was plenty of evidence there. Who was the victim, I asked, some trawler man? Yes, you said. And who did it, I said, the skipper? Yes, you said, the skipper. There you go. I'd solved the case already. But Stien, you made it sound like it was the crime of the century. Evidence from the DNA Gateway, seven weeks of surveillance, a car chase along the E16... Sure enough, the gun came out at the end. Sure enough, it was an MP5. Did you use it, I said, knowing of course that you didn't, Stien. No, you said, I didn't need to. I bet you didn't, I thought to myself.

Anyway, after a while you stopped talking about yourself and asked me what I was doing. I told you I was working on a number of different projects. Including the NOKAS case? you said. Including the NOKAS case, I replied.

You asked me if I knew the theory that the Munch thefts had been carried out to divert attention from the NOKAS case. You said you'd been sifting through names, names from across the criminal spectrum, mostly known names but also unknown names that had come from various intelligence strands. Every single unknown was double-checked against the national database and in most cases nothing came up. But a couple of weeks before you'd got a match with a name that had my details attached. What was the name, I said, knowing the answer of course. Sorensen, you said, Jon Sorensen.

I looked at you, Stien, and wondered how serious a game I was getting into. I wanted to know what you knew about Sorensen yourself and what you knew about what I knew. I wanted to know how long a couple of weeks really was, how much you'd actually gathered, how much you thought I'd share. Mostly I wanted to know how you'd got the name and where from, what grade of intelligence you were talking about, what kind of source. Because if Sorensen's name really had filtered up from the streets, then his connection to the Munch case was a real possibility. But it was just as possible that the name had filtered down from Holm, or from one of us. A loose word from Haugesund to a colleague. A loose word from that colleague to a source. It doesn't take much to make Chinese whispers. Before you know it, the name's gone full circle. Besides, it was a common enough name.

Is he connected to the NOKAS money? you asked.

Honestly, I said, I have no idea.

So he's one of your other cases?

He could be, I said.

What case? you asked.

Come on, I said. Let's not waste our time. Tell me what you know and I'll tell you what I know.

So we began to talk. You went first. That was only fair. You said you couldn't reveal your source but that it was a good source, one that could be trusted. You said you'd made some checks on the name and that the profile was, admittedly, unusual. But you said that naturally the international angle was being pursued by Kripos and that checks suggested the name had travelled to London and New York fairly recently and of course both were money laundering centres. You said Kripos were investigating the possibility that the name might be acting as a go-between for a dealer or a collector and proxies linked to the thefts.

Your level of interest suggested you knew something I didn't but you weren't going to say what it was. Since you wouldn't disclose your source, I decided not to disclose mine either. All I said was that I had it on good authority that the name was in possession of a picture by Munch and that he'd been in and out of the country one weekend in April.

You asked all the usual questions: why I was so interested in the Munch case, why I didn't pass on the intelligence, what I'd found out about this Sorensen guy. I told you more or less what I knew, with a few holes, and this was where we left it. You paid the bill – black coffee for me, three beers for you – and then we went our separate ways. We promised to stay in touch. June passed. Then July. August. Nothing happened.

Then last Sunday, September the 4th, I got a call from an officer at Gardermoen. You were interested in someone called Sorensen? he said. Yes, I replied. Well, he said, he's just left the country. I told him it couldn't be the same guy because if he'd left the country, he'd have entered the country, and if he'd entered the country, I'd have been told. Apparently not. According to the records, the officer said, he arrived early morning on a flight from London and he'd just left on the flight back. To London? I asked. Yes, he said, to London. And was he searched? I asked. No. Where was he now? Somewhere over the North Sea, the officer said, booked onto a flight to New York.

That was when I called you, Stien. You were in a car watching someone. Can this wait? you asked. No, I said. Go on then, you said, and I told you what I knew. You asked the usual questions Stien: why the hell Gardermoen waited until he was on the flight back to make the call; what we knew about his movements when he arrived in Oslo (nothing); what we knew about his projected movements in London (nothing); whether he had anyone accompanying him (no).

I called Holm and the Bristol Hotel. No contact. Then I called the deputy director.

He said I'd got three minutes. I didn't make any great claims. I just told him there was this guy touting a Munch a few months ago, how we did some checks, made some searches but nothing was found. How it turned out he'd been back in the country, slipped through the net, was on a flight back to London and booked onto a connecting flight to New York in a few hours' time. After that, I said, the trail will only get colder.

There was silence. He said it was a Kripos investigation, said it wasn't our business, asked why we were getting involved. I told him I'd been pursuing various lines on the NOKAS case and he said what lines and I said money laundering. I told him that Kripos were aware, that they'd had a separate tip-off about the suspect, that they too wanted to make a move. So he said he'd speak to Brørs. And he asked why the intelligence hadn't come past his desk and I said it wasn't significant up to this point but now we had corroborating information. Again he said he'd speak to Brørs. Then he said we'd need international assistance and that was the moment I knew I'd clinched it. Olsen, he added, make sure you've got this right. After that he put the phone down.

Brørs is the one at Kripos who makes all the decisions. The Hamburger they still call him. He weighs one hundred and forty kilos. When I was at Kripos he was a junior detective and the bosses were always trying to get him to diet. You can't be a good cop, they'd say, if you can't run after the bad guys. Rubbish, he told them, I'll chase them in the car. He crashed a lot of cars. He was known for crashing cars. He was known for crashing cars and eating hamburgers and for sleeping at his desk, among the wrappers. He wore big thick spectacles and a brown woollen hat and snow boots all year round. But he solved a lot of cases. Nowadays when you see him he's in a suit and he wears black polished shoes. His glasses are thin and wiry. That's Brørs.

Anyway Brørs said we should proceed but he stopped short of sending Stien and I to London. Interpol were informed. So were Scotland Yard. We alerted the airline but of course he never made it past the desk. He went to check-in then changed his mind. Instead he booked a flight for the following week: that's tomorrow. We told Scotland Yard the basics, that he was a person of interest in the Munchmuseet theft. They traced him to three separate hotels and alerted various contacts. But they said they didn't want to question him without clearer evidence. We'd already gone back to the hut: this time Kripos did the job. They turned the place over but once again found nothing. I told the deputy director we needed someone in London. He spoke to Brørs. Send them both, Brørs said. Brørs spoke to Interpol. Interpol spoke to Scotland Yard. Scotland Yard spoke to Brørs. Brørs spoke to the deputy director. The deputy director and Brørs spoke to the office of the Police Commissioner. The office of the Police Commissioner spoke to the office of the Ministry of Justice. They took a week deciding what to do and then the call from Drammen came through.

Provincial business. If only I had listened to this provincial business. When Magnussen came back in the afternoon and started talking about the hut, I was ready to go mad. I couldn't believe Sorensen was back in the country. I couldn't believe they let him through again. I told Magnussen to get back to the officer in Drammen and check every single bloody detail. Then I got on to Immigration. But their dates were the same: Sorensen had come in on the Sunday morning and returned to London in the afternoon. He'd not been in the country since he left. If he'd come back in, it was under a false name or a different passport. I checked whether he might have used an American passport or a Mexican one but not a single Mexican had entered Norway for weeks and no American citizen under his name or even near it. If he'd entered on a false passport, they told me, tracking it would take time. I called Holm and checked whether he'd had any contact but when he finally answered the call, the answer was no. I checked the Bristol but they'd no records of him since his visit in April. I checked the car hire companies but they'd no records either. Then you called, Stien, and said you'd booked two tickets for London and that we were waiting for the green light from Brørs. I spoke to the deputy director who said Brørs was waiting for a call from the Ministry of Justice. Then I went over to Magnussen's desk to find out what he'd gathered. But when I got there he had the Klaus Clausen case file on his desk and he was trying to get through to a number in New York. I told him not to waste time on that crap, what had he got from Drammen?

Magnussen looked up, with that stupid expression on his face, and said that he didn't have much. What do you mean not much, I shouted, what do you mean not much? Not much, he said, very calmly, just a couple of reports about two boys riding bicycles around the area. Magnussen, I said, this is not a bloody joke. Do you know what we are bloody looking for? I know, he said, but reports are reports. There were reports of a stolen boat. The boat was found. There were noises at this hut. The hut showed no sign of forced entry, everything was clean and tidy. Clean and tidy? I said. Kripos had turned the bloody place over! Who are these bloody boys? What are their names? How old are they? Where are they now? Oh, said Magnussen, I've written their names down somewhere, but they're not in Norway, he said, they've already left the country. Left the country, I shouted, where the hell are they? They are in London, Magnussen says, they flew to London yesterday.

Then, Stien, you called to say Brørs had given us the green light and I said well there were now two additional suspects and as I said this to you I looked at Magnussen and I could see him dial that number to New York again and something inside me didn't feel right at all.

Stien, you're still snoring. Wake up, we're coming into London. I should have told you about Magnussen but it's too late now. Let's forget about Magnussen for the time being. We need to go and find those boys. Wake up, Stien. We need to go and find those boys.

ANNA VIG

After I put the phone down I put on my warmest coat, which is Balenciaga and which I bought last year for two and a half thousand dollars, the most I have ever spent on a coat, and I walk like I did when I first came to this city, when I used to walk until I got lost. Out of the door, down Bethune Street and Bleecker Street, across towards Washington Square, then over Fourth Avenue. Now I am approaching Tomkins Square Park and soon I will see the red towers of Stuyvesant Town and after that the East River and I wonder where my memory will have taken me by the time I get home, back to the other side.

At the moment all I can think of is Jon Sorensen. Of course I shouldn't be thinking of Jon. I should be thinking of my sister Katharine. After all, I've just been told she's dead. But Jon has been in my head ever since I saw him in that gallery on West 25th nearly five years ago. What the hell was he doing in a gallery on West 25th five years ago? What the hell was he doing in New York? How long had he been living here? Why had fate waited fifty years to bring us together again? And why, at the last moment, had it failed us? No, I reasoned afterwards, that wasn't Jon. That was just someone who looked like Jon, fifty years on. You can't tell what someone is going to look like, fifty years on, can you? Look at me at twenty, look at me at seventy. Even I'm not sure the same person's there.

He calls three times, the cop. His name is Magnussen. I am just fixing my breakfast when the phone rings the first time. To begin with, he doesn't say who he is. He just says he's trying to reach someone called Anna Vig. Are you Anna Vig, madam? he asks.

Anna Vig, I say, yes I am Anna Vig. And why not? All sorts of strangers call my number. This is New York, after all. Who's this? I ask.

He starts talking. Straightaway I get his accent. He says he's a policeman, an investigator, that he is calling from Norway, from Oslo. The line is crystal clear but his English is poor. He says there is nothing to worry about but that he is trying to contact someone called Anna Vig who lived in Norway in the 1950s.

I'm an American, I tell him, you can hear it in my accent. Of course, he says apologetically. But do you have, he asks, do you have, but I interrupt him. Once more I tell him I'm an American, a citizen of the United States. I'm sorry I have been a bother to you, he says. Then he hangs up.

Did I happen to have what? All that stuff I got rid of years ago! Why is he calling me now?

Two minutes later I am sitting down a little confused and he calls again. I am sorry to phone you once more, he says, but I am wanting to know are you a relation of someone called Katharine Vig?

I don't speak, I cannot speak, so he carries on and I listen. He says Katharine – he calls her Mrs Vig – died a couple of years ago and among her possessions was a picture, a stolen picture of some value, one missing for many years. They are trying to speak to any relatives who may know where the picture had come from, to see whether there are other – he pauses and breaks out of English and uses the Norwegian word instead: *eiendeler.*

Assets? I said, translating without realising it.

That's it, he says, assets. Then the line goes quiet, as quiet as those mornings when I'd wake in my bunk early and there'd be ice on the insides of the window panes and I'd wait patiently until Katharine woke and when finally she stirred I'd say please Katharine can I climb in with you but usually she would say no Anna, later, let me sleep.

Did you know her? the man says, his tone changing. Can I ask how old you are madam?

Me? I reply. What has this got to do with me? No, I tell him, I think you have the wrong person. You must have the wrong number. The wrong person. A different Anna Vig. There is another pause. Of course, he says, I understand. I am very sorry madam. I am very sorry to disturb you. And then he says goodbye and hangs up a second time. But afterwards, just as I am about to go out, he calls again and makes me write down his name and his number. Please contact me, he says, if there's anything you want to tell us. I have nothing to tell you, I say.

I had plenty to tell, plenty to tell about Katharine, but instead I was thinking of Jon. I should have been thinking of Katharine, my big sister dead two years. Maybe it was the shock. But I thought of Jon and the moment he walked into that gallery asking for directions to Fifth Avenue and 79th.

It was around about this time, five years ago. I was talking to McGill the owner about an exhibition I was planning, when this man walked in. Go to 23rd Street, the girl at the desk told him, and take the subway up to 77th. No, the man said, I'd rather walk if that's okay. I just need to know roughly which way I should be heading. I've lost my bearings, he told her. He was a tall man, very tall, way beyond six foot, and he wore a long dark overcoat made of expensive cloth and a pair of old, well-made brogues and on his head he wore a homburg. His voice was mixed: East Coast, plus a little of something else. I couldn't see his face. His back was turned. The receptionist drew some directions for him on an exhibition flyer. He thanked her, took the directions and left. When he took the directions I saw his hands and I knew at once it was him.

Those enormous hands. I remember staring at those hands as he slept and thinking how incongruous they looked, how detached they seemed from the person they belonged to. They seemed capable only of physical, even brutal acts. And yet if you followed the line up his arms, to his shoulders, his back, the rest of his body – he always slept on his front, taking up so much of the bed – you realised that his hands were just another part of him, another part of the man that I loved.

All this was many years ago.

What was I to do? Everything happened in delay. By the time I realised who he was, he had disappeared out of the door. I was meant to be meeting McGill. We were meant to be making plans. But I excused myself from McGill and instead I went up to the receptionist. I asked her where the man had said he was heading and she said the Met but that he'd wanted to walk. I asked her what directions she'd given him and she said she'd told him to go straight up Fifth Avenue but that it was three, four miles and much easier to take the subway.

I walked up Fifth Avenue, looking. Afterwards I took the subway at 23rd Street and went the way the girl had suggested. I imagined him deciding to take the train too. I imagined both of us taking the same train together. When I got down to the platform, the train's lights were scuttling down the tunnel. This is a city of millions, I told myself, don't be crazy. But then I thought if our paths had crossed once already in a day there was no reason why they couldn't cross again.

The rest of the day I spent in the Met. I went to something on life in Paris which had paintings by Chagall and Balthus and these kinds of people. There was something else on Chardin. I thought through numerous possibilities: I had taken the subway and gotten a head start. But he might have taken lunch. He might have bumped into a friend on the way. He might have decided against the whole thing and gone home. He might have left it until the following day. He might have spent the whole afternoon inside the museum, like me, looking for something and never finding it. He'd appeared, then disappeared.

I prepared to explain my own disappearance, half a lifetime ago. When I disappeared I bought a single berth to New York and the ship crossed in a week. I got my ticket by selling the Johannessen to a man who worked for Norwegian American, and the Fjell and the Nesch I carried in my suitcase all the way to Brooklyn. The Nesch went to some pawnbroker in the first week and the Fjell went to a dealer. Years later I saw it in a catalogue going for twenty thousand dollars. But I was happy to be rid of the lot, reminders as they were of my theft.

The theft I could be forgiven for, but not the way I killed Jon's love. The victim of my theft, Petersen, loved me but I did not love him back. The man I loved, Jon, I betrayed with the victim of my theft. My parents would neither countenance the man I loved nor the fact I was a thief. I was young and my instinct was to run, to disappear. My country was scarred by years of occupation. Across the ocean lay untainted opportunity. On the boat I met my future husband. We were married for nearly fifty years.

But even after fifty years, the heart remains a fragile object. It should be the one thing in our bodies that grows stronger while everything else decays. It flutters and pounds young before striking a dependable beat. But the longer the beat goes on, the softer it becomes until you barely realise it is there: love becomes commonplace, everyday. Never again do you experience the shock of love until you experience the shock of grief and then you experience it with the same staggering rawness because grief is love reversed.

My husband Moti died the year the century ended. Poor Moti. My heart was ill-prepared. Afterwards, in an attempt to kill the grief, I lost my married name – I never quite got used to being a Kreutzer, much as they're part of me. I reclaimed the simple single syllable of my Norwegian forefathers: Vig. I tried to contact my sister but my actions were slow, too cautious. I put this down to age. These things are so tiring, I told myself. In truth I feared what I might discover. My parents, I found along the way, had died two decades before: one day after the other, my mother first, then my father. They are buried at the church in Vestby. I could find nothing of my sister. No trace. Nothing at all. I went to libraries first, reference centres. I spent hours at computers. All my searching was fruitless. Then today, she came to me.

Dead two years. What had I imagined? I had imagined Katharine still alive. Living in Norway: I had got that right. Family: husband, children, grandchildren. This is what I had hoped. Not living alone. In the absence of other family members, they had reached out to me. Had she lived her final years alone, unloved? How else would the Karsten have fallen into their hands, a picture worth tens of thousands of dollars? *Among her possessions*, the policeman had said. Perhaps the painting they found in her flat wasn't the Karsten. Perhaps it was something else, something of enough value for other people to be interested in. But Katharine wasn't taken by art. She wasn't impressed by pictures. When I told her I wanted her to look after it for me, she knocked a nail in the wall of her kitchen and hung it. No ceremony at all. Perhaps over the years she learned to love it. Or perhaps she knew it was stolen. I told her it was a gift from Petersen. I wrote from the deck of the *Stavangerfjord* that I wanted nothing more to do with him and that the painting was hers to keep. I wrote that I wasn't sure when I'd be back, and when I didn't return she probably felt she knew the reason. Of course the Karsten was stolen. And the Nesch. And the Johannessen. And the Fjell. And the Munch.

I remember Petersen showing the Munch to me, telling me how beautiful it was. He was right, it was beautiful. It showed two lovers, kissing in a field. Perhaps, he said, one day soon, it will be yours. He was asking me to be his lover. I answered him by stealing his pictures.

I was flattered by Petersen's attention. He was an important man, a powerful man and I was young, very impressionable. He was the kind of man who got what he wanted. I was old enough to work out that he wanted me but I wasn't so old to resist him. I'd only been working with him for a week when he invited me into his office and said how valuable I was to him, as if I was part of his collection. He told me I was beautiful. I took the Nesch. He asked me out for dinner. I took the Fjell. He asked if he could kiss me. I took the Johannessen. He invited me to his place in the mountains. I took the Karsten. He said he was in love with me. I stole the Munch.

I remember getting home and looking at the Munch in a kind of panic. There was something so amazing and yet so sad about that picture. It was mine and yet not mine. It was me and yet it wasn't me. I had it yet I couldn't keep it and I couldn't take it back. I didn't know what to do. I wanted to tell Jon but if I'd told Jon I would have had to have told him everything. I could never in a million years have bought it for myself. Neither of us had any money. He'd have guessed it was a gift and if it was a gift, he'd have wanted to have known why, why was Petersen giving away pictures from his collection? I couldn't answer that without lying. I looked at that picture and I wanted Jon and I back where we belonged, back in that barley field. But when I looked at it I saw Petersen in that picture, not Jon.

The barley field was near my parents' house in Vestby. Every weekend that summer he'd take the train from Oslo and we'd meet under this great oak tree. It stood in the middle of the field. He was always there before me, his head in a book. Once I arrived and he was asleep. He looked so young, like a baby. Sometimes he'd hide in the barley and jump out and surprise me. Sometimes he'd hide high in the tree. I can see you, I would say, even if I couldn't see him. Often he'd sit lower down and watch me as I approached and then the branches of the great oak would shake and this beautiful man, all leanness and youth, would jump out and run towards me. Then we would kiss.

We met in January 1951, on the train between Oslo and Trondheim. Jon was twenty-one. I was eighteen.

I had left school and was living at home with my

parents. I spent the days trying not to think about what I was going to do with my life.

They were changing the locomotive, decoupling the train. We were outside, on the platform at Oppdal. It was late afternoon and there was little light left in the day.

As soon as I left I realised I had packed too few clothes. The snow was starting again. I had left home in a hurry.

Only a few people got off the train, mostly those who'd been on board since Oslo. It was too cold to stay outside for long.

I cannot even remember what we had argued about, my parents and I. We argued all the time. But I remember feeling the need to get as far away from them as possible.

I had trouble lighting my cigarette and he came and lit it for me. He wore a woollen suit with a scarf and thick, heavy socks and boots.

I took the train into Oslo and stayed the night with Katharine. She had told me to go home. One night, I said, all I want to do is stay one night. Okay, she said.

He asked me where I was travelling to. Trondheim, I told him. He said he was going there too. Are you at the university? he asked. No, I said, I'm visiting a friend.

In the morning I woke before dawn and walked to the station. There were trains back to Vestby but instead I bought a ticket to Trondheim. I don't know why.

Who is your friend, he asked, where does your friend live? We stamped our feet against the snow, to keep warm.

I had no friend. I had planned to take the train to Trondheim, spend the night somewhere cheap, then take the first train back to Oslo. That was all.

I am not sure where she lives, I told him. I have the

address somewhere in my purse. She's someone I used to go to school with.

After Oslo I would return to Vestby and show my father my ticket and tell him next time I would travel to Tromsø. Or Sweden. And stay there. You don't have the money, he would say, and he'd be right.

Shall we go back inside? he said. It's too cold to be standing around. Where are you sitting? he asked.

My ticket I have kept. It was among the few things I took with me to America. *Tur og retur, Oslo Trondheim* it says, and a number, 00727. I was in the second coach, in a seat looking back.

I am in the fourth coach, he said, looking forward. Perhaps, he said, you would like a cup of chocolate?

You may think that I had barely looked at a man. Well, I had been to some dances. But I had never danced with a stranger.

Thank you, I said, but I have a letter to write and we will be in Trondheim soon. I turned from him and walked down the corridor, back to my seat. When I looked back he was standing there, smiling at me. But I did not write a letter. Instead I thought about what I would do when I got to Trondheim. The next train was the following morning. There must be a hotel by the station. One that was hopefully not expensive. In fact, there were several. I had not stayed in a hotel before. I went to three and picked the second. It was the cheapest, some distance from the station. Is everything all right young lady? the woman at the desk asked. Perfectly fine, I told her. The station porter had asked the same thing when I stayed behind in the carriage until everyone had left, to avoid seeing him on the platform. Perfectly fine, I had told him.

Why had I behaved in that way? Perhaps it was

shyness. Perhaps the adventure of getting on the train and going somewhere I had never been, for no particular purpose, was enough for me. My imagination needed no further stimulus. Perhaps I felt vulnerable in my freedom. Perhaps a sense of caution had crept in.

I lay in bed that night and cursed myself. I thought how silly the trip had been, how purposeless. I could not sleep and listened to the city grow dark and quiet about me. The snow continued to fall. When I woke it was past seven and the only train back to Oslo had already left. It was a Sunday. The snow had stopped and the skies were clear. I paid the bill at the hotel – I had no money for a second night – and walked back to the station, where I pleaded with them to issue me with a new ticket for the following morning. I remember counting my money and realising I had barely enough for a meal. I bought an apple and sat down in the station and tried not to think about my parents or about where I would sleep that night. When I stopped crying I walked into the city and that was when I saw Jon again. He was waiting for the tram to Bymarka, his skis on one shoulder. He stood taller than the others. I stared at him. Eventually he saw me.

I'm going to the mountain, he said, will you come? I have nothing, I replied. Don't worry, he said, I will find you something.

We stood next to each other on the tram (how long that short journey was) as it wound through the city's suburbs towards Gråkallen, the little mountain where people spent their weekends. They chatted noisily of routes and rendezvous and compared the latest gear and fashions while the sides of the carriage rattled with skis. We hardly said a word. I looked down at the floor and thought how silly I would look in my long overcoat.

I had not expected Jon to be shy but he looked away too, onto the houses as they passed. Sometimes he whistled nervously. I decided when we got there to make my excuses and take the first tram back.

But when we got there Jon collected his skis and gave them to me and told me to wait, said he'd be back in five minutes. I could not leave them and run. So I waited and watched as people marched towards the slopes or into the woods and thought that perhaps the day would not be so bad. When he returned he had skis and poles and boots that fitted and everything else he said he'd put in his bag. After that we set off.

I cannot remember a happier day in my life. Of course I was nervous, so nervous to begin with. I know the best trail, he said, I did it last semester. Before long we were into the wilderness, no other people, just us and the sun and the sky so blue and the snow like scattered diamonds.

I lost my nervousness. We skied across a frozen lake and stopped in the middle to share a cigarette. We went up to the highest point and looked across to Sweden. We sat on the branches of a tree and ate the lunch that he'd brought: *geitost*, crackers, coffee from a thermos, fruit, chocolate. When I drifted into heavy snow he came back up the slope to help me. When he fell after making a jump I laughed and said he was a fool.

I told him everything. I told him I was from Vestby and that I had argued with my parents. I told him my friend in Trondheim had existed only in my imagination. I told him how I had missed my train back to Oslo that morning and that I'd spent nearly all my money and that I had no place to stay. I told him that I was quite happy despite all this.

I told him my sister Katharine was at university in

Oslo studying and that my parents had wanted me to follow her there but that I wanted to enrol at the Kunstakademi. They'd said they weren't wasting their money on me drawing pictures. So I stayed at home and drew pictures at home and I told him of the pictures I drew, the view from my bedroom mostly, at different times of the day. The line of the hills I'll remember to my dying day. He asked would I draw a picture of him and I said perhaps and that I'd bought a little sketch book with me but that I hadn't drawn a single line. Then I realised that I hadn't my case with me and I started to panic and he told me the case was safe, that the case was back in the hut where he'd picked up my skies and boots. Did it cost you? I asked. No, he said, I know the man.

I told him that I was going to find a job, any old job, and save up so I could enrol at the Kunstakademi and that I'd work while I studied and stay with Katharine in Oslo although Katharine thought I was silly too and that I should please my parents. I told him I wasn't sure if Katharine would let me stay for so long. He asked what kind of job I'd get and I said there were jobs like typing jobs or doing paperwork or I could work in a shop. He said that he had some money, a little money, and that he could lend me some if I really needed it because he thought it was very important that I did what I wanted to do. And I looked at him and I wanted to smile on account of his kindness but I did not smile because I did not want the money.

Later we sat in a cafeteria and drank chocolate and I drew a picture of him fresh-faced, tall, jagged in looks, with his woollen suit and polo neck and wavy hair and constant smoking and his large hands always holding a cigarette, usually a Petterøe. I don't know what happened to the pictures. I remember him placing them on the mantelpiece in his room which was chaos, full of unpacked bags, a trunk, books, his gramophone, records and I remember thinking I must take them, I must take them back to Oslo but I must have left them or perhaps I took them back and lost them, two pictures, a picture of his hands, a picture of him.

You will sleep in my room, he said, and I will sleep elsewhere. I nodded my head, having nowhere else to go. But getting in was no easy task. He took the porter around the corner to look at a dead fox and wedged the door open with my case. I ran up the stairs and waited and eventually he came. I have no idea where he slept. When I woke it was dark and he was knocking on the door. Anna, he whispered, you must catch your train now. I dressed in three minutes and together we walked to the station.

I remember our farewell only for what it wasn't. We shook hands and exchanged addresses. I gave him our neighbour's, Thorsen. Jon gave his address in Trondheim and his address in Stavanger. As soon as he got back to his room he wrote to me in twelve pages. He told me that he loved me. I waited three days for the letter to arrive. Thorson I could trust. He was an old man and was no great friend of my parents. He understood what life was about. He left the letters in a bird box in a tree at the end of his garden, hidden from view. I baked him biscuits, *serinakaker*, in return.

Throughout the spring and most of the summer I managed to keep secret our love. My brief disappearance had created torment but inside I could not have been happier. I floated above the turbulence happy to know I was in love. My sister Katharine was jealous but she kept her word and said nothing to my parents. We wrote and wrote and wrote and when the holidays came we wrote no more but met, embracing, at first on station platforms and then in places agreed and at times arranged: somewhere on Karl Johans mostly, Birkelunden, Bygdøynes, the bridge at Åmotbrua... I worked two days a week at the Engebret restaurant, waiting tables. Jon would arrive at the end of the day and wait and then we'd go out. I'd take the last train back to Vestby and he'd head east, to the place he stayed.

One weekend towards the end of the summer we went to Copenhagen to visit one of Jon's aunts. The trip was awful. His aunt was dying, although we didn't know that when we set off. She lived somewhere on the coast. When we got back to the city there was nowhere to stay and in the only hotel we could find we made a bad job of pretending we were married and it cost so much we didn't have enough to eat supper. The pressure made me ill. For the first time we argued. When we returned to Oslo I told Katharine and afterwards she told my parents and after that, life became very difficult. I had no money, at least not enough to enrol and Jon returned to Trondheim for his final year. Then, out of the blue, I got the job with Petersen. I calculated that a year's work would pay for my first year of study. I slept on the floor in the flat that Katharine rented and paid her a little rent. I cooked meals, cheap meals. She seemed happy that Jon and I were apart.

Something had happened during that trip to Copenhagen. I could have travelled up to Trondheim but I did not. I wrote and told Jon I was saving money. He wrote back and said he'd pay for my fare. I told him I was tired from work, that I needed to rest at the weekends, recuperate. What's so tiring about making lists, he'd ask. I don't think he understood what I was doing.

I'd started by cataloguing the collection but after

a while Petersen gave me other jobs to do. I'd look at pictures he was thinking of buying, attend auctions, sometimes even bid on his behalf. I discovered another life outside the lives I'd known. I had money, not much, but a little left over once I'd saved what I needed.

I felt like I knew everything, that I was in control. I was grown up now: I had fallen in love, got a job. But Petersen showed me how young I really was. I sometimes think he changed the course of my life but that's too simple, too obvious. I might have shrugged him off, stayed a year, enrolled at the Kunstakademi, worked my way through the course. Jon and I might have gotten married. Or I might have left the job, returned home to Vestby and done whatever my parents wanted me to do.

Instead I found myself on the deck of the *Stavangerfjord* in early November 1951, drawing the bow of the ship and the horizon and writing letters to them: my parents, my sister Katharine, Jon. Many long letters would follow, many of them unanswered. I told my parents in seventeen pages that I was moving to America, that I was going to be an artist and that I loved them. The same I said to Katharine, in nineteen. I told her I was sorry and asked that she look after our parents. We wrote for many years until she stopped replying. To Jon I wrote just once, one page, no more. I told him I had destroyed our love and for that I would be sorry for the rest of my life. And I told him he should look at the Munch once and then burn it. On my first morning in New York, I went to the Farley Building and spent thirty cents on a cardboard tube. I wrote his Trondheim address on the outside and posted the picture to him, along with the letter. Then I spent the rest of the day walking the city that would become my new home.

The following year I bumped into Moti Kreutzer

again. Moti was a lovely man. He'd given me his father's business card the morning we disembarked and said if there was anything he could do to assist in my new life, then all I needed to do was pay a visit. His father Mr Kreutzer, he said, was an influence. I was wary of new influences and those first six months were the hardest of my life. I kept my head low, fearful of the knock on the door. But of course the knock on the door never came. There was always the chance that Petersen might consider his losses best kept to himself. After a while I began to worry less about what the pawnbroker might have said to the dealer and what the dealer might have said to the private investigator. I worried less about the life I had left behind in Norway and more about the life in front of me. I had a room in a boarding house and a job working in a department store. I saved up for a Rolleiflex. At weekends I walked around the city taking photographs, making sketches.

I liked Staten Island most of all. I liked the views back to the city. And on the ferry one Sunday afternoon I saw Moti. Moti said he'd been looking for me all over New York. It's the kind of thing any young man might have said but it just happened to be true. Get over it son, old man Kreutzer had told him, and stop driving the whole family crazy. Find yourself a good Jewish woman like everyone else. But when Kreutzer met me for the first time the first thing he said was *Son, I see you have a point.*

Kreutzer was a dry goods man and he had other things besides, a bit of property, part-share in a tyre business, interests in construction. Moti was learning to be a lawyer and Kreutzer was thankful that his youngest was doing something that might be of use to the family business, since the eldest son was all math and physics and the middle one was a poet. Moti was Kreutzer's great hope.

We married in the late fall of 1953, two years to the day that I arrived in New York. We honeymooned in Acapulco with bundles of cash in our suitcases, cash that Kreutzer had given us after selling some street concession. This was the deal; he'd get us going while Moti qualified and spent time at a firm downtown and in return Moti would start taking over the business. Moti was happy with the arrangement and within five years we'd moved from our little apartment in Williamsburg to a house in Brooklyn Heights. Moti became an influence. I carried on taking photographs, of people, of things, and when the pictures came back I drew them out, one-by-one. Someone once told me they were good, that I should do something with them. But by then I was pregnant with Daniel and Moti said it wasn't the time.

Sometimes I wondered if the time would ever come. After Daniel there was Thomas. After Thomas, Laurence and then Ronald. By the time little Ron was at school we were already into the back half of the sixties. It wasn't until 1971 that I picked up my Rolleiflex again. It wasn't until '74 that I started showing my pictures to other people. It wasn't until '79 that I got my first exhibition.

1979 was the year Petersen died. There was a paragraph in *The New York Times*. It wasn't like I was waiting for his death or anything, it just prompted me. I decided it was time to tell Moti. We were over twenty-five years married by this time: something from my distant past wasn't going to break everything up.

I used to tell the children that I'd argued with my family, ran away thinking I'd return, met their father, written home every month, never received a reply. All this was kind of true and the children just accepted these things as facts. After a while they stopped asking why they only had one set of grandparents. Obviously Moti had more questions. He knew there'd been someone else. Why wouldn't there have been? I told him I'd fallen in love, I'd fallen out of love, I'd argued with my parents, I'd never had huge numbers of friends, I'd tried to keep in touch, my sister had become estranged. He offered to help. He offered to write to my parents, write to my sister. When we started to have some money, he offered to fly me over, even come himself. He couldn't believe someone could become separated in this way from their family. You are my family, I told him.

I could have told him everything in those first years. Sometimes I wish I had. But I kept all the Petersen stuff out. Once I decided this was what I was going to do, it became difficult doing anything different. After a while I almost convinced myself that the whole thing never happened: that I'd never met Petersen, that I'd never had that stupid affair, that I'd never stolen those stupid paintings, that I'd left my country because that's what people did then, not because it was the only option left to me.

Moti laughed when I told him. But my God it was serious for me. We were out at Orsini's and when he cracked up it seemed like the whole restaurant was looking at us. I began to cry. This great sadness I'd kept secret for three decades and all he could do was laugh! I don't care, he said. It's all ancient history. It's not like you've murdered someone. Then he told me his own little secret: that his father had always thought there was someone else involved. Don't ask questions, his father had said, the answers will only make you unhappy.

So we all put our heads in the sand. The last letter from my sister was in 1960. She wrote so seldom and I was

175

used to waiting but I remember very clearly the shock when I realised she had not been in contact for over a year. The longer the silence, the more futile the letters seemed. I stopped writing to my parents the following year, 1962, and then, a few years later, to my sister. My contact with her was my only contact with my parents. When I lost her, I lost my parents.

Of course I thought a lot about returning in those early years. Of arriving on a doorstep alone, suitcase in hand. But every year that passed, the more difficult a prospect it became. The risks felt too great. I had a family of my own and the bigger it grew, the greater those risks became. I could have flown in and out but I was scared of getting stuck, stuck in another country, paralysed by a guilt so strong it couldn't be broken. I was scared of being found out, of getting caught, of having to stand trial for theft, of going to jail. It seemed so stupid, so far away, but it still felt real. I was scared of seeing Petersen and scared of seeing Jon, and when all these fears eventually disappeared – when Jon simply became my first love, something beautiful and distant, and when Petersen became just one of those things that happened in my life – when all these fears had disappeared, it was far too late to turn back. There was too much silence, too much silence which could not be undone.

What I expected from Jon, that day in the gallery, I cannot tell you. Why I was so intent on seeing him, on speaking to him, I do not know for certain. Moti had not been dead so long and the grief felt raw: much had gone missing from my life. But I did not need these things replacing, far from it. I was simply adapting to the changes, as I have always done. My sons looked after me and I was starting to enjoy life on my own, perverse though it sounds. Following that man across

New York was out of character. Either I wanted to establish the coincidence or else I wanted something more: reconciliation perhaps.

Looking for him amongst the pictures, down the corridors, waiting for him to pass through an entrance or an exit, I wondered what I would say to him, whether he'd recognise me. I wondered if he was visiting, or if he lived here, if he'd left Norway, if he ever went back. I wondered where life had taken him, whether he'd married, had children. I wanted to know what he'd felt when I left, whether he'd ever received the Munch, what he'd done with it, burnt it as I told him to, or kept it? And the letter?

I had sometimes imagined him lying on his bed in his little room at university in Trondheim with the letter on the floor and the picture a pile of ashes. I'd imagined him in the weeks before, when I'd disappeared and left nothing, no clues, and I'd imagined him calling in on my parents, calling my work, gradually putting two and two together. It took a long time for mail to get there in those days. After the uncertainty would have come the betrayal, the anger, the heartbreak and finally the sadness.

But the picture was never burnt. I know that now. I know that because however important that other picture was, the one by Ludwig Karsten that I gave to Katharine, it was never so important that a detective from Oslo would trace me to New York and call me up. It wouldn't be the others that I stole either. That man must only have been interested in the Munch. So, thinking of Katharine, who never did anything wrong, I picked up the phone and called the number that he left, and he picked up – the same man, he picked up the phone and said Magnussen – and I said to him, in Norwegian, that my sister did not steal the picture, that it was me who had stolen the picture and that if he was still looking for it then he should know that I posted it in 1951 to a man I used to love called Jon. After that I put the phone down, pulled the line out of the socket, put on my warmest coat, which is Balenciaga and which I bought last year for two and a half thousand dollars, the most I have ever spent on a coat, and I went out into the morning of the day, to walk the city like I used to, to walk the city that became my home.

But I have long left behind the East River and the red towers of Stuyvesant and I have passed through Gramercy and the Village and still as I walk the city, on my way home, all I can think of is Jon Sorensen.

Jon Sorensen

The taxi driver is pointing up ahead, saying something about something, and I am asking myself what a man of my age is doing, sitting in the back of a taxi, lost in a city I barely know, with only a stuffed owl for companionship? The owl's right next to me, lying down, looking pretty inert, taking in London from an angle. How do you like the view of London, Mr Tecolote? Pretty unusual, hey?

My bags are packed. I'm heading home, whatever happens.

I know this might sound strange, but it's nice to have you back Mr Tecolote. Poor old Mr Tecolote. The process of evisceration seems so unnatural at times. But you were good, very patient, adapting to your new role. Didn't bat an eyelid. Just lay there on the kitchen table and looked at me. Very stoical. In fact, you looked at me then in much the same way as when you looked at me through the crosshairs. A yes I get it kind of look. Then I lowered the sights and pulled the trigger and you got it, in the tummy of course. I didn't want to mess up your face.

It took me a while to find you, clever Mr Tecolote. I thought I knew what tree you were on but there was no sign of you at the bottom. I didn't hear the tell-tale

179

thud of bird hitting ground. I traipsed back to my hiding point and double checked I'd got the right spot. There's nothing worse than losing your tree. If you lose your tree you can lose your kill. Then I checked you hadn't got caught in the branches on the way down. But no, you hadn't got caught in the branches, you'd fallen into a gorse bush and were hiding there. That's why it took me so long to find you. Poor old Mr Tecolote. Spending your last moments in a gorse bush. But by the time I got my hands on you, you were gone. Or near enough gone. It wasn't until I got back to the hut and laid you out on the kitchen table that I realised what a lovely specimen you were. Your disc quite perfect and your plumage barely touched by the shot which had missed your heart, sliced through your liver, shaved your proventriculus and pierced your lung before flying out of your ass with very little fuss. In the gizzard I found your final meal: a field mouse, curled in a ball, patiently awaiting the next stage of the digestive process.

It had been a while since I'd stuffed a bird and I wasn't sure what kind of gear I'd left in the hut. I'm more into butterflies now. But it was all there, just where I'd left it in the bathroom. It might have been easier to have used one of the other owls, unstuffed it, performed the necessary, stuffed it up again, job finished. But they were old friends whom I hadn't seen in a while. I didn't want to mess them up and besides, reverse taxidermy is a complicated business.

I felt bad for you though, Mr Tecolote. You were clearly a very special bird and I didn't have much time to make you look real nice. It wasn't that I was going to rush the job, I just wasn't going to spend as much time on you as I would have liked. I needed to get back home and the police, it seemed, were sniffing around. So I got to work, cutting (bill to anus, every time), removing the meat, degreasing, draining the eye juice, lining up what marbles I had (eighteen millimetre straws I went for in the end), all the time calculating in my head the measurements needed for the surgery, happy, Mr Tecolote, that you were tall enough, being sixty-three centimetres in height, but worried that the tubing I had – just forty-two centimetres of acrylic – left little space at the ends for the picture, the Munch being thirty-seven. You see, two and a half centimetres at the top and the bottom isn't much to play with. I was worried too about the tube's diameter, just twenty-two millimetres, whether it was wide enough to house the picture without it being damaged (the original cardboard tube with Anna's neat hand and its 1951 New York postmark was four, five times its width). I was worried whether it would sit happily inside the bird, whether it would keep its place within the wiring, whether my plan of access to the tube – a kind of trap door around Mr Tecolote's sphincter – was viable. These were my concerns.

But if I had planned the surgery in the first place I would hardly have done it any differently, so good were my improvisations. The wove paper was easier to manipulate than I had imagined and fitted snugly into the tube. The wire frame which I wound around the tube was neither so tight that it prevented the acrylic from being extracted nor so loose that the tube rattled inside the bird's interior. The ends of the tube I stuffed with cotton wool and cast two strong, thin lids from glue and used surgical tape to seal.

That wasn't the end of it though. I had always thought the woman detective in the hotel was just the prelude. To think at one stage I'd thought that she was wanting to go to bed with me. Ha! The vanity of man! Well,

Maria-Paz is thirty-seven so why not? This woman was older, in her forties, and no more attractive. But as soon as it clicked, as soon as I realised what she was up to, it all became very obvious: her questions about the hut. I realised I would have to take precautions. I realised I had been foolish to take the picture straight out of the bank, and from there to the dealer's. I was foolish to have gone to the dealer's. I should have just taken it out of the vault and got on the next flight home. Of course the thing was stolen and of course the dealer would know that. Of course he would tell the cops and of course the cops would come calling.

Mr Tecolote then was not my first piece of cleverness. I cancelled Hertz and went with a local firm. It wasn't until the following day that they caught up with me. Two bruising guys, trying to act casual. Some cover story about looking for a car similar to mine. A routine search, nothing more, they claimed. I acted the old man. A little indignant but mostly cooperative. I let them get on with it. When I got back to the hotel, someone had cased my room too. They tried a third time at the airport, searched me once more, stuck my name on a list. Well it could stay there as long as they wanted. I didn't have the picture. Mr Tecolote had the picture. And what a good place to hide it, up the ass of a snowy owl. They might come looking in the hut but I figured they wouldn't bother a snowy owl. It's a bird of myth in Norway. No one touches a snowy.

I was right as well. When I returned last Sunday, four months later, he hadn't been touched. He was there, up on the wall with his friends, just where I had left him. I didn't even need to take him off. I just poked my finger in, like it was yesterday, and out slid the tube. I unrolled the picture, it was pristine, and put it on the kitchen table. Then I unrolled the copy Dr Alvarez had made for me – the copy I'd let them find if they ever came knocking again – and placed it alongside. What a remarkable job he'd done. Could I distinguish between the two? Only with both in front of me, but the doctor had gotten very close. How he'd done the signature I do not know. His version looked newer, which it was, by a hundred years. The ink, the paper, the cut, the feel: it was just too perfect. But if one had been framed and hung on my wall, after a dozen mornings looking at it I probably wouldn't have known whose it was. But of course that wasn't the point.

It had taken a long time to find Dr Alvarez. I wasn't after a masterpiece, just something that would fool at first glance, a good enough approximation to the original. I wanted something I could hand back to the bank, something that could go back in their vault for safekeeping, something I could point the police to if they came knocking again, which I was certain they would.

There were a couple of decent versions kicking about, in private collections and museums. There was one in the Met and there was Schiefler's book, which I had photocopied and included in the little dossier I passed to Dr Alvarez. All the necessary details were there: type of paper, size of paper, size of print, date and methodology. Woodcuts are not so hard, Dr Alvarez had told me, and the signature was not so technical. Two thousand dollars he charged. I figured if that was the price for getting the picture safely back home then it was money well spent. Dr Alvarez asked no questions, a true professional. Perhaps he was not that interested, having more important clients. His studio in Toluca was discreet but busy – he employed understudies.

I warmed to the project and became an expert in

concealment. From a thrift store on West 17th I picked up the walking stick, a perfect piece of whimsy with a finely carved eagle's head for a handle. Twenty dollars this antique cost me. Pressing the eagle's beak unlocked the handle which unscrewed to reveal a hollow cylinder. Simple. From a Walmart I bought identical Perspex tubing to that used in Mr Tecolote – two point two in diameter – and cut forty-five centimetres in length, which slotted inside the stick with plenty of extra. I put bottle stoppers either end. I was in business.

Walking with it was another matter. I had no limp or defect and had to make one up. At seventy-five years old I would certainly look the part. But it felt unnatural, fake, almost comical. Everywhere I walked, it walked too, but as soon as I was alone I would throw it down and curse.

Whenever I considered the bother I went to, the time and money spent, miles travelled, enquiries made, I imagined the picture hanging in my kitchen in the farm, with the cloud forest beyond it, and I became more and more determined to retrieve it. Of course it would have been easier to have just flown over, picked it up, flown back. But the police had other ideas.

Second time around I had no problems until I got to London. There were no unsolicited conversations with detectives, no casual encounters on minor roads. I had made it my plan to enter on the Sunday, drive up to the hut, stay the night and fly out again on the Monday, dropping Dr Alvarez's copy at the bank, where I paid a yearly rate on a safety deposit box. A straight swap. If they asked me for the picture, I'd tell them it was in the bank.

But while I was up at the hut I got it into my head that it wasn't the dealer who'd tipped off the police back in April, but the bank. The more I thought about it, the more likely it sounded. I had signed everything out, sitting in a back room with an official, applying my name and signature to triplicate documents, estimating the approximate value of the work, about seventy thousand dollars for an original Munch print, and not giving a thought to any suspicions I once harboured that the work had, all those years ago, been stolen by Anna. Anyway, why would anyone care now? Did the police not have better things to do? Surely all suspicion had been erased by the passage of time?

But time was not on my side and neither were circumstances. Art theft, I realised from reading the newspapers, was in vogue amongst Norway's criminal class. The police were twitchy, alert. The banks would have been given the nod. It would have been stupid walking into that bank Monday morning and signing all those documents again, putting my name back out there, letting it be known to the whole world that I was in possession of a Munch, or as it happened to be, a Dr Alvarez.

So I put the Munch in the walking stick and Dr Alvarez's copy I put in Mr Tecolote, another straight swap. Why not? If they ever asked where the picture was, I could always direct them to the owl as a last resort. Or I could keep my mouth shut. Either way, it felt safer to be without it. I junked the trip to the bank and took the next flight out of Oslo and booked myself onto the late flight to New York.

But then I panicked. Everything was fine until I got to Heathrow when the woman at the desk of American Airlines looked at me in a funny way and told me over-apologetically that she had to make a call to a colleague. I decided to cut my losses. I rescheduled the flight for the following week, made my way to the taxi rank and asked to be taken somewhere central, somewhere small.

Maybe it was paranoia. Maybe it was instinct. I didn't want to take the risk. Sure I needed to get back to New York but I was in no great hurry. First I needed to go back and retrieve Dr Alvarez. I needed the copy back. If they searched me on the flight out to New York, I'd let them find Dr Alvarez. Well they could keep Dr Alvarez if they wanted to. But they'd be less interested in a fake than in something genuine, something stolen. Once they realised it wasn't real – their experts would find out pretty quick – they'd either charge me with some minor felony or let me go. It was a reasonable decoy. But how to retrieve Dr Alvarez? I knew they'd search me proper if I went back in again and I couldn't leave the original in London.

Then there was a knock at the door and the boy walked in, like it was all meant to happen.

(I liked the look of the boy right from the start. He reminded me of an old friend, someone I worked with, a guy called Mullane, freckles, red hair, lean as hell Mullane was. Mullane was one of the engineers when I worked in Argentina. We had some times together. He was a bit older than the boy but still young, late twenties or something. I had just turned forty and was divorced for the second time. I wanted to get away from it all. The job came up and I went for it: a few years out of the cold and if I missed Norway there was always Patagonia. It could have been Africa but South America sounded easier. I'd had two years in Houston before, when Isabelita was in charge. Not that she was in charge of much. The country was a mess, the Left were running amok. The generals restored a bit of order. They offered up a whole load of drilling concessions in the Magellan fields and because exploration was my area, they asked me to go: just to

186

get the ball rolling, they said. It was fine but I worked too much, spent too much time in Rio Grande, Rio Gallegos: windy dumps, horrible places. But when I wasn't in these places I was in Buenos Aires and I loved Buenos Aires. Mullane loved it too and we drank together. He was a borderline alcoholic, probably the wrong side of the border. Hooked on the aguardiente and obsessed with books. Crime books. American writers mostly, of the hard-boiled school. He had some bookshop in New York that would send them over. Once he'd read them he'd try to pass them on to me but after a while I told him not to bother. I found them too melodramatic. Anyway, one day I returned to the city from a trip down south and they told me he'd disappeared. Hadn't turned up to work for several days. The company weren't too bothered at first. There'd not been a foreign kidnapping since '74 and Mullane wasn't exactly a target. He'd never needed a bodyguard. He travelled a fair bit and was never the most reliable of guys. Sometimes he went fishing, up on the Paraná. But a week passed and still he didn't return. The bosses back home started to get nervous. They called me. You're his friend, they said, go look for him. Find out which bar he's hanging out in and haul his ass back to the office. Make a few enquiries, they said, it's part of procedure, until we send someone proper to look for him. So I flew down south, looked round the usual hotels, had a few drinks with a few people, went up to Santa Fe, spent some days there, met some guys who ran angling clubs, took an afternoon on the water, caught some dorado, put them back. Ridiculous. I felt dumb, clueless, like the parody of a private dick in one of those books of his. But the books, it turned out, held the clue. I got back to BA and was typing up this ridiculous report when I got it into my head to contact the store in New York that had been sending him trash for the last two years. Their address and number were printed on a bookmark tucked into every copy they sent. So I called up the shop, explained who I was, and asked if Mullane had called recently with an order. Oh yes, went the guy at the other end, just a couple of days ago in fact. I asked him where the books had been sent. Not the usual address, the guy said, let me have a look. There was this long pause as the guy ruffled through some papers. Eventually he picked up the receiver again and read out an address somewhere in South Dakota. *South Dakota*. Any phone number, I asked? No number, he said. So I took down the address and said goodbye. For the first time I was worried. What was an East Coast boy like Mullane doing in South Dakota? I passed the address to Head Office and they put a real Sam Spade onto the next flight to Sioux Falls and he drove north to a place called Aberdeen and found the address: a tiny rented house with a tiny rented lawn. Nothing much happening inside. He pressed the buzzer, knocked the door a few times. No reply. Curtains drawn. He checked the back door and the windows. All firmly closed. He went back into town, had lunch, then returned. Same scene but this time he decides to force the back door and creeps inside, shoes off like the spook that he is. It's dark with cheap furniture, tidy as hell. Nobody downstairs. He creeps upstairs. Two bedrooms. Silence. Checks the first. Nothing doing. Creeps into the second and there, in the middle of the room is a single bed and next to it a suitcase, full of these detective books. A hundred of them, maybe two hundred. And there's Mullane, sitting up in bed, reading under a spotlight, looking ill as hell but calm not intimidated, not distressed at all by the sudden appearance of the private dick, like he's been expecting him. The detective looks at Mullane and Mullane looks at the detective and there is this long silence until eventually the detective raises his eyebrows as if to say, well, it's your turn not mine and what does Mullane say in response? What he says – and these were his exact words – he says *I needed to go somewhere quiet to read*. He needed to go somewhere quiet to read. Somewhere quiet like South Dakota. Of course the private eye goes back into town and files a verbal report to the company and the company holds a meeting and decides Mullane has gone crazy and fires him with immediate effect. There was, after all, little oil in South Dakota. And the dick goes back to the house to relay the news to Mullane, this time knocking on the front door out of an unusual politeness and then, when he gets no answer, forcing the back door again. As soon as he's inside he senses something is wrong and he runs up the stairs to the second bedroom and he opens the door to find the bed neatly made and no sign of the runaway reader. Afterwards, anyone wanting out of the company would use Mullane's great excuse, *I needed to go somewhere quiet to read. Somewhere quiet to read.*)

With Mullane in my head I had asked the boy whether he liked reading. But he didn't seem to understand the question. So I asked if he was room service, because that's what I'd assumed he was even if he didn't look much like it. But he wasn't room service, he was some kind of courier, and he'd come to the wrong door, the wrong room, even the wrong hotel perhaps, I didn't know. I thought, here was the kind of person who might jump at the job, as long as enough cash was dangled in front of him. So I started to sound him out, playfully. I needed somebody who was honest and not too worldly-wise. He was not too worldly-wise. He had a kind of cockiness about him which I took to be a lack of confidence. He was sharp, asked most of the right questions and money was important to him, which I liked. He was worried about his job but once he relaxed and we got talking, he struck me as someone who was probably decent although mostly interested in the cash I was offering. Whether he clocked my falsehoods, I don't know. Sure I've had a stroke before. Sure I've attended taxidermy conferences and competitions although not for many years. None of what I said would have come out as totally crazy, and if it was, picking up Mr Tecolote would have been double the surprise. But as I say, he was more interested in the money.

As for the consequences, I had thought through a number of possibilities.

One, that the boy would walk out of the room and I'd never see him again. I'd lose some money and end up back at the beginning, having ventured but not gained.

Two, that the boy would be caught at the airport trying to take the owl out. I told him the owl was no problem but that he should keep the thing in his main luggage because the bureaucracy was very boring, which it is if I remember rightly. If they put Mr Tecolote under the X-ray, they'd certainly spot the wire and if they spotted the wire, they'd find the picture and it would all come back to me. And when they found it was a copy I'd say hell I've had the thing for years I didn't realise it was copied and I'd tell them I'd put it in the owl for safe keeping. Eventually they'd leave me alone.

Then there was the third, more remote possibility: that the boy would actually make it through. That he'd squirrel Mr Tecolote over, hand him back to me, take the rest of his money and disappear. This was what I needed. If they stopped me at the airport, I had the copy to present if anyone was interested. If they thought that was sinister, well what could I do? I was a man of seventy-five and of good character. They were only interested in me if what I had was real. What I didn't want was them to find what I really had. I didn't want to risk going back into Norway with the original in my stick. I didn't want that stick touched until I was back in my kitchen on the farm, making a frame and a border on the table, cutting the glass, placing it down on the frame on the linen, then the border, then the woodcut, then the backing and the wire: simple, a nail on the wall, ready.

Anna and I, up on the wall. First love. It was a straightforward desire that shouldn't have required all the subterfuge: the work's concealment inside a bird of prey, the commissioning of a copy, the creation of a medical condition, the work concealed within a stick. Then lying to a boy who walked into my hotel room and paying him money to pick up the bird then changing hotels to keep moving and then changing again because the walk across the park to visit the butterflies was too long for an old man with a stick. Because much as I loved the view from the balcony I couldn't stay all day in my hotel room. So I spent my days, stick in hand, looking at butterflies at the museum round the corner. In the afternoon I'd come back, take a swim then dine. Occasionally I wondered whether the boy would return or not. I wondered whether he might have got lost.

But no, Mr Tecolote, he didn't get lost. He found you there at the hut, and brought you back to me. He found you along with all the others, all the others I'd brought home over the years. I remember the first, a doe I shot the day after I moved in. I remember carving my name and the date on the beam above the front door before I went out. I didn't go out to shoot anything in particular.

I just walked out, early, round the lake, through the snow, into the mountains, gun in hand. I came across her as I sat and ate lunch. I was looking down at the lake, at the hut, through my binoculars and she walked into vision. She felt too far to shoot but I thought I'd have a go anyway so I lined up, pulled the trigger and down she went.

I thought I might be able to dress her back at the hut but it was too long a walk and she was bigger than she looked. As soon as I saw her proper, I knew she'd need dressing straight away. But even without her stomach and her guts and her organs she was still heavy work. I tied up her legs to a fallen branch and slung her over my shoulders. When I got back I washed her out a little bit more then I took her inside and hung her from the rafters. She would have frozen or gotten eaten outside. There were buckets in the bathroom for the blood.

My plan was to come back the following weekend and skin her then. She was young and didn't need hanging for so long. But that week the Kielland disaster happened and I never got back until late the following month. Every time I thought about the dead animal hanging from the beams with the winter finally turning to spring and the weather getting warmer and warmer, I thought of the men on the rig in their terror and of the sea that all oilmen fear but never think will take them.

When I eventually returned I imagined the worst. Sure the place stank but the animal was still hanging there in a reasonable state and the blood had not spilt over the bucket. I dumped the carcass back on the hills and mounted her head by way of apology. She was the first to go up on the wall: Mary Helen, named after my first wife. That summer, every weekend I went back and forth from Stavanger, arriving late on the Friday, unloading the car with new things I had bought: furniture, carpets, bedding, wardrobes, shelves, washing machines, kitchenware, tins of food, all these kinds of necessities. On the Saturday morning I'd work on the roof, unwrap the tarpaulin, mend the beams that needed mending, board up, lay the bark which I straightened by driving over in my car and then eventually the turf: *torvtak*. I went to a meadow and picked the flowers I wanted to grow on my roof: *rødkløver*, *røsslyng*, *bjørnbrodd* and in the afternoon I'd head out with my gun and shoot something. It didn't matter what. If it was edible I'd cook it in the evening and if it was beautiful or interesting, I might stuff it the next day. Then I'd drive back to Stavanger.

My second wife, Hilde, ended up on the wall after a wildly successful day in the hills. I shot nine ptarmigans, three grouse and a hare. I'd not stuffed a hare before. It definitely had the look of Hilde. By September the hut was pretty much done, the roof finished, the place furnished, warm, the walls full of animals. I had two elks, a few deer, a moose, a lynx, a wolf, a few foxes, the owls and a bunch of other birds. I was ready to retire as an oil man. I was fifty and had plenty of money. I could have quit if I'd wanted to. Then came the call from America and there was something about the Gulf of Mexico that appealed.

Mr Tecolote then was a final act. In the twenty years that passed I'd been back only a handful of times and each time I'd added another beast to the wall and wondered whether it would be the final one: '83, '88, '98, 2001... When I bought my place in New York and sold my house in Stavanger it was like I was leaving my country behind. I'd married an American. I'd become a citizen of the United States. But I couldn't let go of the hut and had distant visions of the two of us retiring to the hills.

Instead, being thirty years younger, she found someone else thirty years younger. So I replaced one dream with another and moved myself to Mexico. Did a man in his seventies need four properties at once? I liked New York and Mexico City and I could never have left the farm. It was time to let go.

The picture was safe in the bank. I'd been mindful of its worth and unhappy that it was up on the wall, free for anyone to take, anyone who could be bothered to break into a little wooden house in the middle of nowhere. So I had it put in a vault.

The elk I called Petersen.

As for the letter, I hated the letter and burnt it instead of the picture. The picture I would never have burnt. I saw it as proof of our love. A friend of mine brought it down from Trondheim and gave it me in Oslo where I had a holiday job. I almost threw the thing down the chute. It had been five, six weeks of no answers and I didn't want any more pain. For a while I thought about going to the States but I knew it would end in misery.

So the picture I kept. Eventually it went up on the wall in the house in Stavanger and then down again when I couldn't tell Mary Helen where it had come from and then after that it went back in the tube for a couple of decades and then finally it went up on the wall in the hut. Now I must hang it in the farm because that's where I'll end up dying and at my age it helps to be able to see the memories. And what finer memory than the bittersweet memory of first love.

Mr Tecolote, my co-conspirator. I am going to move you onto your back because the taxi driver's just noticed you and he's looking a little surprised. Well you do like to spring a surprise, Mr Tecolote. Getting you back was a surprise in itself. As I said, I thought the boy would have

194

got lost. Then there was the surprise when I opened you up. Immediately I assumed the police had found the picture. That useless Pia Haugen woman. But then I doubted myself. So I called up the boy and left a message on his cell phone. I asked him to call me, at the hotel. I said I was sure he knew what it was about and that I wanted to sort things out. I told him to come over as soon as he could.

That was yesterday. Today is Tuesday. When I woke this morning I was more relaxed. I thought if my friend the detective had the picture, she would quickly find out what it really was and bother me no more.

So I spent the morning in the swimming pool and after that I lunched and took my afternoon nap and when I woke I noticed the phone by my bedside was flashing. The recorded message said a young gentleman was at reception and that he had something for me. I called the concierge but he told me the boy had left several hours before. He also said there were two people from Norway – a man and a woman – who had been asking after me.

Then I looked for my stick and it was gone. So they had found what they were after, God knows how. While I was sleeping. Or the boy...

Now the taxi driver is pointing up ahead, saying something about something. And I am asking myself what a man of my age is doing, sitting in the back of a taxi, lost in a city I barely know? We are heading to an intersection somewhere east of the centre. I have told the driver he must wait then take me straight to the airport if I'm not to miss my flight. All the time as we snake our way through the traffic I am thinking of Anna and I am thinking of the picture and I am thinking what if life had continued in the way it was meant to have continued? Would I be sitting in the back of a taxi, lost in a city

I barely know, seventy-five years of age, with only a stuffed owl for companionship?

Why was I not content to sit upon a chair? Or look for butterflies in the forests? Why did I feel the need to try and bring the past back, the past of fifty years? Could I not have brought it back as easily in my head as I could by having it in my hands, having it on my wall, having it when I woke up in the morning, when I went to sleep at night? Was I so worried about losing love's memory that I needed it in my hands, in a picture whose power and meaning would never fade? Could I not be content in the knowledge that I had loved, that I had been that person in the picture, that I had lived that kiss? First love is first love. Let it be, perfect and imperfect. Don't ruin it with more dreams.

Anna, wisely, had thrown it all away.

But I had kept hold of it, let it sleep in my heart until my heart, decades on, had jolted it awake. I thought I had found an answer: something of beauty, something sacred, something precious. More than an object, something that encapsulated a moment, the most important of my life, that kiss in the barley at Vestby. I had never been happier, would never be happier again. Now, in pursuit of that moment for myself, I had lost it for good, undone by my own cleverness. I had lost it in this city, amongst the wide-eyed gangsters and the confidence tricksters and illegal workers and the filthy-rich bankers and those just wanting a little bit extra to help them get by in life. I didn't need the money. I could have bought the picture several times over. But other people did. Bus drivers and newspaper sellers and sandwich-board carriers – they all needed the money. Coffee dispensers and peanut vendors and charity workers – they all needed the money. Cycle couriers needed the money.

Hotel workers needed the money. Even the suited commuters with their fitted shirts and leather luggage could have done with the extra fifty. Amongst these people, I had lost it. Where was it? On the top of a London bus, propped up against a seat? Left on an underground train, heading west as I headed east? Was it in the hands of a man older than me, oblivious, hobbling down the street? Had it made its way back to a thrift store, an antiques shop, a place where they sold canes and umbrellas, its secret hidden within? How long might that secret hold? Was the picture in a bin, forgotten forever? In a pile of ashes, burnt? Being examined, underneath a magnifying glass, by a young man wearing white cotton gloves? I had no answers.

Five minutes, the taxi driver is saying, but we've stopped and he's craning his neck out of the window. Of course I will see the boy, I think, but what is the likelihood that he has anything, anything other than the crap that Alvarez created?

The police, the driver is saying. The police are there.

What do you mean, the police? I say.

The police, he replies. The police. We won't get through, no chance. Can I walk? I ask. I can hear their sirens. Is it far? I ask. Too far, he replies. Too far for a man of your age, Sir, he says.

So I tell him to find another route. And he sucks his lips and goes forward a bit and then left and then first right down a little narrow side street and over another little road onto a bigger road again and when he gets onto the bigger road to turn left I look right and of course that's when I see the boy, that's when I see the boy.

PUSHPENDRA SINGH POYNTZ

You're at the rendezvous in Clerkenwell (for fuck's sake the *rendezvous*, like it's some Cold War bollocks) and it's a quarter to eight which is to say you're early for once and you're trying to decide whether you're lucky or whether you're heading into gigantic amounts of trouble. On the face of it, you're lucky. Nothing's really happened. But you've got a funny feeling something's about to happen. Something like gigantic amounts of trouble.

You crashed a set of lights going down Copenhagen Street and they were on to you straight away. They were hiding round the corner, City of London coppers, and they put their lights on and flashed you and you thought Poyntz, a stop is okay. Even a stop and search because you don't have anything on you. But not a fine, please God, not a fine. One of the officers, the tall one, gets out of the car and pulls out his little pink book and you think, well it may not be a little bollocking but at least it's not a fine. Because sometimes they just give you a little bollocking and you say what a dick you've been and that you were in a rush to get to your mum's or your nan's or whatever and that you'll be more careful next time officer, much more careful. And they let you on your way. Sometimes they stop you, that's the little pink book, a stop or a stop-and-search and sometimes they give you an on-the-spot.

Anyway, to begin with, it worked how it normally works: they ask you your name and then they ask you where you live and then they take your mobile number and your date of birth and where you were born and they record your height and your build and your hair colour and what you're wearing. Just the usual fascist stuff. Then they ask if you've ever been in trouble with the law and you're not exactly going to say yes, you're not going to mention the night you spent in the cells when you were fifteen for laughing at a police horse or the business of the book stealing business, so naturally you say no. Then they ask you for your ID and you're careful not to hand over your fake ID, the Grover Watrous, you hand over your genuine ID, the Pushpendra Singh Poyntz. They hand your life story over to their mate, the one who's behind the wheel, and he taps your life story into the Police National Computer and normally after that they say don't be idiot and they let you cycle off, and you're thankful the horse stuff's gone off the record and that the book stuff never got to court.

But this time after he's checked your details the dude behind the wheel, the small one, gets out of the car and comes over. He asks you to step inside the car for a moment and you say what about my bicycle because you aren't going to leave a Bianchi Mega Pro leant against a curb, just like that. He says don't worry about the bicycle for the moment, just get in the car like I said, and you think how dumb they're being since all you've done is crash a light and suddenly you're getting the third fucking degree. But you are hardly in a position to disobey an officer of the law.

So you get in the car and the two of them stand outside and have a little natter and you think about Sam and wonder how near he is with the rendezvous being just round the corner. He'll be there soon enough, the dick, handing the picture over to the old man as you wait for a ticket in the back of a squad car. You realise you should have called the hotel, what was it, the Mandarin Oriental? I'm trying to get through to a Mr Sorensen. I beg your pardon, Sir? Mr Sorensen. He's a guest of yours. Certainly sir, I'll put you through. My name's Poyntz, you'd say. I'm a friend of Sam's. When you see him, please tell him to go back home. Tell him to forget it. Tell him you're happy with what you've got. Tell him the whole thing was a big joke. Tell him you're heading back to Mexico City and that you don't have time to talk. Whatever you do, don't take what he's about to give you.

You call Sam again and leave a fourth message on his voicemail. You tell him you're in the back of a police car, that you've been caught crashing a light. You tell him not to give the picture to Sorensen. You tell him how he double-crossed us and that it was our turn to double-cross him. You tell him to cast his principles aside. You tell him to call right away. Then you text him, a seventh time

Don't do anything until I get there

because he needs to be persuaded not to hand over the fucking picture and as you send the text, the officers get back into the car. They ask you once more if you've ever been in trouble with the law. Once more you say you haven't. Then they ask you where you've been in the last few days. London, you reply. They ask you whether you're sure you've been in London. One hundred percent sure, you reply. You've not been abroad? they ask.

Abroad. Fuck. Yes. I've been abroad.

Well I have recently come back from abroad Sir, you reply. They say where and you say Scandinavia. Which part of Scandinavia? they ask.

Sweden, you say.

So they ask you what you've been doing there and you tell them you've been on holiday. Nice holiday? they say. Very nice, you reply. Go on your own? they say. On my own, you reply. You tell them you have some relatives in Sweden. Of course, they say. Then they ask whether the name Samuel Black means anything to you and you think fucking hell Sam what massive heap of shit have you landed yourself in.

Quickly you realise you are also in the same massive heap of shit and while you are realising this up pops a text from the very same Samuel Black and you think what would Abdoujaparov do in a situation like this and so you try to style it out and you say Samuel Black? I've never heard that name in the whole of my life.

(The Abdoujaparov rule has tended to serve you well although it is the enemy of common sense. In fact, it's more than the enemy of common sense: it's the suicide bomber of rational thought. It's what made you crash the lights. It's what made you challenge Salowitz at backgammon. It's what made you tell your family you were studying to be a lawyer. It's what made you purchase Leibniz, your budgerigar. Leibniz senior may have been a god of logic but what was the logic behind buying a budgerigar? You needed a girlfriend, not a budgerigar. It was impulsiveness in its purest form. Okay, the price you were told by the man was a good one. But then you got home and realised you'd have to do a whole load of things like feed it and water it and clean out its cage and talk to it and that if you forgot to do these things, the bird became very irritable, very tetchy indeed.

But the whole thing about the Abdoujaparov rule is that, more often than not, it pays to follow it. The police would eventually let you go. You became a master at backgammon. You continued to lead a free life because a lawyer is not a free man, a lawyer is a slave to the law. And you made a new friend and called him Leibniz and girls when they came round to your place thought it was cute that you kept a bird and looked after him and fed him and watered him and cleaned out his cage and talked to him *and* gave him Maltesers to eat which made him jump up and down on his little ledge, so happy they made him.)

Of course, there are times when your innate Abdoujaparovism – for want of a better word – creates a very negative situation. You probably shouldn't have climbed Mr and Mrs Nahal's silver birch and jumped fifteen feet down, six feet across, into their swimming pool because when you hit the lip with your heel you broke your ankle in three places and nearly drowned but fuck it you were only thirteen and Hardeep Nahal was the richest boy in school and he bet you ten pounds if you did it and you did it and you won the bet. You probably shouldn't have taken the book stealing business to its logical conclusion (being caught) and you probably shouldn't have tried fire-eating or fought the Brazilian cage fighter or spent all that money on that rare Donald Byrd album when it turned out to be an Earth, Wind & Fire album with a fake label, and not even a good Earth, Wind & Fire album. Maybe it's something to do with an erroneous frontal lobe. But if you don't climb the fucking tree you'll never know how good the view is and if the view's no good then maybe next time you won't bother climbing the tree again. Or as someone else said in a different kind of way, the Bianchi may be safe hanging up in the hall, but that's not what the Bianchi's for.

Anyway, the tall copper gets out of the car again and makes another call and the other one asks what you do for a job and you say you work for a courier company delivering stuff around London on your bicycle and he says what kind of stuff like all you do is shift Class As and you say envelopes and documents and other stuff and that you've delivered on many occasions to Scotland Yard and other stations like Stoke Newington and Ladbroke Grove and Paddington Green but he isn't impressed. So he asks where you're off to and you tell him you're off to see a friend and he says who and you say a friend, just a friend, because it isn't really relevant to the alleged offence, is it, who you are going to see? But he hassles you, doesn't this friend have a name, he says, or is he just *a friend*? And so you string him along, sure he has a name, you say, you just want to keep him to yourself. And eventually he presses you so hard you give up and tell him the first name that comes into your head and that name could have been any old name but it turns out to be Grover Watrous, your alter ego.

How is that spelt he asks and you tell him and he punches G-R-O-V-E-R-W-A-T-R-O-U-S into the Police National Computer and frowns and you're imagining Grover there amongst the crims in the Police National Computer like some character in a Hieronymous Bosch painting, the God-fearing, heavy-smoking, piano-playing clubfoot in the corner of the canvas. Of course he isn't there, dipshit.

Then you ask him what is happening and he says they are just making a couple of checks and you ask if you are going to get a fine and he says yes almost certainly you will be getting a fine and now you are thinking if it's just a fine then probably that's okay.

Then three things happen.

First, the Armenian drives past, at speed, heading south, down towards Pentonville Road. You know it's the Armenian because you recognise his car and because he usually drives pretty quick. This makes you think.

Second, the tall copper who's gone off to make whatever call he's making gets back into the car. And as he turns to speak to you, literally as he is opening his mouth, making his first word, a message comes through on the radio telling them to attend a road traffic collision at the corner of Gray's Inn and Theobalds Road. And as they're listening to the call-out, it's about five minutes away, you see a kid, no more than eleven or twelve years old, calmly making off with the Bianchi. This is the third thing that happens. The little motherfucker isn't even big enough to ride it so he kind of pushes it down the hill in a quick scampy walk. You start yelling at the cops telling them there's a kid nicking your bike and they shout at you to shut up because they are trying to figure out where they are meant to be going. You could have told them straight up: back up to Amwell Street then Rosebery Avenue. You could have stayed in the car and been their fucking satnav but the kid is heading into the estate and you are about to say goodbye to your beloved bicycle. Officer, officer, you are shouting, look, the kid with my bike. But the tall one just looks round at you and says we'll catch up with you later and then he unlocks the door and says piss off. So you get out and run cleats on stone towards the estate. As soon as the kid hears the siren, he drops the bike and starts running. You would dearly love to collar him, give his neck a good squeeze, make some imprints on his arse. But you are thinking what the fuck the Bianchi is back in your hands and you have things to do, you need to get to the rendezvous. So you clip back in and head towards the rendezvous. But first you open up the text Sam has just sent. It says: *Everything is okay. Listen to Charles.*

Fucker, you think, what does that mean? Charles Charles Charles Charles Charles.

Charles, you think, could be many things.

Charles Charles Charles Charles Charles. Charles who? Who is Charles? You don't know anyone called Charles. Charlie? You don't know anyone called Charlie. You don't know anyone called Carlos, you don't know anyone called Carl, you don't know anyone called Carlo, or Carlito, or Carolo or C. You knew a Chad a while back. *Listen* to Charles? Which Charles? Ray Charles? Prince Charles? Charles Ives? Charles fucking Aznavour? Take It Easy My Brother Charles? Carlos Santana? Charles Mingus? Mingus? Mingus! Charles Mingus. Mingus surely. None of the others are close to being amongst your influencers. But which album? You can't just say listen to Mingus. Which track? Which bit of which track? Which fucking note in that multimillion note puzzle that is Charles Mingus?

What does it all mean, the fucker? What does the great cigar chomper have to do with anything?

As you wait for Sam at the rendezvous you are thinking in no particular order of *The Black Saint and the Sinner Lady* and of *Pithecanthropus Erectus* and obviously of *Mingus Ah Um* and of *Blues & Roots* and of *Tijuana Moods* (that's Charlie) and of course you are thinking of *Mingus, Mingus, Mingus, Mingus, Mingus*. You think of 'Freedom' and then you sing it in your head and after that you hum a bit of 'Goodbye Pork Pie Hat' and then the riff to 'Boogie Stop Shuffle' and as you hum this you think of Mingus on the brink of eviction in his ramshackle apartment in Reichman's film brandishing his sniper rifle as his little girl plays around beneath him, and drinking wine, and tuning his bass, and nailing the windows down. That film you must have watched a million times, those isms, those Mingusisms swirl around your head like his notes, his theory about Kennedy's assassination and his theory about women and his theory about white domination, as he fires his gun and makes a hole in the roof. It made Mingus cry and it always makes you sad when they actually come and evict him, the NYPD and the trilby-wearing enforcer from the Sanitation Department a no-jazz-lover who snarls at the newsmen with all of Mingus's things out on the street, furniture and mattresses and sheets of music on the floor, and his bass ready for transportation to 134 Madison Street. He walks to the squad car after being arrested for the possession of hypodermic needles and pills and the newsman asks him about the heroin and Mingus replies, that's not my style, so the newsman asks what is and Mingus replies, *street life.*

Street life. An ambulance rushes past you. Cars stop to let it pass then they move on, cautiously. The pattern of traffic resumes. North to south, south to north, then stop. West to east, east to west, then stop. North to south, south to north, etc. You look for the man from the west, you look for Sam from the east. The siren fades and everything is suddenly quiet. In the vacuum is your rendezvous, like a small bomb waiting to detonate or go *tick tick tick click* and then life goes on.

206

MASHTOTS
HAMBARTZUMIAN

Today I make exception. I drive quickly and not so careful. My car today is not clean. But most of the time I drive
fucking careful and most of the time my car is fucking
clean and most of the time you can have a look motherfucker and what do you see? Nothing motherfucker!
Last time the piggies stop me like last month or whatever
they look everywhere first they open up bonnet check
all them little spaces even fucking windscreen wiper
water then they look underneath carpet front and passenger side and then they take up back chair careful I say
them chair is leather and then they all over the fucking
boot carpet up wheel out looking everywhere even looking to see if something hidden in handle of fucking fire
extinguisher then finally they look underneath and one
of them piggies gets down on his back with a torch and
checks out fucking Porsche Cayenne underbody I fucking laugh my fucking head off Porsche Cayenne is up on
curb and like two tons squish! Oh dear one dead fucking
policeman but Porsche Cayenne is good boy, Porsche
Cayenne stay still and piggy comes out bit oily. I joke

with them you want to do clean and service while you here? What you looking for boys? You lost something? But they don't say nothing they just put their hands underneath their bulletproof and say nothing. Time before they much quicker but I have couple little things underneath spare wheel, two blades no guns. Just in case. They open up boot and I fucking worried they gonna find them but they don't fucking look. They just pull up carpet and give it nice feel and that's it. Give me piece of paper then, fucking stop search, then fuck off. Of course motherfuckers always start with body check first. How many times. Pat pat pat on my tracksuit bottoms. Thigh, crotch, careful, shoe. Looking inside my fucking Reebok. Smelly Reebok. Underneath arm. Feel my fucking muscles motherfucker. You jealous? You see I'm clean. Porsche Cayenne is clean! After a while they gonna stop stopping me because it boring for them every time Porsche Cayenne is clean, every time I am clean. Saint Mashtots! So instead if I want something moved I get Grigor to go in Astra or I go in Astra myself. Okay Astra not five hundred brake horsepower six fucking cylinder engine. Astra seat don't remember shape of Mashtots's bum or warm Mashtots's bum on cold winter morning. Astra stereo two speaker not fourteen speaker. Astra nought-to-sixty fifteen seconds, Cayenne nought-to-sixty is four. But Astra never get stopped by piggies. Astra like horse and cart. Piggies won't touch a horse and cart. In horse and cart you can keep anything. Underneath fascia on driver's side. Blades, shooter, whatever. Just in case. But Grigor does most of that thing and he hate the fucking Astra! Boss he says let me drive the Merc. Merc too fucking obvious I tell him. Astra too slow he says. Fine I say. Next time we buy a fucking Vectra. But Grigor smart guy. Does what Mashtots tell him. Big man, good thief. Meet him at gymnasium. Russian but so what. I can do business with any motherfucker. I can even do business with motherfucking Turk. Prefer not to though. At beginning Grigor help me shift goods after job. Start by giving him TV, DVD player, Blu-ray, this kind of thing. Little gift from Mashtots, gift of friendship. Then I give him different TV, different DVD, bad one, not so good and he says he don't want it. Sell it, I say, then give me half. He get seven hundred for Panasonic fifty-inch or whatever so I think not bad. Then I start sending him more stuff, he sell it nice and quick. Soon I let him come with me one night and we take two, three thousand in three jobs and all gone next day. Easy money motherfucker. Grigor like dog with bone but not too quick I tell him. No need to make big noise. Every night he want to go out but I say if we go every night we get caught. Once, twice a week is enough. Move around the city I tell him. So we move around the city. We start off low division, Leyton, Camberwell, Peckham. Then we move up to Championship, Clapham, Clerkenwell, Islington, Ealing. Soon we are in fucking Premier League, Hampstead, Highgate, Notting fucking Hill. But Premier League needs good preparation. So Grigor goes week before, day then night, finds out when motherfuckers on holiday, when motherfuckers go to country at weekend, when motherfuckers at work in day who in the house during day what protection they have in doors in windows alarms all that shit, where is nearest piggy station. He pick two or three address then he give me list and I go see myself. I pick one and we go do it. But I tell you these jobs difficult, dangerous. Getting into Premier League house is not easy. You cannot use fucking Mickey Mouse telescopic rod through letterbox. You cannot use Tesco reward card on fucking Banham lock. But when

you get in, prize is great. In low league you take everything you can but mostly it is junk. In Championship
you decide what is good, what is not good. TV is good,
computer is good, stereo is not good. In Premier League
everything is good. Fucking toilet roll is good. So in
Premier League you need to know what is very best not
just what is very good. Maybe you take just one or two
things of big value. You leave white goods, electronic to
others. You go for jewellery, gold, pictures, Persian rug,
marble heads. Sometime we make mistake. One time we
get home and tiara is high street rubbish. Grigor's mistake. I take set of silver dinner plate worth five thousand.
Soon we become interested in antique. Not expert, interested. For me art and silver mostly. I go to living room
and Grigor go to bedroom to find jewel and watches.
Normally we have three-minute rule but that depend on
distance to piggy station. If alarm is silent, longer. The
only other rule, next day everything must be gone. I
have people for gold, people for silver, people for art,
people for furniture, people for jewellery, people for
watches, people for books, people for clocks, we have
people for fucking everything. Whatever we sell to these
people is sold again in hours, then again and again until
it so far away it will never be trace. Then sometimes one
of these people asks can we keep eye out for this fucking
thing or that fucking thing and sometimes we are told
look in this place and you get lucky. There is big price
on stealing to order. We fix a big price to get item and
then we have a look and if it possible and not set-up then
we do job. But job like this can take many months prepare. One time we asked to get picture from country
house some place so me and Grigor go to check place
out. Picture is on wall in study some famous cartoon or
whatever and house open to public so we walk in have

a look walk out. When we are driving back in Merc Grigor is talking about plan and I pull out cartoon it is only small cartoon from my tracksuit bottom. Most easy job in world. Eight thousand pound. There are many advantage to being fat man for instance I hid diamond necklace in crack of my big arse when police stop Grigor and me one night after coming back from job. Normal we have many paint tin in back of Astra and most of them are full of gloss, white undercoat all this kind of paint and we have many other things you need for decorate rollers, extension, brushes, white spirit all this kind of thing. Normal we hide jewel and thing in some tins and bang shut but we left in big rush. When piggy start flashing I put everything in passenger foam seat but they bloody quick and I have these diamonds in my hand when they walking towards me. So I stuff them down pants down crack and make my buttock nice and hard. Then piggy ask me to get out I have to shuffle piggy says spread my fucking legs so I make gamble and spread them big yet still this fucking diamond is sitting nice and tight in my arse's crack although all time I am expecting it to drop to floor with a clink clink clink and we are caught. My god how much we laugh Grigor and me. Another time we do a job on a book for one of the book people and it's like first ever print of whatever in a display cabinet in big house somewhere north London. These job always difficult at night finding something small in big house when all you have is torch. So we decide to risk job in day and I go back garden and Grigor knocks on door to see if anyone in and he keep knocking and knocking and then he ring me and I get in through back French window with glass cutter forty-five seconds and I let Grigor in and double lock. But the motherfucker is like a book maniac there are fucking books everywhere and we are upstairs and downstairs looking for fucking book and nowhere. At last we go basement and there it is I don't remember its fucking name and I am just about to break the glass when there's the sound of front door opening. A motherfucker! We freeze and Grigor makes his body big like he wants to fight. No, I whisper. Go up, quietly, and leave through front door, but slam front door. Grigor is smart guy. Does what he is told. Good thief, big man. Hears the motherfucker go upstairs, tip-toes to front door, opens it, slams it and as soon as he slams it, I break glass take book. Man run downstairs, open door goes into street and out I go through back door. Simple. I put book in pants, front pants, baggy tracksuit, climb over garden wall into street. I hide bag under van and go to find Astra. On way to find Astra I bump into the motherfucker looking for Grigor. His book is on top of my cock. You seen a man running, he asks, fat man, looks foreign. I shrug though the mother-fucker's description of Grigor very correct and off he goes. Well the book, I still don't remember name, was fucking hot so I told the book person he needed to shift it quick quick quick. At the book person I met Indian boy. He had five boxes he was wanting to sell. Book person was not interested but I was interested in Indian boy and we chatted a little just about boring stuff not business and I gave him my number because I wanted to know what his other lines were what motherfucking business he was up to and I said call if you need any-thing, I can sort things out, but really I didn't want him getting in my way. Later I asked book person what he was doing but he said he didn't know it was the first time he'd met him and he was trying to flog stolen books that weren't worth handling. Anyway it turned out he wasn't up to nothing but he worked as a courier and occasionally I needed someone to take small items to my people during night time. First couple times I gave him empty parcels to see I could trust him to see he was very reliable and then I'd let him take little things and give him some notes or whatever. Sometimes he asked me for favours sometimes I help. Mostly it was telephone numbers of girls, this girl who worked in this hairdresser, this other girl who he saw on a bus he thought her name was something or her surname was this but he wasn't too sure. One time he wanted some false X-rays and I got Grigor to sort them but most of the time I ignored his calls because they were just a bit motherfucking crazy at times and I was happy to use him when I needed to but he was not going to fucking use me. Like one time he called up and said he wanted me to tell people if he died that he had died because I knew a lot of people which is true I do I know a lot of fucking people but I was Mashtots Hambartzumian I was not a fucking passer of messages that was his job and so I said yes yes I will do that of course and then I gave him a job but didn't pay him because I had helped him out but I would never agree to do that sort of motherfucking thing for anyone not even my dead mother may you rest in peace. That's fucking madness. Anyway I had not heard from him for very long time, months and months until yesterday evening when I get this text message from him and he says he needs to come and see me that he has this picture by artist and can I help him move it on through one of my people. I have never once told him what business I do but he is not a stupid boy and he probably has idea. I have never heard of the motherfucking artist but I say of course and tell him he must bring it to me now because in this matter you have to move quickly. But when he comes I am out I am taking my dog Housep for a walk and I forget about it till follow morning and I call up art person to check it out and art person go fucking mental. You sure it stolen, they ask. I don't know, I say. Art person says there was a big theft very big theft last year very big theft in motherfucking Sweden or whatever and maybe it is one of them stolen pictures. You need to get hold of it quick, he says, and you need to bring it here. So I call up the Indian boy but there's no reply and I call him up again and still there's no fucking reply and never before has he not returned my fucking calls so I find out where the Indian boy lives and then I call up Grigor and tell him we've got a job. But Grigor's motherfucking girlfriend has just had a baby. Congratulations Grigor, I say, we've got a job. Not today, he says. Tomorrow. This is business, I tell him. Tomorrow morning, he says and I think perhaps tomorrow morning because the motherfucker Indian boy may still call me back. But the motherfucking Indian boy does not call me back and tomorrow morning is not okay because when we go this morning some fucker has beaten us to it some fucker has beaten me to it and when we realise he's beaten us we run outside and there he is fucking taking picture of Cayenne and making motherfucking lines on Cayenne bodywork like he wants to get himself fucking killed just like that. But it's okay because Mashtots might not have caught up with him then but Mashtots knows who that mother-fucker is and Mashtots is coming to say hello to him motherfucker, coming to say hello to him right now.

PART THREE

SAM BLACK

24

PEPE'S PIZZAS

On our way back from Heathrow Airport we lost the owl.

It was Poyntz's fault, although he blamed me and it's true I was responsible for attaching the bird to his saddle bag. But he should have noticed when it fell to the ground.

It was a miracle that the owl had not been damaged during the flight. We decided to stick him in the United States Postal Service bag – the bike bag – along with the Pinarello. It meant securing him to the frame but he was bulky and annoying and people started staring at us, reasonably I suppose. In the end Poyntz found one of those self-service cling film wrapping machines and we shrink-wrapped the bird. We must have shrunk him by about 25 per cent but he fitted quite snugly, gaffer-taped between the tubes. On the other side, somewhere on the Inner Ring, we put our bikes back together and the owl looked pretty happy, a bit airless but pristine.

I took the USPS bag on my back and the owl I secured with bungee netting onto Poyntz's saddle bag. I didn't like the fact he was responsible for it but I had no room and he had refused the bike bag. We set off towards

Hounslow, me in front. It was nine o'clock at night. Then somewhere in Brentford Poyntz drew up at the lights and I looked across and asked him where the fuck the owl was.

What owl? he said.

We rode back the way we came, all the way, four, five miles, back to the airport and found the spot where we'd reassembled our bikes and then retraced our journey back into the city. When we weren't scouring the roads for an owl wrapped in plastic we argued. I told Poyntz he was a fuckwit of the highest order for not realising the bird had slipped the net.

You should have ridden behind me, he said.

You should have fucking felt him fall off, I replied.

You should have fucking put him on properly.

I did fucking put him on properly.

How come he fucking fell off then?

How come you didn't fucking feel him fall off?

And so on. Poyntz said he didn't give a shit about the owl. He said if it got totalled by a ten-tonner it wasn't going to get any uglier than it already was and either way he wasn't going to cry about it. He said picking up the owl had been the stupidest job he'd ever done, even more stupid than some of the dockets Fat Barry had given him. He said he didn't even give a shit about the rest of the money and that all he wanted was to go home and have a very long sleep and then get up and go to work and continue his search for the Kashmiri Beauty and failing that drop in on the girl who cut hair at the salon at the bottom of Ridley Road.

You mean Gossip? I said.

Yeah. Gossip.

Then he said he wished me well in my endeavours with Sorensen – he actually used that phrase, the arsehole – but that his association with the whole project had formally ended when we touched down on British soil and that I was on my own. He said I should tell Sorensen that the bird was confiscated by customs in Oslo because it was illegal or whatever to export dead wildlife – which it probably was – and that I should demand the money anyway because there were all sorts of official complications at the airport and that I was very lucky not to have been arrested or even better, I *had been* arrested and detained by customs and subjected to some very brutal cross-examination by the specialist wildlife division of the Norwegian police. And if I really wanted the money badly, Poyntz suggested, I should tell Sorensen that whilst being detained my human rights were cruelly violated, the details of which I would prefer not to go into, being of a sexual nature. If that doesn't get you the rest of the money, said Poyntz, then I don't know what will.

I was only half-listening to this crap and trying to concentrate on finding the bird. But the longer we rode back into London, the more futile the search became and the more I imagined the owl being flattened, the owl being dragged, the owl being shred to pieces, the owl being kidnapped, the owl being kicked by drunkards, the owl being undressed, mounted and stuck on someone's wall, the owl turning up in a provincial museum: Snowy Owl, *Bubo scandiacus*, origin unknown.

About twenty metres short of where we'd first stopped at the lights, at a small parade of shops with the M4 still thundering overhead, Poyntz rode onto the pavement and locked his bike. It's no good, he said. The owl is lost. There's no logic in looking further. Plus, I need to eat.

He walked into Pepe's Pizzas. I felt too sick to eat and went round the corner to a petrol station to buy tobacco.

I looked at the newspapers. They were still running stories about a hurricane in the United States. I picked up a copy of *The Times* and read it until the guy behind the counter asked me if I was going to buy it or not. I put it back, bought twenty-five grammes of Golden Virginia and returned to the bikes.

While I was smoking I could see Poyntz arguing with someone in the takeaway. I couldn't hear what it was about because of the roar of the motorway. I looked at the concrete underside of the flyover with its straight ridges and weather stains. I watched cars whizz by. I read the graffiti and then I read it again. I thought about Sorensen and what his reaction would be. I decided I didn't really care.

But when Poyntz walked out of the shop he had two massive pizzas under his right arm and under his left, the owl, missing its cellophane and looking, well, strange. He explained he'd had to buy two speciality XXLs, which were eighteen inches in diameter, in exchange for the bird. It had been behind the counter on top of a fridge when he walked in. Fifty quid had been the starting point for negotiations, Poyntz being unable to prove to Pepe's satisfaction that the owl was rightfully his. Pepe was a businessman and business was business. Eventually Poyntz knocked him down to thirty quid's worth of pizza: a Master Blaster for me (pepperoni, onions, hot chillies and green peppers) and for him a Bam Bam (green peppers, onions, BBQ chicken and jalapeños). I had to get the biggest, Poyntz explained, or Pepe wouldn't hand it over. That was the deal.

The owl, it transpired, had almost knocked one of Pepe's delivery men off his Honda C90. He'd swerved to avoid it, clipped it, mounted a curb and hit a wall. He put the owl in his moped box and took it back to Pepe to prove that the crack on the front mudguard wasn't his fault. Pepe gave him a bollocking for putting a dead animal in a box that was used for the delivery of hot food before giving him his next order and sending him on his way. Pepe then unwrapped the owl, figured he'd be able to sell it, placed it in an empty tub of cooking oil and stuck it on top of the drinks fridge. Poyntz recognised Mr Tecolote by his ears poking out of the top.

The owl's head was, by all accounts, a little mashed up. I don't know whether the moped alone had caused the trauma or whether something heavier had turned its perfect disc into a face lop-sided and loose on the left, fat and bulbous on the right. And not just bulbous, eyeless too. The left eye was still hanging in there, but the right was gone for good, leaving behind a black gluey socket. Maybe a good taxidermist would be able to perform some reconstructive work and restore twenty-twenty vision. In the meantime, the bird had taken on an even more sinister appearance. I feared for Sorensen's chances at the taxidermy competition.

We ate our pizzas, my appetite restored but not to the level that I could finish all twelve slices. Poyntz polished off the rest of mine, pronounced himself ill, and lit a cigarette. The owl I put inside my saddle bag instead of my clothes which I wrapped into a shirt and bungee-ed onto the outside.

By the way, Poyntz said as we got onto our bikes to go home, you know when I told you I didn't care about the money? Well obviously I was joking. I care a lot about the money. A lot. I'm back on the project. I'm with you. All the way. For starters, I've just spent a fucking fortune on pizza.

Good, I said, I'm glad. Now shall we go?

23

ABDOUJAPAROV

Riding back at night through London, with the heat still coming off the roads although it was past ten o'clock, I thought about Djamolidine Abdoujaparov and I thought about Yelena Zykov and I thought about Mr Bembo and I thought about Sorensen and finally I thought about myself and I wondered what I should do with my life.

The deal with Abdoujaparov, according to Poyntz, was that he started doping because he was fed up with riding bicycles and because he wanted to kick-start his retirement plans, which mostly involved breeding pigeons. He was at the end of his career and probably thought fuck it, what have I got to lose. Or maybe like many other riders the doping was just another part of the sport, not pretty but well-established. He thought there was safety in numbers but got unlucky. He was the only rider to be expelled that year, which was 1997, the year before the Festina affair which properly blew the lid on everything. It's not like it wasn't going on.

Still, I like the theory that he wanted to go out with a bang, one way or another. Look at him on the Champs-Élysées six years earlier. He'd already won the green jersey but went all in for the most beautiful victory of his short career. He's riding like a fucking maniac, elbows out like razor blades but still boxed in by six or seven other riders until he takes the inside, riding as close as possible to the crowd. Then, about a hundred yards from the finish – just as he's nosing in front, just as he's getting ready to take it, just as he's heading back towards the centre of the road – he suddenly looks down at his wheels and in a split second he's lost his line and crashed into a giant inflatable Coca-Cola can and hit the steel barriers at whatever it is, thirty-five, forty miles an hour and the race is lost. *La chute d'Abdoujaparov.* It's inexplicable, the way he changes course so quickly, as if his brain has sent an obviously false command and in the heat and the noise he's blindly obeyed it. It's probably one of the best crashes ever but it's also one of the strangest. Abdoujaparov veers off the road in such an extreme and single-minded way, it's like an act of self-destruction. There he is, motionless on the tarmac, dead or as good as dead after two and a half thousand miles of cycling. The rules dictate that to finish a stage in the Tour de France you must cross the line. So half an hour after everyone else, Abdoujaparov is put back on his bicycle and wheeled over the line by his team. He's broken his collar bone but what the fuck, he's got the green jersey.

The deal with Yelena Zykov was slightly different. She knew the risks better than any of us and she knew the consequences of those risks. She knew that if you ride dangerously there's a good chance you're going to get knocked off, and once you've been knocked off, you're either lucky or you're not. But she also knew that however safely or dangerously you ride, there's a chance you'll get knocked off anyway and that if you ride confidently, if you control the road, if you let the road know who you are and what you're doing, if you assert yourself, then you lessen that chance. So there's a thin line between riding confidently and riding danger-ously and most couriers tread that line.

Then there's the argument about helmets, the argument being that if you don't wear a helmet, car drivers will keep their distance because their perception is that you're not being safe and if you're not being safe you're dangerous and if you're dangerous you should be given a wide berth. So the argument goes that riding without a helmet means you're safer on the road. Yelena Zykov was one of a number of couriers who bought into this argument, which apparently has a bona fide academic study behind it. Well that's okay then. I'm not saying a helmet made of polystyrene would have saved Yelena's life, but it might have done.

There's cause and effect and there's random event. Abdoujaparov's crash on the Champs-Élysées was cause and effect: he lost control and as a result he rode into an inflatable Coke can. Yelena's death was part cause and effect, part random event: she rode fast and unprotected but even if she'd worn a helmet and ridden at seven miles an hour, she might still have been struck by that dumper truck and catapulted into that Victorian brick wall.

The deal with Mr Bembo was very different. He was a random event of the purest kind, like the owl turning up in Pepe's Pizzas. I had travelled to Norway to escape his prognostications and now returned to London with a choice: heed his words and rely upon the gris-gris to protect me from danger. Or ignore them entirely, brave it out, move on. For once, my indecision was short-lived: I realised, with relief and a little shame, that my business with Mr Bembo was finished, that his spell on me, what-ever it was, had either expired or only ever existed in my imaginings. I rode, like Yelena Zykov, with supreme confidence. The voodoo bag, still under my seatpost, I decided to throw away at the first opportunity.

If Mr Bembo had been an arbitrary event that had passed, then, I saw the deal with Sorensen as pure cause and effect. First he had provided the opportunity for me to escape what I thought was my fate. Now he was giving me the chance to change my future. At the same time I was telling myself I could ride without fear, I was also realising how much I wanted to get off my bike and do something different. It was like the accident with the Porsche Cayenne, the visit to Mr Bembo, the trip to Norway and back, all pointed to a single drop, a final delivery, the biggest, the best, the last. I hoped The Bounty would give me money for two weeks or a month, enough time to put down my bicycle for a bit. It wasn't going to set me up for life but it might just draw me a line in the sand. After the owl, I told myself, that was it. I'd take the cash, give Poyntz his share, tell Fat Barry I was done, and move on to the next thing, whatever that was.

22

A Discussion About the Owl

We arrived at Poyntz's flat at midnight and the topics du jour at midnight were the usual topics du jour at midnight in Poyntz's flat: what records to play, where was the dope, where was the cherry brandy.

What records to play: it was always jazz with Poyntz. It all sounds the fucking same I'd tell him. No it doesn't you moron, he'd say, and he'd take out something by Joe Henderson and play it alongside Jelly Roll Morton, as if to make the point.

Where the dope was hidden: in the usual place, an empty Jan Garbarek cassette box, a pirate copy of *Legend of Seven Dreams* although the tracks as Poyntz liked to emphasise were only partially from *Legend of Seven Dreams* some were from *It's Ok to Listen to the Gray Voice* and some were from other albums. The picture on the front showed Garbarek looking young and monkish, smiling at the camera, showing his teeth. In the background was a long road heading into a cold landscape: probably Norway. When Poyntz lost the actual tape, *Legend of Seven Dreams* became a repository for weed.

But sometimes *Seven Dreams*, as it was often abbreviated to, got lost itself. It took a quarter of an hour for Poyntz to find.

Where was the cherry brandy: under Poyntz's bed, again after some looking. I told him he must have gone to bed with the bottle after a lonely night and he said, correct, 100 per cent.

We put the owl amongst Poyntz's vinyl, between Hank Mobley and Lee Morgan. Despite this it still looked unhappy. It was Sunday going into Monday.

What happens now? Poyntz said.

What do you mean? I replied.

What happens to the owl? You're gonna take him to Sorensen tomorrow?

Yep.

What are you going to say about the facelift?

I don't know. I'll tell him I dropped him and ran him over by mistake.

Is he the kind of jerk who'd dock our bounty?

Our bounty?

Yeah. *Our* bounty. Will he dock *our* bounty because we've messed up his owl's face?

I don't know. Maybe. Maybe not. Maybe we just won't get The Bonus. He said there was more money when I returned with the owl but he didn't say exactly how much.

Hold on. I thought you told me it was the same again?

It will be the same again. Plus a bit more, he said, if he was happy.

Well there goes the bit more. I wouldn't be happy if I was brought an owl that looks like it's been in a fistfight. It's missing an eye for fuck's sake!

He might just be happy to see him. The owl's an old friend – he said it himself.

227

Well his old friend's been mugged. Look at that motherfucker. Have you ever seen a more sinister looking animal? It's like asking someone to pick up your Pinarello and they come back with a Genesis. The fucking owl's meant to be up for some taxidermy competition! Not that I believe it.

You don't?

Of course I don't. There's something inside that owl and you know it.

Like what?

I don't know. Money. Diamonds. Drugs. You tell me.

You think I know and I'm not telling you?

Someone's not telling and it's either him or you.

There is nothing inside that owl Poyntz.

How do you know? Have you given it a shake? Have you heard the sweets rattle inside? Have you determined the average weight of a stuffed owl and weighed our friend to compare? Have you given him a prod or a feel? Have you ever touched up that owl? Does he look like he's holding something in? He looks like he's holding something in to me.

Seriously, I said. You're a joke. What does it matter either way? We don't question what's in all the other crap we deliver day in day out.

This is not a normal job, said Poyntz. We've gone to another country to pick up an owl for someone who claims to be big in the world of taxidermy. Fair enough, just about. But neither of us have bothered to check who he is and what he's about. If he's being straight with us, it's unusual, but there's nothing wrong with that. If he's tricking us, then whatever we've done is almost certainly illegal. What if there's a kilo of heroin inside that owl? Where does that leave us?

You're being very sensible.

Me? Sensible?

Listen, I said. I really don't think there's a kilo of heroin inside that owl, and if there was, somehow I think it would have got picked up at the airport. They're quite hot on that kind of thing.

I don't know. Did they X-ray the bikes?

Probably. They must have done . Why wouldn't they?

They're kind of bulky.

That's not a good enough reason not to X-ray something. I really think if there was something funny inside that owl, we'd know about it by now.

Maybe the sniffer dogs were off sick, said Poyntz. Let me double check.

No, I said. I don't want you messing him up any further. He's intact.

Intact?

Intact. His skin is unbroken.

So you HAVE felt him up?

Of course I've felt him up. I felt him up at the hut while you were dealing with your hangover. I felt every single part of him. It was lovely.

I don't believe you.

It's true. Don't you think I would have checked myself? Don't you think I was worried there might be something in there that wasn't meant to be in there? I would have left it behind at the drop of a hat if I thought there was. But there isn't. It's just a fucking stuffed animal. Nothing more, nothing less. It's no different a docket to a letter or a bag of locusts or a bunch of flowers or sheaves upon sheaves of boring legal papers.

But you didn't look inside?

No of course I didn't. He's all sewn up.

So you don't know for sure?

No. I don't know for sure. But I thought at the time it

was unlikely and now that we've got through customs without being charged with trafficking I think it's even more unlikely.

I still think we should check.

Don't fucking open up that bird. Please. I need him looking his best. I don't have time to sort out his face. To be honest I just want him off my hands. Please don't make things worse. If his face is fucked up and he's spilling his entrails we won't get any money at all from Sorensen. I promise you we won't.

Well let me come with you tomorrow.

Not this again, I said. I'm going to clean my teeth.

21

ON POYNTZ'S SOFA

When I woke Poyntz was gone and so was his bike. It was past nine o'clock. He'd be on his first, maybe second or third docket of the day. I thought about work. I thought of Sorensen handing over The Bounty and going to Fat Barry to tell him I was quitting. If there wasn't enough money from The Bounty, I'd tell Fat Barry I was fit again after my crash and ready to work Tuesday.

How much was enough money? Sorensen had promised another seven fifty on return of the owl plus more if the job was done well and on time. I had until lunchtime. Of the seven fifty expenses, we'd precisely zero left over, including a thousand kroner that I was pretty sure I'd lost in the tunnel. Say he gave us two fifty extra, that would be five hundred each, two maybe three weeks to look for something else before I had to go back to Fat Barry.

Lying on the sofa looking at the owl though, I figured I could kiss goodbye to any extra money. And there was always the chance that Sorensen would look at its disfigurements and knock down the seven fifty. I got up, took the owl off the shelf, put it in my bag, picked up the Pinarello, and let myself out.

20

GREEK DREAMS

When I got home the first thing I did was the same thing I always do when I get home: I picked up the picture of my mother and I kissed it three times.

The picture is of her at a picnic when I was eight or nine or something. She's wearing this cotton dress with pink flowers on it and in one hand she's holding a salad bowl like she's just about to serve up or make some dressing. She's smiling at the camera in a really nice but slightly wistful way and there's nothing much more to say about the photograph other than it's a bit dirty now but I never try and clean it because I'm worried I'll mess it up and I don't want to frame it because that's just the way it is and I like it that way.

My parents could have been together then – they separated around about the same time – but I've no idea whether my father was at the picnic or not. I often wonder if he's somewhere in the background or whether he took the photo himself and that there's something about his presence there that's making my mother look wistful.

When my father left my mother it was pretty dramatic: he just walked out of the house and was gone. Because he left all his crap, for a long time we thought he was going to come back. There were all his books and his clothes and all this stuff from his past, suitcases full of letters and photos, prescription sunglasses, used train tickets, that kind of thing. My mother waited a long time before she finally realised he wasn't coming back. I went on holiday with a friend and his family and when I came back all his stuff had been taken to the dump. You had to look really hard to find any trace of him at all and it was in things like kitchen curtains which I remember him putting up one summer's afternoon and it being a big deal. I was kind of annoyed with my mother for throwing away all his stuff. Still, he was a shit to her and he drank too much.

My mother, I thought, would be happier once things had settled down and for a while it seemed like she was and that the two of us had found a life together: we shared the house, I went to school, she went to work, we went away together. We went abroad to Greece and I heard her cry in a bathroom in Pylos. I knocked on the door and asked whether she was okay and she said yes and told me to go away.

After Greece I decided to learn Greek because I liked the way it sounded and because I thought it would get me girls. I didn't learn much. I was fourteen years old. I got into bicycles because my mother didn't drive and I needed to get places. My first proper bike was a Muddy Fox. My first cigarette was with Karl Lake – a Camel Light – and my first kiss was with a girl called Alexa: I wrote out her name in Greek on a piece of paper and handed it to her in class. Αλεξα. She wore a cute fringe.

My second bike was a hybrid, a Trek Multitrack 750 which I sprayed blue and crashed coming down Herne Hill on my way back from a party. My mum told me to take the bus from then on. Around about this time I got into drugs, weekend recreational like everyone else, and stole bicycles to pay for them. I re-sprayed the Trek red and hawked it for twice its market value. This led me to Renzo, an Italian with a rat's tail and a van and a lock-up in South London. He was a good mechanic and a practising Hindu. He persuaded me to drive with him to Cambridge and then gave me a crowbar and instructions. We went early morning and were back in London by lunchtime, a dozen bikes to the good. This was where I got my third bike, a Dawes Super Galaxy, my favourite ever excluding the Pinarello. We pilfered all summer and I learnt how to mend bicycles until my Super Galaxy got stolen and I understood the pain of having your bike nicked. I told Renzo I was retiring and went back to school. Later I heard that Renzo had gone down for trying to steal bikes during a triathlon. He'd got too ambitious.

All the money I had I spent on my fourth bike, a Raleigh Professional. I was entering the big league. I travelled up to Derby one weekend to pick it up from a man who claimed it had been ridden in the Tour of Britain. I paid him one hundred and ten pounds and spent the winter doing it up.

That was the same winter my mother walked into the sea. For fourteen weeks she lay in hospital, breathing through a machine, unable to communicate, never opening her eyes, wearing hospital pyjamas. I spent some of this time at school trying hard not to think about it and most of the time at home trying hard to ignore the ring of the doorbell. I remember spring going into summer and being underprepared for my exams. In the end I stopped going to school and would rise early, revise, eat lunch, revise some more and then bike over to the hospital in the evening. Sometimes I revised by her bedside but mostly I read aloud books by Greeks. This was the start of the Greek Period. I read her all of Homer, all of Sophocles, and a bunch of others. Sometimes I talked to her although I knew she couldn't hear. Sometimes I'd listen to my Walkman with one headphone and give her the other. I played music I knew she liked, violin music mostly. Sometimes I just played stuff I liked and made her listen to it too.

All the time there were adults talking to me like I was a child, which in the eyes of the law I still was. My teachers talked to me like they were my friends, which they were not, and my friends didn't talk to me at all – they didn't know what to say. My father wasn't told until the last minute because everyone feared he'd try and take the money. They were right. He came down in a flash but by then it was too late.

I knew of course that there was never any chance of her coming back. Only right at the beginning, when my fat-arsed head teacher, ashen-faced, took me out of class and told me the news, did I think everything would be okay. But when I got to hospital you could tell from the doctors, the way they looked at you, the way they spoke: *Are you Mr Black? Shall we find somewhere quiet? We're doing everything we can... It's very serious... There's a possibility she may not...* After a week or so the language became bolder. They said she'd be on life support until life support was switched off. When's that? I asked. We need to come to that decision together, the doctors said.

I'm not sure how much I was part of that decision. It's possible I stated a preference but I don't really remember. I remember some conversations we had but I don't ever remember my opinion counting for much. I do remember my aunt ringing the doorbell and me letting her in for once and her telling me that a date had been set and that the whole family – by which I think she meant me – needed to 'move on' and take things to the 'next stage'. I opted out of the bedside vigil as the switch was hit and chose to sit my exam: *he committed him to the arms of the two fleet messengers, Death, and Sleep, who presently set him down in the rich land of Lycia.*

Lycia for my mother was Hogg & Son, Funeral Home. They laid her out in North Hendon, her attendants the Hogg brothers, tall and as grey as death itself. In polite cockney they welcomed me into their dark and functional place of work, sat me down, expressed their condolences, asked if I had any questions, shuffled paperwork and finally told me my mother was ready to be seen.

Someone had organised all this in the manner expected. I didn't know there were different ways of doing things or that I even had an option not to step beyond that thick velvet curtain where my mother lay looking like someone else. She was almost comic in her embalming, bloated, colourless, rigid. They'd put some kind of blusher on her cheeks as if to say let's give her a bit of life why not? although she never wore make-up. They had her in a white shirt, a kind of blouse thing which I did not recognise. They'd closed her eyes and her mouth and brushed her hair so it was nice and tidy. I wondered if they'd cleaned her teeth as well and whether they'd used the right toothpaste.

When I decided I'd seen enough I got on my bicycle and rode north until I stopped crying, which was some-where outside Milton Keynes. It was three days short of May and between the sunshine the rain fell lightly as I pedalled. I thought about riding further, further north or west to Wales but there was the funeral to attend and I risked going feral. I spent the night in a wood between two motorways then cycled back to London in the morning.

The funeral was full of people I didn't know.

The will, as it happened, left everything to me. Not that I cared about any of that stuff. All I wanted to do was pass my exams and go my own way, which I did. I got a place at a university and the house I grew up in was sold and the money went to the lawyers until I became an adult. After their fees and all the rest of that crap it came to one hundred and seventy-six thousand pounds, three pence. It showed up in my bank account on my eighteenth birthday.

My bender lasted all of the summer holidays. I went to Malaysia first, I don't know why, and after that I got it into my head to go back to Greece, but to climb the mountain where Alcibiades was murdered. When I got to Greece I found out the mountain was somewhere in central Turkey. I travelled straight away to Turkey but never found the mountain. When I came home I was dusty and my face was full of freckles and I was just a little bit fucked-up. I slept on people's floors until I ended up in hospital one night having my stomach pumped. After that I thought it was time to stop grieving and stop reading books by Greeks. I also realised I needed to spend my money quickly and on something sensible.

First I bought the Pinarello. She cost me fifteen hundred pounds, shipped over from a dealer in Germany. She was bicycle number five.

Then I bought somewhere to live. I became a man of property, the owner of a flat above a launderette. It had two beds, overlooked a roundabout and cost me one hundred and forty-three thousand pounds. I bought it in cash, paid the rest of my uni fees upfront and put the remainder in a bank account. By the time I'd finished all the money was gone. I was glad it was gone. I had a roof over my head and a bicycle but I needed to find a job.

This is when I became a courier.

In dreams my mother slowly came back to me. To begin with she was completely absent. I'd dream of moments of need: as a boy falling over, gashing my leg, falling from a height, calling her name, sick in bed, lonely, and she'd be nowhere to be seen. Just me, on my own, fighting for myself. Basic.

Then after a while, a few months, she started to make appearances, little cameos in adventures that didn't really concern her. In the background of an office, feeding paper into a photocopier, playing piano in a jazz bar, driving a tube train as it pulled into a station. She winked at me as I stood at the platform, eating a bowl of pasta.

Finally, she turned up in one of my Greek Dreams. I had stopped reading books by Greeks and started dreaming about them instead. Mum, I said, what the fuck are you doing here? No one important ever turned up in my Greek Dreams. She was helping me prepare a libation to some god. I was digging the hole and in her hands she held honey and wine and on her head she was balancing a carafe of water. Pass me the water, I said and the carafe floated over to me. But with the spade in one hand and the carafe in the other I was unable to get out of the giant hole that I had dug. My mother looked down on me with benevolence. Just climb out, she said. So I climbed out.

In another I was riding the Pan-American on a tandem. It was hot as hell and hard work. The road was straight and there was no landscape other than flat desert and faraway mountains. Every now and again a hand would reach out from behind me and pass me the bidon and I'd drink from it and pass it back. The water was cold and sweet. I carried on cycling.

After a while I began to wonder who was riding behind me. I got this strong feeling it was my mother but she wasn't saying anything, just handing me water from the bottle. The strange thing about the bottle was that the water never went down or lost its coolness.

Finally, I looked back and discovered it wasn't my mother, it was Laurent Fignon in his heyday. He was wearing the yellow jersey and his trademark gold specs and stripy headband. He was putting a serious shift in.

You okay? I asked him.

No, he said, in my mother's voice. I've got saddle sores.

How bad? I said.

Pretty bad, he replied.

You've got jelly? I asked.

Sure I've got jelly, he said.

You want me to have a look? I said.

No thanks, he said, let's keep riding.

I couldn't tell whether this was my mother looking like Laurent Fignon or whether this was Laurent Fignon sounding like my mother. But my feeling was that if it was one person more than the other, then it was my mother more than Laurent Fignon, whose saddle sores cost him the Tour in which he lost to Bernard Hinault, by just eight seconds as it happened.

Mostly when I dreamt of my mother she wore the same cotton dress with pink flowers that she's wearing in the photo. This was a recurring dream although it was more variations on a theme, the theme being the cotton dress with pink flowers. Nothing much happened in these dreams. My mother just turned up wearing the same dress and spoke to me about stuff. Sometimes it was stuff in her life, sometimes it was stuff in mine, sometimes it was stuff in neither of our lives. Once she lectured me on the best way to play twenty-one on an opening roll. You have two basic options, she said. 24/23 and 13/11, or 13/11 and 6/5. One is cautious, darling Sam, the other is bold. 13/11 is a given, so the choice you have is between 24/23 and 6/5. 24/23 sets your men running, 6/5 is risky but gives you the option of developing that key five-point. I'd go for this. The advantage outweighs the risk but darling Sam, be careful, you need to get out of your opponent's home board as quickly as you can.

My mother never played backgammon in the whole of her life although this was sound advice.

Another time she talked and talked about her problems, about how lonely she was, about how scared she was about me growing up and leaving her, how she was worried about getting old and getting ill, about living on her own, about a whole bunch of things all of which seemed familiar but alien because she never would have said any of this stuff in real life; she'd have kept it hidden, which she did, and here she was blurting it out in my dreams. The worst thing was I wasn't really interested. She came across as boring, bleating. I didn't want to hear her agony. When I woke up I felt ashamed and started to cry. I asked myself why I didn't do anything about her sadness when she was alive.

My answer: I was a teenager and teenagers only think about themselves.

Of course the irony about recurring dreams is that at some point they stop recurring. Kids are meant to have a lot of recurring nightmares because they're working through their fears. When the fear keeps recurring it becomes commonplace and as it becomes commonplace it begins to wear off. Finally, the fear disappears and so does the nightmare.

When I stopped dreaming about my mother in the cotton dress with pink flowers I wondered if a little bit of the grief had died and if so then maybe this was a good thing. But I missed her terribly, more than ever. In these dreams, however fucked-up they were, she came back to life: her voice, her mannerisms, her being. I'd wake up wanting to return to her and I'd try to will myself back to sleep, never successfully. And as the dream recurred less and less, I felt like I was losing something vital, a memory, a part of myself, and that soon it would be gone for ever.

Eventually the dream did disappear for good and I was left with the photograph: a dream of a memory, a memory of a dream.

19

AT THE
MANDARIN ORIENTAL,
HYDE PARK

(PART ONE)

I left my bike at home and took the Tube to Sorensen's hotel. My plan was to stop in on Fat Barry on the way back.

The Hotel Priam was still standing. The same guy was at reception, the one who'd had cheese on his upper lip, but he didn't recognise me from before.

Mr Sorensen, I said. Could you tell me which is his room number?

Sorensen? He tapped the name into his computer. He checked out six days ago, he said.

Checked out?

That's what the computer's telling me.

Where did he go?

I don't know. He just checked out.

He didn't say where he was going?

No, Sir.

He's expecting a delivery.

Is it something I can help with?

Not really, I said. He didn't leave a forwarding address at all? Any messages?

What's your name?

Sam Black.

He went into an office behind him and came back with someone else who introduced himself as the manager. He had pocked skin and a lazy eye.

What's your name Sir? the manager asked.

Sam Black, I said.

Mr Black?

I guess so.

You know Mr Sorensen do you?

Yes, I said, I do.

Very well, he left this for you. He handed me an envelope with my name on it. Inside was a note. It read:

I have changed hotels. I am opposite, in the Park Central .

Opposite sure enough, was the Park Central Hotel. There was another note for me there.

Mandarin Oriental.

So I walked across the park and found Sorensen in room 312 of the Mandarin Oriental.

They kicked me out for smoking, he said. Twice.

Why didn't you go to the park to smoke? I asked.

The park? I don't want to have to go to the park every time I need a cigarette, he said. Anyway, this is a better hotel. It has a balcony. They don't much like smokers here either but they can't stop you from smoking on the balcony can they?

243

The balcony was small, two chairs and a tiny table but with amazing views of the park straight ahead, the park with its horse lanes made from sand and shit and its triangular paths bisecting the greenery. We sat down and smoked and Sorensen talked about the spa facilities for a while, how good they were, amongst the most comprehensive he'd come across and I asked him how he'd ended up in one of the best hotels in the city after starting in what looked like one of the worst and he said, very simply, that it was all down to the balcony. He would have settled for any hotel with a balcony: this just happened to be the first he came across. Then he talked about some other hotels he'd stayed in: one in Rio, one in Delhi, one somewhere else. He said the views there were better than anywhere else. To be honest, I'd kind of switched off at this point and I was wondering where it was all leading. Finally, he cut to the chase and asked whether I had his owl.

Yes, I said.

And how is he?

He's okay.

And my key?

Yes.

Everything locked up?

Yes.

And how did it all go? Did you like my country?

I said yes and told him his country was very beautiful but that his owl was a bit damaged.

Show me, he said.

We went back inside and I took the owl out of my saddle bag and gave it to him.

Oh, he said, that's nothing. He put the bird on the bed.

It all felt a bit too clever. He'd spent a load of money getting me to pick up the fucker and when he had it in his hands he barely looked at it and then he discarded it like it was any old piece of shit.

You found the hut okay? he said, taking a wad of money out of a bedside table. I looked at the money and decided it was in my best interests to play the game.

It was fine, I replied. You'd left it pretty messy.

Messy?

There was stuff on the floors.

What kind of stuff?

Just stuff. Like your jackets were on the floor. The bookshelves were a bit messed up too. Cupboards were open, that kind of thing. The place wasn't very tidy.

Interesting. And that's how you found it?

Yeah. It was okay. We tidied up.

We?

I pointed to the owl. Me and your friend, I said, smiling weakly.

Oh. Thank you.

No problem, I said.

And did you have any problems with anyone when you were there?

At the house?

At the house or anywhere else. Did you have any problems?

No.

No problems at all?

What d'you mean problems?

Problems with people. People asking you what you were doing?

No.

Neighbours, these kinds of people?

I didn't see any neighbours.

Police?

I can't remember seeing any policemen at all.

And at the airport?

I'm sure there were police at the airport. Why?

You didn't have any problems at the airport?

No. Why?

Well, he said, the thing about owls is that they're kind of special and they attract attention. Snowy owls are pretty common in Norway but people are funny about them. They're like a national symbol for some people.

Oh, I said, playing along. I can believe that. I guess that's why this thing is so important to you.

Exactly.

And what are you going to do with him now?

The owl?

Yes, the owl.

He laughed. I'm on a flight back to New York tomorrow night.

And that's it?

That's pretty much it. I'm hobbling back home. Now let me give you your money.

That's very decent of you.

How much did I say?

In my head the number seven fifty scrolled up to a grand, then twelve fifty. Seven fifty, I said, deciding it would be better to tell the truth.

Here, he said, and he counted out fifteen notes, every single one of them red, and handed them over. I thanked him.

No, he said. The gratitude is all mine. I didn't think you'd make it.

You didn't?

Not really. I trusted you but you're young. Young people make mistakes.

And if I hadn't made it?

What would I have done?

Yeah.

I'd have found you somehow.

How?

Well I've got your cellphone number, haven't I? I know who you work for. I know where you live.

You know where I live?

I think so.

How the fuck do you know where I live?

You told me, didn't you?

No.

Oh. Maybe I don't know where you live then. Anyway, you've got your money, I've got my owl. We're both happy. As long as you keep quiet about it all, as I said.

As you said?

As I said. Didn't I say? Oh well, I'm saying it now. He took a further five notes from the wad and gestured to the door.

So you won't tell me what's in that owl? I said, not taking the hint.

Nothing's in the owl Mr Black, he replied, and he opened the door and held out the money for me to take.

Naturally I took The Bonus and walked.

18

LANZAFUCKINGROTE

I had one thousand pounds in my pocket, half of which was promised to Poyntz. I was in no rush to get to Fat Barry's so I walked through the park and then east through the centre of town, figuring it would take me an hour. In fact, it was nearer two hours by the time I'd stopped for something to eat and bumped into Guzzman on his way to a drop-off in Soho. He warned me Fat Barry was pissed off that I'd been off the radar for such a long time and he wasn't wrong. When I walked into the office he stood up. I'm not sure I'd ever seen him stand up in the office before. He started to harangue me big time. Where the fuck have you been, he said, Lanzafuckingrote?

Look at my face Barry, I said.

And?

I've been in a crash.

That was months ago.

It was ten days ago.

Where's your bike?

At home.

What the fuck is it doing at home? I need you to work.

I need to talk.

About what? What d'you need to fucking talk about? Holy mother of God Sam. I'm your controller not your counsellor. I need you on the road. I've got a fucking massive backlog of jobs. I can't afford you to be off any fucking longer. Seriously.

Just five minutes, I said.

Okay, he said, but hold on. He took a call from a client and assigned another job and swore at a rider out on the roads because another client was chasing a delivery and lit another cigarette and asked Sue for a cup of coffee and Sue said they were out of sugar and he swore and said he'd tried drinking coffee without sugar and it was impossible fucking impossible and he took and assigned another job and then told me to pop downstairs and get a bag of sugar, he'd pay me back. As I went downstairs someone else was coming up. We passed on the landing. You could tell he was a rookie from the way he looked, the clothes he wore and that nervous excitement that all new riders have. He was kind of dressed for work and kind of dressed for something else: he had a pair of trainers no cleats, cycling shorts of the nastiest kind and a base layer from a camping shop. His legs were underdeveloped. If someone's been on the road for a long time their thighs are turkey thighs and their calves are turkey drumsticks but this guy had nothing on him, no muscle at all. He probably rode a Gary Fisher.

We looked at each other as we passed. He was around my age with a bit of a baby face and a hook nose and wavy hair and freckles and in one hand he carried his Specialized helmet and in the other his keys. Do you know what you are letting yourself in for? I wanted to ask him. But instead I nodded and carried on down the stairs.

When I got back I made Fat Barry's coffee – instant,

three sugars – and waited. The rookie sat on the sofa opposite Barry and waited too.

Eventually Barry got off his swivel chair and walked to the back room where we sat down.

This better be good, he said. How many times have I fucking called you over the last few days?

I'm sorry I didn't return your calls. I've been busy.

Busy doing what?

Sorting stuff out. Recuperating.

You've joined another firm, haven't you?

No of course I haven't. You'd know if I had.

Dart?

No Barry.

Gazelle. That cunt's always nicking my best riders.

No.

Central?

Don't be stupid. I'm not that fucking desperate.

Urban?

Barry, I've not been riding for another company.

Excelsior then.

Very good. Yes. I've joined Excelsior and I'm riding a tricycle.

Jesus Christ. How the fuck am I meant to keep this business going when my riders go AWOL all the fucking time? Where've you been then?

Barry. I told you. I had an accident. I needed time to recover.

But it's just your face. Your legs are okay. Your arms are okay. Your face isn't pretty but it's okay. I've seen much worse. What about Poyntz?

What about him?

Where the fuck's he been?

I don't know. You tell me. I'm not his keeper.

You know where he's been. You're his fucking friend.

I've not heard from him for ages.

Fucking hell you've got a nerve. I can just about excuse you when you've had an accident. But covering up for him when he's taken a week off to do whatever you've been doing together. A niece's wedding in Scotland my arse. At least fucking come clean. At least tell Fat Barry the truth. At least don't fucking treat Fat Barry like a fool. Because Fat Barry isn't a fucking fool.

Barry, I said. I don't know where Poyntz has been. I haven't seen him for days.

What you and your best buddy Poyntz?

We're not lovers Barry.

Could have fucking fooled me. Anyway, your five minutes is up. Go home. Get your bike and get on the road.

I can't, I said. I'm sorry.

What d'you mean?

I want to leave.

You want to leave?

I need to hand my radio in.

Why?

I need to go and do something else.

What do you need to do?

I don't know. Something else.

Are you sure?

Not really.

Well then why don't you think about it, and ride for me in the meantime?

No. I need a break.

You've just had a fucking break.

A proper break. A break from riding.

You've joined Alphabet haven't you?

No Barry.

Fucking fuck. The best riders always do this. I'm fed

up with being a courier, they say. I want to go and study. I've met a girl and we're moving to Luxembourg. It's all bullshit. Next week I hear they're riding for the competition. No one has the fucking balls to tell me anything.

You pay chicken shit Barry.

Listen chicken shit. I pay chicken shit because if I paid any fucking more there'd be no fucking chickens and there'd be no fucking shit. I don't make any fucking money out of this job. No one seems to realise that. I do it because it's what I do. I do it because of the bike.

Because of the bike?

Yes. Because of the fucking bike. I love the bike.

I love the bike too, Barry.

You see. You do it because you love the bike. You're a clever fellow, Sam. You could go and do anything. You have a few issues but generally you're okay. I don't blame you for wanting to do something other than ride a bike all day. But you ride a bike all day because you love the bike. All my riders love the bike.

He pointed to the rider I passed on the stairs, the one with the hook nose. He was waiting for a docket.

That boy over there, said Fat Barry, he's called Sam, like you. I call him Other Sam. He joined last week. He doesn't love the bike. He may ride a bike, he may like the bike, but he doesn't love the bike. You can tell. Straightaway.

He might learn to love the bike.

I doubt it, and even if he does, then what? He'll become a half-decent rider before swanning off somewhere else.

For the last time Barry, I'm not going anywhere else.

Then why do you want to leave? And what are you going to do?

I don't know.

Fat Barry paused and looked at me and lit a cigarette and said, I've got it.

Got what? I said.

You think you're living on borrowed time? he said.

Maybe, I replied.

Maybe? You mean yes?

Sometimes it feels like it.

You're thinking I've had a crash and escaped with barely a nick and next time I won't be so lucky.

Next time or the time after that.

How long have you been riding?

I've ridden a lot.

Not as much as some.

No, not as much as someone like Yelena.

Yelena's accident was a freak. Not usual.

What's a usual accident Barry? They're all fucking unusual.

You know what I mean, Samuel. It's very unusual for couriers to get killed. They're better riders than everyone else. And the Black Goddess was one of the very best.

But that didn't stop her getting killed, did it?

No, you're right, it didn't. What happened to her would have happened to anyone. She was just in the wrong place at the wrong time.

She's not the first and she won't be the last.

That's true, Sam, that's true. But the chances are slim.

The chances?

The chances of her and then another courier.

Barry, I got run over last week.

But it was a nick wasn't it?

I ended up in hospital.

Listen, he said. I can't force you to work for me. I can't force you to ride your bike. It's not so strange that you're having a wobble. We all have wobbles now and again.

Accidents sharpen the mind. It's difficult to get back on. You've had a week. Take another. Or take it gently, do a morning. I don't want to lose one of my best.

Shucks Barry.

I'm serious.

The funny thing is, I kind of felt for Fat Barry. He was laying it on thick because me quitting was one hell of an inconvenience for him. It would take months to get a half-decent rider up to scratch and there was no way an off-the-peg messenger would walk into Zenith for the kind of money Fat Barry paid. Zenith was like one of those low league football clubs that had no cash and had to nurture talent to survive. He traded on the kudos of riding for Zenith by paying bottom dollar but riders still went to him because bicycles were in his blood and he treated his staff as specialists not commodities. But the more I looked at Fat Barry back at his desk, doing his job of work, spitting into the phone, whipping his couriers into shape, the greater I felt the heat of that cash in my pocket. Over a grand against two fifty a drop: there was no contest. There are other roads, I thought. Just give yourself space to explore them.

So when Fat Barry turned his back to deal with some or other emergency, I quietly placed my radio on his desk and walked out of Zenith Couriers for the last time.

17

RIDDLES

I had grown so used to walking London's streets with my cycling shoes – feeling the metal pebble of the cleats in the centre of my soles and hearing their tip-tap as I hurried in and out of buildings making my deliveries – that when I was not wearing them and wearing instead my battered pair of Nikes it felt like I was walking on a great lightness, that the pavements were cushion-lined.

Also you do not notice the strangeness of people when you travel at speed. You see the broad strangeness of the city as you weave your way through it, making your crooked lines, and you may catch sight of its equally crooked characters. But you do not see detail on their faces.

(I once sat next to someone on the Tube who revealed to me, as she read, the most amazing tattoo I have ever seen. It was inked upon the underside of her left forearm and I made note of it in case it should ever go out of my head. It showed a stag morphing into the silhou-etted skyline of a city: like New York but not New York. Underneath the city's horizon were the letters RWT fol-lowed by a six-digit number. It was a riddle: there was no way I was going to solve it. Then, as she turned the page, I noticed that written with a black marker on her hand was a list. It said:

> *keg*
> *pen*
> *cat*
> *move morgan*
> *expensis*
> *recepte*
> *padlock*
> *paris*
> *paper*

It was another riddle which I was not going to solve.)

On the Central Line then I found myself wallowing in the humanity bath of a packed carriage. I stood and stared mostly at tourists, fitting them into their stereotypes. Italians in shades of olive, Japanese with baseball caps and cameras, Americans with baseball caps and luggage. I looked at the freak show and enjoyed being part of it too. I counted seven bubbles in a glob of spittle that ran from a sleeping baby's mouth. I examined the contents of someone's bag (lipstick, magazine, Handy Andies). I eavesdropped on a pair of suits discussing a meeting ahead (...they're going to try and play hardball, geezer. Don't let them.). I watched a nun write a text message. Then after two stops I found a seat and this was when I met Bella Meikels.

She was sitting back to the platform, with a friend on her right. I was opposite and to her left, back to the tunnel, reading a book. If the layout of the train was a backgammon board, I was on my one-point, she was on her four-point, and her friend was on her five-point.

In my book a man was telling the story of his life, from beyond the grave. I started a chapter: a black butterfly flies into the man's room and perches on a picture of his father. As I read, I noticed out of the corner of my eye the girl, the one on the four-point, noticing me out of the corner of her eye. I tried to carry on reading: the butterfly is making the man nervous.

Opposite, the girl was talking to her friend. When I looked up a second time, so did she. We exchanged glances.

I was nervous too, super-aware that something was happening, not just to me – my mind was racing sure enough – but also to her. From the corner of my book I could see a girl of high cheekbones and smooth, fair skin. She had chestnut hair that ran right to left across her brow. She wore no make-up save a little gloss on the lips perhaps, and a black V-neck with dark jeans, tight against the hips and the ankles, and shoes a ballet pump, the flat-soled slip-on tininess of a dancer, black with a bow at the top of the vamp, a kind of velvety suede, sockless.

The man's unease about the black butterfly has now turned to anger. He swipes at it with a towel and it falls to the ground, dead. But I had already stopped reading the book. I was concentrated on the stranger and the stranger was concentrated on me. She was making timpani rolls in my ribcage. We were trying to limit the number of eye missiles we were sending each other but we were not succeeding.

There must be an art to the oeillade but I was unseasoned and so must she have been. In the movies it happens on escalators and the look is long and unwavering. There is little unsureness. The moment is anointed, triumphant.

Here though, it was more like a delicious game of cat and mouse. She would look up and catch me looking at her and quickly we'd both look away. I would look up and catch her looking at me and quickly we'd both look away. Then we'd look up at the same time and catch each other looking at each other at the same time and quickly we'd both look away. Our moments were furtive and made in split seconds. But they were full of something I had not felt since that day I jumped into cold water with Kelly Zimmerman and floated in the darkness.

Or so it seemed. Because then doubt crept in and I began to wonder if the whole thing was just another of my imaginings. When I looked up and her back was turned, turned towards her friend, I felt a great pang of sadness. When I looked a second time and she'd not moved, I suddenly felt the full power of rejection.

I tried to continue reading. As my brain chased its tail I noticed, away from the empty words on the page I was reading, that the girl had asked her friend for paper and was writing something down on it. I speculated. It was either a note of invitation or it was something entirely different: some shopping list, an aide-memoire, a drawing of a cat she used to know. When she finished scribbling I busied myself not wanting to appear expectant but still we caught each other's glance again – the last time I would ever see her, I imagined. Well: she was mesmerising and looked at me with declaring eyes.

They got off at the next stop. I looked down and she walked straight past me.

Then, at the last moment, she passed me a note, folded in two. It was a business card in crimsons, brown and magnolia and on it was typed the following:

KONTAKT
THEMATISCHE BUCHHANDLUNG
ZU STADT, POLITIK, POP,
ÖKONOMIE, ARCHITEKTUR,
DESIGN, KUNST & THEORIE

NEUE SCHÖNHAUSER STRASSE 92, 11228 BERLIN
TEL 030 25839631, FAX 030 25839632

GEÖFFNET: MO – FR 12 – 20 UHR, SA 11 – 16 UHR

It was a riddle, in German. There was no way I was going to solve it.

So I turned it over and written in red ink were the girl's name and her number. A real life billet-doux. Her name was Bella Meikels.

16

ROLLAPALUZA

When I got home I put Bella Meikels's card behind the picture of my mother and went to my bedroom and sat on my bed, counting money. I split the money into two piles and put my share under my pillow and Poyntz's in my pocket then went back to the picture of my mother, kissed it, and picked up Bella Meikels's card. I looked at the number then looked for my phone so I could punch in the number and keep it safe. I didn't want to lose the number.

But I couldn't find my phone. It wasn't in my bike bag and it wasn't in my jeans or my top. I'd either left it on the Tube or left it at Fat Barry's. If it was on the Tube, there was nothing I could do about it. I wasn't going back to Fat Barry's. I went to the telephone box across the road and dialled my number. At first it rang out. When I called it again, someone picked it up.

What what? the voice said.

Who's that? I asked.

What do you mean? said the guy. Who the hell are you?

My name's Sam, I said. You've got my phone. Who is this?

Sam who?

Sam Black. Who the fuck are you?

Sam, it's Bolo.

Bolo. Thank God. You at Zenith?

Yeah. Where you been? Fat Barry keeps cussing you and your phone keeps ringing.

It's probably him.

He's not that stupid.

Listen, I said, when are you finishing? Can I come and meet you somewhere?

I'll be at Rollapaluza.

It's today?

This evening. Didn't you know?

I might have done. Where is it?

Usual place.

Okay, I said. I'll see you there. You'll bring my phone?

Of course, he replied.

I didn't want to go to Rollapaluza, which would be full of couriers asking me where I'd been, asking me why I wasn't on my bike, asking me whether I'd really quit Zenith, asking me what I was going to do, asking me what had happened to my face. I didn't want to talk about myself and I didn't want to have to pay the five pounds to get into Rollapaluza.

As it happened I just walked in straight past the queue and nobody noticed. Sometimes good things happen. I found a corner where I could be on my own and look at people, people I knew and people I didn't know, picking out the messengers from the fakengers and fashion riders. There were a bunch of club riders in orange lycra. I liked the fact they were taking it seriously and they'd give the couriers a good run for their money. There was a crew from a cycling magazine too. They were dressed in purple, drinking lager out of cans.

I looked for Bolo and saw Slim gearing up for a qualifying race. He was up against a tall dude, another club rider by the look of things. They were on their rollers, warming up. Slim swung his shoulders and chewed gum. The club rider adjusted his foot straps. I couldn't see the clocks but I saw the flag go down. Five hundred metres of furious pedalling, and Slim went through. The club rider looked pissed off.

Bolo arrived in a rush and climbed onto the rollers straight away. He won two rounds then came and found me. I was still sat in the corner, thinking about stuff. The atmosphere livened up. The MC found his voice. The DJ banged out tunes. People were getting drunk.

Where's Poyntz? asked Bolo, handing me my phone.

No idea, I replied.

Come on, said Bolo, wiping sweat off his brow. Tell me. Where've you guys been? Fat Barry knows something's up.

No he doesn't.

He does. He's just not letting on because he wants to keep you.

I've been resting. Look at my face.

I know, said Bolo. It's bad. But I know riders when they've not been riding. You've been riding and so has Poyntz. He did twenty-eight dockets today. You can't do twenty-eight dockets on no riding.

Poyntz can.

Trust me. No one can. You need edge for that.

He was at a wedding.

Yeah right.

You've been to an Indian wedding?

No.

They take ages.

You went too did you?

Of course I didn't.

We looked at each other. Anyway, I said, what does it matter?

It doesn't really, said Bolo. People are just asking. I'll ask Poyntz. He's probably here by now.

He's coming here?

Yeah. He had to go and see some Argentinian guy first. Then he was going to swing by.

Argentinian?

Yeah.

Definitely Argentinian?

I think so.

You don't mean Armenian?

That's it. Armenian. Some Armenian guy who he calls the Armenian. Funny that.

The Armenian. Poyntz was either in deep shit or stirring deep shit. I looked at my phone. There were seven missed calls. One was from the phone box opposite my flat. Three were from Fat Barry. The other three were from an unknown number. There was a single message on my voicemail. I dialled my voicemail and tried to listen to it but another race had just kicked off and I couldn't hear a thing. So I went outside and listened to it there. The message was from Sorensen. *Oh hello Mr Black,* it said. *Can you call me? I'm sure you know what it's about. I'd like to sort things out if at all possible, before I fly back to New York. I'm flying tomorrow evening in case you forgot. I'd like you to come round now. I'm very appreciative. At the least, please give me a call. Thank you.*

The tone was polite but pissed off, a little bit menacing. Passive aggressive. I was confused. I figured if it was something important there would have been a greater urgency. He sounded calm but hot underneath. I felt a little irritated myself.

I called Poyntz. Where are you? I said.
Why?
What do you mean why?
Why?
Because I've got your fucking money.
You got it? All of it? We got The Bounty?
Yep.
What all of it?
Yep.
Fucking great.
So where are you?
Where am I? I'm doing some stuff.
What stuff?
Oh just stuff.
Where?
Oh, somewhere. Where are you?
At Rollapaluza.
You're at Rollapaluza?
That's what I said. Are you coming?
I might do. I've got a couple of —.

You might do? Poyntz, this fucking money is burning a hole in my pocket. I MIGHT just get mugged on the way home. I MIGHT just spend your money.

No you won't.
I might.
Have you got it on you now?
Yeah.
How much have you got?
Your share. Five hundred.
Five hundred? Fuck. Five hundred each?
Yep.
And you've got mine in your pocket?
Yes, for fuck's sake!
So he topped up The Bounty with The Bonus?

Two fifty on top.

He didn't care about the face?

Nope. He just gave me the money and I left.

And what about —.

What?

No forget it. Listen, he said. I'll be over in a bit.

I'm not hanging around.

Okay. Give me twenty. No wait. I'll be half an hour. No more. I promise.

Fine. I said. No more.

15

TRUST

He didn't arrive for ages. Half an hour passed, then an hour. I sat in the corner, drank beer, and felt nostalgic for the time before Sorensen's message.

I wanted to have left him behind, to have dealt with it all, to have taken the money and gone. I thought I'd done it. I'd got pretty close. But it was all too good to be true. Now there was a complication. I was pretty sure Poyntz had created this complication and that it was me, not him, who would have to sort things out. But because I didn't know what the complication was, I didn't know what needed to be sorted out. Everything felt a little fucked.

I wondered if Sorensen was the type to send a goon round to Zenith. I'm looking for someone called Samuel Black, the goon would ask. You and me both, Fat Barry would reply.

Was this why Fat Barry had called me? Or was he just trying to get me back on my bike? Paranoid, I looked around Rollapaluza for meatheads but all I saw were Rollapaluzaheads: Slim had been knocked out in the quarters and was skinning up; Guzzman was already drunk; the team from the cycling magazine were trying to ignore the couriers and the couriers were ignoring them; two girls – one of them I knew – were preparing for their semi-final with light pedalling and chat; the DJ was mixing up northern soul and hip hop and Early Man was trying to dance to it; the lights dimmed once more.

The girls raced. The one I knew, a Gazelle rider, was an old friend of Yelena Zykov's. I didn't know what her real name was but Maid Maleen was her call-sign. She rode red and her opponent blue. I watched the hands of the giant clocks chase each other. Red led all the way, not that Maid Maleen knew it. She just raced head down long dark hair everywhere and when the race was over she looked back at the dial and found out she'd won. She had a nice smile, serious, shook the hand of the other rider, got off the red roller and high-fived her friends.

After Maleen lost her final – to a girl from a racing club up north – Poyntz turned up. He was in a kind of excitement himself with a little apprehension thrown in. I watched him look for me unsuccessfully amongst the crowd and the noise. I hadn't shifted in two hours except to pick up beer and go for a piss. People had come and gone, asking the same questions, getting the same answers.

Is it true then? said Poyntz, when he eventually found me.

Is what true? I replied.

That you've left Zenith. Fat Barry keeps calling me.

It's pretty much true.

He thinks you've gone elsewhere.

I know.

But you haven't.

Of course I haven't.

I told him that.

Thanks.

So what are you going to do? asked Poyntz.

I don't know, I replied.

How much have you got?

Loads.

Seriously. How much?

No more than you. We've both got the same.

Honestly?

Honestly.

How long will it last?

A month maybe.

That's nothing.

I can always come back.

Not if you want to stop riding.

Who said I wanted to stop riding?

Fat Barry.

I'm only stopping until my face gets better.

Your face? Your face is fine, Sam. You know that.

We set out the board. It felt dumb playing backgammon while everything was going crazy around us but I wanted to play and Poyntz was happy to play along with me. He won the first two games and halfway through the third some dickhead from Premier tripped on the way to the bar and upset the board. I had been ready to roll and was in the driving seat, eleven pips to Poyntz's fifteen. I needed doubles bigger than one while he needed doubles bigger than two. If neither of us rolled doubles I'd win being the first to throw, even if I rolled the worst dice possible, successive twenty-ones, which was unlikely since the probability of that was one-in-six to the power of four. Oh well. I thought of resetting the board but Poyntz always tried to move a piece here or there and I had other things on my mind than an argument over the pip count. So we packed up and went outside for a cigarette and I took the opportunity to play him Sorensen's message.

So that's him? he asked.

That's him, I replied.

He sounds a little creepy.

It doesn't sound nice, does it?

No.

There was a pause as I waited for Poyntz to talk. But instead he asked about the money.

He gave us everything he promised and more, I told him. He honoured his side of the deal.

Seven fifty then an extra two fifty?

That's right. There's a grand between us.

And you've got it on you?

Maybe.

What d'you mean maybe?

I've got your money Poyntz. It's safe.

Then let's see it.

Tell me first what the message means.

What message?

Sorensen's message. What does it fucking mean?

I don't know what it fucking means! You tell me what it fucking means! He's your fucking friend.

He's not my fucking friend and I don't know what his fucking message means. I left my phone at Zenith, picked it up and I've got this fucking menacing message on it and I don't know what it means.

I don't know what the message means either, Sam.

Yes, you do. Cunt.

Okay, said Poyntz, let's just rewind for a moment. You delivered Mr Tecolote?

Yes.

And everything was fine?

Yes.

He was happy to see you?

I guess so. He was a bit surprised.

Surprised?

A bit surprised, yeah. But happy I guess.

How was he surprised?

Well it's like he wasn't really expecting me. For a start he wasn't in the same hotel. He'd moved.

From where?

Before he was in this hotel called the Priam so I went there and they said he'd moved to the hotel across the road but when I went to the hotel across the road there was a note for me saying he was in the Mandarin Oriental. So I wandered across the park and found him in the Mandarin Oriental.

That's a proper hotel isn't it?

Yeah. It's nice.

And?

And nothing.

What about the owl?

The owl was fine.

Did he check it?

What d'you mean?

Did he check it? Did he check his face and stuff?

Not really.

But the face was fucked! It didn't bother him at all?

Not particularly. He didn't seem to care about the owl.

He didn't care about the owl?

No, Poyntz. He didn't care about the owl.

He cared about the owl but he was pretending he didn't care about the owl.

Maybe. What's in the owl Poyntz?

You're fucking asking ME! Why didn't you fucking ask him?

I did.

And what did he say? Nothing?

Yep.

Well there you go. Nothing's in the owl.

How do you know?

Because he said it.

Because you've looked yourself?

No. Because he said it.

And you believe him do you?

Yes, said Poyntz. In your words, I've no reason to disbelieve him.

So he paid us nearly two grand to go and pick up his owl and when we returned it to him, fucked, he didn't give a shit?

Yes Sam. But every time I've questioned you about this strangeness, you shrug your shoulders and say well yeah it's a bit crazy but so what it's fun and it's free money. So can I have my five hundred pounds?

Not until you tell me what that message means.

I don't know what the fucking message means! Here, play it again.

I put my phone on speaker and played the message again: *Oh hello Mr Black. Can you call me? I'm sure you know what it's about. I'd like to sort things out if at all possible, before I fly back to New York. I'm flying tomorrow evening in case you forgot. I'd like you to come round now. I'm very appreciative. At the least, please give me a call. Thank you.*

Okay, said Poyntz. So this is what it is. We've kind of mistreated the owl and he's not so happy with the way that he looks because he's got this fucking taxidermy conference or whatever at the end of the week doesn't he? He needs to make it look nice and owly, yeah, not like it's been punched in the face? So what he wants is for you to return with the money, maybe just the two fifty, and negotiate some kind of compensation deal that will allow him to do all necessary touching up and restoration work to the bird. He might need to buy in some materials or whatever. I'd say give him a hundred and call it quits. Explain the difficulty in getting it through customs and say you had to pay money for some forms or whatever. But don't let him take all The Bounty. A hundred and twenty-five tops I reckon.

Nice try, I replied. If it was a problem with the owl he'd have said something at the time.

Maybe he didn't notice.

He can't not have noticed.

He definitely noticed the owl?

I saw him notice the owl. I was as worried as you that he wasn't going to give us The Bounty.

He gave you The Bounty having noticed the owl?

Yes.

Maybe he took a closer look once you'd gone and changed his mind.

Maybe he looked inside the owl, I said, and discovered that whatever was meant to be in there was actually missing.

He could have checked at the time.

Not if whatever was in there wasn't meant to be in there.

He could have checked while you were out of sight, gone into the bathroom or something.

That would have made it a little obvious, I said.

Wasn't everything a bit obvious anyway?

I don't know. You tell me.

Seriously, said Poyntz. I have no idea what was inside that owl. Promise to God.

So now you're saying there *was* something inside it?

I've always said it was possible.

When he gave me The Bounty he told me to keep everything quiet.

272

What d'you mean? What did he say?

I asked him about what was inside the owl and he said nothing and then he flashed the cash and told me to keep schtum. And he asked me about the police.

The police?

Yep.

What police?

He asked if we'd had any trouble with the police. At the airport or whatever.

Fuck. That doesn't sound good.

No it doesn't, does it Poyntz?

And what did you say?

I said no. I never saw the fucking police. Did you?

No. Wouldn't know what they look like. The Norwegian police that is.

And what do you reckon was inside the bird?

For fuck's sake Sam! When will you let this go? Maybe it fell out.

It?

Whatever was inside the fucking animal.

The bird was sealed.

What do you mean? The bird must have an orifice or two. All birds have holes. Bumholes.

The bird was stuffed for fuck's sake.

Maybe not to professional standards. Maybe its little hole wasn't closed up. Maybe the string of pearls fell out of its bumhole.

And what does the Armenian think about the bumhole theory?

The Armenian?

Yeah. What does the Armenian think?

What's the Armenian got to do with this?

Haven't you just been to see the Armenian?

No.

Oh. I thought you had.

Who told you that?

Someone.

Who?

Someone.

Who?

Bolo.

Bolo?

Bolo.

Bolo told you I'd been to see the Armenian?

Well haven't you?

Poyntz paused. Fucking Bolo, he muttered.

So you *have* been to see the Armenian?

Yeah. I briefly popped my head in to visit my friend the Armenian.

So first you say you haven't seen him then you say you have. What did he do for you?

Nothing.

He's helping you out of a little problem, isn't he?

He's helping me sort out my piles.

What's he helping you with Poyntz?

My piles. They're fucking awful. All that riding in Norway has given me the worst haemorrhoids ever. I can hardly sit down.

And what does the Armenian recommend?

Homeopathy. I think.

I stared at Poyntz. He stared back at me. Neither of us were smiling. We'd reached the end of the road. There was to be no more bullshitting. You can lie to a friend within measure. But there's a line you don't cross.

Okay, he said, lighting a cigarette. Let's make a little deal.

Go on.

I can tell you something. But I can't tell you everything.

I can't tell you everything because you'll fuck everything up if I tell you everything.

I have a right to know Poyntz.

Yes. That's true. I suppose you have a right to know.

So you do know what was inside that owl?

Of course I know.

You cunt.

Yes. I'm a cunt. But I'm a cunt who knows what was inside that owl.

What was inside that owl Poyntz?

This, he said, and he took out his phone and showed me a picture, a picture of a picture. I asked what the fuck it was.

It's a picture, he said.

A picture?

Yeah a picture, like a painting but not a painting.

You're having a fucking laugh, I said. There's no way that was inside the owl.

I extracted it myself.

When?

Last night.

When last night?

When you were sleeping. I woke up and my insatiable curiosity struck.

What did you do?

I put it on the kitchen table and gave it a good fingering around the bumhole.

Sick.

Yep.

And?

I couldn't find the hole. Then you began to stir so I panicked and I got a knife.

You fucking idiot.

It was fine. I made a little surgeon's incision. With

a bread knife. Anyway, it worked. I made a hole big enough to fist the fucking owl and as soon as I started rooting around I felt this plastic tube thing and within thirty seconds I had it out on the kitchen table. That Sorensen dude is pretty fucking ingenious you know. He's a pro.

And the picture?

The picture was inside the tube. It's not big. It's like the size of a computer screen. All carefully rolled and wrapped up.

And this is it? I said, looking at the picture on his phone again.

Yep. That's it, said Poyntz. It's like a print or something. I don't like it very much. Pretty boring. Not one of his best.

His?

Poyntz shrugged. Whoever did it, he said. I don't know.

I looked at the picture and felt a strange kind of relief. I had expected something more explosive, more obvious. Something more criminal. There was only a certain amount of trouble one could get into over a picture. But why? Why hidden inside the owl? What was the point of the deception? Why go to such lengths? Why so elaborate?

It's clearly stolen, I said.

Yep, replied Poyntz.

And it's probably worth something, I said.

Yep.

And you don't know who it's by?

No.

Signature?

Poyntz paused. I couldn't read it, he said.

I looked at the picture again. The resolution was too

poor to make out much. It was kind of black and white and dismal with a streaky sky, mountains in the background and in the foreground what looked like a nun. I asked Poyntz what the Armenian thought of it.

He smiled. The Armenian has many talents, said Poyntz, but art criticism is not one of them. I went to see him about a separate matter.

Don't lie to me again Poyntz.

Seriously. It was nothing to do with this.

What was it to do with then?

It was a private matter. I'm allowed to maintain a certain privacy aren't I?

He's going to make some enquiries for you?

You're barking up the wrong tree Sam.

He's going to see how much it's worth?

Listen, it's probably just an heirloom. It's probably worth nothing.

Best check with the Armenian though? You don't want to throw a money-making opportunity down the drain.

I'm telling you Sam. I went to see the Armenian about a separate matter. Anyway, I couldn't find him. He wasn't about.

I don't believe you.

It's true. I promise you.

I don't believe you.

Fine. Don't believe me.

I don't.

Fine.

Not fine, I said. What the fuck am I going to tell Sorensen you cunt?

Tell him nothing. Don't call him up. Or call him up and say you don't know what he's talking about.

No actually you know what I'm going to do, I said.

I'm going to call him up and say sorry but my friend – if I can call you that – has stolen your lovely picture and here's his number and this is his address. You'll find him hawking the picture on the Portobello Road with a shadowy figure known only as the Armenian.

He does actually have a name the Armenian.

Oh he does, does he?

Yeah, he does. He's called Mashtots.

What?

Mashtots Hambartzumian.

What the fuck?

Exactly. That's why I call him the Armenian.

Right.

And you should know he doesn't have the picture by the way, I've got it.

Well that's nice to know. Where is it?

It's safe.

Where is it?

It's safe.

In your flat?

It's safe.

It's in your flat.

Maybe. Maybe not.

You need to give it to me Poyntz.

No way.

I need to give it back to Sorensen.

No way.

Poyntz, it's not ours.

You're right. It's mine.

Very funny.

I found it.

It's not yours. You've stolen it.

Off who? The owl?

Off Sorensen.

And who did *he* steal it off?

I don't know. Neither of us knows. But it's not ours to keep.

He fucking tricked us.

That's true. But I want to be done with it all. Tell me where the picture is, I'll take it back tomorrow and you can have your five hundred and we can put the whole thing behind us.

You are joking.

Poyntz, if you fuck me over I'll fuck you over.

That is low.

No it's not, I said. It's quite straightforward. He gave us the money on completion of the job. I completed my side of things. You haven't. I'm going to be doing you a favour. I'm giving you the opportunity to hand back your stolen sweets. When you hand over your sweets, I'll hand over the money. I'll go back tomorrow, give him back the picture, apologise, say there was a crazy mix-up and that will be the end of it.

He still fucking tricked us.

Maybe. But we knew the risks.

And now we're just paying him back.

Poyntz, the picture's not ours.

It's not his either.

You don't know that.

I sense it.

I looked at Poyntz. You're making a fucked-up situation more fucked-up, I said.

It's fine, he said. Here's what I'm going to do. Give me until lunchtime tomorrow. The Armenian will have got back to me by then.

Ah. So the Armenian IS involved.

Of course he's involved dipshit. He'll know what we can do with it. If he says it's a pile of crap, take the picture

279

back, be my guest. Don't forget to leave the five hundred on the kitchen table. But if he says it's something, you can keep the five hundred. It's yours. A present from me. I'll deal with the rest. You don't have to get involved. I'll go and find Sorensen, explain the situation. I'll tell him you've had to go to Toronto on business. Or I'll tell him you're fucking dead or something.

Don't joke about that.

Okay fine, I'll tell him you've got chronic fatigue syndrome.

Thanks.

I'll tell him the police have been fishing around, asking questions. I'll tell him he's in a whole load of shit and that he's one move short of a bird-trafficking indictment and if he gets heavy on me I'll call the police and they'll be over in a shot. We've not done anything wrong have we? We just did a job for someone. A run-of-the mill international docket.

You're out of your mind.

Lunchtime tomorrow.

He's flying back tomorrow evening.

That's plenty of time.

Plenty of time to make the wrong decision.

I'm weighing up my options.

You've only got one option and that's to tell me where the picture is.

No Sam, said Poyntz, I can do what I want.

Do what you want then, I said. Do what you want.

I'd had enough. I'd had enough of being deceived, by Poyntz, by Sorensen. I needed my bed. I needed to get away, from everyone, from Poyntz and all the riders who were streaming out of Rollapaluza, riders with medals around their necks, riders zipping up and looking for keys in their saddle bags, riders unlocking their Surlys and their Felts and their Fujis and Cinellis and Dolans and Holdsworths and Shwinns, their Colnagos and their Nishikis, and cycling off into the dark. I needed to get back on my Pinarello and feel the wind behind me. I needed to be home, forgetting about it all. I needed to put my head under the duvet and sleep for forty-eight hours. I needed to wake up having lost two days and for everything to be sorted, a clean slate, no more Sorensen, no more fucking owls, no more deliciously red fifty pound notes, no more scabs on my face.

When I got home I kissed the picture of my mother and put Poyntz's money in the jam jar under the sink, remembering I needed to get rid of the gris-gris. I vowed not to touch any of the money until the job was finished. When the job was finished I'd call up Bella Meikels and ask her out on a date.

Then I sat on the loo, looked in my wallet and counted what I had in real life. I had five pounds and a bunch of receipts from Norway which at one stage I'd thought I'd need to show Sorensen. One-by-one I screwed up the receipts and threw them in the bin, sometimes hitting, sometimes missing, until I came across a folded banknote, a thousand kroner no less. It was the same thousand kroner note that I thought I'd dropped in the tunnel we got lost in the day after the black metal gig. For once the gods were smiling on me. Whoever was on the note was a fucking malcontent but at least I could exchange this fucking malcontent for some sterling. I went to bed, in my head the picture on the flip side of the note: a sun illuminating mountain skies.

14

EGGS

I slept for just six hours, dropping off before midnight and waking at dawn. I felt alert and a little anxious and alone. I got up, made coffee and stood at the window and watched morning happen outside: buses making pilgrimages to Victoria Station, kerbside-sprayers and street sweepers, shift workers, a single vagabond. Then I went back to bed and thought about eggs.

I thought of the spicy eggs Bolo had once made me. Perico eggs he called them. Then I thought of One Eyed Jack which my father would cook, always using the same chipped teacup to create the circle in the white slice, frying one side before flipping and cracking into the hollow. I thought of eggs scrambled and eggs poached and eggs pickled and scotched and I thought of the eggs we'd had in Norway after cycling from Sorensen's hut, eggs which sat on giant slabs of salmon. I thought of the Eggs Wazoffing which Early Man's Austrian girlfriend had once cooked and eggs another messenger, Eugene, had once told me about, Chinese eggs which are soaked and cooked for a day in the piss of prepubescent boys and sold as a delicacy and medicine. Eugene was a shy guy and I was surprised to hear him tell lies. But it turns out they really do make that shit. I thought of the eggs that I sometimes cooked on cold mornings, boiling four, two for each pocket, eggs that would keep me warm for an hour or so which I'd then peel while I rode and eat in three mouthfuls or hand them out to other riders, who always asked for salt. These eggs were good for throwing too. I know a messenger who keeps little pebbles in his back pocket to throw at drivers who piss him off enough, enough to crack a windscreen or dent a panel. I could never be so sure with my aim but a hard-boiled egg never killed anyone.

But I had no eggs in the fridge at all, just cheese and a half-opened pack of sausages that had gone wrong. I went outside and bought ingredients for Bolo's eggs. It was nine, nine fifteen and Poyntz would already be collecting dockets. I needed fortification so I smoked a cigarette and cooked Bolo's eggs. I must have missed something out because my version was way off but I covered the omission with hot sauce. Then I got on my bike, ready to break into Poyntz's flat.

13

AT THE
CHURCH OF ST ANNE'S,
LIMEHOUSE

Before I broke into Poyntz's flat I went down to the river and spent half an hour looking at its gloomy vastness and imagining what it would be like to swim across to the other side, just like that. I would probably strip down to my underpants and drown, being a weak swimmer. It was cold, not so cold that you couldn't stand and watch a river for half an hour but cold enough for the balls to shrink just thinking about swimming.

The water was choppy as fuck for the still, clear day that it was. The cruise boats beetling down towards the Thames Barrier left wake patterns that reached the side of the shore before being swallowed up. I'd get swallowed up too. The captain might see my head bobbing up and down in the milk chocolate but he'd have a timetable to keep to and a fresh set of pleasure seekers upriver, thinking about white wine.

If I made it over to the other side (I might take a breather on a buoy and chat to a seagull or climb one of those floating pontoons whose purpose has never been clear to me) then my first priority – after the slippery ladder that would deliver me onto dry land – would be a fresh set of garments. If I had not already been collared by the river police I might find an obscure alley in which to take stock. My pants would still be dripping bilge water and dead matter. I would be shivering and cadaverous. In the cobbled alley I might find some omni-purpose rag – something someone had once used to wipe a dipstick. I would use this to dry my skin. Then, in a big black wheelie bin that could always be used as a temporary shelter, I would strike gold: some theatrical clobber a prankster had stolen from the Globe Theatre and dumped: a pair of tights, some pantaloons, a doublet, sturdy boots, a feathered cap. Perhaps a sword. In these I would venture forth onto the streets of Rotherhithe or wherever, dispatch a gang or two, find the nearest bridge to cross, and skip back to Limehouse where my Pinarello would be waiting for me, plus my clothes of the future.

Or so my imaginings went.

But instead of swimming the Thames I did something much more unusual: I took myself to church. My intention had been to go straight to Poyntz's and do quickly what I needed to do but when I looked up at his flat there were a couple arguing on the walkway which he shared with his neighbours. They looked like they were from number 29 (Poyntz lived in number 27). So I locked up my bike in the graveyard of St Anne's, full of dead sailors, and resolved to kill some time. The big creaky door was open and the church was empty but fully lit and warm.

I went inside and sat down. What was I meant to do? Pray? It had been a long time since I had uttered a prayer.

I looked up at the ceiling with its gold stucco circles and sky blue paint, the church's celestial promise. Everything was quite magnificent. Four massive pillars kept up the roof and balcony. The walls were peeling and half-plastered but the giant pipes of the organ sparkled. The pulpit was formidable and Jesus looked forlorn but in control, framed in stained glass.

Near the altar there was a little metal table where you could go and buy a tea light and spark it. The candles were ten pence each. None had been lit. I always thought this was a Catholic thing. You lit a candle for the Virgin Mary or a saint. It was like the lowest kind of papal indulgence: light a candle, give money, and you might be spared on reckoning day.

I looked in my pocket and found one pound seventy and a lighter. Some fucker was going to have to take the plunge. I lined up seventeen candles and lit them one-by-one. Then I sat down on the front pew, closed my eyes and made seventeen prayers.

I prayed for my dead mother.

I prayed for my dead mother again.

I was about to pray for my dead mother a third time then I thought I may need some credits so I prayed for all the dead people in the graveyard outside, especially the masons and the ones who had drowned at sea. This prayer counted as one.

I prayed for my bicycle, that it might not be involved in any more crashes. God, I said, look after my bicycle for fuck's sake. Please.

I prayed for me. That was probably a selfish use of a credit but still, I felt I needed it and I wanted to be on the safe side, especially since I was about to jettison the gris-gris.

I prayed for Poyntz. God, I said, look after him even though he is a dick sometimes.

I prayed for all the sick people in all the hospitals, especially Guy's and St Thomas's.

I prayed for Yelena Zykov, who ended up dead in Guy's and St Thomas's.

After this I felt I needed to broaden out a bit so I prayed for the people of Africa. People always pray for the people of Africa.

Then I prayed for things to go okay with Bella Meikels but I thought hell I can make that all happen without divine intervention so I withdrew that prayer and prayed for Fat Barry instead not because he particularly deserved a prayer just because he just happened to come into my head at that moment.

Shit, how many more did I have to go? I'd lost count so I sent two credits to my mum again – four in total wasn't bad going – and then I granted three to Abdoujaparov because probably no one ever prayed for him, not even the Russian Orthodoxy although maybe he followed Islam.

Finally I prayed for the place I was in which was kind of a prayer for Limehouse which Poyntz said was full of criminals but which seemed okay to me but also a prayer for the lovely church which had stood on this spot for hundreds of years and seen lots of motherfuckers like me pass in and out of its doors and hopefully not judged them, just welcomed them with open arms and given them the Christian handshake whatever that was and baptised them and married them and buried them and seen generations and generations through all sorts of shit and misery and still come out of it standing on solid foundations and providing refuge for people waiting to break into people's homes.

When I opened my eyes I almost keeled over so bright was the light streaming in through the stained glass. In amongst the technicolour a man in olive corduroys was looking into me in an angry manner. He must have been the church warden or something.

Did you light all those candles? he asked. His tone was kind of aggressive.

Yes, I replied, still trying to recover from the head spin.

What, every single one of them?

Yes, I said. Every single one of them.

I looked at the candles. There were sixteen candles there, flickering away. One of them had gone out. I wondered which one it was. I wondered which prayer wasn't going to get answered. Then I left the church and made my way to Poyntz's flat.

12

Household Gods

I had broken into Poyntz's flat several times before but only as an accomplice to Poyntz himself, who was good at locking himself out.

There were two techniques. There was the door and the window. The door came first, then the window.

The door was a cinch: a credit card and nothing more. I remember Poyntz swiping us in on a number of occasions. Then Poyntz realised what a dumb cinch it was and got his landlord to install a deadbolt. You can't use a card on a deadbolt.

The window technique followed. You climbed onto the sill, jemmied a gap with a crank tool and used a coat hanger or a bungee to fish the lever up. The rest you could do with your bare hands. When Poyntz installed the deadlock the window became the default technique.

I don't know why Poyntz locked himself out so much. I'm a disorganised fuck was his answer. I told him to leave a key with someone, someone he could trust like his neighbours. But he didn't trust his neighbours and instead kept a spare behind the bar at his local, which was a dumb thing to do since the pub was only open during opening hours and when you lock yourself out it's either first thing in the morning or three in the morning.

Poyntz wouldn't just leave his keys in the house. He'd leave them in the door. He'd leave them in the office. He'd leave them in the Montmorency. He'd leave them under trees in parks. He'd leave them at drop-offs and pick-ups. He'd leave them in his bag and break into his house and empty his bag and find them.

As it happened I didn't need to do much. I carried my bike on my shoulder up to the third floor and thinking he might have forgotten to double lock when he left that morning, got out my wallet and tried a card. What a dick: the door opened. Then I locked it from the inside, put my bike in the hall and made myself a cup of tea. Amazingly, there was milk in the fridge and it had not yet curdled.

Theoretically I had all day to find this fucking picture but I didn't particularly want to hang around. He was my best friend and I knew his flat about as well as I knew my own but it's hard to relax when you're somewhere you're not meant to be. I gave myself two hours. I figured Poyntz would have spent some time considering where best to hide the prize but that he wouldn't have over-elaborated. It was half past ten. Ideally I'd be out by twelve and handing the picture back to Sorensen by one. Then everything would be over.

I looked in the kitchen first because that was where I was. I checked the obvious places, drawers and things, and some unobvious places like the oven and the freezer and inside the boiler. Part of the problem was that I wasn't sure exactly what I was looking for: how big it really was, whether it was wrapped up or not, rolled up or straight. All I'd seen was the picture Poyntz had shown me on his phone.

I moved to Poyntz's bedroom. It was a fucking mess and it stank. The bed was unmade and there were clothes all over the floor. I kicked a sock, lifted a pillow. Then I picked up the mattress and looked underneath. There was a copy of *Cycling Weekly* and a gas bill. I leafed through *Cycling Weekly* and started reading a feature about Jens Voigt. Under the bed there was a holdall full of books. In his desk were a bunch of dockets he'd never completed. On top of the wardrobe was a suitcase but it was empty.

I felt like a copper. This was federal, at the very least, and I didn't have to cover my tracks, no Sir. Fuck I could turn the whole place upside down if I wanted to. But I didn't want to. In the back of my head I was thinking that perhaps the Armenian had the picture all along and that trashing Poyntz's flat wouldn't help.

I looked at Poyntz's household gods, on the wall above his desk. There was a framed picture of Charles Mingus and a framed picture of Djamolidine Abdoujaparov. There was Poyntz's dad shaking hands with the Yogi Ramesh. There was a postcard of a Russian icon and a framed picture of David Lynch. There was a framed picture of Nijinsky and a hermit in a cave and Sir Francis Chichester with his broken teeth and see-through specs. There were various men in beards – Joseph Jongen, Jerry Garcia, Isaac Albeniz – and the photograph of a woman with a broken leg wearing knickers lying down in bed looking out across the Swiss Alps. I knew these people because I had seen them many times. They were what Poyntz called his influencers.

To their right were the pictures that Poyntz took of himself in coin-operated photo booths and the pictures that he took of his friends and the pictures that he took of himself with his friends in coin-operated photo booths.

There was Poyntz with his mate Theodora Winkelstein, the one with the bob; there was Poyntz with his sister and his niece; there was Poyntz with his mother and his father and, inexplicably, there was Poyntz and a Dobermann in the booth together and the Dobermann was licking his face.

There was Poyntz on his own in a boxing robe, Poyntz in a Stetson, Poyntz in drag and Poyntz shaving. There were several of Poyntz in profile, left to right and right to left, Poyntz in specs, Poyntz in sunglasses. There was Poyntz in a number of different turbans. There was Poyntz in black tie, in his Fugazi T-shirt, Poyntz on his way to an English wedding with a flower in his buttonhole and Poyntz on his way to a Sikh wedding in his kurta pyjama. There was Poyntz picking his nose, Poyntz flicking Vs and horns at the camera. There was Poyntz with long hair, when he was sixteen, and Poyntz small and earnest-looking, aged thirteen, sporting bumfluff and a top knot. There was Poyntz drunk, eating a chicken burger.

Bolo was there and so was Fat Barry. Yelena Zykov had been inveigled into a booth and was giggling. There was Guzzman and there was Byron. Then there were a whole bunch of mystery characters. Some were people Poyntz knew, including the man I was convinced was the Armenian (Poyntz always denied it). Others were just passport photos that Poyntz had found on the street or on the floor of the post office or underneath the machine, left in the slot, not deemed flattering enough.

Amongst the fifty or so in this collection was me, me with Poyntz in the booth at a service station on the way down to Brighton. I've decided you're all right, he said, so I'm gonna add you to my wall. And he put the money in the box and told me to sit on the swivel chair. I don't need my fucking passport picture taken, I told him, I'm up-to-date. Relax, he said, just look at the screen and wait for the flash. But just before the flash went off he jumped into the booth and that's the picture: he's grabbed my head, really hard, and I'm trying to move it but it's like my head's in a vice and he's shouting at me to look at the camera for fuck's sake, whatever I do just look at the camera! I'm hitting him but he's behind me pinning my arms with his elbows and squashing my face so it looks warped and fucked up.

Quite a few of them were like that. That was his tactic: immature. There were a lot of people up on that wall with their heads sandwiched between Poyntz's hands.

I went into the tiny room where Poyntz kept his bike stuff. There was half a bike there, an old Cannondale he was doing up. I undid the seatpost and looked down the tube. If the picture could fit inside an owl it could fit inside a seatpost. I looked in some of his bike manuals. I looked inside a pair of panniers but there was just an empty bag of Quavers and an idiot's guide to astronomy, southern hemisphere.

I made myself a cup of coffee. Then I went into the living room, lay down on his sofa, smoked a cigarette and stared for several minutes at Poyntz's record collection. I felt a sense of defeat.

My conundrum was this: I could forget the records and look deeper around the flat, in places someone without a brain might hide an object of value, like underneath a loose floorboard.

Or I could search one-by-one through Poyntz's record collection, but it would take all day. I looked at the vinyl, stacked up neatly, and searched for signs of human interference. Two or three records were out of place so I took them out and looked inside but there was nothing.

Then I looked at the records either side of them. Same.

A criminal psychologist might look at Poyntz and consider whether he'd choose a record randomly to hide his crime or pick something that referenced it. Some Norwegian jazz, perhaps. I looked through all his Garbarek albums and concluded Poyntz was more of a random kind of guy. So I gave myself an hour of random searching. Then, I decided, I'd go and find Poyntz and take him to Sorensen and leave him to sort everything out.

Before the records though I tried Leibniz. I asked him where his master had put the picture. Where did he put it my friend? I asked.

But Leibniz had barely ever acknowledged my presence, let alone uttered words to me. We'd never hit it off. Poyntz claimed he'd taught him to repeat 'Broadsword calling Danny Boy' in the manner of Richard Burton. Of course I didn't believe it. The budgerigar was mute as far as I was concerned. I wondered if I let him out of his cage he might do something clever, like hover over the spot marked X. But if he was really clever he'd find the gap in the window by the front door and make his escape from captivity. So I went back to the records.

I worked section-by-section, picking out three from each. Poyntz would spend whole weekends rearranging his jazz collection from sub-genre to alphabetical, from alphabetical to date, from date to sleeve colour, from sleeve colour to market value, from market value to sentimental value, from sentimental value back to sub-genre, etc. I picked out twenty records but none had anything in them other than what you'd expect. My method felt methodical but was in fact quite arbitrary. I had no idea he'd hidden the picture in a record and if he had hidden the picture I had no clue which of the two thousand or so records in his collection he'd used to hide it. I took out another twenty records, at random. They were all jazz records apart from three: one was a recording of the old Pope, Pope John Paul the Second, singing mass; one was a bunch of Russian songs sung by someone called Oda Slobodskaya. The last record, the twentieth, was some classical thing by a man called Adams, John Adams, born 1947, played by the City of Birmingham Symphony Orchestra, the sleeve was fluffy white clouds on blue skies and a picture of a monk and an oil tanker and a bridge, with four tracks: 'Harmonielehre', 'The Chairman Dances', 'Tromba Lontana' and 'Short Ride in a Fast Machine' – and inside this record I found the fucking picture, pristine, enclosed within a square plastic envelope between the vinyl and its sleeve. I took it out and it curled at the sides so I carried it carefully to the kitchen table and rolled it out. It was quite beautiful really: a pair of lovers, kissing, against a dark sky.

What was so wrong about this simple picture? What was forbidden, what was the evasion, the mystery? I had been duped – as expected I suppose – but why? There must have been a good reason. It must have made economic sense. Or perhaps there was some kind of criminal necessity. Yet Sorensen didn't seem to have given a shit about the owl. In fact, he was almost disappointed when his beloved Mr Tecolote was returned to him. Looking at the picture, I felt Poyntz's impulse to cut and run. Here was the prize and it was ours to keep. I didn't know how we'd make money from it but no doubt the Armenian had ideas: at the least it would make good collateral and there'd be some decent cash in that. Fuck it: we'd been hoodwinked and this was our revenge.

But still I wanted to be shot of everything. If I got some

answers along the way, then even better. But mostly I wanted freedom, freedom from the deal. It was nearly midday. I put the picture back in the sleeve and the sleeve in the record and the record in my bag and I tidied up and after tidying up I took a final little tour of the flat to make sure everything was more or less how it looked when I arrived. I found myself in Poyntz's bedroom staring at the passport picture of the man I took to be the Armenian, the man Poyntz always denied was the Armenian. The more I looked at the picture the more I thought I knew him. First I thought this was because I'd seen the photo a bunch of times and had always made a thing of asking Poyntz who amongst the strangers this mean-looking motherfucker was: bald, corpulent, eyes like a Dobermann.

Eyes like a fucking Dobermann! Was this the same maniac behind the wheel of the Porsche Cayenne? Same build, same baldness, different clothes but a nice flash tan, no smile, just business? Was this the cunt who'd tried to run me over, given me the ugly face, made me believe the soothsayer, left me for dead on the pavement? If it was, then why the fuck when I told Poyntz everything, gave him a picture-perfect description, yellow Cayenne included, did he shrug and say next-to-nothing? Sam, he mumbled, there are some crazy motherfuckers out there.

Poyntz, what if that Dobermann licking your fucking face belongs to the Armenian? Wasn't the Dobermann's picture taken in the same booth as the Armenian's? Tell me, Poyntz, is that the Armenian's dog? Don't say, he was sitting in the back of the tinted Cayenne when it fucked me up the arse?

No, I thought, it can't have been the same guy. It was just another of my imaginings. I had been floating in the air, contemplating death. Could I really be relied upon to provide an accurate description of the car and its driver? The car was definitely yellow but was it definitely a Cayenne? And if it was, there are probably a hundred and one yellow Cayenne drivers in London. There are probably a thousand and one Armenian lookalikes in London. He was just like any other bodybuilder who for too many years had been a casual abuser of anabolic steroids and Piz Buin.

11

ANOTHER INCIDENT WITH THE PORSCHE CAYENNE

But then I met him on the stairs, on the stairs as I left Poyntz's flat for Sorensen's, on the stairs with his breaking-in buddy, another pumped-up meathead as it happened. They were talking under their voices, walking up as I walked down with the Pinarello on my shoulder. They were there as I turned the corner, looking up at me as I looked down on them, the two of them gearing up for the job. They weren't coming to pay Poyntz a friendly visit either, an off-the-cuff. The breaking-in buddy had a Lonsdale holdall which was groaning with tools.

I wanted to tell them to go home: tools would not be required. I wanted to let them know, politely, that their job of work was futile, that they would never find what they were looking for because what they were looking for was in my bag and my bag was on my back and it was staying there. I wanted to explain to the Armenian who I was, flesh out the happy coincidence and talk him away from any clumsy pillaging he was about to embark upon. Then, once we were better acquainted, I wanted to ask him why he ran me over ten days before and didn't stop. I wanted to point to my scars and hear his explanation. There was etiquette, didn't he know, and there was something called the law as well. And when he bristled and baulked and flexed his upper body muscles, looking at his mate as if to say let's do him, then I wanted to fight, learn some martial art from scratch, so I could take the two of them down and teach the Armenian a lesson, have the cunt in an arm lock, twisted in pain, begging for mercy, promising whatever I wanted, which wasn't much, just an apology I suppose.

Instead we looked at each other, a little too long for comfort, and I hurried down the stairs. Was there a flicker of recognition in his eyes? I don't know but there was more than a fucking flicker in mine as I walked out of Poyntz's and saw the Porsche Cayenne in all its yellowness parked right outside: tinted windows and a new back bumper. I called Poyntz and when it went to voicemail I texted him:

Call me. Need to talk. Urgent.

and then I decided it would be wise to take some pictures of the beast and I did this as quickly as I could, looking up all the time to the third floor. I got a nice shot of the car on its own – I was getting to know my enemy – and close-ups of both number plates and the tax disc. Then I got two pence out of my pocket and got on the Pinarello and did a circle of Oast Court's parking facilities and rode up with the Cayenne on my left and the queen between thumb and forefinger and I coined the whole of the near side of the Porsche, four fucking panels' worth, and he must have sensed something or seen me because the next thing I heard was a thick rusky *motherfucker* and the sound of shouting and the two of them running down the stairs, forty stones' worth of flesh, ready for some exercise. But by the time they were down I was away, up the street looking back, and the Cayenne – stupidly for a getaway car – was facing the wrong way. I heard the familiar roar of its engine but by then I was two, three blocks away and the Armenian was never going to catch me, not me nor the Pinarello.

10

GRIS-GRIS

Through Whitechapel and Aldgate and then the City I rode at speed, buzzed by adrenalin and in my head the idea that being chased I would need to practise a little my skills of avoidance and escape.

For my practice run I chose Fleet Street, which was long and had enough arteries to the left and right to escape should escape be necessary. I got up speed down Ludgate Hill and went through the traffic heading to Blackfriars – all the time imagining the Cayenne on my tail – then took the road heading west, this being the path of least resistance. But this wasn't practice proper since there was no real reason to ride against traffic heading east when the traffic heading west was smooth enough. So at St Clement Danes, I made up the problem. I could see the Cayenne poking its nose out of Essex Street. The Armenian had spotted me. He could drive straight and block the road or shunt me, whatever. My only option was to zip across the zebra nearest to the courts and ride against everyone coming the opposite way. This is what I did, clipping a file-carrying clerk en route up Aldwych and riding between four, five lanes of hooting and cunt-calling traffic.

It was so much fun I carried on up the Strand where I felt invincible and clipped two wing mirrors.

Then at Trafalgar Square, which I have always hated, I rode right anti-clockwise-against-clockwise up St Martin's Place then turned (since north was wrong for Sorensen's) and rode the opposite direction clockwise-against-anti-clockwise, all in twenty seconds tops. Straight after this I ended up between two buses with the gap at the back narrowing, wondering very seriously what I was playing at.

One of the things you can do in this situation is to let both drivers know all parties are heading towards a potential calamity and bang your fists against the side of their vehicles to make them stop. Once they've stopped you can either proceed through the gap, assuming it's wide enough; if not you'll have to reverse (easy with a balancing hand) or – even worse – get off your saddle and walk backwards, back-wheeling your bike: a humiliation.

The other option is to pedal through the gap – triumph – but the gap always tapers quicker than you think. What did I have to lose? Sorensen's prize?

Of course like a dick I went for it although the space I was heading for was probably only half a metre wide (the gap between the Pinarello's drop handlebars is precisely forty-six centimetres). But the Cayenne was behind me, wasn't it?

Once I'd made it I glanced back at the gap, smug as fuck, pride intact, and pedalled straight into the driver's side of a Number 3 heading towards Crystal Palace. It was a soft crash this one, my right side handlebar taking the force, sending me off, skidding towards the curb. As soon as I was down I was up, knowing the adrenalin, however fucked I was, would get me back on my saddle and away from the scene: I had no defence for riding the wrong way round Trafalgar Square and I wasn't going to endure the drama of the afterwards, all the finger-pointing and witness-calling and phone calls to the police and incident response and whichever fuckers ran the Number 3. I'd had my punch-in-the-face. In the scenario the Armenian was already onto me with his faux-friendly Dobermann and one of those chain whips. In real life my left-hand side was starting to hurt. I got back on my bike and cycled off down the Mall, slowly, riding on wonky bars. At the fountain outside Buck Palace I stopped and took some road out of my thigh with a pair of tweezers and gave it a wash. My elbow was bleeding too. My face was fine, my helmet a little scratched. I rolled a cigarette and cursed myself. Then I took the seatpost off the Pinarello, extracted the gris-gris, and threw it into the water.

The water in the fountain was still and clear. The gris-gris floated for a bit, then sank. I watched it bubble a little on the bottom. Then I stared at tourists for a while.

It was September and they sat a little cold, huddled on the steps, studying maps, making plans, arguing about what to do next. Suddenly I started crying. I don't know why. I just noticed there was a tear in my eye, a single tear, then another and afterwards there were more. It felt like grief, big amounts of it, but I couldn't figure out who or what I was grieving for. Was it the tourists, huddled on the steps of the fountain? If it was, it was a dumb thing to cry about. Was it some hidden memory connected to where I was – perhaps some visit to look at the Queen's windows – that was so deeply buried that I could only make it up on the spot? I didn't give a shit about the Queen or her windows. Was I crying from the pain in my elbow? My elbow had stopped bleeding and it wasn't painful. My bike? The Pinarello was okay; her handlebars I had already re-aligned. And the picture?

Shit! The picture! But the picture was absolutely fine. I didn't even need to take it out of the record sleeve. I'd landed on my side: a soft crash, as I said. I'm not even sure my bag had touched the ground. I'd successfully protected my drop, despite coming off my bicycle. A good messenger always protects his drop.

I wondered if my mother was the cause of all these tears. An Italian woman, about the age she would have been, came up and asked if I needed an *ambulanza*. Would an ambulance offer on-the-spot grief diagnosis, I wondered? Would they triage my tears and say, yep mister, it's definitely your mother that's triggering all this Category One weepiness? Although it could be gall stones. Or a hernia. Or sciatica. Or saddle sores.

The Italian woman offered me a pocket handkerchief. I accepted it and wiped my eyes. She pointed to my thigh, my elbow. They're fine, I told her, I promise you. She shrugged as if to say, were I her son, she wouldn't let me be so relaxed. Honestly, I said, I'm fine. I told her she was very kind. She shrugged again and walked away and as she walked away I began to cry again. This is ridiculous, I thought. Something has made me into a monster of grief. I looked for the gris-gris in the fountain but the fountain had just come on and I couldn't find it anywhere with the water so disturbed. Then I began to panic and when I began to panic I realised it wasn't grief that I felt, but fear. Grief I could handle but fear, that was the worst.

9

AT THE
MANDARIN ORIENTAL,
HYDE PARK

(PART TWO)

Sorenson's hotel was just round the corner. I locked up the Pinarello outside the Embassy of Kuwait and walked through the lobby to the reception. I asked for Sorensen, in 312, and the man dialled but got no reply.

He's definitely not checked out? I asked.

Not yet Sir, said the man. He was like a Filipino Englishman.

Can I leave a message for him and wait here for a while? I asked.

Certainly, he said. What is the message?

Could you tell him I have something for him? I'll leave my number just in case.

Of course Sir, he said.

He was good, the Filipino Englishman. He was my proof that I wanted everything to be transparent, everything above board.

But I was not patient. After waiting a quarter of an hour and twice calling his room again, I figured it might just be easier to slip the picture under the door and be done with it, or at the least give it a knock. So I took the lift up to the third floor and made my way along the corridor to Room 312.

It was locked. I knocked and waited. I knocked again. I knocked a third time. Then I thought professionally and realised I needed some proof of delivery. I decided to hand my package to the Filipino Englishman, show him the picture even, get some kind of receipt. Then it was out of my hands. But as I walked back down the corridor to the lift I noticed the key to 312 hanging amongst a bunch of others on the back of the maid's trolley. She was in 306, singing softly to herself.

I stopped and thought for a moment. Then quickly I took the key plus a couple of bars of luxury soap for good measure and walked straight back to 312 where I let myself in.

What was I expecting? I was pretty sure he wouldn't be in there. But a part of me wouldn't have been that surprised if I'd walked in and found him slumped in the armchair from a coronary or fallen asleep in the bath or even worse naked on the bed with an orange in his mouth and a carving knife sticking out of his neck. In this scenario I would be doing the maid a favour.

But Sorensen wasn't playing out any scenario. The bathroom was empty and so was the armchair and so was the bed, which was made to perfection. Everything had been tidied, cleaned. The balcony door was locked. The minibar had been replenished. The maid had done me a service and I wasn't going to be interrupted. But was he still in the hotel?

He must have been, because in the cupboards his bags

were still there and his laundered shirts and his cowboy boots and his suit hanging up on the rail and a bunch of other clothes. In the top drawer of his bedside table I found his wallet and two passports, one US, one Norwegian. In his wallet there were over two thousand dollars in hundred dollar bills and around a thousand pounds in the fifties that he'd given me. The rest was just cards. Both passports showed he'd been born in Stavanger, as he'd told me, in 1930. The Norwegian passport was clean. In the US passport I counted stamps for India, Italy, France, Venezuela, Spain, Aruba, Egypt, Saudi, Nigeria, Australia, the Maldives, Argentina, Thailand, Costa Rica and a whole load of other places but mostly there were stamps for Mexico.

In the second drawer of his bedside table were cigarettes, lots of them.

In the bottom drawer of his bedside table was the old book Sorensen had been reading when I first saw him, sitting up in bed looking thin. The book was in German, written by someone called Schiefler, published in Berlin:

Verzeichnis des graphischen Werks Edvard Munchs.

I opened it and went straight to the back, where all the pictures were, and searched a little frantically for Sorensen's. There were skulls a go-go and loads of naked women with long dark hair, some drowning, some swimming, men in top hats looking like death, a woman on a bridge looking shocked. There were beaches and woods and living rooms and a variety show which was the only picture where anyone was fucking smiling. Of course there was The Scream (why the fuck hadn't I recognised that sky, the same sky on the thousand kroner note) and there was kissing: a woman snogging a skeleton; a couple necking by a window and what surely was the picture that until recently had been residing inside Mr Tecolote: a man and a woman so tightly embraced that their faces had become one.

I looked up the number, 102:

DER KUSS

The Kiss: but the rest was nonsense, more German I couldn't even guess at.

I went back to the picture in the book and looked at it again. The couple were the same as in Sorensen's, but the background was different. Sorensen's had been dark with houses in the background. *Der Kuss* was plain. Why the book then?

Why the book? Tucked into the spine, in one of the pages, was a single-ride subway ticket, and on that page, picture number 232:

DER KUSS AUF DEM FELDE

had been encircled lightly in pencil. Underneath was everything you needed to know about *Der Kuss auf dem Felde*, too much for me in fact:

H. In der Mitte des Bildes ein auf freiem Felde stehendes, sich umschlungen haltendes und küssendes bekleidetes Menschenpaar. Der Mann rechts, die frau links. Jenseits der dunkeln Fläche, auf welcher die beiden stehen, im Hintergrunde die Silhouette von Dorfhäusern, welche sich schwarz von Himmel abheben. Am Himmel helle under dunkle Wolkenstreifen. Vorn links ein angedeuteter Felsblock.

And on the next page:

209:266 Druck: Handdrucke des Künstlers und Lassally
Der Bildrand rechts, ca. 7 mm, auf den frühen
Exemplaren nur undeutlich abgedruckt.
Schwarz auf weißem Papier.

I didn't know what it all meant. But I knew enough to know I had this picture in my saddlebag. *Mann. Frau. Silhouette. Der Kuss auf dem Felde*: the kiss in the field.

I put the book on the bed and went to get my saddlebag. I wanted to double check. But as I was taking the record out, I heard the sound of key in door and the sound of Sorensen behind it.

8

BRYSTER

What did I have? I had everything, everything plus the book and an angular view of the bedroom. He had entered so clumsily that I'd even had time to weigh as options the bathroom and under the bed. But in the end I had gone for the wardrobe. The bed would have been safer if there had been clearance but it was impossible to tell since the covers kissed the carpet. The bathroom had more space. But the wardrobe had a comic feel and was by far the best for surprises. In the darkness, my right hand had found his walking stick resting in the corner. I would use it for self-defence if need be.

Good spa, he said to himself as he walked in, good spa. He was dressed in the livery of leisure: white towel gown with the Mandarin logo gold-embossed on the breast pocket; white towel slippers too small for his feet. I wondered what he had had. Acupuncture? A facial? Crystal therapy?

He walked in front and beyond, out of vision, then round the bed to the far side where he opened a drawer in the smaller of the two bedside tables – I'd not looked inside this one – and searched for cigarettes. Not finding them, he walked back to the table on the other side and took a pack from the second drawer down. Then he walked over to the balcony, opened the door and went outside.

While he was smoking, I considered what to do. I was still at this time hoping to hand over the picture. I would need to leave and come back. I couldn't just spring out of the wardrobe. But at some point, fairly soon, he would need to get dressed and I was very aware that next to me hung his suit and his shirts and in their little cubbyholes, neatly separated, his socks and his pants and stuff.

If he went to the bathroom, I could make my escape quite easily. Then I could knock a moment later, give him the picture, and leave. I didn't need to hang around. I could live without explanations. Or I could just slip the record under the door.

But the picture was worth a fucking fortune! It was over a hundred years old! It was by one of the greatest most fucked-up artists of the last century! The king of miserablists! It wasn't some little keepsake for a man too ill to get on a plane. Poyntz and I had expatriated, at great personal cost, a work of national significance, a rare and invaluable example of artistic endeavour at its most...

Fuck, I didn't fucking know. But then something very nasty happened that swung it.

He returned. He closed the balcony door. He drew the curtains. It was dark, fucking dark. I could see the bed and not much more. I heard him shuffle around a little, then get something from the desk that was opposite the bed, on my right-hand side. I heard the drawers open and then close. Fuck, I thought, he actually knows I'm here and he's picked up some implement of death. He's going to open the wardrobe doors and pepper my body with bullets. He's going to open the doors and plunge the knife in. He's got a samurai sword. Or a vial of acid. Or he'll just grab me by the neck and use those fucking massive hands of his to strangle me in seconds. I held the skull of his walking stick tightly and took deep, silent breaths.

What a pussy I am. It was worse. The old man went back to the far side of the bed, turned on the bedside light, took off his robe (but kept his slippers on), lay down on the bed and with one hand on the magazine he'd selected, *Bryster,* started to pleasure himself with the other.

No, I thought to myself, please God no. I do not have to witness this. I can close my eyes and pretend I am actually somewhere else. I can close my eyes and pretend I am in a wardrobe in a motel in Ontario and those Northern European noises I am hearing are in fact the noises of a man outside giving his car a push-start on a particularly snowy morning.

No, I thought to myself, I can close my eyes and close my ears and pretend the wardrobe is flying through the sky, out of the window, over Hyde Park. Look! There's my bicycle attached to the railings of the Kuwaiti Embassy! And look! There is the Queen and there are the Houses of Parliament!

Then I thought, no, I am not even in a wardrobe at all, I am just in a dark place learning Italian. Go! *Uno, due, tre, quattro, cinque, sette, otto, nove, dieci.* Now the teacher is asking me to name the US Postal Service team of 2004: Armstrong, Azevedo, Hincapie, Landis. Ekimov? Shit. I didn't know them all. Something else, something easier. Abdoujaparov's major wins? Green jerseys in the Tour, three, '91, '92 and '94? One each in the Giro and the Vuelta, '92 and '94? No, surely the other way round? '94 and —.

He was still going, and struggling a little. He had cast *Bryster* aside in deference to the power of imagination and he was using both hands. Jesus he had a massive cock. Shitting hell he really did. One of his slippers had fallen off. The whinnying had been replaced by words, Norwegian words, murmured low and indistinct. His face was nearing paroxysm. His toes clenched like an artificial hand. His septuagenarian man-boobs jiggled assiduously. The whole scene required pixellation. The money shot was coming. Look away. I looked away. I looked away. I looked away.

He was still going. At his age, I thought, maybe it always takes this long. I kept looking away and wondered what special kind of coronary I'd trigger if I jumped out now. People die of a broken heart. Can't you die of shame? Not that I was myself without shame. I'd broken into his hotel room and was watching him masturbating through the doors of a fitted wardrobe. That was one charge of voyeurism to add to the burglary and whatever crimes we had committed with Mr Tecolote and his priceless work of art. No pride in that.

Finally, when silence fell upon the room I looked again and saw a buttock heading towards the bathroom. The empty bed was ruffled and losing heat; the *Bryster* centrefold was staring up at the ceiling, unloved. A door opened and closed, there was a pause, then the sound of running water. Should I wait until he was in the shower? Or would he want to get his pants out first and warm them on the radiator? Some people were funny like that.

I felt it was time to seize the moment so I opened the wardrobe gradually and stepped onto the carpet of room 312 and crept out like a cat burglar, my saddle bag slung over my shoulder. It contained everything I needed in life plus the book by Gustav Schiefler about the picture by Edvard Munch which was in the record by John Adams. In the lift on the way down the bellhop looked at me kind of askance. Which was okay because I had just spent fifteen minutes hidden in a wardrobe, a little nauseous and asphyxiated, watching a solo act. So perhaps he was just picking up on the unusual vibe. But then I realised the reason he was looking at me was because in my right hand – I hadn't noticed – I was still clutching Sorensen's walking stick which is a contrary look for a courier: a walking stick, with a silver skull for a knob. I couldn't style it out. But I couldn't return it either. Not even the picture now. Everything had gone too far.

So I walked out, past the lobby where a man and a woman – I won't lie, they looked like detectives and the man was built like a brick shithouse – were talking to my friend the Filipino Englishman. I got on my bike and pedalled, the stick half-in, half-out of my bag, skull amongst the grime and the grease, and as I rode I wondered what the bellhop might be saying to the plainclothes and what the plainclothes might be saying to Sorensen and what Sorensen might be saying to the Filipino Englishman and what the Filipino Englishman might be saying to the plainclothes. But I thought less of the picture and more of the stick since the bellhop had clocked the stick and the stick placed me inside Room 312. The stick made no sense at all. Sorensen had used it during our first meeting like he really fucking needed it and again during our second meeting too. And yet when he came back from the spa he walked unaided and was full of the sprightliest movements.

7

POSSIBILITIES

This was my itch but it was not yet fully developed. I was unsure what to do, where to go. I had time on my hands so I went to scout some places for my date with Bella Meikels. I headed to the river on the slow roads with the idea of finding some possibilities and some lunch too.

Around about this time Poyntz started calling me, leaving messages on my voicemail, texting me. But I wasn't yet ready to speak to him so I let my phone ring and eventually I silenced it.

First I went to the Millennium Bridge, to the middle, which was one possibility. The middles of bridges are good places to go on a date, especially if you live north of the river and your date lives south. Tower Bridge is a good one but you need to check when the bridge is lifting.

There's no timetable for when the bridge lifts so first you need to talk to the bridge people. You call them and you explain you are going to propose to your wife and could they let you know when they are expecting a big schooner or warship or whatever. Not that I was going to propose to Kelly Zimmerman but this is what I did when I met her for a date on Tower Bridge. It was perfect. I told Kelly to meet me on the south side, about five minutes before the bridge was due to lift. But she turned up late, as the bridge was splitting and she got stuck on the north side for half an hour. I called her and said what the fuck you're on the wrong side like it was a big joke but she wasn't impressed and she didn't find it funny. To her it was an inconvenience, an unnecessary delay, being separated by a big ship and a body of water. Those bridge things take ages to come down.

Afterwards we walked along the South Bank and kissed and went to see *Ice Cold in Alex*, which I loved but which she said sucked. How can *Ice Cold in Alex* suck? It's a war film, she said, girls hate war films.

Generally though, the places Kelly and I met for dates were good. The best was Waterloo Station on roller skates. I bought a pair from a charity shop but I didn't try them on (why would you?) and they were too small, size eights so I wore them without socks. I wanted to dump them afterwards because carrying roller skates is a pain but they were about to become retro and Kelly said I should keep hold of them. Kelly had blades. Of course Kelly had blades.

We met on the concourse which is practically designed for rolling and made races from one end of the station to the other. During the third race, which was the decider, I got stopped by British Transport Police who ordered me off the station. I sat by the Victory Arch and waited for Kelly to join me. Five minutes later she came, in her socks, blades in hand. The police had told her to take them off, dirty fuckers.

But roller skating was risky for a first date so I cycled east, looking for more possibilities. I liked the tops and bottoms of parks, bandstands, Japanese gardens, duck ponds, statues of flawed heroes, these kinds of things.

316

Poyntz favoured interiors: the frozen food section of a supermarket (where do you go from there? I always thought), a room in a museum, a section in a reference library, a chair in a barber's shop. How does that work? I asked, when he proposed it for his date with the girl from Gossip, the hairdressers at the bottom of Ridley Road.

It's easy, Poyntz said. It's her area, isn't it?

Not a barber's shop.

A place where hair is cut.

But that's like a busman's holiday.

It will be interesting.

It will be fucking mad. You're having your hair cut?

Yeah.

In Giovanni's?

Yeah.

On Mount Pleasant?

Yeah.

And you're saying to the girl from Gossip, meet me there, while I'm sitting in the chair, chatting to Giovanni or Mario or whatever his name is, the Spurs fan, or the old man who's a genius barber but who never does anything but whistle arias and sigh and you're saying just come in, take a seat, it's a man's world but hey, this is cool for you, I'll just finish my buzz cut and then we can go and eat ice cream and make whoopee?

Yeah.

I think she'll run a mile.

Well if she runs a mile then she's not the One.

But you know she's not the One anyway.

That's true, said Poyntz, that's true.

The Kashmiri Beauty was the One but Poyntz had only met her once, fleetingly at a party, as she was leaving and Poyntz was arriving. They passed in the hallway.

They smiled at each other and he said hi and she said hi and literally that was that. Poyntz spent the rest of the evening asking everyone at the party who she was. But nobody knew. For weeks afterwards I'd call him up and ask what he was up to and without fail he'd reply that he was looking for the Kashmiri Beauty. I tolerated it for a while then told him to forget it or he'd make himself mentally ill.

We'd discussed quite a few times what Poyntz would do if he bumped into the Kashmiri Beauty again and what kind of date he'd go on.

Imagine she's flying back to Kashmir the next day, I said, for an arranged marriage or whatever. The flight's booked, her bags are packed. Then she sees you —.

Hold on, Poyntz interrupted, I'm not sure she's from Kashmir. That's just my hunch.

Okay, I said, whatever. This is a scenario. We're scenario-ising.

Okay. A scenario. But it's pretty unlikely someone like her would settle for an arranged marriage.

This is a scenario, Poyntz.

But scenarios need to be realistic.

Not 100 per cent realistic. Anyway, this is the scenario. She sees you. In the street. You stop her in her tracks. You cycle over. Hey, aren't you the girl etc. etc. You get talking. You make her laugh. You ask her out that evening. She ums and ahs, all coy. Eventually she agrees. What's the date?

It's a good question, said Poyntz, thinking.

So?

No frozen food?

No.

Can I take her to the velodrome?

She hates bicycles.

She can't.

She does.

Then she's not the One.

Okay. She likes bicycles but she's already been to the velodrome that week.

Wicked. I like her even more. Is the London Planetarium open in the evening?

I'm not sure. Anyway, it's closed for refurbishment.

Damn. How about that museum full of surgical instruments... whatsitsname?

No. The Kashmiri Beauty is squeamish.

Then she's not the One. If she's squeamish she'd be bad in bed.

She's amazing in bed. That museum just makes her feel funny.

Okay, said Poyntz. I've got it.

Go on.

We meet at London Bridge station.

No stations.

No wait. We meet outside London Bridge station.

Where?

Dunno. Wherever. By the cathedral.

Okay.

I have two tickets to Leith Hill. I've got a lantern and a wicker hamper full of fine wine. We take the slow train with all the commuters. Our seats have been reserved. We get off at Dorking or whatever the stop is and trek to the top of the hill. I have a key to the gothic tower. We watch shooting stars and the planes coming into land at Gatwick.

It's nice, I said, but it's not reassuring.

What do you mean?

She doesn't know you.

She trusts me.

How can she? She doesn't know you. You can't take someone to the middle of a wood in Surrey on a first date for fuck's sake.

She's adventurous.

Maybe, I said, but she's not mad.

So it went on and on and on. But it was all pie in the sky. Because how was Poyntz going to ever bump into the Kashmiri Beauty? I at least had the prospect of a date with Bella Meikels. But I still needed to find some more possibilities.

6

At the
Golden Syrup Factory,
Silvertown

This was how I ended up in Silvertown. I'd left Bankside behind me and wound my way through Bermondsey and Rotherhithe and Deptford and Greenwich and rode as far as Charlton and beyond, looking all the time for possibilities.

There were possibilities enough along the way but none which filled me with great boldness. There were clay pipes on Deptford Beach and the view to Canary Wharf from the alleyway mooring next to the Master Shipwright's House. There were the forbidden swimming ponds in Repository Woods where we could rendezvous on Ha-Ha Road but that wasn't so far from Poyntz's trip to Leith Hill and invading private property might be problematic on a first date. There were safe options like the Meridian Line at Greenwich where Poyntz and I had raced in our first alleycat and there was the walk from Plumstead to Erith but I didn't know Bella Meikels so well and she might take exception to gas works and pumping stations and sewage depots.

This got me onto the view across the river, a land of promise where the smells were of hops and sugar and where I could see the twin turrets of the Tate and Lyle factory, the most beautiful sight in London. If I couldn't smell the molasses (there must have been a northerly wind) I could at least imagine the smell of the molasses and suddenly I had my date with Bella Meikels right in front of me. In my imaginings it went like this:

We meet underneath the Monument, right underneath it, where the inscription gives directions to St Magnus the Martyr but where instead we walk in the opposite direction, up King William Street past St Mary Wool-noth to Bank, to ride the DLR together. She is dressed as she was, the only way that I know her, dark jeans and a sweater, black pumps with bows but this time dark socks and as we get onto the train she says to me, smiling, I think it is going to snow.

We get off and change trains. Where are we going? she says. Pontoon Dock, I tell her. It's only two stops away. She looks up at the map.

Outside snow is falling heavily. It is starting to settle on buildings, on cars, in the parks. Children are looking up at the pink-and-grey sky in surprise, holding out their hands, catching flakes as they fall.

Will you be cold? I ask.

I don't think so, she replies.

We get off at Pontoon Dock. It's a funny place, more of a non-place: there's a concrete train station in the sky and that's it.

We're heading to the river? she asks.

In that direction, I reply.

Where to?

322

It's a surprise, I tell her.

When will I find out? she asks, a little nervous.

Soon, I say, a little nervous.

It's not pretty where we are. It's a dual carriageway, busy and all that's ahead is the roundabout and the Texaco. The road's longer than I remember. If we can just get to the roundabout, I think to myself, everything will be okay.

I want to take her arm but it feels too soon. Instead we walk side-by-side and find ourselves bumping into each other, just a little. Every time it happens it's a thousand volts. Our footsteps in the snow are making a record of our date, but when I look back – we have finally made the roundabout – the snow is falling so thick that the record is already being erased.

There, I say, pointing to the factory. It's where they make Golden Syrup.

You're taking me on a date to the Golden Syrup factory?

Yeah, I say. What do you think?

I think that's great, she says.

There's a sign that reads: Visitors Please Report to Reception so we walk in and report to reception and the receptionist makes a call and straightaway a man in a green blazer with gold piping appears. You must be Mr Black, he says. I've been expecting you. Then he looks at Bella and bows his head and smiles and says welcome.

There's a long walk along corridors with doors either side that have names and job titles embossed onto gold plates. They say things like:

RODDY McDOUGALL
DISTRIBUTION MANAGER, MOLASSES

and

RANDOLPH SAVAGE JNR
ACQUISITIONS AND OPERATIONS, CANE SUGAR

and

DR DOLORES CORTEZ-DOMINGUEZ
HEAD OF GRANULATION RESEARCH

At the end of the corridor there's another room where the man in the green blazer gives us a safety briefing and we're issued with white overalls and hats. Bella's hat has a net at the back which she uses to tie up her hair and for the first time I see the nape of her neck and I am smitten.

You can hear the roar of the factory. We take a lift to the third floor, walk another set of corridors and emerge onto a gantry that encircles the entire hall. Everything is down below. There are four steel vats with tiny lids that clap with steam and they're linked to a giant mixing chamber where a horizontal arm rotates three and a half thousand litres of syrup at two revolutions a minute. From the chamber, tube tentacles run to ten separate production lines where the green-gold tins are given their final wash, dried and pushed along one-by-one to the feeding terminal. Nine hundred and seven grams of partially inverted refiner's syrup is poured, with mechanical precision, into each tin. The lids are stamped and off they roll. At the end of the line they're laser-marked and weighed and the workers check for indentations, scratches, spillages, stickiness and then they're packed into boxes, thirty in each and forklifted off the shop floor to the distribution depot.

We take the metal lift down to the ground and while the

man in the green blazer is trying to explain the process of passing linear polarised light through a sucrose solution Bella looks down onto the mixing chamber and says what if?

What if what? I ask.

What if you fell by mistake into that thing?

To do that you'd have to dive from the gantry.

Not if you were chief tester or something. Or if there was a fly in the mix and your manager told you to fish it out.

You'd have to hang onto the giant arm and climb up. Don't worry, I'd come and save you.

How?

I'd jump in, pull you out.

Then we'd both be stuck, she says.

On the floor of the factory I watch her as she wanders amongst the machines. There is something very beautiful about the way that she wanders, transfixed, hands stuck in the pockets of her overalls. Myself, I cannot concentrate. Every time I look at a tin of syrup my focus moves to her. I am not in control of my eyes. They have a sugary craving: the study of her legs, her hips, her hands, her arms, her breasts, her lips, her hair.

Her chestnut-coloured hair which runs right to left across her brow.

She is nodding to the man in the green blazer who is explaining things to her. They walk down the line together. She points to things, he talks. She asks a question, he replies. She makes a joke, he laughs. Then she has stopped listening although he is still talking and she is looking for me, like she has suddenly remembered our date. She looks behind her, beyond her and to either side. She cannot see me because I am behind a machine, watching her. I move a little so she can see me.

We are two lines from each other, twenty metres or so and in amongst the noise. When she catches me she stops and stares. She is framed by pistons and pouring systems, bright steel, dark gold. I stare back at her and for several moments we are lost in the gaze that we hold. Here is something bigger than reality, something bigger and better than the continuous noise and industry, the striving and the work, the destination-making and opportunity-taking. Something amazing has happened.

Our parting gift, inevitably, is a tin of syrup each. That's very kind, she tells the man in the green blazer. It's been very interesting, thank you.

You're very welcome, he smiles, it's a pleasure. Then he looks outside and tells us to be careful. Be careful, he says, with the snow.

She pops to the loo. I wait outside the gates and try to roll a cigarette but my hands are too cold and the snow is spoiling the papers. It's thick on the ground now: ten, fifteen centimetres have fallen and it carries on falling. The factory is covered, the car park, the long road down to the river, the trees that line the old tram track are covered. I shiver and watch a plane coming into City Airport, its lights twinkling away, and I think about where to go next. Around here, it's just Terry's: all the pubs are long boarded up, the California then Cundy's where even the strippers couldn't bring in the punters. As I am thinking Pontoon Dock and drinks somewhere along the line – Limehouse or all the way back to Bank with the Square Mile weekend-deserted and covered in a delicious carpet of white – and as I am finally lighting my cigarette and taking that first pull into my lungs, I turn around to look for Bella and she is there quite suddenly coming towards me in a half-run, not letting her eyes away. She stops just short of me and looks down for a second, nervous, and then looks up again straight into my eyes. She says thank you that was fun and we are holding each other, hands clasped, her head on my chest with the snow falling upon it in great volume and the smell of perfume on her neck and then we part a little and she takes the cigarette out of my mouth where I had forgotten it was and she takes a quick drag and then throws it into the snow and after that we kiss.

After we have kissed she looks at me again and says, by the way.

By the way what? I say.

By the way, she says, dropping the tin on the ground, I don't really like Golden Syrup.

That's okay, I say. Neither do I.

This was how I imagined my date with Bella Meikels.

5

MESSAGES

At Terry's cafe I ordered tea and two eggs and after I'd eaten my eggs I thought it was probably the moment so I took the stick, its tip on the ground, and had a go at unscrewing the skull. I didn't really care if anyone was watching but Terry's was empty anyway: lunch was over, even for latecomers, and the tables had been wiped clean, ready for breakfast tomorrow.

The skull wouldn't budge until I found the catch, a tiny thing hidden just above the line where the silver met the cane. After that it was no more difficult than opening a bottle of water. I placed the skull on the table and looked inside the hollow and finding nothing, turned it upside down. Out fell the picture, just like it was meant to be.

This was confusing as fuck. Initially I didn't know what it was and the Perspex casing I found a little sinister. But I had been brave today – I'd suffered watching a man masturbate from inside a fitted wardrobe – and so I removed the little seal at the top and with my fingertips a little greased from eating eggs poked my way in and took out what was clearly another picture. Perhaps it was one of those madonnas, I thought, or the men in hats or maybe it was the one where someone actually smiles.

But it was the same fucking picture.

Exactly the same fucking picture: same scene, same couple kissing, same houses in the background, same style, same technique, same everything.

Well they were prints weren't they? Maybe this was number seventy-three and the other one was number one hundred and eighty-nine and in fact they were two-a-penny and hanging in living rooms all around the world or probably they were sitting in attics, stuffed into suitcases and shoeboxes, forgotten and practically worthless.

Why the fuck then had he felt the need to hide one of them inside an owl and the other inside a walking stick? Was this how he got his kicks, aside from *Bryster* magazine?

I put version A, the stick's, on the table using a sugar, a salt, a ketchup and a brown sauce for weighting purposes. I consulted the book for some clues but it was no less German than when I'd looked at it in Sorensen's hotel room. Then I got version B, the owl's version, and using a pepper, a vinegar, a spanner and a wrapped-up, packed-up inner tube, I put the two pictures side-by-side.

The old dear was looking at me quizzically. You know we close at five, she said.

Sure, I said. Just give me a second. I was concentrating on my game of spot-the-difference.

It's not that I want to rush you, she was saying, but I need to be home to make me mum's dinner you see. She shuffled back and forth from the kitchen, J-cloth in one hand, broom in the other. She worries if I'm not there on the dot, she went on. Always a worrier, my mum. If there's anyone —.

But I'd got it, spotted the difference, and was already

out of the door. I had packed up, left money on the table, turned my phone back on and got back on my bike. I had thirteen missed calls, ten messages on my voicemail and six texts, all of them from Poyntz. In reverse chronology:

> This is seriously important. Don't give it to him.
> What is your fucking problem?
> Where the fuck are you?
> Call me you fucker.
> Call me now. Now = now. NOW.
> Call me.

The voice messages I listened to as I rode; the first message was from Poyntz:

What the fuck. The Armenian keeps calling me. He says you've got the fucking picture. He needs it Sam. Don't ask me why. He just needs it. Listen dude I'm sorry. I should never have told him about it. I got it into my head that he might have helped us. Now he just wants it for himself. Give me a call for fuck's sake. I can explain everything. And listen I don't know how you fucking found it. I can only assume you have broken into my fucking place. For the record I am fucking pissed about you breaking into my place. You owe me some talking so call. Call now. Before it gets too late.

The second message was from Sorensen:

Thank you for your message. I would very much like the picture, thank you. My flight leaves tonight. Perhaps you can call the hotel immediately and tell me where I can meet you. I think it might be worth your while.

The third message was from Guzzman:

Hey Sam. It's Guzz. I think I saw the Black Goddess last night. Give me a call.

The fourth message was another from Poyntz:

I'm seriously worried about you now. It's quarter to three, give me a fucking call dipshit.

The fifth message was from Sorensen:

I need you to call me at the hotel urgently please. I need that picture now.

The sixth message was from Fat Barry:

Sam. It's Barry Gardiner here. Listen I don't know what the fuck you've been up to but none of it sounds any good mate. All sounds a bit fucking bad to me. I've just had a fucking call from some yank asking me where you live. I told him to fuck right off. Then he said it was about a job you did for him and that you'd got something of his and he wanted it back. So I asked him what the job was and he said it was a pick-up from the Hotel Priam last Monday. Funnily enough, Monday was your last job, Sam, at the Hotel Priam. Funny that. But here's the funniest thing. I got a call from the client later that day, different man, saying no fucking rider ever turned up. I remember clear and I'll tell you why: because I had to fucking defend you, say you'd not been well, say you'd had an accident and all the crap and once I'd given it my best, I sent another rider. In fact, I sent Other Sam. He picked up, Room 35, everything hunky-dory. The job's done, finished, I told the yank. No it ain't, he said. You've still got his stuff. But he won't fucking

331

tell me what it is and he won't fucking tell me where you went to get it. So I'm hoping you will fucking tell me what the fuck is going on because I haven't a fucking clue. Then the cunt tells me he's going to come over and talk to me in person. I'm not going to let any old fucker through my fucking door and I didn't, for your information, let him know where you live. But Samuel, I'm minded to, if you don't tell me what's going on. And by the way, I know you wanted to quit and all that. Well just in case you've changed your mind, don't fucking bother. Because you are never ever going to work for Zenith Couriers again. Period. You cunt.

The seventh message was from Early Man:

Sam. It's me. I don't know what's going on but you should know the police have just walked into the office asking for you and Fat Barry's going fucking mental. Laters.

The eighth message was from Kelly Zimmerman:

Er. Yeah. I'm not sure if this is the right number but if it is, if it's Sam's number, Sam Black, Sam it's Kelly here. Long time etc. Listen Sam I've just had a fucking weird call from some guy called Barry. Barry I didn't catch his surname. Said he was your boss or something. For some reason he seemed to think I was your mum which is a bit fucked up. He wanted to know where you were. I don't know how the fuck he got my number. How the fuck did he get my number Sam? And why's he calling me? Anyway. Bye.

The ninth message was from Poyntz again:

Call me. I am genuinely concerned for your welfare.

The final message, the tenth, was from the Armenian:

Motherfucker. My name is Mashtots. I am like associate of your friend Pushpendra. This is my number. Give me call. Then we can be friend. If you don't give me call, let me say I will come and say hello to you. Okay. We are friend. Okay. Goodbye.

4

LEIBNIZ UNDONE

In normal circumstances it might have been difficult to take someone called Mashtots Hambartzumian seriously but on this occasion I had decided to make an exception. My principal concern was that he'd be at Poyntz's when I turned up. He wasn't but he'd made his presence known, turning the place over and killing Leibniz in the process.

I don't know why he killed Leibniz. He didn't need to. It's not like the bird had any of the answers. I'd asked him myself for fuck's sake.

Leibniz was lying on the floor, rigor-mortised, eyes open, beak closed, one wing tucked under his body, the other sticking up in the air, broken and immovable. Maybe the Armenian had opened the door of the cage just to top off his rampage and the poor bird suffered a heart attack on feeling freedom. But it looked like he'd been grabbed and crushed by that ham of a hand.

The rest of the place was like a bomb site. The sofas, beds, chairs had all been overturned. Everything was on the floor: books, records, pictures, lamps, mirrors, everything. All the cupboards in the kitchen had been cleared out and there was broken crockery all over the tiles. The bathroom was a fucking mess and in his bedroom every single passport photo had been ripped off the wall, every single photo save mine. It was the crappiest stitch-up ever.

I didn't want Poyntz to see this but he had to. I needed him to know what this animal was capable of. I didn't get it. I didn't understand the spite. It didn't seem to be the most intelligent way of looking for what was missing. There was no method, just a blind random free-for-all which probably got more and more violent the longer it went on. Leibniz was probably the coup de grâce.

I felt sad and regretful. With nothing on my mind I would have taken it room-by-room, working on what felt right and all the pictures in my memory. Some things couldn't be put right: all the crap that was broken and the budgie of course. Another dead bird I had on my hands.

But there was too much on my mind, far too much, so I decided I should just do something little, whatever it was, to repair the damage and then finish the business with Sorensen once and for all. I called the hotel and left a message for him to meet me in person at half past seven. I said he should be at the crossroads between Clerkenwell Road and St John Street and that I would give him his picture then. I texted Poyntz and told him to be at the same place at eight. After that I picked up every single record that was on the floor, there must have been several hundred, and returned them to where I thought they lived. This took me a whole hour. I put the original Munch – version A, the one Sorensen had put in the stick – in Poyntz's copy of Charles Mingus's *Epitaph*, the record he'd just bought, plus the five hundred pounds I owed him, and put the record in amongst all the others. I left the fake, version B, the one we'd carried all the way back from Norway, in the John Adams record in my bag. Finally, I picked up Leibniz – he was so light and his bright little feathers so smooth – and I put him in a sock and put the sock in the bag too. Then I got on my bike and headed for the rendezvous. It was seven o'clock.

3

SHORT RIDE
ON A
FAST MACHINE

This beautiful city, this beautiful city I have loved all my life would be the death of me, Mr Bembo had warned.

As I rode in my SIDIs and yellow socks and my favourite white shorts and my favourite black top and my favourite cap I thought of the great hoodwinker sweating away in his tower, eating bad food and putting pins into my own little voodoo doll: Samuel Black in white shorts astride a *spumoni*-sprayed Pinarello, no gris-gris in his seatpost.

I switched on my lights and rode.

It was almost dark and in my stomach I had a faint sickness, an empty pit and my beats felt higher than normal. The professional cyclist's heart is enlarged, his rate's abnormal: Indurain rested at 30 beats per minute. I rested at 56. Take out my heart and put it on a platter, take Indurain's and spot the difference: child and adult. What had fear done to their hearts? Made them stronger, bigger, girded their arteries? Or had it a thrombotic effect, crowding the chambers, blocking the avenues, dashing all that high altitude training in Tenerife? What wasn't there to fear when you were riding down Mount Teide at sixty, seventy miles an hour? Did the heart still beat slow when death lay round the corner? Or were they normal human beings, the professionals, who feared normal things: terminal illness, the loss of a loved one?

To ride these streets, you cannot be a pussy. These streets do not smile on nervousness. You learn to cycle through the nerves and you lose your fear. New fears replace old fears but they in turn are vanquished. Your heart grows stronger as you make the journey. That's the theory at least.

One big crash, two crashes, three: you have everything under your belt. You have near-misses, minor prangs, confrontations with drivers, confrontations with pedestrians. You have confrontations with police officers and fellow riders and shouting matches with controllers. You have felt the pain of being doored and floored and capsized by black ice and slicks of oil. You have learnt who to respect and who to disdain. You have ridden eighty miles through pouring rain and thought at the end of the day, no more, and the following morning you have got back on your saddle with the skies clear blue. You have felt invincible, untouchable: nothing can shake you. You are supreme and greedily suck up respect and hatred in equal measure: both taste delicious and you don't give a shit about either because you are in your own world, the world of you, your bicycle and the road on which you ride. You make your own way in that world, your own path is the one *you* take and there is nothing better than the taste of freedom.

At night, everything is heightened. This is when you love riding most of all. The roads are emptier, quicker.

You luxuriate in the space you have been given, there's less need to assert your dominance and instead you can be playful. Plus, there is more grain to life at night: all the characters are out, the life-dancers and danger-mongers and bottom-feeders. Amongst orange everywhere are the neon pinks and blues. You may be fuelled yourself: a little high, a little drunk. There is no place here for fear.

Yet fear I felt. Not that I rode with fear: I rode as if I felt no fear. But the fear I felt was in my head and it did not make itself known to my arms or my legs. My arms and my legs had thoughts of their own, they were dancing to their own tune. They were dancing to a seven/eight time or a five/eight, something that wasn't a fucking waltz. They were dancing to the full symphonic sound, the orchestra of noise: first a woodblock tapping out a pulse at one hundred and fifty-eight, four taps then the rest of the band strikes up, loud as hell, the animals entering ten-by-ten: percussion, wind, strings, brass. Quick-ass brass too, everyone playing double-time like the conductor's lost the plot. Slow down, whoever's wielding the baton! What's with the heavy beats? The gratuitous fanfaring? All that damned syncopation? Why so fast? Too much tension! Too much build-up! Too much heaviness! Too serious! And hey! What was that? A kettle drum? Give me a fucking rest! Kettle drums hurt my fucking ears! Stop, please! When will you quit, wrong track?

Somewhere near Aldgate it quit, 'Short Ride in a Fast Machine', one final blast of imagined noise followed by a final blast of silence and then I've cross-faded to the song I always play in my head-funeral, a track Poyntz once played to me nine times in a row, when we were stoned. I actually quite like it. As my coffin is carried in – Poyntz front right, Fat Barry front left, Guzzman and Early picking up the rear, four bicycles carrying the sixteen-bar cycles – those dreamy D minor chords bring up a nice slow four/four, then the five-note descending riff and as the fat languorous bass says hi at the beginning of sixteen-bar cycle two, joined by the snare, it looks like the boys are stepping into the rhythm, even Fat Barry who has no off-saddle rhythm: they walk in sync up the aisle at Limehouse where I made seventeen prayers. And on the fourth sixteen-bar cycle, through the DFG and E sax, in comes Rodney and all the beautiful girls are crying. All of the women, all the children. My pall is black velvet, a *spumoni* Pinarello embroidered on top and the real thing is being carried behind my coffin, battered, scraped and bent. Inside the coffin I'm okay. I'm dead but I'm okay. I'm wearing my SIDIs and my yellow socks and my favourite white shorts and my favourite black top made from merino wool and my favourite cap. Well actually I'm wearing my second favourite cap but there you go: something must have happened to my favourite.

I can hear Fat Barry's heavy breathing and see the tears rolling down his face and the tears rolling down Poyntz's face and the tears rolling down Early's and Guzzman's and all the beautiful girls' faces, all of them are crying especially the ones I never managed to kiss which is pretty much all of them apart from Kelly Zimmerman who's there at the back but she's not shedding any tears. All the Zenith crew have turned up and there's a big crew from Gazelle and a crew from Dart and a whole posse of people from the other firms: riders from Premier, London Wheels, Excelsior, these kinds of riders. Spinks is there, picking his nose, Byron too. John Heimerdinger's in rapture, Mitsu, Bolo, Little Jonathan. Slim's crying, Salowitz is impassive. There's Salowitz's girlfriend Sara or Zara or Cara and her fit mate Hannah

or is it Anna. There's Bobby Gottlieb and Anders Thor-
bjorn and Franco and Alisha Conn what a bitch and
the lovely Jeanne-Marie and the lovely Geraldine and
lovely Mary Big Tits, who married the Brazilian cage
fighter who once beat up Poyntz. Big Nuts is there too
plus Belgian Jim and Solomon Weisendanger and Louis
and Malcolm and there's Mauricio who can't swim and
who cycled into the canal drunk on a freezing January
night and owed his life to a zookeeper. There's Sue from
the office with her husband Derek next to her, he's a
postman.

Some of my relatives are there too but my dad is not
there or if he is there the bastard is hiding behind a pil-
lar. At the back of the church is that new rider, Other
Sam, and next to him is Yelena Zykov.

2

THE BLACK GODDESS

Yelena Zykov. The Black Goddess. At the crossroads in Clerkenwell, out of my head-funeral, I watched her pass me at speed, heading west.

I had stopped and was waiting for Sorensen, good boy that I was. I had parked up and was early, a whole fifteen minutes early. I had rolled a cigarette and smoked it and rolled another and I had waited for every passing black cab to stop and disgorge a tall and elderly Scandinavian confidence-trickster. I had a wrench with which to defend myself or attack, should attack be necessary. I was visible and ready to do battle or preferably just hand over the fake, express ignorance about the real one, and get on with my life. I would reason with the Armenian if the Armenian came my way and if he didn't I would try to forget about him. If I couldn't, I would seek him out in the presence of an independent witness and explain the situation. I was putting my affairs in order.

I was putting my affairs in order. I decided to call Bella Meikels. Then I decided not to call her until I had handed over the picture and wrapped things up with Sorensen. Then I thought, don't be a pussy just call her so I got her card from my wallet, the crimson brown and magnolia card which I'd put next to the picture of my mother, and I dialled the number.

After this I pressed red and thought hold on, what am I going to say?

Twice more I dialled and pressed red and finally I let it ring and it rang eight times then went to voicemail. So I left her a message: Hello, I said. My name's Sam. You left me your number on the Tube. I was thinking perhaps we could go for a date. I've got somewhere in mind. I think. Anyway. This is my number. Text me or something. Bye.

Then I texted Poyntz. I wanted to be super cryptic. I didn't want anyone to understand the message apart from me and him. I wasn't going to let anyone go near it, not Sorensen or the Armenian or the cops who were looking for me. So no mention of Mingus, not even of the record. No mention of that fuckhead Munch, no mention of either of the fucking pictures. I just said:

Everything is okay. Listen to Charles

and I left it there. And as I sent it, the very moment it pinged, I saw the Black Goddess pedal right through the crossroads, right in front of my eyes.

Of course I had to follow her.

Straightaway I ran to my bike and clipped in and started to pursue. I had ten minutes to spare and I could always be a little late for Sorensen. I didn't want anything more than confirmation, a little glimpse of the legend, maybe some taster of the afterlife. If it wasn't her, well it wasn't her and I could put one final nail in the coffin of my mumbo-jumboism.

I couldn't tell. To begin with she was a speck ahead of me and didn't once look back. She certainly rode like Yelena, more than a maniac, weaving and deceiving, bum in the air, head bobbing, shoulders feinting. I thought perhaps it could be Missy Miller who rode for Dart but when I got closer I saw that the bike was all wrong for Missy. She took me halfway up the hill and then left onto Hatton Gardens and from there led me a merry dance, a *danse macabre* you could say: a circuit of Hatton Wall, Leather Lane, St Cross Street, Kirby Street, Greville Street, Saffron Hill, St Cross again, Hatton Place, and then back onto Hatton Wall to do the whole safari all over again.

I followed and every time I turned a corner, she turned the one ahead. Not once was she ever more or less than a turn or a block away. Every time I changed direction she changed direction too. I couldn't catch up, make speed. It was like she was fixed ahead of me. I glimpsed her then she disappeared.

We rode quick, very quick, then quicker. There were no cars, few people. The pubs were open and noisy, the Bleeding Heart, the One Tun – pubs couriers would sometimes drink in when they were fed up with the Duke of York – but everyone was shuttered inside. The one-way markings the Black Goddess ignored. I followed my siren slavishly. The song she sang was more a kind of Ukrainian Hope Sandoval on a sit-up-and-beg than the Yelena Zykov that I knew, battering her Bob Jackson and listening to hardcore. I was stuck to my Pinarello all right, stuck like Odysseus to his mast, prisoner to his ship, listening to the liquid music, and finally drawing nearer. The Black Goddess sang soft and slow, a lament from ancestors' past, a threnody in Ukrainian, wailing, dirge-like, pretty damn awful in fact – not my kind of music at all – but kind of beautiful at the same time. I moved to within ten metres of her back wheel. Surely it was her: same bike, same get-up, same riding style, same refusal to engage, to look back, same aloof no-one-can-touch-me Yelena, the *noli me tangere* Yelena, this was the Black Goddess all right. But I had yet to see her face.

Quickly, we abandoned the circuit, right at St Cross instead of left and then right again onto Gray's Inn Road: it was like I was being taken back to Zenith or up to Percy Circus on that alleycat victory of hers. I felt I had never ridden faster in my life but everything was slowing down to zero, to a standstill, to nothing. The hymn she still sung, louder and louder as I approached her. At the crossroads which I had traversed every which way a thousand times the lights were green, turning to amber and red. I should head back to Sorensen, I thought, it was almost half past seven. He may be there, waiting for me. He may be anxious, perturbed, needing to catch his flight. Big man wanted his picture. I was going to give him his fucking picture.

Another right turn, three minutes downhill, I'd be there. Could I say I'd seen the Black Goddess? Surely I could. I had seen her bike, her clothes. What had she looked like? Fit as fuck? That face, that crazy beauty? I didn't see her face, I'd admit. I couldn't catch her up.

Couldn't catch her up? A ghost? A little sprite of the mind? No wonder, people would say, she doesn't exist. They'd laugh. You're right, I'd reply, lamely. I sometimes get confused.

She doesn't exist, she does. She does, she doesn't.

She did! She existed! I saw her! With my own eyes! As we crossed the line, the lights long gone red, I saw her. Racing up to it. Just a glimpse, I told myself, before I peel off. Just the face. That's all I wanted to see. Her face. Her crazily beautiful face.

But her crazily beautiful face was very suddenly beautiful no longer but a gorgon, a death mask, freshly fucked-up by the two-tonner that had totalled her on Tower Bridge Road, newly bruised, boss-eyed and bloodied, contorted, de-toothed, half-tongued, gums flailing, the kind of picture best left in the mortuary or the grave, six feet under, lid closed, end of story. As I stared at this horror transfixed, unable to shift eyeballs, unable to move, stuck in time, staring at this cracked-up fucked-up mirror, I heard in the Black Goddess's threnody a different kind of melody, a blasting screech and hiss to my left – had I moved off the fucking road or not? – the kind of screech and hiss that is so long and unfavourable that every muscle in your body locks up in grim readiness for what's coming next, the portent, the crisis, the spectacular. Has it come yet? *Not yet.* Is it coming soon? It has to! *Be patient.* But the screeching is still there, I can still hear it! *I know, the screech is still...*

After this, my ears will tell you, there were four noises, all in quick succession. There was the noise of my Pinarello being struck, and both of us were flung high into the air. Then there was the noise of the yellow car that struck me striking the shop on the corner. There was the noise of my bag – which somehow had gone its own way – hitting the ground and spilling its contents. Then there was the noise of me, basically doing the same thing.

There would have been other noises after that, plenty of other noises I am sure, but I can only imagine what those noises were.

My Pinarello would never be ridden again. You see those two carrying her up the aisle? That's pretty much the long and short of it. It's not a recoverable situation. You can see there's a crack in the top tube and her stays are all warped and buckled. You might salvage the brake levers and the rear derailleur is not so bad, plus the tyres

I suppose, perhaps the crank. But the frame is what the Pinarello is all about, and her frame is fucked.

Second, the yellow car. The yellow car I saw just a little of, as I hovered and floated above everything. It was the same car I'd been thinking of too much: the Porsche Cayenne. It had hit the curb at the back and flipped, rolled, crashed into the shop and uprighted itself again. The Armenian had stumbled out of the car and was lying on the pavement, dead.

Third, the bag, my Ortleib Zip City, much-loved, much-used, not so great for big packages but perfect for smaller ones. My habit was to leave it unzipped and by the time it thudded to the ground there was nothing much inside but air. My wallet, my phone, Sorensen's picture and Poyntz's budgerigar-in-a-sock and all my bike tools and all manner of other crap: they were all happily scattered, across the happy scene.

Finally there was me. Well I floated. For a hell of a long time. Because it's really true what they say, you know, about your life flashing in front of you, just like it does in the movies. I saw everything I didn't see in my first crash (the carving knife thrown at me by the rotisserie chef, the peep show merchant, the tears running down my face, etc.). And then I saw more: the eggs I'd had for breakfast, Poyntz drunk eating a chicken burger, the Armenian and his housebreaker chum surprised on the stairs. But mostly I saw Yelena Zykov, my Pinarello locked onto her back wheel, her Bob Jackson frame and her scuffed SIDIs; the Black Goddess in her black shorts, black T-shirt, black Le Bourget stockings (woollens in winter, fishnets in spring and late autumn). As I drew alongside her, I saw that she was as remarkable as ever I remembered, looks of angularity and darkness, figure full and heavenly, eyes bejewelled, majestic on two wheels. And as I looked at the Black Goddess she looked back at me and winked. But when I tried to return the compliment I realised I could not, because I could not open my eyes, they would not open at all, however hard I tried.

1

ZIPP WHEELS/TIGERS

I dreamt I was at Delphi: I had an appointment to see the Oracle there. But I was early for my appointment with the Oracle so I was killing time, reading a magazine.

(I flew over Delphi once, on the way back from Athens. I was watching *The Big Lebowski* and had a window seat. During the hallucination scene, after the Dude's White Russian is spiked, I looked out of the window and saw this great big peninsula jutting out of Greece like a bunion. I looked it up on the in-flight magazine and realised that the mountain beyond was Mount Parnassus and that somewhere on the slopes below was Delphi, home to Mr Bembo's predecessors.)

Anyway I was early, killing time, reading Poyntz's copy of *Cycling Weekly* in fact, the one with the feature about Jens Voigt. There were a bunch of other people also waiting to see the Oracle: it was like a doctor's surgery and the ticketing system seemed pretty strict. I was number one hundred. Every five or ten minutes a voice called a number, and someone got off their stone bench, ticket in hand, and took the hot dusty path round the corner.

A few of the people I knew. There was Phyllis, the

landlady at the Montmorency. She was number eighty-seven. Early Man was there, taller than everyone else, looking vacant and a little worried. Fat Barry was there too. His number was after mine, number one hundred and six or something. I asked him what he wanted from the Oracle. What d'you think? he said, aggrieved. I want to know if you're coming back to Zenith Couriers or not!

What an idiot, what a waste of a question! Why didn't he just ask me himself? I'd already told him I wasn't coming back and I'd meant it when I'd said it. Besides, he'd bloody sacked me!

It's true, said Barry, I sacked you. But it's not official or anything. Let's go and get an ice cream and talk about it while we wait. It's pretty hot out here.

You go, I said. I don't want to miss my slot.

I read more of *Cycling Weekly* and heard Early Man's number come up. When he returned he was wearing a hospital robe and looking kind of sad.

What's up? I said. Bad news?

He paused.

Go on tell me, I said, what did she say?

It's fine, he said. It's nothing.

Come on, I told him, I'm your friend. Open up for once.

No honestly, he said, it's fine. He looked at me, shrugged his shoulders, then disappeared into some olive grove. I thought about my own question to the Oracle. I wanted to know if I could get my old life back. Not the one I may or may not have recently lost, but the one I had before that. I wanted to know if I could be free from external control, free from people like Mr Bembo. His prophecy had turned out to be true, twice, and I was fed up with being hit by yellow cars.

350

I realised my question to the Pythia was slightly paradoxical. I was asking one oracle – the Oracle of Delphi – if I could wrest control of my life from another – the Oracle of Stepney Green. If she said yes and she was right, didn't it mean that she was now in charge? And if she said no, then wasn't I back to square one?

But you don't have choices in dreams. That was my question, and before Fat Barry returned with my 99 Flake my number had already been called.

I took the hot dusty path round the corner, following the signs to the temple. My God it was hot, white hot and bright. I looked to take my jumper off but all I was wearing was a hospital robe. Shit, hadn't Early Man returned wearing hospital robes too? Around the corner there was another little path, then another. The nearer I got to the temple the more people there seemed to be. Everyone was wearing hospital robes and the Pythia was calling my name. *Samuel Black. Road traffic collision.* Yep that was me. I headed towards the light of the temple. It felt like I was walking towards the sun. What was I expecting? The usual variation of a Greek Dream: a beautiful woman sits on a big tripod, some laurel leaves in her hand, gazing into a bowl of water around some noxious fumes, the omphalos nearby, more noxious fumes. Probably some gibberish answer to my question, maybe a riddle, hopefully a straight answer. A yes or no would be nice.

But instead of asking her my question about self-determination, I asked her how to play an opening roll of sixty-four.

Idiot.

Now of course this is an interesting question for any backgammon player and a definitive answer with all the appropriate reasoning would have been pretty useful, but it wasn't the question I wanted and it surprised me. The Oracle's answer surprised me too: why the fuck should I tell you, the voice said, when you're the one who's fucking winning?

A riddle then, yet another riddle I wasn't going to solve.

The thing is, the voice continued, it's all very well you lying there in your stinking hospital gown with your leg in plaster and your panda eyes and your nose more than a little out of joint but I don't buy the argument that you need assistance in this or any other game of backgammon because I know and you know and the doctors know – in fact the doctors have said quite categorically – that your brain is in fine form Sam. Indeed, on the basis of your current play I would argue that your brain capacity has, by some fucking annoying miracle of nature, been enhanced by your recent trauma. So to ask me what's the best way of playing an opening roll of sixty-four, the kind of move that can set the tone of a game, is totally absurd Sam. Of course I could tell you what you know already: that 24/14 opens you up to an outfield point on the next roll; that 24/18 and 13/9 is pretty risky but you're running if you survive; that the safe option is 8/2 and 6/2 but that an anchor on two sucks. However, why am I going to tell you something you *don't* know if it helps you gain an advantage when already the advantage is yours? Unless you already know what you're going to play and you're bluffing, you're lulling me into a false sense of security. Sorry Sam, I won't fall for that.

I had woken. The voice belonged to Poyntz. I looked at him and blinked.

Don't be a dick, I said. It was a genuine question: how do you play an opening roll of sixty-four?

Fine, he said. I'll give you a genuine answer. Play 8/2 and 6/2.

Nice try, I said, playing 24/18 and 13/9.

Risky, he said.

I was in a hospital bed, sitting up, being kept in under observation, playing backgammon with Poyntz. The doctor had said I was probably up to it and every time I played I won, not just by a little, by a lot. Since Poyntz's first visit we'd played nine sessions of six games and in each session I'd beaten him.

In the bed to my left an elderly woman was chatting to her dog, a Teacup Pomeranian. In the bed to my right a construction worker who'd been hit by a falling crane read the football scores. Opposite a broken neck watched hospital TV.

I rolled twenty-one and moved two men onto seven. It wasn't all bad for Poyntz. In my absence he'd finally got his revenge on Salowitz. He'd been back in the Crown and Salowitz, short of cash, had approached him for an easy hit. Poyntz had wavered, bluffed, then once Salowitz had downed a couple of drinks, reluctantly agreed. Poyntz drunk three Cuba Libres, all without rum. A board was found and Salowitz got greedy: five pounds a pip, plus doubles. Poyntz played pure, Salowitz played the back game: but he overstretched his cube play and rolled badly and when Poyntz bore off Salowitz still had a man in Poyntz's home board. Salowitz's pip count was embarrassing: fifty-eight with the doubling cube at eight. That was fifty-eight x eight x five. Two thousand, three hundred and twenty pounds.

That's nonsense money, I told Poyntz. You'll never get it.

I will eventually, Poyntz replied. But I don't exactly need it right now.

I looked at him. Suddenly our game of backgammon seemed quite unimportant. It had lost out in the grand scheme of things.

What do you mean you don't need it? I said. When have you ever not needed money, Poyntz?

Right now, he said. We're rolling in it. He paused and made his move, casually. You see, I finally got to meet your friend Mr Sorensen.

I looked at him. And?

We came to a deal, quite a good one.

You sold him the picture?

He nodded.

You found it?

Listen to Charles, you said. Of course I found it.

And how much did he pay, for his own picture?

A lot.

How much?

Enough to send him on his way, happy, enough for us to go to India.

India?

Yes, I think we should probably go to India.

We?

When you're a bit better. Then we can head out. Like soonish. We can go and stay at my grandfather's place in Nagpur. He's got a lodge as well, in a tiger reserve. The tigers are very beautiful. We can go and hang out there, you can convalesce. We can probably both have a Mercedes-Benz and if things get tough, I'll take the job managing the lingerie factory. Have a think about it. Take some Lucozade, he said, and have a think about it.

Poyntz had brought me Lucozade. The nurses brought me toast and Marmite in the morning and cups of weak tea and Weetabix singles, four of them, for my breakfast.

The doctors looked at my leg and my nose and shone lights into my eyes and glossed over my test results.

During the day when I wasn't playing backgammon, I slept and dreamt dreams, Greek dreams mostly, and when I wasn't sleeping I daydreamt about the new bicycle I was going to get: a Cinelli Supercorsa with Dura-Ace componentry and a pair of Zipp wheels.

During the night when I wasn't sleeping, I lay awake, unable to sleep, and listened to noises in the ward. Sometimes the noises were patients snoring, patients talking to themselves, patients moaning, humming, turning in bed, laughing, shuffling to the loo. Sometimes there would be vomiting, sometimes screaming, sometimes whimpering and tears. Often a nurse arrived and reassurance was whispered or a glass of water brought or a second opinion sought. One time a patient was removed. Rarely was it silent but when it was, it was most often silent in the hour before dawn when even the sick and the dying gave way to the natural rhythm of the night and the restless city rested. But during this hour for some reason I never failed to be awake, even if I'd slept beforehand. Often during this hour I'd just lie there and enjoy the silence, enjoy the solitude, enjoy the darkness of the moment. When dawn broke it broke behind me, behind the window behind my pillows, and filled my little cubicle with gradations of light, so that by the time I was ready to drift off again I could already make out the end of the bed and the washbasin and the plastic jug of water with its vertical indentations. At the end of the tenth night and beginning of the eleventh day I decided I'd seen enough of everything, regardless of what the doctors did or did not say, and so I put on what clothes I had and on top of them I put on my hospital robe and I wrote a little thank-you note and, leaving it on my bed which I had dutifully made, I walked out on my crutches, through the ward and beyond, through endless corridors and eventually out through the back doors, into the cold morning air. And in my head I had the intention of going to see some tigers.